For Jackson and Harvey

FOUNDRYSIDE

ROBERT JACKSON BENNETT

First published in Great Britain in 2018
This edition published in 2019 by

Jo Fletcher Books
an imprint of Quercus Editions Ltd
Carmelite House
50 Victoria Embankment
London EC4Y 0DZ

An Hachette UK company

A CIP catalogue record for this book is available from the British Library

PB ISBN 978 1 78648 785 8
EB ISBN 978 1 78648 787 2

10 9 8 7 6 5 4 3 2 1

Printed and bound in Great Britain by Clays Ltd, Elcograf S.p.A.

I

COMMONS

All things have a value. Sometimes the value is paid in coin. Other times, it is paid in time and sweat. And finally, sometimes it is paid in blood.

Humanity seems most eager to use this latter currency. And we never note how much of it we're spending, unless it happens to be our own.

– KING ERMIEDES EUPATOR,
'REFLECTIONS UPON CONQUEST'

1

As Sancia Grado lay facedown in the mud, stuffed underneath the wooden deck next to the old stone wall, she reflected that this evening was not going at all as she had wanted.

It had started out decently. She'd used her forged identifications to make it onto the Michiel property, and that had gone swimmingly – the guards at the first gates had barely glanced at her.

Then she'd come to the drainage tunnel, and that had gone . . . less swimmingly. It *had* worked, she supposed – the drainage tunnel had allowed her to slink below all the interior gates and walls and get close to the Michiel foundry – but her informants had neglected to mention the tunnel's abundance of centipedes, mud adders, and shit, of both the human and equine variety.

Sancia hadn't liked it, but she could handle it. That had not been her first time crawling through human waste.

But the problem with crawling through a river of sewage is that, naturally, you tend to gain a powerful odour. Sancia had tried to stay downwind from the security posts as she crept through the foundry yards. But just when she reached the north gate, some distant guard had cried out, 'Oh my God, what is that *smell*?' and then, to her alarm, dutifully gone looking for the source.

She'd avoided being spotted, but she'd been forced to flee into a dead-end foundry passageway and hide under the crumbling wooden deck, which had likely once been a guard post. But the problem with this hiding place, she'd quickly realised, was it gave her no means of escape: there was nothing in the walled foundry passageway besides the deck, Sancia, and the guard.

Sancia stared at the guard's muddy boots as he paced by the deck, sniffing. She waited until he walked past her, then poked her head out.

He was a big man, wearing a shiny steel cap and a leather cuirass embossed with the loggotipo of the Michiel Body Corporate – the candle flame set in the window – along with leather pauldrons and bracers. Most troublingly, he had a rapier sheathed at his side.

Sancia narrowed her eyes at the rapier. She thought she could hear a whispering in her mind as he walked away, a distant chanting. She'd assumed the blade was scrived, but that faint whispering confirmed it – and she knew a scrived blade could cut her in half with almost no effort at all.

This was such a damned stupid way to get cornered, she thought as she withdrew. *And I've barely even started the job.*

She had to get to the carriage fairways, which were probably only about two hundred feet away, behind the far wall. And she needed to get to them sooner rather than later.

She considered her options. She could dart the man, she supposed, for Sancia did have a little bamboo pipe and a set of small but expensive darts that were soaked in the poison of dolorspina fish – a lethal pest found in the deeper parts of the ocean. Diluted enough, the venom should only knock its victim into a deep sleep, with an absolute horror of a hangover a few hours later.

But the guard was sporting pretty decent armour. Sancia would have to make the shot perfect, perhaps aiming for his armpit. The risk of missing was far too high.

She could try to kill him, she supposed. She did have her stiletto, and she was an able sneak, and though she was small, she was strong for her size.

But Sancia was a lot better at thieving than she was killing, and this was a trained merchant house guard. She did not like her chances there.

Moreover, Sancia had not come to the Michiel foundry to slit throats, break faces, or crack skulls. She was here to do a job.

A voice echoed down the passageway: 'Ahoy, Nicolo! What are you doing away from your post?'

'I think something died in the drains again. It smells like death down here!'

'Oh, hang on,' said the voice. There came the sound of footsteps.

Ah, hell, thought Sancia. *Now there are two of them . . .*

She needed a way out of this, and fast.

She looked back at the stone wall behind her, thinking. Then she sighed, crawled over to it, and hesitated.

She did not want to spend her strength so soon. But she had no choice.

Sancia pulled off her left glove, pressed her bare palm to the dark stones, shut her eyes, and used her talent.

The wall spoke to her.

The wall told her of foundry smoke, of hot rains, of creeping moss, of the tiny footfalls of the thousands of ants that had traversed its mottled face over the decades. The surface of the wall bloomed in her mind, and she felt every crack and every crevice, every dollop of mortar and every stained stone.

All of this information coursed into Sancia's thoughts the second she touched the wall. And among this sudden eruption of knowledge was what she had really been hoping for.

Loose stones. Four of them, big ones, just a few feet away from her. And on the other side, some kind of closed, dark space, about four feet wide and tall. She instantly knew where to find it like she'd built the wall herself.

There's a building on the other side, she thought. *An old one. Good.*

Sancia took her hand away. To her dismay, the huge scar on the right side of her scalp was starting to hurt.

A bad sign. She'd have to use her talent a lot more than this tonight.

She replaced her glove and crawled over to the loose stones. It looked like there had been a small hatch here once, but it'd been bricked up years ago. She paused and listened – the two guards now seemed to be loudly sniffing the breeze.

'I swear to *God*, Pietro,' said one, 'it was like the devil's shit!' They began pacing the passageway together.

Sancia gripped the topmost loose stone and carefully, carefully tugged at it.

It gave way, inching out slightly. She looked back at the guards, who were still bickering.

Quickly and quietly, Sancia hauled the heavy stones out and placed them in the mud, one after the other. Then she peered into the musty space.

It was dark within, but she now let in a little light – and she saw many tiny eyes staring at her from the shadows, and piles of tiny turds on the stone floor.

Rats, she thought. *Lots of them.*

Still, nothing to do about it. Without another thought, she crawled into the tiny, dark space.

The rats panicked and began crawling up the walls, fleeing into gaps in the stones. Several of them scampered over Sancia, and a few tried to bite her – but Sancia was wearing what she called her 'thieving rig', a homemade, hooded, improvised outfit made of thick, grey woollen cloth and old black leather that covered all of her skin and was quite difficult to tear through.

As she got her shoulders through, she shook the rats off or swatted them away – but then a large rat, easily weighing two pounds, rose up on its hind legs and hissed at her threateningly.

Sancia's fist flashed out and smashed the big rat, crushing its skull against the stone floor. She paused, listening to see if the guards had heard her – and, satisfied that they had not, she hit the big rat again for good measure. Then she finished crawling inside, and carefully reached out and bricked up the hatch behind her.

There, she thought, shaking off another rat and brushing away the turds. *That wasn't so bad.*

She looked around. Though it was terribly dark, her eyes were adjusting. It looked like this space had once been a fireplace where the foundry workers cooked their food, long ago. The fireplace had been boarded up, but the chimney was open above her – though she could see now that someone had tried to board up the very top as well.

She examined it. The space within the chimney was quite small. But then, so was Sancia. And she was good at getting into tight places.

With a grunt, Sancia leapt up, wedged herself in the gap, and began climbing up the chimney, inch by inch. She was about halfway up when she heard a clanking sound below.

She froze and looked down. There was a bump, and then a crack, and light spilled into the fireplace below her.

The steel cap of a guard poked into the fireplace. The guard looked down at the abandoned rat's nest and cried, '*Ugh!* Seems the rats have built themselves a merry tenement here. That must have been the smell.'

Sancia stared down at the guard. If he but glanced up, he'd spy her instantly.

The guard looked at the big rat she'd killed. She tried to will herself not to sweat so no drops would fall on his helmet.

'Filthy things,' muttered the guard. Then his head withdrew.

Sancia waited, still frozen – she could still hear them talking below. Then, slowly, their voices withdrew.

She let out a sigh. *This is a lot of risk to get to one damned carriage.*

She finished climbing and came to the top of the chimney. The boards there easily gave way to her push. Then she clambered out onto the roof of the building, lay flat, and looked around.

To her surprise, she was right above the carriage fairway – exactly where she needed to be. She watched as one carriage charged down the muddy lane to the loading dock, which was a bright, busy blotch of light in the darkened foundry yards. The foundry proper loomed above the loading dock, a huge, near-windowless brick structure with six fat smokestacks pouring smoke into the night sky.

She crawled to the edge of the roof, took off her glove, and felt the lip of the wall below with a bare hand. The wall blossomed in her mind, every crooked stone and clump of moss – and every good handhold to help her find her way down.

She lowered herself over the edge of the roof and started to descend. Her head was pounding, her hands hurt, and she was covered in all manner of filthy things. *I haven't even done step one yet, and I've already nearly got myself killed.*

'Twenty thousand,' she whispered to herself as she climbed. 'Twenty thousand duvots.'

A king's ransom, really. Sancia was willing to eat a lot of shit and bleed a decent amount of blood for twenty thousand duvots. More than she had so far, at least.

The soles of her boots touched earth, and she started to run.

The carriage fairway was poorly lit, but the foundry loading dock was ahead, bright with firebaskets and scrived lanterns. Even at this hour it was swarming with activity as labourers sprinted back and forth, unloading the carriages lined up before it. A handful of guards watched them, bored.

Sancia hugged the wall and crept closer. Then there was a rumbling sound, and she froze and turned her head away, pressing her body to the wall.

Another enormous carriage came thundering down the fairway, splashing her with grey mud. After it passed, she blinked mud out of her eyes and watched it as it rolled away. The carriage appeared to be rolling along of its own accord: it wasn't pulled by a horse, or a donkey, or any kind of animal at all.

Unfazed, Sancia looked back up the fairway. *It'd be a pity,* she thought, *if I crawled through a river of sewage and a pile of rats, just to get crushed by a scrived carriage like a stray dog.*

She continued on, and watched the carriages closely as she neared. Some were horse-drawn, but most weren't. They came from all over the city of Tevanne – from the canals, from other foundries, or from the waterfront. And it was this last location that Sancia was most interested in.

She sunk down below the lip of the loading dock and crept up to the line of carriages. And as she approached, she heard them whisper in her mind.

Murmurings. Chatterings. Hushed voices. Not from the horse-drawn carriages – those were silent to her – but from the scrived ones.

Then she looked at the wheels of the closest carriage, and saw it.

The interiors of the huge wooden wheels had writing upon them, a sort of languid, joined-up script that looked to be made of silvery, gleaming metal: 'sigillums' or 'sigils', as the Tevanni elite called them. But most just called them scrivings.

Sancia had no training in scriving, but the way scrived carriages worked was common knowledge in Tevanne: the commands written upon the wheels convinced them that they were on an incline, and so the wheels, absolutely believing this, would feel obliged to roll downhill – even if there was actually no hill at all, and the carriage was actually just rolling along, say, a perfectly flat (if particularly muddy) canal fairway. The pilot sat in the hatch of the carriage, adjusting the controls, which would tell the wheels something like, 'Oh, we're on a steep hill now, better hurry up,' or, 'Wait, no, the hill's flattening out, let's slow down,' or, 'There's no hill at all now, actually, so let's just stop.' And the wheels, thoroughly duped by the scrivings, would happily comply, thus eliminating the need for any horses, or mules, or goats, or whichever other dull creature could be coaxed into hauling people around.

That was how scrivings worked: they were instructions written upon mindless objects that convinced them to disobey reality in select ways. Scrivings had to be carefully thought out, though, and carefully wrought. Sancia had heard stories about how the first scrived carriages didn't have their wheels calibrated properly, so on one occasion the front wheels thought they were rolling downhill, but the wheels in the back thought they were rolling *uphill*, which quickly tore the carriage apart, sending the wheels hurtling through the streets of Tevanne at phenomenal speeds, with much mayhem and destruction and death ensuing.

All of which meant that, despite their being highly advanced creations, hanging around a carriage's wheels was not exactly the brightest of things to do with one's evening.

Sancia crawled to one wheel. She cringed as the scrivings whispered in her ears, growing louder. This was perhaps the oddest aspect of her talents – she'd certainly never met anyone else who could hear scrivings – but it was tolerable. She ignored the sound and poked her index and middle finger through two slits in the glove on her right hand, baring her fingertips to the moist air. She touched the wheel of the carriage with her fingers, and asked it what it knew.

And, much like the wall in the passageway, the wheel answered.

The wheel told her of ash, of stone, of broiling flame, of sparks and iron.

Sancia thought, *Nope.* The carriage had probably come from a foundry – and she was not interested in foundries tonight.

She leaned around the back of the carriage, confirmed the guards hadn't seen her, and slipped down the line to the next one.

She touched the carriage's wheel with her fingertips, and asked it what it knew.

The wheel knew soft, loamy soil, the acrid smell of dung, the aroma of crushed greenery and vegetation.

A farm, probably. *Nope. Not this one either.*

She slipped down to the next carriage – this one your average, horse-drawn carriage – touched a wheel, and asked it what it knew.

The wheel knew of ash, and fire, and hot, and the hissing sparks of smelting ore . . .

This one came from another foundry, she thought. *Same as the first. I hope Sark's source was right. If all of these came from foundries or farmland, the whole plan's over before it began.*

She slipped down to the next carriage, the horse snuffling disapprovingly as she moved. This was the penultimate one in line, so she was running out of options.

She reached out, touched a wheel, and asked it what it knew.

This one spoke of gravel, of salt, of seaweed, of the tang of ocean spray, and wooden beams soaking above the waves . . .

Sancia nodded, relieved. *That's the one.*

She reached into a pouch on her rig and pulled out a curious-looking object: a small bronze plate inscribed with many sigils. She took out a pot of tar, painted the back of the plate with it, and reached up into the carriage and stuck the little bronze plate to the bottom.

She paused, remembering what her black-market contacts had told her.

Stick the guiding plate to the thing you want to go to, and make sure it's stuck hard. You don't want it falling off.

So . . . what happens if it falls off in the street or something? Sancia had then asked.

Well. Then you'll die. Pretty gruesomely, I expect.

Sancia pressed on the bronze plate harder. *Don't you scrumming get me killed*, she thought, glaring at it. *This job's offering enough damned opportunities as it is.* Then she slid out, slipped through the other carriages, and returned to the fairway and the foundry yards.

She was more careful this time, and made sure to stay downwind of any guards. She made it to the drainage tunnel quickly. Now she'd have to trudge back through those foetid waters and make straight for the waterfront.

Which was, of course, where the carriage she'd tampered with was also bound, since its wheels had spoken to her of sea spray and gravel and salty air – things a carriage would only encounter at the waterfront. Hopefully the carriage would help her get into that highly controlled site.

Because somewhere on the waterfront was a safe. And someone incomprehensibly wealthy had hired Sancia to steal one specific item inside it in exchange for a simply inconceivable amount of money.

Sancia liked stealing. She was good at it. But after tonight, she might never need to steal again.

'Twenty thousand,' she chanted softly. 'Twenty thousand. Twenty thousand lovely, lovely duvots . . .'

She dropped down into the sewers.

2

Sancia did not truly understand her talents. She did not know how they worked, what their limits were, or even if they were all that dependable. She just knew what they did, and how they could help her.

When she touched an object with her bare skin, she understood it. She understood its nature, its makeup, its shape. If it had been somewhere or touched something recently, she could remember that sensation as if it had happened to her. And if she got close to a scrived item, or touched one, she could hear it muttering its commands in her head.

That didn't mean she could understand what the scrivings were *saying.* She just knew something was being said.

Sancia's talents could be used in a number of ways. A quick, light touch with any object would let its most immediate sensations spill into her. Longer contact would give her a physical sense of the thing she was touching – where its handholds were, where it was weak or soft or hollow, or what it contained. And if she kept her hands on something for long enough – a process which was deeply painful for her – it would give her near-perfect spatial awareness: if she held her hand to a brick in the floor of a room, for example, she'd eventually sense the floor, the walls, the ceiling, and anything touching them. Provided she didn't pass out or vomit from the pain, that is.

Because there were downsides to these abilities. Sancia had to keep a lot of her skin concealed at all times, for it's difficult to, say, eat a meal with the fork you're holding spilling into your mind.

But there were upsides, too. A facility with items is a tremendous boon if you're looking to steal those items. And it meant Sancia was phenomenally talented at scaling walls, navigating dark passageways, and picking locks – because picking locks is easy if the lock is actually telling you how to pick it.

The one thing she tried hard not to think about was where her talents came from. For Sancia had got her abilities in the same place she'd got the lurid white scar that ran down the right side of her skull, the scar that burned hot whenever she overextended her talents.

Sancia did not exactly like her talents: they were as restrictive and punishing as they were powerful. But they'd helped her stay alive. And tonight, hopefully, they would make her rich.

The next step was the Fernezzi complex, a nine-storey building across from the Tevanni waterfront. It was an old structure, built for customs officers and brokers to manage their accounts back before the merchant houses took over almost all of Tevanne's trade. But its age and ornate designs were useful for Sancia, offering many sturdy handholds.

It says something, she thought, grunting as she climbed, *that scaling this big goddamn building is the easiest part of this job.*

Finally she came to the roof. She gripped the granite cornices, clambered onto the top of the building, ran to the western side, and looked out, panting with exhaustion.

Below her was a wide bay, a bridge crossing it, and, on the other side, the Tevanni waterfront. Huge carriages trundled across the bridge, their tops quaking on the wet cobblestones. Almost all of them were certainly merchant house carriages, carrying goods back and forth from the foundries.

One of the carriages should be the one she'd marked with the guiding plate. *I scrumming well hope so,* she thought. *Otherwise I hauled my stupid arse through a river of shit and up a building for no damned reason at all.*

For ages the waterfront had been as corrupt and dangerous as any other part of Tevanne that wasn't under direct control of the merchant houses – which was to say, incredibly, flagrantly, unbelievably corrupt. But a few months ago they'd gone and hired some hero from the Enlightenment Wars, and he'd booted out all the crooks, hired a bunch of professional guards, and installed security wards all over the waterfront – including scrived, defensive walls, just like those at the merchant houses, which wouldn't let you in or out without the proper identification.

Suddenly it'd become difficult to do illegal things on the waterfront. Which was quite inconvenient for Sancia. So she'd needed to find an alternate way into the waterfront for her job tonight.

She kneeled, unbuttoned a pouch on her chest, and took out what was likely her most important tool of the night. It looked like a roll of cloth, but as she unfolded it, it gained a somewhat cuplike shape.

When she was finished, Sancia looked at the little black parachute lying on the rooftop.

'This is going to kill me, isn't it?' she said.

She took out the final piece of the parachute: a telescoping steel rod. Set into the ends of this rod were two small, scrived plates – she could hear them chanting and whispering in her head. Like all scrived devices, she had no idea what they were saying, but her black-market contacts had given her strict instructions on how all this would work.

It's a two-part system, Claudia had told her. *You stick the guidance plate to the thing you want to go to. The guidance plate then says to the plates in the rod, 'Hey, I know you think you're your own thing, but you're actually part of* this *thing that I'm attached to – so you need to get over here and be part of it, fast.' And the rod says, 'Really? Oh gosh, what am I doing all the way over here? I need to go be a part of this other thing right away!' And when you hit the switch, it does. Really, really fast.*

Sancia was vaguely familiar with this scriving technique. It was a version of the method the merchant houses used to stick bricks and other construction materials together, duping them into thinking they were all one object. But no one tried to use this method over distances – it was considered unstable to the point of being useless, and there were far safer methods of locomotion available.

But those methods were expensive. Too expensive for Sancia.

And the parachute keeps me from falling, Sancia had said when Claudia was done explaining it all.

Uh, no, Claudia had said. *The parachute slows it down. Like I told you – this thing is going to go really,* really *fast. So you're going to want to be high up when you turn it on. Just make sure the guidance plate is actually where you need it to be, and nothing's blocking your path. Use the test piece first. If it's all lined up, turn on the rod and go.*

Sancia reached into yet another pocket and pulled out a small glass jar. In this glass jar was a bronze coin, and inscribed on this coin were sigils similar to the ones on the parachute rod.

She squinted at the coin. It was stuck firmly to the side of the glass facing the waterfront. She turned the glass over, and, as if magnetised, the coin zipped across the jar and stuck itself to the other side with a tinny *tink!* – again, the side facing the waterfront.

If this thing is attracted to the guiding plate, she thought, *and if the guiding plate is on the carriage, then it means the carriage is at the waterfront. So I'm good.*

She paused. *Probably. Maybe.*

She hesitated for a long time. 'Shit,' she muttered.

Sancia hated this sort of thing. The logic behind scriving always seemed so stupidly simple – barely logic at all, really. But then, scriving more or less bent reality, or at least confused it.

She put the jar away and threaded the rod through the tapered end of the parachute.

Just think of what Sark told you, she thought. *Just think of that number – twenty thousand duvots.*

Enough money to fix herself. To make herself normal.

Sancia hit a lever on the side of the rod and jumped off the roof.

Instantly she was soaring through the air across the bay at a speed she'd never thought possible, hauled along by the steel rod, which, as far as she understood, was frantically trying to join the carriage down in the waterfront. She could hear the parachute whipping out behind her and finally catching the air, which slowed her down some – first not much at all, but then a little more, and a little more.

Her eyes watered and she gritted her teeth. The nightscape of Tevanne was a whirl around her. She could see water glittering in the bay below, the shifting forest of masts from the ships in the harbour, the shuddering roofs of the carriages as they made their way to the waterfront, the smoke unscrolling from the foundries clutched around the shipping channel . . .

Focus, she thought. *Focus, idiot.*

Then things . . . dipped.

Her stomach lurched. Something was wrong.

She looked back, and saw there was a tear in the parachute.

Shit.

She watched, horrified, as the tear began to widen.

Shit! Double shit!

The sailing rig lurched again, so hard that she barely noticed she'd flown over the waterfront walls. The rig started speeding up, faster and faster.

I need to get off this thing. Now. Now!

She saw she was sailing over the waterfront cargo stacks, huge towers of boxes and crates, and some of the stacks looked high indeed. High enough for her to fall and catch herself. Maybe.

She blinked tears out of her eyes, focused on one tall stack of crates, angled the rig, and then . . .

She hit the lever on the side of the rod.

Instantly, she started losing momentum. She was no longer flying but was instead drifting down toward the crates, which were about twenty feet below. She was slowed somewhat by the rapidly dissolving parachute – but not enough to make her comfortable.

She watched as the giant crates flew up to her.

Ah, hell.

She hit the corner of the crate so hard that it knocked the wind out of her, yet she still retained sense to reach out and snag the wooden corner, grabbing hold and clutching to its side. The sailing rig caught some wind, and was ripped out of her hands and went drifting away.

She hung fast to the side of the crate, breathing hard. She'd trained herself to fall, to catch onto walls in an instant, or bounce or slide off of surfaces – but she'd rarely had to use such training.

There was a *clank* from somewhere to her right as the sailing rig fell to the ground. She froze and just hung there for a moment, listening for any alarms being raised.

Nothing. Silence.

The waterfront was a big place. One noise was easy to disregard.

Hopefully.

Sancia took her left hand away from the crate, dangling by just one hold, and used her teeth to pull off her glove. Then she pressed her bare left hand to the crate, and listened.

The crate told her of water, and rain, and oil, and straw, and the tiny bite of many nails . . .

And also how to climb down it.

Step two – getting in the waterfront – had not gone quite as planned.

Now on to step three, she thought wearily, climbing down. *Let's see if I can avoid screwing that one up.*

When Sancia made it to the ground, at first all she did was breathe hard and rub her bruised side.

I made it. I'm inside. I'm there.

She peered through the cargo stacks at the building on the far side of the waterfront: the Waterwatch offices – the police force for the waterfront.

Well. Almost there.

She pulled off her other glove, stuffed both of them in her pockets, and placed her hands on the stone surface at her feet. Then she shut her eyes and listened to the stone.

This was a hard trick, for Sancia: the ground around her was a wide area, so it was a lot to listen to all at once. But she could still listen, still let the stones spill into her mind, still feel the vibrations and trembling all around her as people . . .

Walked. Stood. Ran. Shifted feet. Sancia could feel all of them just as one could feel fingers running down one's own bare back.

Nine guards nearby, she thought. *Heavy ones – big men. Two stationary, seven on patrols.* There were doubtlessly many more than that on the waterfront, but her abilities could only see so far through the stones.

She noted their positions, their directions, their speed. For the ones close to her she could even feel their heels on the stones – so she knew which way they were facing.

The scar on the side of her head started getting painfully warm. She winced and took her hands away – but the memory of the guards remained. Which meant this would be like trying to navigate a familiar room in the dark.

Sancia took a breath, slipped out of the shadows, and started off, dodging through crates, slipping under carts, pausing always just-so as guards made their rounds. She tried not to look at the crates as she moved. Most bore markings from the plantations, far out in the Durazzo Sea, and Sancia was well acquainted with such places. She knew that these raw goods – hemp, sugar, tar, coffee – had not been harvested or produced with anything resembling consensual labour.

Bastards, thought Sancia as she slipped through the crates. *Bunch of rotten, scrumming bastards . . .*

She paused at one crate. She couldn't read its label in the dark, but she placed a bare finger against a wooden slat, listened carefully, and saw within it . . .

Paper. Lots of it. Blank, raw paper. Which should do nicely.

Time to prepare an exit strategy, she thought.

Sancia pulled her gloves on, untied one pocket on her thigh, and pulled out her final scrived tool for the evening: a small wooden box. The box had cost her more than she'd ever spent on a job in her life, but without it, her life wouldn't be worth a fig tonight.

She placed the box on top of the crate. *This should work well enough.* She hoped so. Getting out of the waterfront would be a hell of a lot harder if it didn't.

She reached back into her pocket and pulled out what looked like a simple knot of twine, running through a thick ball of lead. In the centre of this ball was a tiny, perfect clutch of sigils – and as she held it, she heard a soft whispering in her ear.

She looked at the ball of lead, then the box on the crates. *This scrumming box,* she thought, putting the lead ball back in her pocket, *had damned well better work. Or I'll be trapped here like a fish in a pot.*

Sancia jumped the short fence around the Waterwatch offices and ran to the wall. She crept to the corner of the building, then ducked her head out. No one. But there was a large, thick doorframe. It stuck out about four or five inches from the wall – plenty of room for Sancia to work with.

She leapt up and grabbed the top of the doorframe, then pulled herself up, paused to rebalance, and placed her right foot on the top of the frame. Then she hauled herself up until she stood on the doorframe.

Two second-floor windows were on her right and left, old and thick with oily, yellowed glass. Sancia pulled out her stiletto, slipped it into the crack in one window, flipped back the latch, and pulled the window open. She sheathed her stiletto, lifted herself up, and peered in.

Inside were rows and rows of shelves, filled with what looked like parchment boxes. Probably records of some kind. The area was deserted, as it ought to be at this time of night – close to one in the morning by now – but there was a light downstairs. A candle flame, perhaps.

Downstairs is where the safes are, thought Sancia. *Which won't be unguarded, even now . . .*

She crawled inside, shutting the window behind her. Then she crouched low and listened.

A cough, then a sniff. She crept through the shelves until she came to the railing at the edge of the second floor, and peered down into the first floor.

A single Waterwatch officer sat at a desk at the front door, filling out paperwork, a candle burning before him. He was an older man, plump and timid-looking, with a slightly lopsided moustache and a crinkled blue uniform. But it was what was behind him that really interested Sancia, for there sat a row of huge iron safes, nearly a dozen of them – and one of them, she knew, was the safe she'd come for.

But now, she thought, *what to do about our friend down there?*

She sighed as she realised what her only option was. She took her bamboo pipe out and loaded it with a dolorspina dart. *Another ninety duvots spent on this job,* she thought. Then she gauged the distance between herself and the guard, who was tsking and scratching out something on the page before him. She placed the pipe to her lips, aimed carefully, breathed in through her nose, and then . . .

Before she could fire, the front door of the Waterwatch offices slammed open, and a large, scarred officer strode through, clutching something wet and dripping in one hand.

She lowered the pipe. *Well. Shit.*

The officer was tall, broad, and well-muscled, and his dark skin, dark eyes, and thick black beard suggested he was a pureblood Tevanni. The hair atop his head was cut close, and his appearance and bearing immediately made Sancia think of a soldier: he had the look of a man used to having his words listened to and acted upon immediately.

This new arrival turned to the officer seated at the desk, who looked no less surprised than Sancia to see him. 'Captain Dandolo!' said the officer at the desk. 'I thought you'd be out at the piers tonight.'

The name was familiar to Sancia. Dandolo was the name of one of the four main merchant houses, and she'd heard that the new waterfront captain had some kind of elite connections . . .

Ah, she thought, *so this is the striper who's taken it upon himself to reform the waterfront.* She drew back into the shelves, though not so far that she couldn't see.

'Something wrong, sir?' said the officer at the desk.

'One of the boys heard a sound out in the stacks, and found this.'

His voice was terribly loud, like he spoke to fill up every room he was in with whatever he had to say. Then he held up the ragged, wet thing – and Sancia immediately recognised it as the remains of her air-sailing rig.

She grimaced. *Shit.*

'Is that a . . . kite?' said the officer at the desk.

'No,' said Dandolo. 'It's an air-sailing rig – what the merchant houses use for mercantile espionage. It's an unusually poor version, but that's what it seems to be.'

'Wouldn't the walls have notified us if someone unauthorised crossed over the barrier?'

'Not if they crossed over high enough.'

'Ah,' said the sergeant. 'And you think . . .' He looked over his shoulder at the line of safes.

'I'm having the boys comb the stacks as we speak,' said Dandolo. 'But if they're mad enough to fly into the waterfront with this thing, maybe they're mad enough to go for the safes.' He sucked his teeth. 'Keep an eye out, Sergeant, but stay at your post. I'll look around. Just to see.'

'Right, sir.'

Sancia watched with growing horror as Dandolo mounted the stairs, the wood creaking under his considerable weight.

Shit! Shit!

She considered her options. She could go back to the window, open it up, slip outside, and stand on the doorframe below, waiting for Dandolo to leave. But this took a lot of risks, since she could be seen or heard by the man.

She could shoot Dandolo with the dolorspina dart. That would likely cause him to go tumbling back down the stairs, alarming the sergeant below, who could then raise the alarm. She debated if she could reload in time to hit him too, and found this plan no better.

Then she had a third idea.

She reached into her pocket and pulled out the knot of twine and the scrived lead ball.

She'd intended to save this final trick as a distraction while she made her escape. But then, she *did* need to escape from this current situation.

She put away her pipe, gripped each end of the twine knot, and looked up at the approaching captain, who was still climbing the stairs in front of her.

You're an arsehole for scrumming this up for me, she thought.

She gripped the ends of the twine knot, and ripped it untied in one fast motion.

Sancia vaguely understood how the scriving mechanism worked: the interior of the lead ball was lined with sandpaper, and the twine was treated with fire potash, so when it was ripped through the sandpaper, it ignited. Just a small flare, but that was enough.

Because the scrived ball in her hands was linked with a *second* lead ball, which was far, far away in the box atop the paper crates in the cargo stacks. Both balls were altered to be convinced that they were actually the *same* ball – and thus, whatever happened to the one happened to the other. Dunk one in cold water, and the other would grow rapidly cool. Shatter one, and the other would shatter as well.

So this meant that when she pulled the twine and ignited the flare inside, the second ball in the cargo stacks suddenly grew burning hot too.

But the second ball was packed in *quite* a lot more fire potash – and the box it sat in was filled to the brim with flash powder.

The instant Sancia ripped the twine through the lead ball, she heard a faint *boom* way out in the cargo stacks.

The captain paused on the stairs, bewildered. 'What the hell was *that*?' he said.

'Captain?' called the sergeant downstairs. '*Captain!*'

He turned away from Sancia and called down the stairs, 'Sergeant – what was that?'

'I don't know, Captain, but, but . . . There's smoke.'

Sancia turned toward the window and saw that the scrived device had worked quite well – there was now a thick column of white smoke out in the cargo stacks, along with a cheery flame.

'Fire!' shouted the captain. 'Shit! Come on, Prizzo!'

Sancia watched, pleased, as the two of them sprinted out the door. Then she dashed downstairs to the safes.

Let's hope it keeps burning, she thought as she ran. *Otherwise I might crack the safe, and get the prize – but I'll have no tricks left to get me off the waterfront.*

Sancia looked at the line of safes. She remembered Sark's instructions – *It's safe 23D. A small wooden box. The combinations are changed every day – Dandolo is a clever bastard – but it should be no issue for you, girl. Should it?*

She knew it shouldn't. But then, she was now working with a much tighter deadline than she'd previously planned for.

Sancia approached 23D and took her gloves off. These safes were where civilian passengers stored away valuables with the Waterwatch – specifically, passengers unaffiliated with the merchant houses. If you were affiliated with one of the merchant houses, it was assumed you'd store your valuables with them directly, because they, being the manufacturers and producers of all scrived rigs, would have far better security and protection than just a bunch of safes with combination locks.

Sancia placed one bare hand on 23D. Then she leaned her bare forehead against it, took the tumbler wheel in her other hand, and shut her eyes.

The safe blossomed to life in her mind, telling her of iron and darkness and oil, the chattering of its many toothed gears, the clinkings and clankings of its stupendously complicated mechanisms.

She slowly started turning the wheel, and felt instantly where it wanted to go. She slowed the combination wheel down, and . . .

Click. One tumbler fell into place.

Sancia breathed deep and started turning the wheel in the opposite direction, feeling the mechanisms clicking and clanking inside the door.

There was another *boom* out in the cargo yard.

Sancia opened her eyes. *Pretty sure I didn't do* that *one . . .*

She looked back at the window on the western side of the offices, and saw that the greasy glass panes were dancing with greedy firelight. Something must have caught out there, something *much* more flammable than the paper crate she'd intended to set alight.

She heard shouting, screaming, and cries out in the yard. *Ah, hell,* she thought. *I need to hurry before the whole damned place burns down!*

She shut her eyes again and kept turning the wheel. She felt it clicking into place, felt that perfect little gap approaching . . . and the scar on her head burning hot, like a needle in her brain. *I'm doing too much. I'm pushing myself too damned far . . .*

Click.

She sucked her teeth. *That's two . . .*

More screams from outside. Another soft *boom.*

She focused. She listened to the safe, letting it pour into her, feeling the anticipation of the mechanism within, feeling it wait with bated breath for that one final turn . . .

Click.

She opened her eyes and turned the handle on the safe. It opened with a *clunk.* She swung it open.

The safe was filled with an abundance of items: letters, scrolls, envelopes, and the like. But at the back was her prize: a wooden box, about eight inches long and four inches deep. A simple, dull box, unremarkable in nearly every way – and yet this bland thing was worth more than all the precious goods Sancia had ever stolen in her life combined.

She reached in and picked up the box with her bare fingers. Then she paused.

Her abilities had been so taxed by the evening's excitement that she could tell something was curious about the box, but not immediately what – she got a hazy picture in her mind of pine wood walls within walls, but not much more. It was like trying to look at a painting in the dark during a lightning storm.

She knew that wasn't important, though – she was just meant to get it, and not ask questions about its contents.

She stowed it away in a pouch on her chest. Then she shut the safe, locked it, and turned and ran for the door.

As she exited the Waterwatch offices, she saw that the little fire was now a full-on blaze. It looked like she'd set the entire damned cargo yard alight. Waterwatch officers sprinted around the inferno, trying to contain it – which meant likely all of the exits were now available for her to use.

She turned and ran. *If they find out I did this,* she thought, *I'll be harpered for sure.*

She made it to the eastern exit of the waterfront. She slowed, hid behind a stack of crates, and confirmed that she was right – all the officers were tending to the blaze, which meant it was unguarded. She ran through, head aching, heart pounding, and the scar on the side of her head screaming in pain.

Yet just as she crossed, she looked back for one moment, watching the fire. The entire western fifth of the waterfront was now a wild blaze, and an unbelievably thick column of black smoke stretched up and curled about the moon above.

Sancia turned and ran.

3

A block away from the waterfront, Sancia slipped into an alley and changed clothing, wiping the mud from her face, rolling up her filthy thieving rig, and putting on a hooded doublet, gloves, and hosiery.

She cringed as she did so – she hated changing clothes. She stood in the alley and shut her eyes, wincing as the sensations of mud and smoke and soil and dark wool bled out of her thoughts, and bright, crunchy, crispy hemp fabric surged in to replace them. It was like stepping out of a nice warm bath and jumping into an icy lake, and it took some time for her mind to recalibrate.

Once this was done, she hurried away down the street, pausing twice to confirm she'd not been followed. She took a turn, then another. Soon the huge merchant house walls swelled up on either side of her, white and towering and indifferent – Michiel on the left, Dandolo on the right. Behind those walls were the merchant house enclaves – commonly called 'campos' – where the merchant houses ran their clutch of neighbourhoods like their own little kingdoms.

Clinging to the bases of the walls was a tall, rambling stretch of ramshackle wooden tenements and rookery buildings and crooked chimneys, an improvised, makeshift, smoky tangle of soaking warrens stuffed between the two campo walls like a raft trapped between two converging ships.

Foundryside. The closest thing Sancia had to a home.

She passed through an alley, and was greeted by a familiar scene. Firebaskets sparked and hissed at the street corners ahead. A taverna on her left was still thriving even at this hour, its old yellow windows glimmering with candlelight, cackles and curses spilling through the drapes across the entrance. Weeds and vines and rogue nut trees tumbled out of the flooded alleys as if launching an ambush. Three old women on a balcony above watched her passage, all picking at a wooden plate, upon which sat the remains of a striper – a large, ugly water bug that turned a rather pretty, striped violet pattern when boiled.

The scene was familiar, but it didn't make her any more relaxed. The Tevanni Commons were Sancia's home, but her neighbours were just as ruthless and dangerous as any merchant house guard.

She took back passageways to her rookery building, and slipped in through a side door. She walked down the hallway to her rooms, felt the door with a bare index finger, then the floorboards. They told her nothing unusual – it seemed things hadn't been tampered with.

She unlocked all six of the locks on the door, walked in, and locked it again. Then she crouched and listened, her bare index finger stuck to the floorboards.

She waited ten minutes. The throbbing in her head slowly returned. But she had to be sure.

When nothing came, she lit a candle – she was tired of using her talents to see – crossed her room, and opened the shutters of her windows, just a crack. Then she stood there and watched the streets.

For two hours, Sancia stared out the tiny crack at the street below. She knew she had good reason to be paranoid – she'd not only just pulled off a twenty-thousand-duvot job, she'd also just burned down the damned Tevanni waterfront. She wasn't sure which was worse.

If someone had happened to look up at Sancia's window and catch a glimpse of her, they likely would've been struck by the sight. She was a young girl, barely older than twenty, but she'd already lived more than most people ever would, and you could see it in her face. Her dark skin was weather-beaten, the face of someone for whom starvation was a frequent occurrence. She was short but muscular, with bulky shoulders and thighs, and her hands were callused and hard as iron – all consequences of her occupation. She sported a lopsided, self-applied haircut, and a lurid, jagged scar ran along her right temple, approaching close to her right eye, whose white was slightly muddier than that of the left.

People did not like it when Sancia looked at them too hard. It made them nervous.

After two hours of watching, Sancia felt satisfied. She closed her shutters, locked them, and went to her closet and removed the false floor. It always discomfited her to open up the floor there – the Commons had no banks or treasuries, so the whole of her life's savings was squirrelled away in that dank niche.

She took the pine box out of her thieving rig, held it in her bare hands, and looked at it.

Now that she'd had some time to recover – the screaming pain in her skull had subsided into a dull ache – she could tell right away what was odd about the box, and it bloomed clear in her mind, the shape and space of the box congealing in her thoughts like wax chambers in a beehive.

The box had a false bottom in it – a secret compartment. And inside the false bottom, Sancia's talents told her, was something small and wrapped in linen.

She paused, thinking about this.

Twenty thousand duvots? For this thing?

But then, it was not for her to think about. Her purpose had been to get the box, and nothing more. Sark had been very clear about that. And Sancia was well favoured by their clients because she always did as she was asked – no more, no less. In three days, she'd hand the box off to Sark, and then she'd never think about it again.

She put the box in the false floor, closed the floor, and shut the closet.

She confirmed that her door and shutters were secure. Then she walked over to her bed, sat, placed her stiletto on the floor beside her, and breathed deep.

Home, she thought. *And safe.*

But her room did not look much like a home. If anyone had happened to peer inside, they'd have thought Sancia lived like the most ascetic of monks: she had only a plain chair, a bucket, an unadorned table, and a bare bed – no sheets, no pillows.

Yet this was how she was forced to live. She preferred sleeping in her own clothes to sleeping in sheets: not only was it difficult to adjust to lying in yet more cloth, but bedsheets were prone to lice and fleas and other vermin, and the feeling of their many tiny legs picking their way across her skin drove her absolutely mad. And when her scar burned hot, she couldn't bear to have any of her other senses overloaded either – too much light and too many colours were like having nails in her skull.

Food was even worse. Eating meat was out of the question – blood and fat did not taste delicious to her, but instead carried an overpowering sensation of rot, decay, and putrefaction. All those muscle fibres and tendons remembered being part of a living creature, of being connected, whole, bright with life. To taste meat was to know, instantly and profoundly, that she was gnawing on a hunk of a corpse.

It made her gag. Sancia lived almost entirely off of plain rice mixed with beans, and weak cane wine. She did not touch strong alcohol – she needed total control over her senses just to function. And any water found in the Commons, of course, was not to be trusted.

Sancia sat on her bed, bent forward, rocking back and forth with anxiety. She felt small and alone, as she often did after a job, and she missed the one creature comfort she desired the most: human company.

Sancia was the only person who'd ever been in her room, or in her bed, for touching people was unbearable: it wasn't quite like she heard their thoughts, because people's thoughts, despite what most believed, were not a smooth, linear narration. They were more like a giant, hot cloud of bellowing impulses and neuroses, and when she touched a person's skin, that hot cloud filled up her skull.

The press of flesh, the touch of warm skin – these sensations were perhaps the most intolerable of all for her.

But perhaps it was better, to be solitary. There was less risk that way.

She breathed deep for a moment, trying to calm her mind.

You're safe, she said to herself. *And alone. And free. For another day.*

Then she pulled her hood over her head, tied it tight, lay down, and shut her eyes.

But sleep never came.

After an hour of lying there, she sat up, took off her hood, lit a candle, looked at her closed closet door, and thought.

This . . . bothers me, she thought. *A lot.*

The problem, she decided, was a matter of risks.

Sancia lived her life very carefully – or at least as carefully as one could while making a living climbing towers and breaking into places full of dangerous, armed men – and she always sought to minimise any potential hazards.

And the more she thought about it, possessing something small that was worth the nigh-inconceivable sum of twenty thousand duvots while not knowing what that thing actually *was* . . .

Well. It now felt mad. Especially if she was going to hold on to it for three scrumming days.

Because the most valuable things in the city of Tevanne were undoubtedly scriving designs: the strings of sigils that made scrived rigs work. Scriving designs took a great deal of effort and talent to compose, and were the most protected property of any merchant house. Get the right scriving design and you could instantly start making all kinds of augmented devices at a foundry – devices that could easily be worth a fortune. Though Sancia had often been offered work to go after merchant house designs, she and Sark always turned it down, since house-breakers who ran such jobs often wound up pale, cold, and bobbing in a canal.

And though Sark had assured her that this job had *not* been about scriving designs – twenty thousand duvots could make anyone too stupid for their own good.

She sighed, trying to quell the dread in her stomach. She walked over to the closet, opened it, opened her false floor, and took the box out.

She looked at it for a long time. It was unadorned pine, with a brass clasp. She took off her gloves and felt it with her bare hands.

Again, the box's form and shape bled into her mind – a large cavity, full of papers. Again, she sensed the box's false bottom, with the linen-wrapped item beneath. Nothing else – and no way for someone to *know* she'd opened the box, then.

Sancia took a breath and opened it.

She felt sure the papers would be covered in sigil strings, which would have been as good as a death warrant for her – but they were not. They were elaborate sketches of what looked like old carved stones with writing on them.

Someone had written notes on the bottom of a sketch. Sancia was only a little better than literate, but she tried her best, and read:

Artefacts of the Occidental Empire

> It is common knowledge that the hierophants of the old empire utilised a number of astounding tools in their works, but their methods remain unclear to us. While our modern-day scriving persuades objects that their reality is something that it is not, the Occidental hierophants were apparently able to use scriving to alter reality directly, commanding the world itself to instantly and permanently change. Many have theorised about how this was possible – but none have conclusive answers.
>
> More questions arise when we study the stories of Crasedes the Great himself, first of the Occidental hierophants. There are many tales and legends of Crasedes utilising some kind of invisible assistant – sometimes a sprite, or spirit, or entity, often kept in a jar or box that he could open at his discretion – to help him in his labours.

> Was this entity another alteration that the hierophants had made to reality? Or did it exist at all? We do not know – but there seems to be some connection to the greatest and most mysterious of the tales of Crasedes the Great: that he built his own artificial god to govern the whole of the world.
>
> If Crasedes was in possession of some kind of invisible entity, perhaps it was but a rough prototype for this last and greatest iteration.

Sancia put the paper down. She understood absolutely none of this. She'd heard something once about the Occidentals during her time in Tevanne – some kind of fairy story about ancient giants, or maybe angels – but no one had ever claimed the hierophants were *real*. Yet whoever had written these notes – perhaps the owner of the box – certainly seemed to think so.

But she knew these papers weren't the real treasure. She dumped them out and set them aside.

She reached into the box with two fingers and slid the false bottom away. Below was the small item, wrapped in linen, about as long as her hand.

Sancia reached for it, but paused.

She couldn't afford to screw up this payout. She needed to get the money together to pay a physiquere who could fix the scar on her head, fix what was wrong with her, make her somewhat . . . normal. Or close to it.

She rubbed the scar on the side of her head as she looked inside the box. She knew that somewhere under her scalp, screwed into her skull, was a fairly large metal plate, and on that plate were some complicated sigils. She didn't know anything about the commands there, but she knew that they were almost certainly the source of her talents.

She also knew that the fact that the plate had been forcibly implanted inside her would not matter one whit to the merchant houses: a scrived human was somewhere between an abomination and a rare, invaluable specimen, and they'd treat her accordingly.

Which was why her operation would be so expensive: Sancia would have to pay a black-market physiquere more than the merchant houses were willing to reward them for handing her in – and the merchant houses were willing to pay a lot.

She looked at the linen-wrapped item in her hand. She had no idea what it was. But despite Sark's warnings, the risks of not knowing were just too high.

She put the box down, took out the item, and began unwrapping it. As she did so, she caught a glint of gold . . .

Just a gold piece? A piece of gold jewellery?

But then she pulled the cloth away, and saw it was not jewellery.

She looked at the item lying on the linen in the palm of her hand.

It was a key. A large, long key made of gold, with an intricate, terribly strange tooth, and a rounded head that sported an oddly carved hole. To Sancia, the hole faintly resembled the outline of a butterfly.

'What in hell?' she said aloud.

Sancia peered closely at it. It was a curious piece, but she couldn't see why it would be worth all this . . .

Then she saw them – there, along the edge of the key, and curling around the tooth: etchings. The key was scrived, but the commands were so slender, so delicate, so *complex* . . . They were like nothing she'd ever seen before.

But what was stranger still – if this key was scrived, why couldn't she hear it? Why didn't it murmur in the back of her mind like every other scrived device she'd ever encountered?

This doesn't make any sense, she thought.

She touched a single bare finger to the gold key.

And the second she did, she heard a voice in her mind – not the usual avalanche of sensations, but a real, actual *voice,* so clear it sounded like someone was standing right next to her, speaking rapidly in a bored tone: *<Oh, great. First the box, and now this! Aw, look at her . . . I bet she's never even heard of soap . . . >*

Sancia let out a gasp and dropped the key. It fell to the floor, and she jumped back from it like it was a rabid mouse.

The key just sat there, much as any key would.

She stared around herself. She was – as she knew full well – completely alone in this room.

She crouched down and looked at the key. Then she reached down and carefully touched it . . .

Instantly, the voice sprang to life in her ear.

<*. . . can't have heard me. It's impossible! But ah yeeaaahh she's definitely looking at me like she heard me, and . . . Okay. Now she's touching me again. Yeah. Yeah. This is probably bad.*>

Sancia took her finger away like it had been burned. She looked around herself again, wondering if she were going mad.

'This is *impossible,*' she muttered.

Then, throwing caution to the wind, she picked up the key.

Nothing. Silence. Maybe she'd imagined it.

Then the voice said: <*I'm imagining this, right? You can't actually hear me – can you?*>

Sancia's eyes shot wide.

<*Oh, hell. You* can *hear me, can't you?*>

She blinked, wondering what to do. She said aloud, 'Uh. Yes.'

<*Crap. Crap! How can you do that? How can you* hear *me? I haven't met anyone who could hear me in . . . Hell, I don't know. I can't remember the last time. Then again, I can't really remember all that much, truth be to—*>

'This is impossible,' said Sancia for the second time.

<*What is?*> said the voice.

'You're a . . . a . . .'

<*A what?*>

'A . . .' She swallowed. 'A key.'

<*I'm a key. Yes. I didn't really think that was under dispute.*>

'Right, but a . . . a *talking* key.'

<*Right, and you're some grimy girl who can hear me,*> said the voice in her ear. <*I've been talking for a hell of a lot longer than you've been alive, kid, so really* I'm *the normal one here.*>

Sancia laughed madly. 'This is insane. It's *insane.* That's got to be it. I've gone insane.'

<*Maybe. Maybe. I don't know what your situation is. But that wouldn't have anything to do with me.*> The voice cleared his throat. <*So. Where am I? And, ah, oh. That's right. I'm Clef, by the way. Now – who in the hell are you?*>

4

Sancia put the key back in the false floor in her closet, slammed it shut, and then slammed the closet door closed.

She stared at the closet for a moment, breathing hard. Then she walked over to her apartment door, unlocked the six locks, and peered out into her hallway.

Empty. Which made sense, since it was probably three in the morning by now.

She shut the door, locked it, went to the shutters, unlocked them, and looked outside, panic fluttering in her rib cage like a trapped moth. Again, no movement in the street.

She didn't know why she was doing this. Perhaps it was sheer compulsion: to have something so wild, so insane, so unbelievable happen to her *had* to invite danger.

Yet she could see none coming – not yet, at least.

She closed her shutters and locked them. Then she sat on her bed, holding her stiletto. She wasn't sure what she was going to do with it – stab the key? – but it felt better to be holding it.

She stood, walked back to her closet door, and said, 'I'm . . . I'm going to open the door and take you out now – all right?'

Silence.

She let out a shuddering breath. *What the hell did we get mixed up in?* She was used to scrived devices muttering things, sure, but to have one directly address her like an overcaffeinated street vendor . . .

She opened the closet door, opened the false floor, and looked at the key. Then she gritted her teeth, stiletto still in her left hand, and picked it up with her right.

Silence. Perhaps she'd dreamed it, or imagined it.

Then the voice spoke up in her mind: *<That was kind of an overreaction, wasn't it?>*

Sancia flinched. 'I don't think so,' she said. 'If my chair starts talking to me, it's going out the goddamn window. What the hell are you?'

<I told you what I am. I'm Clef. You never told me your name, you know.>

'I don't need to tell a damn object my name!' said Sancia angrily. 'I'm also not going to introduce myself to the doorknob!'

<You need to calm down, kid. You're going to give yourself a fit if you stay this worked up. And I don't want to be stuck in the saddest apartment in the whole world with some grimy girl's decaying corpse.>

'What merchant house made you?' she demanded.

<Huh? House? Merchants? What?>

'What merchant house made you? Dandolo? Candiano? Morsini, Michiel? Which one of them made this . . . this thing you are, whatever it is?'

<I don't know what the hell you're talking about. What thing is it that you think I am?>

'A scrived device!' she said, exasperated. 'Altered, augmented, elevated, whatever damn term the campo people use! You're a rig, aren't you?'

Clef was silent for a long while. Then he said, *<Uh, okay. I'm trying to think of how to answer that. But, quick question – what's 'scrived' mean?>*

'You don't know what scriving is? It's the . . . it's the symbols that are drawn on you, these things that make you who you are, what you are!' She looked closer at his tooth. She didn't know much about scriving – as far as she was aware, it took about a thousand certifications and degrees to do it – but she hadn't ever seen sigils like these. 'Where did you come from?'

<*Ah, now* that *question I can answer!*> said Clef.

'Okay. Then tell me.'

<*Not until you at least tell me your name. You've compared me to a doorknob and a chair, and you've also said I was a . . . a 'rig.'*> He said the word with palpable contempt. <*I feel like I'm entitled to* something *resembling decent treatment here.*>

Sancia hesitated. She wasn't sure why she was so reluctant to tell Clef her name – perhaps it felt like something out of a children's story, the foolish girl who gives her name away to the wicked demon. But finally she relented, and said, 'Sancia.'

<*Sahn chee yuh?*> He said the word like it was the name of a grotesque dish.

'Yes. My name is Sancia.'

<*Sancia, huh?*> said Clef. <*Terrible name. Anyways. You already know I'm Clef, so—*>

'And where did you come from, Clef?' she said, frustrated.

<*That's easy,*> said Clef. <*The dark.*>

'You . . . what? The dark? You're from the dark?'

<*Yeah. Someplace dark. Very dark.*>

'Where is this dark place?'

<*How should I know? I don't have much frame of reference here, kid. All I know is that between it and here is a whole lot of water.*>

'So they shipped you over the ocean. Yeah. I figured that. Who shipped you over here?'

<*Some guys. Dirty. Smelly. Jabbered a lot. I expect you'd have got on pretty well with them.*>

'Where were you before the dark?'

<*There's nothing before the dark. There's just the dark. I was always in the dark, as . . . as far as I can recall.*> There was a note of anxiety in his voice at that.

'What was with you in the dark?' asked Sancia.

<*Nothing. There was just me, and the dark, and nothing else. For . . .* > He paused.

'For how long?'

Clef laughed miserably. *<Think of a long time. Then multiply that times ten. Then multiply* that *times a hundred. Then a thousand. That still doesn't come close to how long I was there, in the dark, alone.>*

Sancia was silent. That sounded like something akin to hell to her – and it sounded like Clef was still shaken by it.

<Still, not sure if this place is an improvement,> said Clef. *<What is this, a prison? Who'd you kill? It must have been someone really great to be punished like this.>*

'This is my apartment.'

<You live this way voluntarily? *What, you can't get yourself even, like, one picture?>*

Sancia decided to cut to it. 'Clef . . . You know I stole you – right?'

<Ah – no. You . . . stole me? From who?>

'I don't know. From a safe.'

<Ah, now who's got the shitty, unsatisfying answers? How's it feel? I guess that's why you're acting so damned panicked.>

'I'm panicked,' said Sancia, 'because to get you, I had to do a ton of things that could get me harpered in a blink.'

<Harpered? What's that?>

Sighing, Sancia quickly tried to tell Clef that 'harpering' referred to a method of public torture and execution in Tevanne: the subject was placed in a stockade, and the harper – a long, thin piece of extremely strong wire, attached to a small, scrived device – was placed in a loop around their neck, or perhaps their hands or feet or delicates. The scrived device would then, much to the subject's distress, begin cheerily retracting the wire, tightening the loop inch by inch, until finally the wire bit into and completely amputated the chosen extremity.

It was an extremely popular spectacle in Tevanne, but Sancia had never attended a harpering. Mostly because she knew that, in her line of work, there was a not-insignificant chance it could be her bits in the loop.

<Oh. Well. I can see how that makes this all pretty urgent.>

'Right. So. You don't know who owned you, do you?'

<Nope.>

'Or who made you.'

<That presumes I was made, which is something I'm not sure of yet.>

'That's insane. Someone had to have made you!'

<Why?>

She couldn't come up with a good answer to that. She was mainly trying to figure out exactly how much danger she was in. Clef was obviously, undoubtedly the most advanced scrived device she'd ever seen – and she *was* pretty sure he was a scrived device – but she wasn't sure why someone would be willing to pay forty fortunes for him. A key that did little more than insult you in your mind would have pretty low value to the merchant houses.

Then she realised there was an obvious question she hadn't asked yet.

'Clef,' she said, 'since you're a key and all . . . what exactly do you ope—'

<You know you don't have to talk out loud, right? I can hear your thoughts.>

Sancia dropped the key and backed away to the corner of her room.

She stared at Clef, thinking rapidly. She did *not* like the idea of a scrived item reading her mind, not one damned bit. She tried to remember all the things she'd thought since she'd started talking to him. Had she given away any secrets? Could Clef even hear the thoughts she hadn't known she'd been thinking?

If there's risk in exposing yourself to him, she thought, *it's a risk you've already taken.*

Glowering, she walked back over, knelt, touched a digit to the key, and demanded, 'What the hell do you mean, hear my thoughts?'

<Okay, wait, sorry. Poor phrasing. I can hear some *of your thoughts. I can hear them if – if! – you think them hard enough.>*

She picked him up. 'What does *that* mean, think them hard enough?'

<Why not try thinking something hard, and I'll let you know?>

Sancia thought something very hard at Clef.

<Very funny,> said Clef. *<Obviously I can't do as you suggest, as I don't have the necessary orifices.>*

<Wait,> thought Sancia. *<You can really hear this?>*

<Yeah.>

<You can hear what I'm thinking right now?>

<Yeah.>

<Every single word?>

<No, I'm just saying 'yeah' for no reason. Yes, yes, I can hear you!>

She wasn't sure how she felt about this. It was as if Clef had moved into a room upstairs inside her mind, and was whispering to her through a hole in the ceiling. She struggled to remember what she'd been talking to him about.

<What do you open, Clef?> she asked him.

<What do I open?>

<You're a key, right? So that means you open something. Unless you don't remember that, either.>

<Oh. No, no, I remember that.>

<So . . . what do you open?>

<Anything.>

There was a silence.

<Huh?> said Sancia.

<Huh what?> asked Clef.

<You open anything?>

<Yes.>

<What do you mean, anything?>

<I mean what I said. Anything. I open anything that has a lock, and even a few things that don't.>

<What? Bullshit.>

<It's true.>

<Bullshit, it's true.>

<You don't believe me? Why not try it out?>

Sancia considered it, and had an idea. She walked over to her open closet. Sitting in the corner was her collection of practice locks, specimens she'd ripped out of doors or stolen from mechanists' shops, which she laboured over every other night, refining her skills.

<If you're lying,> she said, *<you've picked the exact wrong person to lie to.>*

<Watch,> said Clef. *<And observe.>*

Sancia picked up one of the locks, a Miranda Brass, which was generally considered to be one of the more formidable conventional locks – meaning not scrived – in Tevanne. Sancia herself, with all her talents, usually took about three to five minutes to pick it.

<*What do I do?*> she asked. <*Just put you in the keyhole?*>

<*What else would you do with a key?*>

Sancia lined Clef up, gave him a mistrustful glance, and slid the golden key into the lock.

Instantly, there was a loud *click*, and the Miranda Brass sprang open.

Sancia stared.

'Holy shit,' she whispered.

<*Believe me now?*> said Clef.

Sancia dropped the Miranda Brass, picked up another – this one a Genzetti, not as durable as a Miranda, but more complicated – and popped Clef in.

Click.

'Oh my God,' said Sancia. 'What in all harpering hell . . . how are you *doing* that?'

<*Oh, it's easy. All closed things wish to open. They're* made *to open. They're just made to be really reluctant about it. It's a matter of asking them from the right way, from inside themselves.*>

<*So . . . you're just a polite lockpick?*>

<*That's a really reductive way of thinking about it, but sure, yeah, whatever.*>

They went through the rest of the locks, one by one. Every time, the second Clef penetrated the keyhole, the lock sprang open.

<*I . . . I don't believe it,*> said Sancia.

<*This is what I am, girl,*> said Clef. <*This is what I do.*>

She stared into space, thinking. And an inevitable idea quickly captured her thoughts.

With Clef in her hands, she could rob the Commons absolutely blind, build up the savings to pay the black-market physiqueres to make her normal again, and skip town. Maybe she didn't even need the twenty thousand her client was dangling in front of her.

But Sancia was pretty sure her client was from one of the four merchant houses, since that was who dealt in scrived items. And she couldn't exactly use a lockpick to fend off a dozen bounty hunters all looking to lop her to pieces, and that was precisely what the houses would send her way. Sancia was good at running, and with Clef in her hand, she could maybe run quite far – but outrunning the merchant houses was difficult to ponder.

<*Well, that was boring,*> said Clef. <*You don't have any better locks than that?*>

Sancia snapped out of her reverie. <*Huh? No.*>

<*Really? None?*>

<*No mechanist has ever dreamed up anything stronger than a Miranda Brass. There's no need to, not with scrived locks available for the really rich people.*>

<*Huh. Scrived locks? What do you mean?*>

Sancia pulled a face and wondered how in the hell to explain scriving. <*Okay. Well. There's these things called sigils – it's some kind of angelic alphabet that the scrivers discovered, or something. Anyways, when you write the right sigils on things, you can make them . . . different. Like, if you write the sigil for 'stone' on a piece of wood, it becomes more like stone – a little stronger, a little more waterproof. It . . . I don't know, it convinces the wood to be something it isn't.*>

<*Sounds tedious. What's this got to do with locks?*>

<*Hell . . . I don't know how to put this. The scrivers figured out a way to combine sigils to make a bunch of new languages. Ones that are more specific, more powerful – ones that can convince items to be really,* really *different. So they can make locks that only open for* one *key in the whole world, and they're completely unpickable. It's not a matter of pressing and pulling on the right lever, or something – the lock* knows *there's only one key it's supposed to open for.*>

<*Huh,*> said Clef. <*Interesting. You got any of those lying around?*>

<*What? Hell no, I don't have a scrived lock! If I was rich enough to afford a scrived lock, I wouldn't be living in a rookery where the latrine is just a bucket and a window!*>

<*Yeesh, I didn't want to know* that*!*> said Clef, disgusted.

<*It's impossible to pick scrived locks, anyways. Everyone knows that.*>

<*Eh, no. I told you, everything closed wants to open.*>

Sancia had never heard of a rig that was capable of picking scrived locks – but then, she'd never heard of one that could see and talk either. <*You really think you can pick scrived locks?*>

<*'Course I can. You want me to prove that too?*> he said, smug. <*Think of the biggest, meanest scrived lock you can, and I'll bust it down like it was made of straw.*>

Sancia looked out her window. It was almost dawn, the sun

crawling over the edge of the distant campo walls and spilling across the leaning rooftops of the Commons.

<I'll think about it,> she said. She put him in her false floor, shut the door, and lay on her bed.

Alone in her room, Sancia thought back to her last meeting with Sark, at the abandoned fishery building on the Anafesto Channel.

She remembered navigating all the tripwires and traps that Sark had set for her – 'insurance,' Sark had called it, since he'd known that Sancia, with all her talents, would be the only one who could safely circumvent them. As she'd gingerly stepped over the last tripwire and trotted upstairs, she'd glimpsed his gnarled, scarred face emerging from the shadows of the reeking building – and to her surprise, he'd been grinning.

I've got a corker for you, San, he'd rasped. *I've got a big fish on the line and no mistake.*

Marino Sarccolini, her fence, agent, and the closest thing she had to a friend in this world. Though few would have thought to befriend Sark – for he was one of the most disfigured people Sancia had ever seen.

Sark had one foot, no ears, no nose, and he was missing every other finger on his hands. Sometimes it seemed about half his body was scar tissue. It took him hours to get around the city, especially if he had to take any stairs – but his mind was still quick and cunning. He was a former 'canal man' for Company Candiano, an officer who'd organised theft, espionage, and sabotage against the other three merchant houses. The position was called such because the work, like Tevanne's canals, was filthy. But then the founder of Company Candiano had gone mysteriously mad, the company had almost collapsed, and nearly everyone had got fired except for the most valuable scrivers. Suddenly all kinds of people who'd been used to campo life found themselves living in the Commons.

And there, Sark had tried to keep doing what he'd always done: thieving, sabotaging, and spying on the four main merchant houses.

Except in the Commons he hadn't had the protection of a merchant house. So when he'd finally got sniffed out by agents of Morsini House after one daring raid, they'd taken him and ruined him beyond repair.

Such were the rules of life in the Commons.

When she finally saw him that day in the fishery, Sancia had been taken aback by the look on Sark's face – for she'd never seen him . . . delighted. A person like Sark had little to be delighted about. It was unsettling.

He'd started talking. He'd vaguely described the job. She'd listened. When he'd told her the price tag, she'd scoffed and told him that the whole thing had to be a scam – no one was going to pay them that much.

At that, he'd tossed her a leather envelope. She'd glanced in it, and gasped.

Inside had been nearly three thousand in paper duvots – an absurd rarity in the Commons.

An advance, said Sark.

What! We never get advances.

I know.

Especially not in . . . in paper money!

I know.

She'd looked at him, wary. *Is this a design job, Sark? I don't deal in scriving designs, you know that. That shit will get us both harpered.*

And that's not what this is, if you can believe it. The job is just a box. A small *box. And since scriving designs are usually dozens of pages long, if not hundreds, then I think we can rule that out.*

Then what is *in the box?*

We don't know.

And who owns the box?

We don't know.

And who wants the box?

Someone with twenty thousand duvots.

She'd considered it. This hadn't been terribly unusual for their line of work – usually it was better for all parties involved to know as little as possible about one another.

So, she'd said. *How are we supposed to get the box?*

He'd grinned wider, flashing crooked teeth. *I'm glad you asked . . .*

And they'd sat and hashed it all out right then and there.

Afterward, though – after the glee of planning it out, preparing it, discussing it there in the dark of the fishery – a queer dread had seeped into Sancia's stomach. *There anything I should be worried about here, Sark?*

Anything I know? *No.*

Okay. Then anything you suspect?

I think it's house work, he'd said. *Those are the only people who could toss around three thousand in paper. But we've done work for the houses before, when they need deniability. So in some ways, it's familiar – do as they ask, and they'll pay well, and let you keep your guts where they are.*

So why is this different?

He'd thought for a moment, and said, *With this price tag . . . well, it's got to be coming from the top, yeah? A founder, or a founderkin. People who live behind walls and walls and walls. And the higher you go in the houses, the richer and madder and stupider these people get. We could be stealing some princeling's plaything. Or we could be stealing the wand of Crasedes the Great himself, for all I know.*

Comforting.

Yeah. So we need to play this right, Sancia.

I always play it right.

I know. You're a professional. But if this is coming from the echelons, we need to be extra cautious. He'd held out his arms. *I mean, look at me. You can see what happens when you cross them. And you . . .*

She'd looked at him, eyes hard. *And me?*

Well. They used to own you. So you know what they can be like.

Sancia slowly sat up in bed. She was achingly tired, but she still couldn't sleep.

That comment – *They used to own you* – it had bothered her then, and it bothered her now.

The scar on the side of her head prickled. So did the scars on her back – and she had a lot more there.

They don't own me still, she insisted to herself. *My days are free now.*

But this, she knew, was not entirely true.

She opened the closet, opened the false floor, and picked Clef up.

<*Let's go,*> she said.

<*Finally!*> Clef said, excited.

5

Sancia ran a string through Clef's head and hung him around her neck, hidden in her jerkin. Then she walked down her rookery stairs and slipped out the side door. She scanned the muddy fairway for any watchful eyes, and started off.

By now the streets of Foundryside were filling up with people, tottering or skulking over the wooden sidewalks. Most were labourers, staggering off to work with their heads still aching from too much cane wine the night before. The air was hazy and humid, and the mountains rose in the distance, steaming and dark. Sancia had never been in the uplands beyond Tevanne. Most Tevannis hadn't. Living in Tevanne might be rough, but the mountainous jungles were a lot worse.

Sancia turned a corner and spotted a body lying in the fairway up ahead, its clothes dark with blood. She crossed the street to avoid it.

<*Holy shit,*> said Clef.

<*What?*>

<*Was that guy dead?*>

<How can you see, Clef? You don't have eyes.>

<Do you know how your eyes work?>

<. . . that's a good point, I guess.>

<Right. And . . . and you did *see that, right? That guy was dead?>*

She looked back and observed how much of the man's throat was missing. *<For his sake, I sure hope so.>*

<Whoa. Is . . . Is anyone going to do something about it?>

<Like what?>

<Like . . . I don't know, take care of the body?>

<Eh, maybe. I've heard there's a market for human bones in the Commons north of here. Never found out exactly what they wanted them for, though.>

<No, I mean – is anyone going to try to catch the killer? Don't you have any authorities who try to make sure that stuff doesn't happen?>

<Oh,> said Sancia. *<No.>*

And she explained.

Since it was the merchant houses that made Tevanne great, it was probably inevitable that most city property would wind up being owned by them. But the houses were *also* all competitors who jealously protected their scriving designs; for, as everyone knew, intellectual property is the easiest kind to steal.

This meant that all the land the houses owned was fiercely guarded, hidden behind walls and gates and checkpoints, inaccessible to all except those who possessed the proper markers. The house lands were so restricted and controlled they were practically different countries – which the city of Tevanne more or less acknowledged.

Four walled-off little city-states, all crammed into Tevanne, all wildly different regions with their own schools, their own living quarters, their own marketplaces, their own cultures. These merchant house enclaves – the campos – took up about eighty per cent of Tevanne.

But if you didn't work for a house, or weren't affiliated with them – in other words, if you were poor, lame, uneducated, or just the wrong sort of person – then you lived in the remaining twenty per cent of Tevanne: a wandering, crooked ribbon of streets and city squares and in-between places – the Commons.

There were a lot of differences between the Commons and the campos. The campos, for instance, had waste systems, fresh water, well-maintained roads, and their buildings tended to stay standing, which wasn't always the case in the Commons. The campos also had a plethora of scrived devices to make their lives easier, which the Commons certainly did not. Walk into the Commons showing off a fancy scrived trinket, and you'd have your throat slit and your treasure snatched in an instant.

Because another thing that the campos had that the Commons did not was laws.

Each campo had its own rules and law enforcement, all of which fully applied within their rambling, crooked boundaries. But because each campo's individuality was considered sacrosanct, this meant there was no defined set of citywide laws, nor was there any real citywide law enforcement, or judicial system, or even prisons – to establish such things, the Tevanni elite had decided, would be to suggest that the power of Tevanne superseded the powers of the campos.

So if you were part of a merchant house, and resided on a campo, you had such things.

If you didn't, and you lived in the Commons, then you were just . . . there. And, considering all the disease and starvation and violence and whatnot, you probably weren't there for long.

<*Holy hell,*> said Clef. <*How do you live like that?*>

<*Same way everyone lives, I guess,*> said Sancia, taking a left. <*One day at a time.*>

Finally they came to their destination. Up ahead, the wet, rambling rookeries of Foundryside came to a sharp stop at a tall, smooth white wall, about sixty feet high, clean and perfect and unblemished.

<*We're coming up on something big and scrived, aren't we?*> said Clef.

<*How can you tell?*>

<*I just can.*>

That disturbed her. She could tell if a rig was scrived if she got within a few feet of it – she'd start hearing that muttering in her head. But Clef seemed to be able to do it from dozens of feet away.

She walked along the wall until she found it. Set in the face of the wall was a huge, engraved bronze door, intricate and ornate, with a house loggotipo in the middle: the hammer and the chisel.

<*That's a hell of a big door,*> said Clef. <*What is this place?*>

<*This is the Candiano campo wall. That's their loggotipo in the door.*>

<*Who are they?*>

<*Merchant house. Used to be the biggest one, but then their founder went mad, and I hear they had to lock him away in a tower somewhere.*>

<*Probably not good for business, that.*>

<*No.*> She approached the door and heard a faint chanting in her head. <*No one really knows what they use this door for. Some say it's for secret business, when the Candianos want to snatch someone out of the Commons. Others say it's just so they can sneak their whores in and out. I've never seen it open. It's not guarded, because they think no one can break it – since it's scrived, of course.*> She stood before the door. It was tall, about ten feet high or so. <*But you think you can, Clef?*>

<*Oh, I'd* love *to try,*> he said with surprising relish.

<*How are you going to do it?*>

<*I dunno yet. I'll have to see. Come on! Even if I can't, what's the worst that can happen?*>

The answer, Sancia knew, was 'a lot'. Tampering with anything related to the merchant houses was a great way to lose a hand, or a head. She knew this wasn't like her, to be walking around the Commons with stolen goods in broad daylight – especially considering this particular stolen good was the most advanced scrived rig she'd ever seen.

It was unprofessional. It was risky. It was stupid.

But that nonchalant comment of Sark's – *They used to own you, you know what they're like* – it echoed in her head. She was surprised to find how much she resented it, and she wasn't sure why. She'd always known when she was doing work for the merchant houses, and it'd never inspired her to play the job wrong before.

But to have him just come out and say that – it burned her.

<*What are you waiting for?*> begged Clef.

She approached the door, eyeing the scrivings running along its frame. She heard the faint muttering in her head, as she did whenever she was close to anything altered . . .

Then she knelt and put Clef into the lock, and the muttering turned into a scream.

Screaming questions poured into her mind, all of them directed at Clef, asking him dozens if not hundreds of questions, trying to figure out what he was. Many of them went by too fast for her to understand, but she caught some of them:

<BE YOU THE BEJEWELLED SPUR OF WHICH THE LADY WROUGHT ON THE FIFTH DAY?> bellowed the door at Clef.

<No, bu—>

<BE YOU THE TOOL OF THE MASTER, THE WAND FERROUS WITH THE WIDDERSHINS ETCHINGS, WHO SHALL HAVE ONLY ACCESS ONCE A FORTNIGHT?>

<Well, see, I—>

<BE YOU THE TREMBLING LIGHT, FORGED TO FIND THE FLAWS OTTONE?>

<Okay, hold on now, but . . . >

And on and on and on. It all went too fast for Sancia to really understand – and how she was even *hearing* it was stupefying to her – but she could still catch snatches of the conversation. It sounded like security questions, like the scrived door was expecting a specific key, and it was slowly figuring out that Clef was not that key.

<BE YOU AN ARMAMENT FERROUS, FORGED FOR THE BREAKING OF THE OATHS WHICH HAVE BEEN LAID UPON ME?>

<Partially,> Clef said.

A pause.

<PARTIALLY?>

<Yeah.>

<HOW ARE YOU PARTIALLY AN ARMAMENT FERROUS FORGED FOR THE BREAKING OF THE OATHS WHICH HAVE BEEN LAID UPON ME?>

<Well, it's complicated. Let me explain.>

Information poured back and forth between Clef and the door. Sancia was still trying to catch her breath – it was like trying to swallow an ocean all at once. She suspected that, as long as she was touching Clef, she could hear whatever he heard as well.

But all she could think was: *That's what a scrived device is? That? It's . . . like, a mind? They* think*?*

She'd never have expected this. Certainly, she was used to hearing a faint muttering when she was close to scrived items – but she'd still assumed they were just *things*, just objects.

<Explain it to me again,> said Clef.

<WHEN THE SIGNALS ARE GIVEN,> said the door, now uncertain, *<ALL SHAFTS ARE RETRACTED, AND OUTWARD PIVOT IS PERFORMED.>*

<Okay, but at what speed do you pivot outward?> asked Clef.

<W . . . WHAT SPEED?>

<Yeah. How hard do you pivot outward?>

<WELL . . . >

More messages poured back and forth between the door and Clef. She began to understand: when the proper scrived key was inserted into the door, it would send a signal to the door, which would tell it to withdraw its bolts and pivot outward. But Clef was confusing it, somehow, asking it too many questions about which direction it was supposed to pivot, and how fast or hard.

<Well, obviously I've got past the second rung,> Clef said to the door.

<THIS IS TRUE.>

<And the frame triggers are still in place.>

<ONE SECOND . . . THIS IS VERIFIED.>

<So what I'm saying here is . . . >

A massive amount of information coursed through the two entities. Sancia couldn't understand a bit of it.

<ALL RIGHT. I THINK I SEE. SO. BE YOU CERTAIN THAT THIS DOES NOT COUNT AS OPENING?>

<Positive.>

<AND BE YOU CERTAIN THAT THE SECURITY DIRECTIVES ARE MAINTAINED?>

<They look maintained to me. Don't they look that way to you?>

<I . . . SUPPOSE.>

<Listen, there's no rule against *any of this, is there?>*

<WELL, I GUESS NOT.>

<So let's give it a shot, eh?>

<I . . . ALL RIGHT.>

Silence.

Then the door started quivering. And then . . .

There was a loud *crack*, and the door opened. But it opened *inward*, and astonishingly hard – so hard that, since she was still holding Clef, and Clef was still in the lock, she was almost jerked off her feet.

Clef popped out as the door fell backward, its bronze face falling away . . . and then she saw the streets of the Candiano campo within.

Sancia stared down an empty Candiano street, alarmed, terrified, and bewildered. It was a totally different world on the other side of the wall: clean cobblestone streets, tall buildings with sculpted façades of dark moss clay, colourful banners and flags hanging from cords running over the paths, and . . .

Water. Fountains with just *water* in them, real, clear, running water. She could see three of them, even from here.

Even though she was stunned and terrified, she couldn't help but think: *They use water – clean water – as decoration?* Clean water was impossibly rare in the Commons, and most people drank weak cane wine instead. To just have it bubbling away in the streets for no reason was incomprehensible.

She came to her wits. She stared at the door, and saw a ragged hole in the wall beside it. She realised the door had never retracted its bolts – it had just swung backward so hard that the shafts had torn right through the wall.

'Holy . . . Holy *shit*!' whispered Sancia.

She turned and ran. Fast.

<*Ta-daa!*> said Clef in her head. <*See! I told you I could do it.*>

<*What the hell, what the hell!*> she thought, running. <*You broke the door! You broke the goddamn door to a goddamn campo wall!*>

<*Well. Yeah? I told you I'd get in.*>

<*What the hell did you do, Clef? What the hell did you do!*>

<*Uh, I convinced him that opening inward didn't really count as opening?*> said Clef. <*So it wouldn't trigger a whole host of his warding questions about me breaking it open. It's not breaking open the door if the door doesn't actually think it's opening, right? And then I just had to convince him to open inward hard enough that we didn't have to bother with any of his bolts, which were the most protected.*> He sounded relaxed, even drunk. She got the mad idea that cracking a scrived device gave Clef something akin to a powerful sexual release.

She dashed around a corner, then leaned up against the wall, panting. <*But . . . But . . . I didn't think you'd scrumming break the door in!*>

<*Scrumming? What? What's that mean?*>

Sancia then quickly attempted to explain that a scrum hole on a ship referred to the vents that allowed waves to wash out the fecal matter in the latrines. But some matter inevitably built up in the scrum hole, so crewmen would have to shove poles down into the holes to clear it out, which, sailors being somewhat filthy-minded people, inevitably became slang for the sexual practice of . . .

<Okay, crap, I get it!> said Clef. *<Stop!>*

<You . . . you can do that to scrived devices?> she asked.

<Sure,> said Clef. *<Scrived rigs, as you call them, are filled with commands, and the commands convince the object to be something it's not. It's like a debate – the debate has to be clear and make sense for you to be persuaded. But you can argue with the commands. Confuse them. Dupe them. It's easy!>*

<But . . . how did you know to do that? How do you know any *of that? You'd only just heard of scrived devices last night.>*

<Oh. Ah. Right.> There was a long pause. *<I . . . don't know,>* he said, and he sounded somewhat unsettled.

<You don't know.>

<N--No.>

<Do you remember any more, Clef? Or is it still just the dark for you?>

Another long silence. *<Can we talk about something else, please?>* asked Clef quietly.

Sancia took that as a no. *<Can you do that to any scrived device?>*

<Ahh, well. My speciality is stuff that wants to stay closed. Apertures. Doors. Barriers. Connection points. For example,> he said, *<I can't do anything about the plate in your head.>*

Sancia froze. *<What?>*

<Uhh,> said Clef. *<Did I say something wrong?>*

<How . . . How'd you know about the plate in my head?> she demanded.

<Because it's scrived. It's talking. It's convincing itself it's something it isn't. I can sense it. Just like you can hear other scrived things.>

<How can you sense it?>

<I just . . . do. It's what I do.>

<You're saying . . . feeling out and tricking scrived items is what you do? Even though you didn't know what it was you did, just five minutes ago?>

<I . . . I guess?> Clef said, now sounding confused again. *<I can't . . . I can't quite remember . . . >*

Sancia slowly leaned back against the wall. The world felt wobbly and distant to her as she tried to process all of this.

To begin with, it now seemed abundantly clear that Clef was suffering from some kind of memory loss. It felt odd to diagnose a key with a mental affliction, given that Sancia still didn't understand how or even if he possessed something resembling a mind. But if he did have a mind, that long time spent trapped in the dark – decades, if not centuries – would have been more than enough to break it.

Perhaps Clef was damaged. Either way, it seemed Clef did not know his own potential – and that was troubling, since Clef already seemed stupefyingly powerful.

Because though few understood how scriving worked, everyone in the world understood that it was both powerful and *reliable.* When merchant house ships – scrived to part the waters with incredible ease, and sporting altered sails that always billowed with the perfect breeze at the perfect angle – pulled up in front of your city and pointed their vast, scrived weaponry at you, you understood that all those weapons would work perfectly well, and you'd promptly surrender.

The alternative – the idea that those ships might malfunction, or fail – was inconceivable.

But it wasn't anymore. Not to Sancia, clutching Clef in her hand.

Scriving formed the foundation of the Tevanni empire. It had won countless cities, built up an army of slaves, and sent them to work in the plantation isles. But now, in Sancia's mind, that foundation was beginning to shift, and crack . . .

Then her skin went cold. *If I were a merchant house,* she thought to herself, *I'd do everything in my power to destroy Clef, and make sure no one ever,* ever *knew he'd existed.*

<*So,*> said Clef cheerily. <*What now?*>

She was wondering that herself. <*I need to make sure all this means what I think it means.*>

<*And . . . what do you think this means?*>

<*Well. I* think *it means that you and I and probably Sark are in a shitload of mortal peril, Clef.*>

<*Ahh – oh. And . . . uh, how can we confirm that?*>

She rubbed her mouth. Then she stood up, hung Clef back around her neck, and started off. <*I'm taking you to see some friends of mine. Ones who know a lot scrumming more about scriving than I do.*>

6

Sancia slipped down alleys and passageways and crossed the carriage fairways of Foundryside until she came to the next Commons neighbourhood – Old Ditch. Foundryside might have been unpleasant to live in because of the residents – the neighbourhood was notorious for its dense concentration of criminals – but Old Ditch was unpleasant due to its environment: since it was situated next to the Tevanni tanneries, the whole area smelled like death and rot.

Sancia did not mind such odours, however, and she wandered down a meandering alley, peering through the staggered rookeries and wooden shacks. The alley ended in a small, bland door, but hanging above it were four lit coloured lanterns – three red, one blue.

Not here, she thought.

She returned to the main street, then walked around a block until she came to a basement door. Four lanterns hung outside – again, three red, one blue.

Not here, either. She walked back to the main thoroughfare.

<*Are you lost?*> asked Clef.

<*No,*> she said. <*The people I want to see . . . They're kind of mobile.*>

<*What, like gypsies or something?*>

<*In a way. They move around a lot to avoid raids.*>

<*Raids from who?*>

<*The campos. The merchant houses.*>

She peered through a leaning iron fence at a crumbling stone courtyard. At the very back was a long stairwell down, and hanging above it were four lanterns – yet unlike the others, these were three blue, one red.

<*Here we are.*> Sancia hopped the fence and crossed the courtyard. She walked down the dark stairwell to a thick wooden door and knocked three times.

A slot in the door opened. A pair of eyes peered out, narrowed in suspicion. Then they saw Sancia and crinkled into a smile. 'Back so soon?' said a woman's voice.

'Not by choice,' said Sancia.

The door fell open and Sancia walked in. Instantly, the murmuring of hundreds of scrived objects filled up her ears.

<*Ah,*> said Clef. <*The merchant houses don't like your friends having quite so many toys?*>

<*Exactly.*>

The basement within was long, low, and strangely lit. Most of the luminescence came from the ten or so scrived glass lights that had been carelessly laid down on the stone floor. The corners were stuffed with books and piles of paper, all of them covered with instructions and diagrams. In between the lights were rolling carts that would, to the untrained eye, appear to be covered with rubbish: ingots of metals, loops of leather bands, strips of wood, and so on.

The room was also incredibly hot, thanks to the large scrived bowls at the back that heated copper and bronze and other metals into a broiling liquid, though someone had set up a fan to circulate the hot air out – cleverly powered, Sancia saw, by stolen carriage wheels, which ran and ran in place, operating the fans. About a half dozen people sat around the bowls of molten metals, plucking at the metals with long, stylus-like tools, which they then used to paint symbols on . . . Well. All kinds of things. Small, bronze balls.

Wooden boards. Shoes. Shirt collars. Carriage wheels. Hammers. Knives. Anything and everything.

The door shut behind Sancia, revealing a tall, thin, dark-skinned woman with a pair of magnifying goggles on top of her head. 'If you're looking for a custom job, San, you'll have to wait,' she said. 'We've got a rush order.'

'What's happening?' asked Sancia.

'The Candianos are mixing up their sachet procedures,' said the woman. 'Totally redoing everything. So a lot of our clients are desperate.'

'When are your clients ever *not* desperate?' asked Sancia.

She smiled, but Claudia was always smiling a little. This mystified Sancia, since in her own estimation Claudia didn't have much to smile about: scriving in such circumstances – hot, dark, and cramped – was not only uncomfortable, but also incredibly dangerous. Claudia's fingers and forearms, for instance, were spotted with shiny, bubbly burn scars.

But that was what the Scrappers had to do. To do their work in open environs would be to invite violence, if not death.

Scriving was a difficult practice. Painting dozens and hundreds of sigillums upon objects, all carefully forming commands and logic that would reshape that object's reality, required not only years of study but also a mind both calculating and creative. Lots of scrivers failed to secure employment at a merchant house campo, and many others washed out. And there'd been recent changes in the scriving culture that had made it suddenly quite difficult for a woman to find employment on the campos. Most merchant-house applicants who didn't make it went to other Tevanni fealty states to do undignified, dull work out in the backwaters.

But not all. Some moved to the Tevanni Commons and went independent: forging, adjusting, and stealing the designs of the four prime merchant houses.

This wasn't easy – but everyone had their contacts. Some were corrupt campo officials who could pass along the right designs and strings. Others were thieves like Sancia, who could steal merchant house instructions on how to make a sigil *just* right. But bit by bit, people had begun to share knowledge, until a small, nebulous group of dilettantes, ex-campo employees, and frustrated scrivers had built up a library of information in the Commons, and trade had flourished.

That was how the Scrappers got started.

If you needed a lock fixed, or a door reinforced, or a blade altered, or if you just wanted light or clean water, the Scrappers would sell you rigs that could do that – for a fee, of course. And that fee was usually pretty high. But it was the only way for a Commoner to get the tools and creature comforts reserved for the campos – though the quality was never totally reliable.

This was not illegal – as there were no laws in the Commons, it couldn't be. But it was also not illegal for the merchant houses to organise raids to kick down your door, destroy everything you'd made, and also maybe break your fingers or your face in the process.

So you had to stay quiet. Stay underground. And keep moving.

<*Not bad stuff,*> Clef said in Sancia's ear as they walked through the messy workshop. <*Some of it's trash, but some of it's pretty ingenious. Like the carriage wheels. They've figured out all kinds of uses for those.*>

<*The foundries did that first,*> said Sancia. <*Apparently that was where they first experimented with gravity, just so they could get all their machines to move around and work better.*>

<*Clever stuff.*>

<*Kind of. I hear it didn't go totally flawlessly at the start, and a few scrivers accidentally quintupled their gravity or something.*>

<*Meaning?*>

<*Meaning they got crushed into a vaguely flesh-like object about as thick as an iron pan.*>

<*Okay, maybe not so clever.*>

Claudia led Sancia to the back of the room, where Giovanni, a veteran Scrapper, was seated before a small desk and was carefully painting sigils onto a wooden button. He glanced up from his work, ever so briefly. 'Evening, San.' He smiled at her, his greying beard crinkling. He'd been a venerated scriver before he'd washed out of Morsini House, and the other Scrappers tended to defer to him. 'How'd the goods hold up? You seem all in one piece.'

'Somewhat.'

'Somewhat what?'

Sancia walked around and, with an air of quaint civility, moved his desk aside. Then she sat down in front of him and smiled into his face, her muddy eye squinting unpleasantly. 'They *somewhat* worked. Right up until your goddamn sailing rig nearly fell apart, and dumped me over the waterfront bridge.'

'It *what*?'

'Yeah. If it were anyone else, Gio, *anyone* else, I'd gut you stern to crotch for what happened out there.'

Giovanni blinked, then smiled. 'Discount next time? Twenty per cent?'

'Fifty.'

'Twenty-five.'

'Fifty.'

'Thirty?'

'*Fifty.*'

'All right, all right! Fifty it is . . .'

'Good,' said Sancia. 'Get stronger material for the parachute next time. *And* you overdid it on the flashbox.'

Giovanni's eyebrows rose. 'Oh. *Oh.* So *that's* what caused the waterfront fire?'

'Too much magnesium in the box,' said Claudia. She tsked. 'I told you so, Gio.'

'Duly noted,' he said. 'And . . . my apologies, dear Sancia. I shall correct the formulas accordingly for future rigs.' He moved his desk back and returned to the wooden button.

Sancia watched. 'So, what's going on? Your customers need new sachets that quick?'

'Yes,' said Claudia. 'Apparently the Candiano campo is . . . an unusually promiscuous one.'

'Promiscuous.'

'Yes. There is, how shall I say, a strong appetite there for discreet arrangements.'

'Ahh,' said Sancia, understanding. 'Night ladies, then.'

'And men,' added Giovanni.

'Yes,' said Claudia. 'Them too.'

This was well-trodden ground for Sancia. Merchant-house walls were scrived so that the entrances only allowed in people with specific identifying markers called sachets – wooden buttons with scrived permissions on them. If you walked through the wrong door with the wrong sachet or no sachet at all, you'd get accosted by guards, or even killed by them; or, in some of the inner walls of the campos, where the richest, most protected people lived, rumour had it you could spontaneously explode.

As someone who frequently needed illegitimate access to the campos, Sancia usually had to go to the Scrappers for forged sachets. But their biggest customers were undoubtedly prostitutes, who just wanted to go where the money was – though the Scrappers could usually only get you past the first wall or two. It was a lot harder to steal or forge the more elite credentials.

'Why'd the Candianos change up their sachets?' she asked. 'Did someone spook them?'

'No idea,' said Claudia. 'Rumour has it mad old Tribuno Candiano is about to pull up the eternal blanket at last and begin his final sleep.'

Giovanni clucked his tongue. 'The Conqueror himself, about to be conquered by old age. How tragic.'

'Maybe it's that,' said Claudia. 'Elite deaths often cause some campo shuffling. If so, with everything in flux, there's probably a lot of easy targets on the Candiano campo . . . If you were willing to take a side job, we'd pay.'

'*Not* market rates,' said Giovanni pointedly. 'But we'd pay.'

'Not this time,' Sancia said. 'I've got some pressing matters. I need you to look at something.'

'Like I said,' Claudia told her, 'we've got a rush job here.'

'I don't need you to copy the scrivings,' said Sancia. 'And I'm not sure you *can*. I just need . . . advice.'

Claudia and Giovanni exchanged a glance. 'What do you mean, we can't copy the scrivings?' asked Claudia.

'And since when do you ever ask for advice?' asked Giovanni.

<*Ah,*> said Clef in her ear. <*So. This is when I make my grand entrance?*>

⁂

'Neat,' said Claudia. She peered at Clef over the scrived lights, her pale eyes huge and enlarged by her magnifying goggles. 'But also . . . very weird.'

Giovanni looked over her shoulder. 'I've never seen anything like it. Never, in all my days.'

Claudia glanced sideways at Sancia. 'You say it . . . talks to you?'

'Yeah,' said Sancia.

'And it's not your . . .' She tapped the side of her head.

'I think that's *why* I can hear him – when I'm touching him, that is,' said Sancia. Besides Sark, Claudia and Giovanni were the only people who knew that Sancia was a scrived human. They'd had to know, since they were the ones who'd put her in touch with the black-market physiqueres. But she trusted them. Mostly because the Scrappers were just as hated and hunted by the merchant houses as she herself would be, if they ever found out what she was. If the Scrappers gave her up, she could give them up in turn.

'What does it say?' asked Giovanni.

'Mostly he asks what all of our swears mean. Have you ever heard of anything like this?'

'I've seen scrived keys before,' said Claudia. 'I tinkered with a few myself. Yet these etchings, these sigils . . . They're totally unfamiliar to me.' She looked up at Giovanni. 'Sieve?'

Giovanni nodded. 'Sieve.'

'Huh?' said Sancia. She watched as Giovanni unrolled what appeared to be a largish sheet of leather. She saw it had buttons sewn into the corners, brass ones, with faint, complicated sigils on their faces. He picked up Clef as if the key were a small, dying bird, and gently placed him in the centre of the leather.

'Whatever this is . . . this isn't going to hurt him, is it?' asked Sancia.

Giovanni blinked at her through his spectacles. '*Him?* You're suddenly sounding very attached to this object, San.'

'That object is worth a whole harpering heap of money,' she said, feeling suddenly defensive about Clef.

'One of Sark's jobs?' asked Giovanni.

Sancia said nothing.

'Stoic little San,' he said. He began slowly folding up the leather around Clef. 'Our grim, tiny spectre of the night. One day I will get a smile out of you.'

'What is this thing?' Sancia asked.

'A scriving sieve,' said Claudia. 'Place the object within it, and it'll identify some – but usually not all – of the major sigils being used to shape the object's nature.'

'Why not all?' said Sancia.

Giovanni laughed as he placed a thick plate of iron on top of the wrapped-up leather. 'One of these days, San, I will teach you *something* about the tiers of scriving. It's not one language, so it's not like you can just translate each sigillum individually. Rather, each sigil is its own command – which calls up a whole string of *other* sigils on the nearby lexico—'

'Yeah, I didn't ask you to give me a degree in this stuff,' said Sancia.

Giovanni paused, miffed. 'One might imagine, Sancia, that you'd show more interest in the languages that power everything around y—'

'One also might imagine my arse getting to bed at a reasonable time.'

Grumbling, Giovanni grabbed a pinch of iron filings from a small cup and sprinkled them over the face of the plate. 'Now, let's see what we've got . . .'

They sat there, watching.

And watching. Nothing seemed to be happening.

'Did you do it right?' asked Sancia.

'Of course I damned well did it right!' snapped Giovanni.

'So what should we be seeing?' asked Sancia.

'The filings *should* be rearranging themselves into the shapes of the primary commands being used in the object,' said Claudia. 'But – if we are to believe this – it'd imply there *are* none.'

'Which, unless I'm mistaken,' said Giovanni, 'is impossible . . .'

Giovanni and Claudia looked at the iron plate for a while before turning to stare at each other, bewildered.

'So, uh, right,' said Claudia. She cleared her throat, then knelt and began wiping the plate clean. 'So . . . it seems like there are, somehow, no sigils or commands on Clef that our methods can identify. Like, none.'

'Meaning what?' asked Sancia.

'Meaning we don't know what the hell it – or he, or whatever – really is,' said Giovanni. 'His sigils are talking a language we don't know, in other words.'

'Would a merchant house be interested in this?' said Sancia.

'Oh, holy monkeys, yes,' said Claudia. 'If there's a whole new scriving language out there, and they get ahold of it, they . . . they . . .' She trailed off. Then she looked at Giovanni, troubled.

'What?' said Sancia.

'I was thinking the same thing,' said Giovanni to her quietly.

'What?' said Sancia. 'Thinking what?'

The two of them sat in silence, staring at each other and occasionally glancing at Sancia.

'Thinking *what*?' she demanded.

Claudia glanced nervously around the workshop. 'Let's . . . take this somewhere private.'

Sancia followed Claudia and Giovanni into the back office, stuffing Clef back down her jerkin as she did so. The back office was filled with tomes and books of sigil strings and scriving commands, reams and reams and reams of papers covered in symbols that made no sense to Sancia.

She watched as Claudia shut the door behind them and locked it.

<*That . . . doesn't seem good,*> said Clef.

<*No. No, it doesn't.*>

Giovanni pulled out a bottle of a potent, noxious cane wine, poured three glasses, and picked up two. 'Drink?' he said, extending one to Sancia.

'No.'

'Sure?'

'Yes,' she said testily.

'You never have fun, San. You deserve some. Especially now.'

'Fun is a luxury. What I deserve is to know how big of a pot of shit I'm in.'

'How long have you lived in Tevanne now?' asked Giovanni.

'A bit over three years. Why?'

'Mm . . . Well.' Giovanni tossed one glass back, then the other. 'This will take some explaining, then.'

Claudia took a seat behind a stack of tomes. 'Ever heard of the Occidentals, Sancia?' she asked quietly.

'Yeah,' said Sancia. 'The fairy giants. They built the ruins across the Durazzo, in the Daulo countries. Aqueducts and the like. Right?'

'Hm. Kind of,' said Giovanni. 'To put it plainly, they were the people who invented scriving, long, long, *long* ago. Though no one's even sure if they really were *people*. Some say they were angels, or something a lot like angels. They were also called hierophants, and in most of the old stories they're regarded as priests or monks or prophets. The first of them – the most notable of them – was Crasedes the Great. They weren't giants, though. They just used their scriving to do some very, very big things.'

'Like what?' asked Sancia.

'Like move mountains,' said Claudia. 'Carve out oceans. And annihilate cities, and build a massive, massive empire.'

'Really?' said Sancia.

'Yes,' said Giovanni. 'One that makes the merchant house empire we've got today look like a piddling pile of shit.'

'This was a long time ago, mind,' said Claudia. 'A thousand years or so.'

'What happened to this empire?' she asked.

'It all fell apart,' said Claudia. 'Nobody knows how, or why. But when it fell, it fell *hard*. Almost nothing survived. No one even knows the real name of the empire. We just call it the Occidental Empire because it was to the west. Like, *everything* to the west. The hierophants owned all of it.'

'Supposedly Tevanne was just a backwater jungle port for this empire, ages and ages and ages ago,' said Giovanni, pouring himself another drink.

Claudia frowned at him. 'You've got work tonight, Gio.'

He sniffed. 'Makes my hands steadier.'

'That's not what the Morsinis said when they tossed you out on your arse.'

'They misunderstood the nature of my genius,' he said airily. He slurped down cane wine. Claudia rolled her eyes. 'Anyways. Apparently Tevanne was far-flung enough that when the Occidental Empire collapsed, and all the hierophants died out, it escaped the damage.'

'And it just stuck around,' said Claudia. 'Until about eighty years ago, when some Tevanni found a hidden cache of Occidental records in the cliffs east of here, detailing in vague terms the art of scriving.'

'And *that*,' said Giovanni with a theatrical flourish, 'is how the Tevanne of today was born!'

There was a moment of silence as this sank in.

'Wait . . . what?' said Sancia. 'Really? You're saying that what the merchant houses do today is based on some notes from some ancient, dead civilisation?'

'Not even *good* notes,' said Giovanni. 'Boggles the mind, doesn't it?'

'It boggles a whole hell of a lot more than that,' said Claudia. 'Because the merchant houses today can do a lot of stuff with scriving – but they don't hold a scrumming candle to what the hierophants could do. Like fly or make things float.'

'Or walk on water,' said Giovanni.

'Make a door in the sky,' said Claudia.

'Crasedes the Great would point his magic wand . . .' – Giovanni mimed the action – 'and – poof! – the seas themselves would part.'

'They say Crasedes even kept a genie in a basket at his waist,' said Claudia. 'He'd open it up and let it out and it'd build a castle for him, or tear down walls, or . . . You get the idea.'

Suddenly Sancia recalled a passage from the note she'd found in the box with Clef: *If Crasedes was in possession of some kind of invisible entity, perhaps it was but a rough prototype for this last and greatest iteration . . .*

'No one knows how the hierophants did what they did,' said Claudia. 'But the merchant houses are desperately, *desperately* searching for ways to figure it out.'

'To graduate from making scrived toilets,' said Giovanni, 'to making tools and devices that can, say, smash mountains or drain the sea – maybe.'

'No one's got close. Until recently.'

'What's happened recently?' asked Sancia.

'About a year ago, a band of pirates stumbled across a tiny island in the western Durazzo,' said Giovanni, 'and found it covered with Occidental ruins.'

'The nearby town of Vialto went absolutely barking mad with treasure hunters,' said Claudia.

'Agents of the merchant houses,' said Giovanni, 'or anyone who wanted to *be* a merchant house.'

'Because if you can find more records, more notes . . .' said Claudia.

'Or, better yet, a real, whole, *functional* Occidental tool . . .' said Giovanni.

'Well, then,' said Claudia quietly. 'You'd change the future of scriving forever. You'd make the merchant houses themselves obsolete.'

'You'd make our whole damn *civilisation* obsolete,' said Giovanni.

Sancia felt nauseous. She suddenly remembered Clef saying: *There's nothing before the dark. There's just the dark. I was always in the dark, as . . . as far as I can recall.*

And it would, after all, be very dark in an ancient ruin.

'And . . .' she said slowly. 'And you think Clef . . .'

'I . . . I think Clef doesn't use any language that the houses use,' said Claudia. 'And if what you say is true, he can do some pretty amazing things. And I think if you nabbed him from the waterfront . . . Which would be, of course, where people would ship in anything from Vialto . . .' She trailed off.

'Then you might be walking around with a million-duvot key hanging from your neck,' said Giovanni. 'Feel heavy?'

Sancia stood there, totally still. <*Clef,*> she said. <*Is . . . is any of this true?*>

But Clef was silent.

⁂

They said nothing for a while. Then there was a knock at the door – another Scrapper, asking for Giovanni's assistance. He apologised and departed, leaving Claudia and Sancia alone in the back office.

'You . . . seem to be dealing with this well,' said Claudia.

Sancia said nothing. She'd barely moved.

'Most people . . . they would have had an absolute nervous breakdown if—'

'I don't have time for nervous breakdowns,' said Sancia, quietly and coldly. She looked away, rubbing the side of her head. 'Damn it. I was going to get this payout, and then . . .'

'Get yourself fixed?'

'Yeah. But I don't see that happening now.'

Claudia absently fingered a scar on her forearm. 'Do I need to say that you shouldn't have taken the job?'

Sancia glared at her. 'Claudia. Not now.'

'I warned you about merchant house work. I told you they'd scrum you in the end.'

'Enough.'

'But you kept doing it.'

Sancia went silent.

'Why don't you hate them?' said Claudia, frustrated. 'Why don't you *despise* them, for what they did to you?' There was a brittle fury in her eyes. Claudia was an immensely talented scriver, but after the house academies had stopped accepting women, all her prospects had vanished. She'd been forced to join the Scrappers and spend her days working in dank basements and abandoned lofts. Despite her cheerful demeanour, she'd never been able to forgive the merchant houses for that.

'Grudges,' said Sancia, 'are a privilege I can't afford.'

Claudia sank back in her chair and scoffed. 'Sometimes I admire how you can be so bloodlessly practical, Sancia,' she said. 'But then I remember that it doesn't *look* very pleasant.'

Sancia said nothing.

'Does Sark know?' asked Claudia.

She shook her head. 'Don't think so.'

'What are you going to do?'

'Tell Sark when I go to debrief with him in two days. Then we skip town. Grab the first boat out of here and go somewhere far, far away.'

'Really?'

Sancia nodded. 'I don't see another way around it. Not if Clef is what you say he is.'

'And you're taking him with you?'

'I'm not leaving him behind. I'm not going to be the arsehole who lets the merchant houses assume godlike powers out of sheer scrumming negligence.'

'You can't get to Sark earlier?'

'I know one of his apartments, but Sark's even more paranoid than I am. Getting tortured has that effect on you. He vanishes after I've done a job for him. Even I don't know where he goes.'

'Well – not to make your options any more complicated – but leaving Tevanne might not be *quite* as easy as you think.'

Sancia raised an eyebrow.

'There's all the stuff with Clef,' said Claudia. 'That's one thing. But . . . there's also the fact that you burned down the waterfront, Sancia. Or at least a lot of it. I have no doubt that some powerful people are looking for you right now. And if they find out who you are . . . no ship's captain in Tevanne is going to take you anywhere. Not for all the cane wine and roses on this earth.'

7

Captain Gregor Dandolo of the Tevanni Waterwatch held his head high as he walked through the throngs of Foundryside. He did not really know another way to walk: his posture was, at all times, absolutely pristine, back arched and shoulders thrown back. Between this, his large size, and his Waterwatch sash, everyone in the Commons tended to get out of his way. They didn't know what he was here for, but they wanted no part of it.

Gregor knew it was odd to feel so jaunty. He was a thoroughly disgraced man, having allowed nearly half the waterfront to burn down under his watch, and he was now facing suspension from the Waterwatch, if not outright expulsion.

Yet this was a situation that Gregor was quite comfortable with: a wrong had been done, and he intended to set it right. As quickly and as efficiently as possible.

A musty wine-bar door opened on his right up ahead, and a soused woman with smeared face paint staggered out onto the creaky wooden walkway in front of him.

He stopped, bowed, and extended an arm. 'After you, ma'am.'

The drunken woman stared at him like he was mad. 'After what?'

'Ah. You, ma'am. After you.'

'Oh. I see.' She blinked drunkenly, but did not move.

Gregor, realizing she had no idea what the phrase meant, sighed slightly. 'You may walk ahead of me,' he said gently.

'Oh. Oh! Well, then. Thanks to you.'

'Certainly, ma'am.' Again, he bowed.

She tottered ahead of him. Gregor walked up beside her, and the wooden walkway bent slightly under his sizeable bulk, which made her stumble. 'Pardon me,' he said, 'but I had a question.'

She looked him over. 'I'm off duty,' she said. 'Least till I find someplace quiet to spew up a bit and dab my nose.'

'I see. But no. I wanted to ask – would the taverna The Perch and Lark be somewhere nearby?'

She gaped at him. 'The Perch and Lark?'

'Indeed, ma'am.'

'You want to go *there*?'

'Yes, ma'am.'

'Well. S'up thataway.' She pointed down a filthy alley.

He bowed once more. 'Excellent. Thank you so much. Good evening to you.'

'Wait,' she said. 'A fine man such as y'self won't want to go *there*! That place is a damn snake pit! Antonin's boys will chew you up and spit you out soon as look at you!'

'Thank you!' sang Gregor, and he strode off into the evening mist.

It had been three days since the waterfront fiasco. Three days since all of Gregor's efforts to make a decent, functional, law-abiding civilian police force – the first of its kind in Tevanne – had quite literally gone up in smoke. There'd been a lot of finger pointing and accusations in that handful of days since, but only Gregor had had a mind to actually do some investigating.

What he'd found was that his initial instincts on the night of the fiasco had been correct: there *had* been a bad actor on the premises, they had indeed targeted the safes of the Waterwatch, and they'd even successfully stolen something. Specifically, a small, bland box from safe 23D had gone missing. How they'd managed to do that, Gregor couldn't imagine – every safe was outfitted with a Miranda

Brass tumbler lock, and Gregor himself changed the combinations on a fixed schedule. They must have been a master safe cracker to pull it off.

But a theft *and* a fire, on the same night? That was no coincidence. Whoever had done one had also done the other.

Gregor had checked the Waterwatch logs regarding the box, hoping that the owner might suggest the identity of the thief. But that had been a dead end – the owner's name had been submitted just as 'Berenice', nothing more, with no contact information included. He could find nothing more about this Berenice, either.

But he was well acquainted with the criminal element in Tevanne. If he could find nothing about the box's owner, then he would start making headway on potential thieves. And this evening, here in the south end of Foundryside, he could get started.

He stopped at one thoroughfare, squinting through the mist, which turned mottled colours from the lanterns hanging overhead. Then he saw his destination.

The sign hanging above the taverna door read THE PERCH AND LARK. He didn't really need to see the sign, however – the large, scarred, threatening-looking men loitering outside the door were enough to tell him he was in the right place.

The Perch and Lark was base of operations for one of the most pre-eminent crime lords in Foundryside, if not all the Commons: Antonin di Nove. Gregor knew this because his own reforms at the waterfront had directly affected the economics of Antonin's ventures, which had displeased Antonin to the point that he'd sent some hired steel out after Gregor – though Gregor had sent them back very quickly, with many broken fingers and one shattered jaw.

He had no doubt that Antonin still harboured lots of bad feelings about this. Which was why Gregor had brought five hundred duvots of his own money, and Whip, his scrived truncheon. Hopefully the duvots would entice Antonin into giving Gregor some information about what thief could have hit the waterfront. And hopefully Whip would keep Gregor alive long enough to ask.

He marched up to the four glowering heavies before the taverna entrance. 'Good evening, gentlemen!' he said. 'I'd like to see Mr di Nove, please.'

The heavies glanced at each other, somewhat baffled by Gregor's politeness. Then one – who was missing quite a lot of teeth – said, 'Not with that, you aren't.' He nodded at Whip, which was hanging by Gregor's side.

'Certainly,' he said. He unbuckled Whip and held it out. One of them took it and tossed it into a box, where it had company with a simply staggering number of knives, rapiers, swords, and other, grislier armaments.

'May I enter now, please?' asked Gregor.

'Fifty duvots,' said the toothless heavy.

'I beg your pardon,' said Gregor. 'Fifty?'

'Fifty if we haven't seen your face afore. And I don't know your face, sir.'

'I see. Well.' Gregor glanced at their weapons. Spears, knives, and one even had an espringal – a sort of mechanised, heavy crossbow that you had to crank – though its gears hadn't been set correctly.

He made a note of it. Gregor always made a note of such things.

He reached into his satchel, took out a handful of duvots, and handed them over. 'Now may I enter?'

The heavies exchanged another glance. 'What's your business with Antonin?' asked the toothless one.

'My business is both pressing and private,' said Gregor.

The toothless guard grinned at him. 'Oh, very professional. We don't see too many professional types here, do we, chaps? Not unless they've come down here to scrum the night lads, eh?'

The others laughed.

Gregor waited calmly, meeting the man's gaze.

'Fair enough,' said the toothless heavy. He opened the door. 'Back table. But move slow.'

Gregor smiled curtly, said, 'Thank you,' and walked inside.

Immediately inside was a short flight of steps. He bounced up the steps, and as he did the air got smokier, louder, and much, much more pungent. At the top of the steps was a blue drape, and he shoved it aside and walked into the taverna.

Gregor glanced around. 'Hum,' he said.

As a former career soldier, Gregor was accustomed to tavernas, even ones as filthy as this. Reeking candles burned on all the table-tops. The floor was little more than a loose grid of wooden slats, so that if someone spilled anything – cane wine, grain alcohol, or any number of bodily fluids – it would drain right through to the mud below. Someone was playing a set of box pipes in the back, albeit very badly, and the music was loud enough to drown out most conversation.

But then, people did not come to tavernas like this for conversation. They came to fill their skulls up with so much cane wine that they forgot for one brief moment that they lived in shit-spattered, muddy ditches clinging to the clean white walls of the campos, that they shared their living quarters with animals, that they awoke every morning to fresh insect bites or shrieking monkeys or the putrid scent of rotting striper shells in the alleys – if they awoke at all, that is.

Gregor barely blinked at the sight. He had seen many horrors in war, and he did not count the sight of the impoverished among them. He himself had once been far more desperate than any of these people.

He glanced through the crowd, looking for Antonin's men. He counted four straightaway, taking up positions at the edges of the taverna. All of them had rapiers, except for the one in the far corner, who was huge and thickset, and leaned against the wall with a threatening black axe strapped to his back.

A Daulo axe, Gregor saw. He'd seen many of their like in the Enlightenment Wars.

He crossed the taverna, spied a table in the back, and approached – slowly.

He could tell which one of them was Antonin right away, because the man's clothes were clean, his skin unblemished, his thin hair combed neatly back, and he was hugely, hugely fat – a rarity in the Commons. He was also reading a book, something Gregor had *never* seen anyone do in such a place. Antonin had another guard sitting beside him, this one with two stilettos stuffed in his belt, and the guard tensed as Gregor neared.

Antonin's brow furrowed slightly and he looked up from his book. He glanced at Gregor's face, then his belt – which held no weapons – and then his sash. 'Waterwatch,' he remarked aloud. 'What's Waterwatch doing in a place where the only waters to watch are wine and piss?' Then he peered closer at Gregor's face. 'Ahh . . . I know you. It's Dandolo, isn't it?'

'You are a knowledgeable man, sir,' said Gregor. He bowed

slightly. 'I am indeed Captain Gregor Dandolo of the Waterwatch, Mr Antonin.'

'Mr Antonin . . .' he echoed. Antonin laughed, showing off black teeth. 'Such a well-mannered gent here among us! I'd have wiped myself better this morn if I'd known you'd deign to bless us with your presence. If I recall, I tried to have you killed once . . . Didn't I?'

'You did.'

'Ahh. Here to return the favour?'

The thickset guard with the axe wandered over to take up a position behind Gregor.

'No, sir,' said Gregor. 'I've come to ask you a question.'

'Huh.' His gaze lingered on Gregor's Waterwatch sash. 'I will assume your question has something to do with your waterfront disaster?'

Gregor smiled humourlessly. 'It would, sir.'

'Yes. It would.' Antonin gestured to the seat across him with one pudgy finger. 'Please. Do me the honour of sitting.'

Gregor bowed lightly and did so.

'Now – why would you come to *me* to ask about that?' said Antonin. 'I gave up the waterfront a long time ago. Thanks to you, of course.' His black eyes glittered.

'Because it was an independent,' said Gregor. 'And you know independents.'

'What makes you so sure?'

'They used an improvised sailing rig. They planted a construction scriving on one of the carriages – something used for adhesives and mortars – and this acted as a rudimentary arrangement to power their rig. It was shoddily made, and did not seem to work well.'

'Something no real canal operator would ever use, then.'

'Correct. A real one could get the real thing. So. An independent. And independents tend to live in one place – Foundryside. Or close to it. Which is your domain, unless I'm mistaken.'

'Makes sense. Very clever. But the real question is . . . why would I help you?' He smiled. 'Your Waterwatch experiment seems to have failed. Wouldn't it be in my interests to make sure it stays that way, and reclaim the waterfront?'

'It has not failed,' said Gregor. 'That remains to be seen.'

'I don't need to see,' said Antonin with a laugh. 'So long as the merchant houses run their campos like kings, Tevanne won't *ever* have anything resembling a policing system – no matter how excellent you make the Waterwatch. And that will fail too, in time. So, my noble captain, I really just need to wait. And then I'll find my way back in – won't I?'

Gregor blinked slowly, but did not react – though Antonin was now needling a sensitive wound of his. He had done a lot of work to build up the Waterwatch, and he did not appreciate hearing it threatened. 'I can pay,' he said.

Antonin smirked. 'How much?'

'Four hundred and fifty duvots.'

Antonin glanced at his satchel. 'Which, I assume, you've brought yourself. Because I wouldn't believe you'd pay if you hadn't.'

'Yes.'

'So what's keeping me from putting some steel in your ribs and taking it now?' asked Antonin.

'My last name,' said Gregor.

Antonin sighed. 'Ah, yes. Were we to expire the sole progeny of Ofelia Dandolo, I've no doubt that all hell would come down on us.'

'Yes.' Gregor tried to swallow his self-disgust. His mother was a direct descendant of the founder of Dandolo Chartered, which made them something akin to royalty in Tevanne – but he thoroughly disdained leveraging his family's reputation for his own ends. 'And I would not give up the money easily. You would have to kill me, Antonin.'

'Yes, yes, the good soldier,' said Antonin. 'But not the best strategist.' He smiled wickedly. 'You were at the siege of Dantua – weren't you, Captain?'

Gregor was silent.

'You were,' said Antonin. 'I know. They call you the Revenant of Dantua – have you heard that?'

Again, he said nothing.

'And I'm told they called you that,' said Antonin, 'because you *died* there. Or came damn close. They even had a memorial service here in the city for you. Thought you were rotting in a mass grave somewhere in the north.'

'I've heard the same,' said Gregor. 'They were wrong.'

'So I see. I get a lot of veterans working for me, you know,' said Antonin. 'And they tell me *so* many stories.' He leaned closer. 'They told me that when your cohorts were holed up in Dantua, with all your scrived armaments ruined . . . Why, they say you resorted to eating rats and garbage. And worse things besides.' He grinned wide. 'Tell me, Captain Dandolo – how does Tevanni long pig taste?'

There was a long silence.

'I would not know,' said Gregor calmly. 'What does this have to do with my proposal?'

'I suppose I'm just a filthy gossip,' said Antonin. 'Or maybe I like telling you you're not as righteous as you act. You killed my profit from the waterfront, brave Captain Dandolo. But no fear, friend – I've made up the difference. Any enterprising man must. Would you like to know how?'

'Would this involve our independent thief?'

Antonin stood, ignoring him, and gestured to a set of rickety wooden stalls in the back, with drapes drawn across their entrances. 'Come with me, sir. Yes, yes, come on.'

Gregor grudgingly obliged, following him.

'Tough economy, these days,' said Antonin. 'Tough market. That's what the campos talk about all day long, market conditions. We all play the same game. One opportunity dries up, so one must look for another.' He walked over to one stall, grabbed a drape, and pulled it open.

Gregor looked inside. The stall was dark, but he could see a pallet on the floor, and a single burning candle. At the far back was a boy, wearing a short tunic, legs and feet bared. The boy stood when the drape opened. He was maybe thirteen. Maybe.

Gregor looked at the soft pallet on the floor, and then at the boy. Then he understood.

'You take away my waterfront work,' said Antonin merrily, 'so I expand my enterprise into a new market. But this market is *so* much more profitable than the waterfront. High margins, low capital. I just needed the nudge to give it a go.' He stepped closer to Gregor. The scent of his rotting teeth was overwhelming. 'So, Captain Dandolo . . . I don't need a single duvot of your damned money.'

Gregor turned to look at Antonin, his fists trembling.

'Welcome back to Tevanne,' said Antonin. 'The only law in the

Commons is might, and success. Those who win are the ones who make the rules. Perhaps an elite child such as yourself forgot.' He grinned, his greasy teeth glimmering. 'Now. Get the hell out of my taverna.'

⸙

Gregor Dandolo walked out of The Perch and Lark in a daze. He retrieved Whip from the toothless thug at the door, ignoring the other guards as they cackled at him.

'Fruitful meeting?' asked the toothless heavy. 'Did he give you a handful of minutes in the stalls? Was there any pull left when you pushed?'

Gregor walked away without a word, buckling Whip back to his belt. He walked a bit down the alley, and stopped.

He thought for a moment.

He took a breath, and thought some more.

Gregor Dandolo did his utmost to follow the laws: both the laws of the city, and his own moral laws of the universe. But more and more these days, one seemed to disagree with the other.

He took off his Waterwatch sash, folded it up, and carefully placed it on a nearby windowsill. Then he took Whip off his belt, and began the process of securely buckling its many leather straps to his forearm. Then he turned and marched back toward the taverna.

The toothless heavy saw him coming and squared himself. Then he cawed out a laugh, and whooped. 'Look here, lads! We've got one who thinks he ca—'

But he never finished his sentence. Because then Gregor used Whip.

⸙

Gregor had made sure that when he'd had Whip commissioned, all of its sigils were carefully concealed, so no one who looked at it would know it was altered in any way. With the sole exception of the straps for buckling it to your wrist, it mostly looked like an ordinary truncheon – with a shaft of about three and a half feet, and a ridged, four-pound steel head at the end – but in truth, it was much more than that.

For when Gregor pressed a button on Whip and snapped it forward, the four-pound head would detach and fly forward, connected to the shaft of the truncheon by a thin but strong metal cable. The truncheon's head had been scrived to believe that, when it was detached from the shaft, it was actually falling straight *down* toward the earth, and so was simply obeying gravity – unaware that it was actually flying in whatever direction Gregor had tossed it. It would smash into anything in its path before Gregor clicked a small lever on the side of Whip's handle, at which point Whip's head would remember how gravity actually worked, the cable would start rapidly retracting, and the head would come zipping back to the shaft with tremendous speed.

This is what Gregor did as he approached the taverna. He was so familiar with Whip that he almost didn't have to think while he was doing it: he just made the motion, and then the toothless heavy was lying on the ground, screaming through a bloody, ravaged mouth.

He hit the lever, and the straps tugged against his forearm as Whip's head came hurtling back to Gregor with a soft, rabid *zzzzip*. His arm shook as it connected with the shaft, but his attention was fixed on the thug on his right, a short, pockmarked man with a black-bladed machete, who looked down at his fallen comrade, looked up at Gregor, and screamed and sprinted at him.

Gregor, still marching down the alley, flicked Whip forward again, aiming for the man's legs. The head of the truncheon connected soundly with his kneecap, and the man fell to the ground, howling in pain. Gregor retracted Whip, and as he passed him he brought the truncheon down sharply on the man's forearm, either bruising or breaking his radius or ulna, which made him howl quite a bit louder.

There were two left, one on each side of the taverna door. One had the espringal, though he looked shocked when he pulled the trigger and nothing happened – ignorant, of course, that he'd prepared it wrong. Before he could do anything else, Gregor hurled Whip forward, and the dense, heavy head of the weapon went crashing into the guard's right hand, smashing his fingers. He dropped the weapon, cursing and screaming.

This left the fourth and final guard, who had picked up a battered steel shield and a small spear. The guard crouched low and advanced on Gregor down the alley, hiding almost all of his body behind the shield.

Served in the wars, Gregor thought. He'd had training, certainly. But not enough.

Gregor flicked Whip out again, and the head of the truncheon sailed over the guard's head, landing behind him, and brought the metal cable down with it. The cable fell over the top of the guard's shield, which made the man pause – until Gregor pressed the lever to retract it.

The head of the truncheon hurtled back with its usual enthusiastic *zzzip!*, cracking into the guard's shoulder along the way, which sent him tumbling forward, sprawling facedown in the alley. He groaned as he looked up at Gregor, who walked up and kicked the guard in the face.

Gregor Dandolo picked up the shield. The guard with the espringal tossed away his weapon and pulled out a stiletto with his good hand. He assumed a fighting position, crouching low. Then he seemed to reconsider his position, and turned and ran away.

Gregor watched him go. Then, with the air of someone on a quick errand, Gregor walked up the stairs of the taverna, lifted his shield, brushed aside the drape, and waged war on The Perch and Lark.

It helped that there were only five guards. It helped more that they hadn't moved since he'd left, so he knew exactly where they would be. It helped even more that it was dark and loud, and Whip's attack was fairly quiet, so Gregor took down two of his opponents before anyone in the room even understood what was happening.

When the second guard hit the floor, blood streaming from his nose and mouth, the whole taverna erupted into chaos. Gregor lowered his shield, which made him an obvious target, and skirted the edges of the screaming, drunken crowd until he came up on the flank of a guard with a spear. The guard saw him at the last minute, eyes widening. He thrust his spear forward, but Gregor had already raised his shield, deflecting the blow. Then he thrust Whip forward, smashing in the man's jaw. The man crumpled to the ground.

Two left. The guard with the Daulo axe and one with an espringal – and this latter one, he could tell, had been trained properly with the weapon. Which was bad.

Gregor raised the shield and sought cover behind a table just as a bolt slammed into his shield. The point of the bolt actually pierced the damn thing, penetrating three inches through – any more and it would have almost certainly punched through Gregor's neck. Muttering discontentedly, Gregor strafed to the right and flung Whip forward. He missed his target, but the head of the truncheon smashed through the wall just over the guard's shoulder, which sent the man diving for cover behind the bar.

The two of them stayed low, waiting for the screaming crowd to evacuate. Gregor glanced up and saw a shelf of bottles above the bar, and, above that, a flickering oil lamp. He estimated the distance, and flicked Whip forward twice: once to smash the bottles of alcohol, and again to shatter the oil lamp.

Hot, burning oil rained down, which quickly set the pools of alcohol alight. There was a shriek, and the guard with the espringal came sprinting out from behind the bar, slapping at his smoking clothes. He never even saw Whip hurtling toward his face.

Once the man was down, Gregor crouched low and looked around. Antonin was still there, cowering in the back, but the guard with the Daulo axe was nowhere to be seen . . .

Gregor felt footsteps through the floorboards on his right. Without thinking, he turned and raised his shield.

There was a loud scream, and then his shield arm lit up with pain. It had been a long time since he'd been hit with a Daulo axe, and he found he didn't enjoy it any more now than he had back during the wars.

Gregor rolled out from the bar and raised his shield again, just in time to catch another blow from the guard with the axe. His whole arm went numb with the strike, and he heard a *snap* – but it turned out to be the wooden slats under his feet, which could hardly bear the pressure.

Which gave Gregor an idea.

Keeping his shield up, he backed away. The guard with the axe charged at him – but before he could bring the axe down, Gregor flicked Whip at the slats at his feet.

The head of the truncheon punched through the wooden slats like they were water reeds. Before the guard could even realise what had happened, he'd put his foot in the gaping hole that Whip had created. Then he slipped, crashing down, and as he did, the entire floor collapsed underneath him.

Gregor leapt back as the wooden slats gave way. When the creaking stopped, he retracted Whip and peeked over the edge of the hole, wrinkling his nose. He couldn't see the guard in the muddy darkness below – but he knew that the taverna latrines emptied into the filthy space under the building.

Gregor took stock of the situation. The taverna was now mostly empty except for the moaning guards – and the large, fat man trying to hide behind a chair.

Gregor grinned, stood up straight, and marched over. *'Antonin di Nove!'* he called.

Antonin shrieked in terror as Gregor approached.

'How did you like my experiment?' Gregor asked. 'You said that might makes right in the Commons.' He ripped the chair away, and Antonin quailed in the corner. 'But might is so often illusory, isn't it?'

'I'll tell you anything you want!' shrieked Antonin. 'Anything!'

'I want the thief,' said Gregor.

'Ask . . . ask Sark!' said Antonin.

'Who?'

'An independent! Former canal man! He's a fence, he sets up jobs and I'm almost positive he did the waterfront!'

'And why would that be?' asked Gregor.

'Because only a damned canal man would think of trying to use a damned sailing rig!'

Gregor nodded. 'I see. So. This Sark. Where would he reside?'

'The Greens! Selvo Building! Third floor!'

'Greens,' said Gregor quietly. 'Selvo. Third floor. Sark.'

'R–right!' said Antonin. Face quivering, he cringed and looked up at Gregor. 'So. Will you . . . Will you let me go?'

'I was always going to let you go, Antonin,' said Gregor, sheathing Whip. 'This is Tevanne. We have no prisons, no courts. And I am not going to kill you. I try hard not to do that anymore.'

Antonin sighed with relief.

'But,' said Gregor, clenching a fist and cracking his knuckles, 'I do not like you. I do not like what you do here, Antonin. And I will show you how much I dislike it, using the only language men like you understand.'

His eyes shot wide. 'N–no!'

Gregor raised his fist. 'Yes.'

Gregor turned, shaking his hand, and walked back to the rickety stalls with the drapes. He pulled them aside, one by one.

Four girls, two boys. None of them older than seventeen.

'Come on, then,' said Gregor gently to them. 'Come on.'

He led the children down the hallway, across the battered, broken taverna, and down the stairs to the alley, where the three guards were still whimpering. The children watched as Gregor searched the body of the unconscious, toothless guard for his fifty duvots.

'Now what?' asked a boy.

'You have nowhere else to go, I assume?' said Gregor.

The line of children stared at him. This question, clearly, was preposterous.

He wondered what to do. He wished there were some charity or home he could send them to. But the Commons, of course, had no such thing.

He nodded, and pulled out his satchel. 'Here. This is five hundred duvots. You lot could put this to far better use than Antonin ever could. If we divide it evenly, we ca—'

But he never finished, because then one of the youngest girls snatched the satchel out of his hand and ran for it.

In a blink of an eye, all the other children were chasing her, screaming threats: *'Pietra, if you think you're keeping all that, we'll cut your damned throat!'*

'Try to catch me, you worthless stripers!' the girl howled back.

Gregor watched, stunned, as the children ran away. He started after them, about to shout at them to stop, when he remembered he had other things to do tonight.

He sighed deeply, listened to the fading sounds of these bickering children, so monstrously abused. He liked to imagine he was accustomed to such horrors, but sometimes the futility of it all overwhelmed him. *No matter how I try, Tevanne remains Tevanne.*

Then he walked down the alley to where he'd hung up his Waterwatch sash. He unfolded it, then slid it back over his head. As he adjusted it, he noticed a splotch of blood on his shoulder. Frowning, he licked a finger and rubbed it clean.

His shield arm hurt. A lot. And it was likely he'd made a good deal of enemies tonight. But it was wisest to move before word could spread.

Now, thought Gregor, *on to this Sark.*

8

Sancia sat on her building's rooftop and stared out at the crooked Foundryside streets below. She came up here only occasionally, usually to make sure she wasn't being watched. And tonight, she needed to be sure, since tonight was her night to meet Sark at the fishery and tell him they needed to get the hell out of Tevanne.

She wondered how she'd explain Clef to him. Despite all the Scrappers had told her, she still didn't know much about him – about what he really was, or could do, or why. And Clef had not spoken to her since that night. She almost wondered if she'd imagined their conversations.

She looked out at the city. All of Tevanne was smeared with starlit smoke and steam, a ghostly cityscape sinking into the fog. The huge white campo walls surfaced among the ramble of the Commons like the bones of a beached whale. Behind them stood the towers of the campos, which glowed with soft, colourful luminescence. Among them was the Michiel clock tower, its face a bright, cheery pink, and beyond that was the Mountain of the Candianos, the biggest structure in all of Tevanne, a huge dome that reminded her of a fat, swollen tick, sitting in the centre of the Candiano campo.

She felt lonely, and small. Sancia had always been alone. But feeling lonely was different from just being alone.

<*Kid?*>

Sancia sat up. <*Clef? You're talking again?*>

<*Yeah. Obviously.*> He sounded sullen.

<*What happened to you? Where did you go?*>

<*I've always been right here. I've just been . . . thinking.*>

<*Thinking.*>

<*Yeah. About what those people said. About me being a . . .* >

<*A tool of the hierophants.*>

<*Yeah. That.*> There was a pause. <*Can I ask you something, kid?*>

<*Yes.*>

<*Wine tastes . . . sweet, right?*>

<*Huh?*>

<*Wine. It tastes sharp and yet sweet on your tongue – doesn't it?*>

<*I guess. I don't really drink.*>

<*It tastes like that. I'm sure it does. I . . . I* remember *that sensation, that feeling of cool wine on a hot day.*>

<*Really? How?*>

<*I don't know. How can I know that? How can I remember that if I'm just a key? And, more, a key that was made to break things open, to break open scrivings and locks and doors? I mean . . . It's not just the idea of being a tool – it's the idea of being a tool* and not knowing it. *Of having things built into you by someone else, things you can't resist obeying or doing. Like when you put me in that lock in that door, I just . . . started. Instantly. And it felt* good. *It felt so good, kid.*>

<*I could tell. Do you remember anything more? About being . . . I don't know, some artefact?*>

<*No. Nothing. I just have the dark, and nothing else. But it bothers me.*>

They sat in silence.

<*I'm dangerous for you, aren't I?*> he said quietly.

<*Well. My client either wants to destroy you, or take you apart and use what they discover to destroy everybody else. And I'm willing to bet they want to kill everyone who knows about you. Which includes me. So – that's a yes.*>

<*Shit. But tonight's when you make a run for it, right?*>

<*Yeah. I meet Sark in two hours. Then I either convince him to jump on*

a ship with me, or I beat him into submission and drag him to the piers. I'd rather have him cooperate – Sark has all kinds of forged documents that can get us out of Tevanne fast. But one way or another, you and I are gone. To where, I don't know yet. But gone.>

<*Well.*> Clef sighed. <*I always did like the idea of an ocean voyage.*>

She moved from Foundryside to Old Ditch, and then on to the Greens, which earned its name due to a curious fungus that merrily feasted on all the wood in this neighbourhood, turning it a dull lime colour. The Greens ran along the Anafesto, one of the main shipping channels, and the area had once been the thriving heart of Tevanne's fishing industry. But then the merchant houses had built up a surplus of scrived ships for the wars, and they'd started to use them to fish instead, which drove everyone else out of business, since they were about a hundred times more efficient. The Greens looked a lot like Foundryside – lots of rookeries, lots of low-slung slums and shops – but rather than being constrained by the campo walls, all the housing came to a sharp stop at the decaying industrial ramble running beside the channel.

Sancia walked along the Anafesto, eyeing the dark, decrepit fisheries ahead. She kept looking to her left, toward the lanes of the Greens. This area was a lot quieter than Foundryside, but she took no chances. Every time she spied someone, she stopped and watched their movements, sensitive to any suggestion that they might be there looking for her, and she didn't move on until satisfied.

She was anxious because she had Clef, of course, and knew all the threats that invited. But she also had her life savings in the pack on her back – three thousand duvots, almost entirely in coinage. She'd need every penny of it to get out of Tevanne, provided she even got that far. And though she carried her usual thieving kit, this offered little in the way of defence beyond her stiletto. It would be darkly funny if, after all she'd been through, she wound up getting mugged in the Greens by the luckiest street urchin of all time.

Once she got close enough she took the back way to the fishery, crawling across crumbling stone foundations and rusting pipes until she approached it from a narrow, shadowy passage. Probably no one thought she'd come at it from this angle, including Sark. The fishery was a two-storey mouldy stone structure, a place so rotted and decayed it was hard to tell its original purpose anymore. Sark was waiting on the second floor, she knew, and the first floor would be riddled with traps – his usual 'insurance'.

She looked at the dark windows, thinking. *How in hell am I going to convince Sark to run?*

<*This place is a shithole,*> said Clef.

<*Yeah. But it's our shithole. Me and Sark have done a lot of business here. It's as safe as we're going to get.*> She started toward it, feeling somewhat comfortable for the first time that night.

She silently crept around the corner, then past the big iron doors – which she knew she shouldn't use, since Sark had trapped them – and slipped through a broken window. She landed softly, took off her gloves, and touched her bare hands to the stone floor and the wall beside her.

Bones, blood, and viscera flooded her mind. The fishery had been the site of so much fish gutting that it almost always bowled her over every time, all the accumulated sensations of so much gore. There were still piles of fish bones here and there throughout the first floor, delicate tangles of tiny, translucent skeletons, and the scent still lingered, of course.

Sancia concentrated, and soon the traps lit up in her mind like fireworks, three trip wires running across the room to three hidden espringals that were almost certainly loaded up with fléchettes: paper packets of razor blades that would turn into a lethal cloud when fired.

She sighed in relief. <*Good.*>

<*All these traps make you feel* better?> said Clef.

<*Yes. Because they mean Sark's here. So he must be alive, and safe.*>

<*You have a weird relationship with your colleagues. I'll just say that.*>

She moved forward to delicately step over the first trip wire . . .

Then she stopped.

She thought for a moment, and peered throughout the darkness of the room. She thought she could spy the trip wires in the dim light – tiny, dark filaments stretching across the shadows.

One, she counted. *Two. Three . . .*

She frowned. Then she knelt to touch the floor and wall again with her bare hands.

<*Something wrong?*> asked Clef.

<*Yes,*> said Sancia. She waited until her talents confirmed it once more. <*There are three trip wires.*>

<*So?*>

<*Sark always uses four traps. Not three.*>

<*Oh? Maybe . . . he forgot one?*>

She didn't answer. She looked around the first floor again. It was dark, but she couldn't see anything unusual.

She looked out the windows at the building fronts beyond. No movement, nothing strange.

She cocked her head and listened. She could hear the lapping of waves, the sigh of the wind, the creaking and crackling as the building flexed in the breeze – but nothing else.

Perhaps he's forgotten it, she thought. *Perhaps he overlooked it, just this one time.*

But that was not like Sark. After his torture at the hands of the Morsinis, he'd become wildly paranoid and cautious. It was not in his nature to forget a safeguard.

She looked around again, just to be sure . . .

Then she spied something.

Was that a glint of metal, there in the wooden beam across the room? She narrowed her eyes, and thought it was.

A fléchette? Buried there in the wood?

She stared at it, and felt her heart beating faster.

She knelt again and touched her hands to the floor for a third time.

Again, the stone told her of bones and blood and viscera, as they always did. Yet now she focused to find out . . .

Was any of that blood *new*?

And she found it was. There was a big splotch of new blood just a few feet from her. It was almost impossible to see with the naked eye, since its stain blended in with the much older, larger stain of ancient fish blood. And her talents hadn't initially spotted it, as it'd been lost in the larger memory of so much gore.

She took her hands away as her scar began to throb. She felt cold sweat prickling across her back and belly. She turned again to the windows, staring out at the streets. Still nothing.

<Uh. Kid?> said Clef. *<You know how I could tell you had a scrived plate in your head? How I just sensed it?>*

<Why?>

<Well . . . I figured I'd let you know that I'm sensing three scrived rigs upstairs.>

She felt faint. *<What?>*

<Yeah. Right above us. And they're moving. Like someone's carrying them and walking around. They just walked overhead.>

Sancia slowly lifted her eyes to stare at the ceiling. She took a deep breath, and slowed her thoughts.

It was obvious what was happening now. The question was what to do next.

What resources do I have? What tools are available?

Not much, she knew. All she had was a stiletto. But she looked around, thinking.

She silently crept along one trip wire, and found its espringal hidden in the corner – yet it was unloaded. Normally it would have had a fléchette pack sitting in its pocket, ready to be hurled forward – but now it was gone. Just a cocked espringal with nothing to shoot.

She grimaced. *I guess I shouldn't be surprised.* She silently dismantled the trap and slung the espringal across her back.

<What are you doing?> Clef asked.

<Sark's dead,> she said. She crept along a second trip wire and started disarming it, but she didn't completely dismantle it.

<What?> said Clef, astonished.

<Sark is dead. And this is a trap.> She did the same to the third trip wire. Then she set them both up so they ran across the base of the stairs, and positioned the espringals so they were pointed right at the stairway.

<How do you know?>

<Because someone set off a trip wire, very recently,> she said. *<There's a fléchette stuck in the wood over there and a decent amount of fresh blood on the ground. That's why there are three trip wires, not four. My guess is they followed Sark here, waited a bit too long to follow him in, and lost some flesh for it. But they must have got him, eventually.>*

<Why are you so sure?>

<Because Sark doesn't walk around with any scrived armaments – so that's not him up there. They tried to clean up, to put everything just as he'd left it so I wouldn't get spooked and bolt – though they weren't stupid enough to leave me down here with loaded weapons. They're upstairs, waiting for me.>

<Really?>

<Yeah.>

<Why didn't they just shoot you as you approached?>

<Probably because there's always a chance I didn't have you, and then they'd have a dead girl and no answers. They wanted me to walk upstairs, right into their arms. Then they'd torture and kill me. All to find you.>

<Oh God! Now what the hell do we do?>

<We're going to get out of this. Somehow.>

She looked around. *I need a weapon*, she thought. *Or a distraction. Anything.* But one stiletto and three espringals with no ammunition didn't get her very far.

Then she had an idea. Grimacing – for she no longer had any idea how much she'd have to use her talents tonight – she touched her bare hands to the wooden beam above her.

Saltwater, rot, termites, and dust . . . but then she found it: the crackling old bones of the beams were shot through with iron spikes in a few places . . . and several of them were quite loose.

She quietly paced over to one loose nail, took out her stiletto, and waited for the breeze to rise. When it did, and the creaking and groaning of the old building rose with it, she gently pried the nail out of the soft wood.

She held it in her hands, letting it spill into her thoughts, iron and rust and slow corruption. It was big, about four or five inches long, and about a pound in weight.

Not aerodynamic, she thought. *But it wouldn't need to be, over short distances.*

She pocketed it, then pried out two more nails and carefully, *carefully* placed them in the pockets of the two espringals pointed at the stairwell door.

Maybe this will kill, she thought. *Or disable. Or something. I just need to slow them down.*

Again, she looked at the street outside. Still no movement. But that didn't necessarily mean much. These people were prepared.

<*Clef?*> she asked.

<*Yeah?*>

<*Can you tell me where they are?*>

<*I can tell you where their rigs are – and if they're carrying the rigs, that's where they'll be too. What are you going to do?*>

<*Try to survive. What are these rigs?*> asked Sancia. <*What do they do?*>

<*They . . . convince something that it's been falling. Or they will, when a certain action is performed.*>

<*Huh?*>

<*It's not like I can see the device,*> said Clef. <*I can only tell you what the scrivings do. And for these, someone does something that activates them. Pulls a lever or something. Then the scrivings convince, uh, some other thing that it's been falling through the air for thousands and thousands of feet, even if it's actually been sitting still. In other words, they make the thing go really, really,* really *fast, all of a sudden, in a perfectly straight line.*>

Sancia listened to this closely. <*Shit.*>

<*What?*>

<*Because it sounds like they're carrying scrived espringals,*> said Sancia. <*They shoot bolts that go very far, very fast. Some of the more advanced ones can punch through stone walls.*>

<*Wow. I . . . don't* think *these do that.*>

<*You don't think? I'm going to need you to be more certain than that.*>

<*I'm, like . . . maybe eighty per cent sure they don't.*>

She took her espringal and huddled at the window at the back, but did not exit yet. <*What are they doing up there?*>

<*I think . . . patrolling, mostly,*> said Clef. <*Walking in circles from window to window.*>

She did some quick thinking. She knew there was a window just above this one. <*Is one of them right above me?*>

<*No. But he will be in a bit.*>

<*Tell me when he's close.*>

<*All right.*>

She'd reviewed her weapon. The espringal was a clunky, powerful weapon, one of the old models you had to crank four or five times. And a big, rusty iron nail was not the best ammunition to use. She'd have to be close.

<He's coming this way,> said Clef. *<He's about ten feet to your left now, upstairs.>*

She slipped the iron nail in her espringal's pocket.

<He's standing right above you now,> said Clef. *<Looking out . . . >*

She did her best to convince herself she was going to do what she needed to do.

It felt insane. She was no soldier, and she knew it. But she knew there were no other options.

Don't miss, she thought.

Then she leapt out, raised the espringal at the window above her, and fired.

The espringal kicked far harder than she thought it would, and it responded so *fast.* She thought there'd be some delay when she squeezed the lever on the bottom, some moment before the gears would engage – but at the slightest pressure, the espringal's cords snapped forward like a crocodile trying to snag a fish.

There was a dark blur as the iron nail hurtled up at the window, then a wet *thud* – and the dark window exploded with agonised screams.

<I think you got him!> said Clef, excited.

Sancia shrank back up against the wall. *<Shut up, Clef!>*

Someone upstairs cried, '*She's here! She's downstairs!*' Then there was the sound of rapid footfalls.

Sancia hugged the wall, heart beating like mad. The screaming above her kept going on and on. It was an awful sound, and she tried her best to ignore it.

<Where are they now?> she asked.

<One scriving is on the ground up there – the guy you shot must have dropped it. There's a second rig at the window at the corner, facing the channel, and the third . . . I think they're going downstairs.>

<Are they moving fast?>

<Yeah?>

<Good.>

She waited, not even breathing. The man above kept shrieking and howling in pain.

Then there was a harsh *snap* from somewhere inside the first floor, and the interior lit up with fresh screams – but these tapered off pretty quickly. Probably because those traps had delivered more of a direct hit, which was likely lethal.

One left – but it was dark. She'd have to risk it.

She dropped the espringal and ran, sprinting through the passageways back to the channel, dodging through all the crumbling buildings and rotting wood, her satchel of duvots bouncing on her back. Finally her feet hit soft mud and she picked up the pace, frantically running along the water's edge.

A voice echoed out from behind her: '*She's loose! She's gone, she's gone!*'

She glanced to her right, up the street, and saw a dozen men pouring out of two buildings and sprinting for the channel. It looked like they were fanning out, so maybe they didn't know exactly where she was. Maybe.

They were waiting for me, she thought as she ran. *It's a whole damn army. They called out a whole damn army for m –*

Then the bolt hit her square in the back, and she fell forward.

The first thing she knew was the taste of blood and earth in her mouth. The rest of the world was dark and smeared and indistinct, noise and screams and distant lights.

Clef's voice cut through the blur: *<Kid! Kid! Are you all right? Are . . . are you dead?>*

Sancia groaned. Her back hurt like it'd been kicked by a horse. Her mouth was thick with blood – she must have bitten her lip as she fell. She stirred, pulled her face from the mud, and sat up, faintly aware of a tinkling sound.

She looked at her back, and saw her satchel of duvots was now little more than a rag. The mud around her was covered in shiny coins. She stared at this, trying to understand what had happened.

<*You caught a scrived bolt right in the back!*> said Clef. <*Your big bag of coins stopped it! Holy hell, it's a miracle!*>

But it didn't feel like a miracle to Sancia. This glittering metal in the channel mud represented the whole of her life's savings.

<*Did you mean for that to happen, kid?*> asked Clef.

<*No,*> she said wearily. <*No, Clef, I did not mean for that to happen.*>

She looked back and saw a dark figure running along the channel toward her – the third man from the fishery building, probably. He must have been the one to fire the shot. He cried, '*She's over there, over there!*'

'Damn it all,' said Sancia. She staggered to her feet and sprinted up the hill and off into the Greens.

Sancia ran blindly, thoughtlessly, drunkenly, hurtling through the muddy lanes, her head still spinning from the scrived bolt. Clef chattered madly in her ear as she ran, spitting out directions: <*They're up the street from you, two alleys down! Three more behind you!*>

She dodged and turned to avoid them, running deeper and deeper into the Greens, her chest and legs aching with the effort. She knew she couldn't run much farther. Eventually she'd stumble, or collapse, or they'd catch up to her. <*Where can I run to?*> she thought. <*What can I do?*> She was close to Foundryside by now, but that didn't mean much. Foundryside Commoners would sell her out in a heartbeat.

<*Use me, use me!*> cried Clef. <*Anywhere, anywhere!*>

She realised what he meant. She glanced ahead, picked a building that looked secure and commercial – so hopefully it'd be empty in the middle of the night – ran up to a side door, and stuck Clef into the lock.

There was a *click*. She shoved the door open, darted inside, and locked it behind her.

She glanced around. It was dark in the building, but it seemed to be some kind of clothier's warehouse, full of musty rolls of cloth and flittering moths. It also appeared to be empty, thankfully.

<*Are they outside?*> asked Sancia.

<*Two are . . . Moving slow. I don't think they know where you went, or they aren't sure. Where do we go now?*>

<*Up,*> said Sancia.

She knelt, touched a hand to the floor, and shut her eyes, letting the building tell her the layout. This was pushing her abilities – her head felt like it was full of molten iron – but she didn't have a choice.

She found the stairs and started climbing until she came to the top window. She opened it, felt the wall outside, let it bleed into her thoughts. Then she slipped out the window and climbed up until she rolled onto the roof. The roof was rickety, old, and not well built – but it was the safest place she'd been yet. It might as well have been paradise.

She lay on the roof, chest heaving, and slowly pulled her gloves on. Every part of her hurt. The scrived bolt might not have penetrated her flesh, but it'd hit her so hard it felt like she'd strained muscles she didn't even know she had. Still, she knew she couldn't relax now.

She crawled to the edge and peered out. She was about three floors up, she saw – and the streets were crawling with heavily armed men, all waving and signalling to one another as they scoured the neighbourhoods. It was the sort of thing professional soldiers did, which didn't reassure her.

She tried to count their number. Twelve? Twenty? A lot more than three, and she'd barely escaped three.

Some of the men were being followed by a curious type of rig she'd heard about, but never seen: floating paper lanterns, which had been scrived so they levitated about ten feet off the ground, glowing softly. They were scrived so they knew to follow specific markers, like a sachet – you put one in your pocket and the lantern would follow you around like a puppy. She'd heard they used them as streetlights in the inner enclaves of the campos.

Sancia watched as the lanterns bobbed through the air like jellyfish in the deep, following the men and spilling rosy luminescence into the dark corners. She supposed they'd brought them in case she was hiding in the shadows. They were prepared for her, in other words.

'Shit,' she whispered.

<So – we're safe, right?> said Clef. *<We just stay here until they leave?>*

<Why should they leave? Who's going to make them leave?> She looked at the remnants of her pack. Not only were the coins gone, but so

was her thieving kit. It must have fallen out as she ran. <*We're basically stuck on a scrumming roof, penniless and unarmed!*>

<*Well . . . Can we sneak away?*>

<*Sneaking's not as easy as you think.*> She poked her head up and took stock of her surroundings. The rooftop was bordered by three rookery buildings, one on either side and one behind. The two on the sides were both too tall and too far away, but the building behind was doable – about the same height as the warehouse, with a stone tile roof. <*Looks like about a twenty-foot jump to the other rooftop.*>

<*Can you make that?*>

<*That's a big maybe. I'd try it if I had to, but only then.*> She looked out farther, and spied the white campo walls and smokestacks of a campo a few blocks beyond. <*The Michiel campo's just a few blocks away. I still have one of their outer-wall sachets from the job I took to get you, Clef. Maybe it still works. Probably does.*>

<*Would we be safe from them there?*>

That was a good question. <*I . . . have no idea, really.*> She knew that a merchant house had to be behind this – that was the only force that could deploy a small army in the Commons just to find her. But which one? None of the assassins she'd seen had worn a house loggotipo – but it would have been supremely stupid for them to do that.

All this meant she could go to ground in the Michiel campo only to find out that the men down there were Michiel house guards, or someone employed by the Michiels. There was no place she could deem truly safe.

Sancia shut her eyes and rested her forehead against the roof. *Sark . . . damn you. What in hell have you got me mixed up in?*

Though she knew she was just as much at fault as he was. He'd been upfront about the job, and she'd still taken it. The money had been too good, and despite all her care and caution, it'd made her stupid.

But she likely wouldn't have survived this long without Clef. If she hadn't opened the box, she realised, she'd be trussed up like a hog right now, about to be butchered.

<*Have I told you thank you yet?*> she said to Clef.

<*Hell, I don't know,*> said Clef. <*I haven't been able to keep up with all this crazy shit.*>

Then she heard a rattling sound in the street below. She poked her head back over the edge of the roof.

An unmarked, black scrived carriage was slowly trundling down the tiny mud pathway in the Greens. Such rigs were about as frequent as a yellow striper here – and the sight of it made her uneasy.

Now what?

She watched with growing dread as the carriage approached. Anxious, she pulled off one glove with her teeth and touched a bare palm to the rooftop. It told her of rain, mould, and piles and piles of bird shit, but nothing more – it seemed they were alone up here.

The carriage finally stopped a few buildings down. The door opened, and a man climbed out. He was tall and thin, and not dressed ostentatiously. His posture was stooped – perhaps a man used to sitting, to indoors work. It was hard to see his face in the shifting lights of the floating lanterns, but he had curly locks that looked somewhat reddish.

And clean. Clean hair, clean skin. That gave it away.

He's campo, she thought. *Got to be.*

One of the soldiers ran up to the campo man and started talking. The campo man listened and nodded.

And he's the man running the show. Which meant he was probably the one who'd arranged the trap that had almost got her killed.

She narrowed her eyes at him. *Who are you, you son of a bitch? Which house do you work for?* But she could glean nothing more about him.

The campo man gestured at a rookery building to the left of the clothier's warehouse – which Sancia didn't like. But then he did something odd: he peered at the buildings around him, then reached into his pocket and took out something . . . gold.

She leaned forward slightly, straining to see. It looked like a round, golden device of some kind – like a big, awkward pocket watch, perhaps, slightly larger than his hand.

A tool made of gold, she thought. *Like . . . Clef?*

The campo man examined the gold pocket watch, and frowned. He kept looking at the tool, then up and around, and then back at the tool.

<*Clef – can you see what that is?*> asked Sancia.

<*Too far away,*> said Clef. <*But it seems li—*>

She heard a shout, this one close, from the rookery to her left –

someone crying, *'Stop, stop, you can't just come in here!'* She looked up just as the window shutters of one room banged open, about three floors above her, and a glowering man wearing a steel cap stuck his head out.

The man spied Sancia immediately, pointed, and cried, *'There! She's there, on the rooftop, sir!'*

Sancia looked back at the campo man in the street below. The campo man looked at the guard in the rookery – and then at her.

Then he held up the golden pocket watch and appeared to hit a button on the side. And everything changed.

The first thing Sancia noticed was that all of the floating lanterns in the streets below abruptly went dark and fell to the ground.

The other thing was that her mind went suddenly . . . quiet. A sort of quiet she hadn't heard in a long, long time, like when you live in the city for years and then spend a night out in the country, and hear simply nothing at night.

<*Whoahhhhh,*> said Clef. <*Gugh. I don't . . . I don't feel so, uhhh, so great . . .* >

<*Clef? Clef, we've been spotted, we've got t—*>

He kept talking. <*I feel like . . . like, I had a stroke, or, or . . . somepin . . .* >

But though she was frantic, Sancia couldn't help noticing that her abilities had . . . changed.

Her hand was still pressed to the rooftop – but now it told her nothing. Just silence.

Then she heard the screaming.

Gregor Dandolo strode through the alley in the Greens, muttering, 'Selvo Building, Selvo Building . . .' as he went. It was harder to find than he'd anticipated, since nothing in the Commons was properly labelled – there were no street names, nor signage of any kind. He needed to hurry – he had to get ahold of this Sark before the man heard he was looking for him.

He stopped in his tracks when he heard the *thump* beside him. He looked down to see that Whip's dense metal head had just fallen off its shaft, and its metal cable was unspooling beside it.

'What?' he said, confused. He hit Whip's lever to retract it.

Nothing happened.

'What the devil?' he said.

In an abandoned loft in Old Ditch, the Scrappers were carefully testing out a new scrived device, one that Giovanni hoped would be his masterpiece: a rig that, when attached to a scrived carriage, would give them remote control of the wheels – or it *should*, in theory, but it was persistently failing to work.

'Something's wrong with the commands again,' said Claudia, sighing.

'What's not expressing correctly?' asked Giovanni. 'Where have we made the wrong ste—'

Then all the scrived lights in the loft blinked off.

There was total silence. Even the hums from the fans were gone.

'Uhhh,' said Giovanni. 'Did *we* do that?'

People did not have many scrived devices in Foundryside and the Greens, and those who did kept them secret. But as some of the residents checked on their hidden treasures, they found something . . . strange.

Lights went out. Machines that had previously worked just up and died. Musical trinkets went silent. And a few of the larger scrivings simply failed – some with disastrous results.

Like the Zoagli rookery in Foundryside. Though the residents didn't know it, the supports beneath the building that kept it upright were actually scrived with commands that convinced the wooden pieces they were dark stone, immune to the rotting effects of moisture and waste.

But when those scrivings stopped, the wooden beams remembered what they really were . . .

The wood creaked. Groaned. Moaned.

And then snapped.

In an instant, the entire Zoagli Building collapsed, bringing all the roofs and all the floors down on its residents before they could even understand what was happening.

Sancia looked up when she heard the enormous *crack* from Foundryside, and stared as a building collapsed. It was like watching a big stack of books slowly slump to the side and then tumble to pieces – yet she knew that dozens and dozens of people had to be inside that structure.

'Holy shit,' she whispered.

<*Urrghhh,*> said Clef drunkenly. <*Some . . . sumthin's not right, Sanchezia . . .* >

She looked back at the campo man. He looked surprised by the sound of the building's collapse, even nervous, and stowed the golden pocket watch away in his vest – a curiously guilty gesture.

Sancia looked at the dead lanterns lying in the street.

<*I can't . . . think,*> Clef muttered. <*Can't do . . . anything . . .* >

Her bare hand was pressed into the rooftop, but the rooftop was still silent to her.

A mad idea wriggled into her thoughts.

No, said Sancia, horrified. *That can't be . . .*

Then a voice to her left: '*Scrumming little bastard!*' She looked up, and saw the man in the rookery window lifting up an espringal.

'Shit!' she cried.

She sprang to her feet and started to run toward the building behind the warehouse.

<*I thoughted you . . . uhh, you weren't sure you cuhh-could make that jump!*> said Clef.

<*Shut up, Clef!*>

A bolt thudded into the rooftop just ahead of her. She screamed and covered her head as she ran – not like that would stop the next shot – but in some calm, distant corner of her mind, she recognised that it had not been a scrived bolt. A scrived bolt likely would have punched right through the poorly built roof.

Sancia ran faster, faster. She took note of the stone shingles of the rooftop beyond, imagining how she'd land on them, how the soles of her boots would grip them.

I really goddamn hope, she thought as she madly pumped her arms, *that I was right about it being twenty feet . . .*

She came to the corner and jumped.

The alley soared beneath her, dark and yawning, passing ever so slowly like a cloud traversing the face of the sun. She'd pushed off with her left foot and stretched out with her right, pointing the arch of her foot at the edge of the distant rooftop, every tendon in her leg and hip and back extending to connect with that one spot, like a sprouting plant reaching toward a sunbeam.

She lifted her arms as she leapt and pumped them back down, maximising her propulsion. She lifted her left foot to join her right. She pulled her knees up. The edge of the roof flew closer to her.

The man in the rookery screamed, '*No scrumming way!*'

And then . . .

She compressed her legs as she landed, lessening the impact. She'd made it – almost. For one splinter of a moment she seemed to hang here, the edge of the roof biting into her feet, her arse dangling over the alley below.

Then momentum, that oh-so-fickle friend of hers, carried her forward just a little, until . . .

Sancia found her equilibrium, and stood up.

Her body was still. She'd made it.

A voice in the alley below shouted, '*Shoot! Shoot her!*'

She started running as the bolts thudded into the wall below her, up from the alley – they must have surrounded the clothier's warehouse. She leapt forward and skidded along the slimy stone roof until she came to a small raised hatch, leading down.

The hatch was locked. She fumbled for Clef again, but screamed as a bolt slammed into the roof right beside her shoulder.

'*She's over there!*' cried the man from the rookeries. She peeked over the hatch and saw him signalling to someone below as he reloaded, cranking his espringal once, twice. *'On the roof, on the other roof!'*

She finally pulled Clef out and jammed him into the lock in the hatch.

<*Now,*> said Clef. <*Lemme see here . . .* >

Another bolt came hurtling down, this one a handful of feet away.

<*Right now now* now *would be just terrific, Clef!*> she said.

<*Huh? Uhh right . . . There!*>

A sharp *click.* Sancia wrenched the hatch open and leapt down the dark stairs to the floor below, flying from floor to floor.

But she wasn't alone. Sancia could hear footsteps below.

She came to the second floor. She glimpsed someone running up the stairwell just below her – a woman's face, a dagger in her hand. She screamed, *'Stop! Stop, you!'*

'Not a harpering chance,' whispered Sancia.

She leapt herself through the door to the second floor, then slammed it shut behind her.

<*Lemme lock it!*> said Clef drunkenly.

Sancia threw her shoulder against it as she ripped Clef off the string around her neck. She tried to slip him into the lock, but then . . .

Bang. Someone on the other side hit the door hard, almost knocking Sancia to the ground. She gritted her teeth, threw herself against the door again, and wriggled Clef into the lock . . .

Click.

Someone slammed into the door again. But this time, because it was locked, it didn't move. A voice on the other side moaned in surprise and pain.

She ran down the hallway as people poked their heads out their doors. She took a left, kicked down one door, and ran into the room.

The apartment was small and filthy. A young couple was lying on a pallet, quite nude, and Sancia could not see much of the man's face, as most of it was obscured by the woman's thighs. Both of them screamed in abject terror as Sancia darted inside.

'Pardon,' she said. She ran through the apartment, kicked open the wooden shutters, climbed up onto the window, and jumped across the alley to the next building.

It was an ageing structure – her favourite kind, as it offered plenty of good handholds and niches to stuff her toes into. She crawled down its side slowly and awkwardly, since she'd lost her ability to sense the walls at a touch, then leapt into the muddy alley below and started running north, away from the Anafesto channel, away from the Greens, away from the Commons and the fisheries and the smell of rot and the hissing bolts . . .

Screams echoed in the distance. Maybe another building had fallen down.

Again, she thought about the dead lanterns, Clef's slurred words, and how all the world was dead to her touch – and, again, the mad idea returned to her.

But it was impossible. Just impossible.

No one could just turn scrivings *off.* No one could just hit a switch or a button and make every rig in a whole neighbourhood just *stop.*

But though it might be impossible, thought Sancia, *so is a key that can open anything . . .*

She remembered the wink of gold as the man played with his contraption . . .

What if he already had something like Clef? Something that could do . . . something else?

Smokestacks soared into the sky ahead of her like a cindery forest – the Michiel campo foundries. She had a sachet, but most of the entryways would be closed and locked by now, since it was well after nightfall.

Then she realised she had an easy solution. <*I hope you're up to the task, Clef.*>

<*Whuzzuh?*> said Clef.

She ran along the smooth, white campo wall until she came to a large iron door, tall and thick and elaborately decorated with the Michiel loggotipo. She took Clef out and was about to stuff him into the lock when suddenly things . . . changed.

There was a scrived lantern just on the other side of the wall. She hadn't been able to see it before, because it'd been dark. Yet it had just come back on, flickering to life.

<*Ugh,*> said Clef, suddenly articulate. <*Whoa. I feel like I had a fever or something. What the hell* was *that?*>

A whispering filled her mind. Sancia looked at the iron door.

She reached out with her bare hand and touched it. The whispering filled her mind, as did a thousand other things about the door.

'Scriving's back on,' she said out loud. 'It's back.'

It seemed as if the effects of . . . well, of whatever the campo man had done back there were fading. This was both good and bad. Good, because both she and Clef now had their abilities back. But also bad, because that meant the scrived lock in this door would now also be fully functional – and though she didn't know how long it'd take for Clef to pick it, she could tell from the calls and shouts behind her that she didn't have much time before her pursuers found her.

<*No other choice,*> she said. <*Ready, Clef?*>

<*Huh? Whoa, wait, are you going to—*>

She didn't let him finish the question. She slid Clef into the lock.

Just like with the Candiano door, a thousand questions and thoughts poured into her mind, all of them directed at Clef.

<*BORDER ARGUMENTS . . . COMMANDS ARE SLOW TO RESPOND,*> the door shouted. <*BUT THE SEVENTEENTH TOOTH REQUIREMENT STILL REMAINS.*>

<*Oh, seventeenth?*> asked Clef.

<*AFTER THE TWENTY-FIRST HOUR OF THE DAY, ALL UNLOCKING IMPLEMENTS MUST POSSESS THE SEVENTEENTH TOOTH, INDICATING PROMINENCE,*> said the door. <*ONLY APERTURATION SHALL BE GRANTED . . . AFTER THE TWENTY-FIRST HOUR . . . TO THOSE BEARING THE SEVENTEENTH TOOTH.*>

Sancia glanced down the alley as she listened. She somewhat understood this: apparently after nightfall, only someone with a specific scrived key – one with an important seventeenth tooth – was allowed to unlock and open the door.

<*How do you know it's after the twenty-first hour?*> asked Clef.

<*TEMPORAL SCRIVING PRORATION RECORDS THE NUMBER OF HOURS PASSED.*>

<*And how long's an hour?*>

<*IT IS RECORDED AS SIXTY MINUTES.*>

<*Oh, that's wrong. They changed all that. Listen . . .* >

A huge exchange of information took place between Clef and the door. The distant sounds of shouts were drifting toward her. 'Come on,' she whispered. 'Come on . . .'

<*WAIT,*> said the door. <*SO THEY REALLY CHANGED AN HOUR TO BEING 1.37 SECONDS?*>

<*Yep!*> said Clef.

<*OH. SO IT'S ACTUALLY TEN IN THE MORNING? WELL, ELEVEN IN THE MORNING NOW. AND NOW IT'S NOON . . .*>

<*Yep. Yep. So, uh, go ahead and open, okay?*>

<*I SEE. CERTAINLY.*>

Silence. Then there was a *click*, and the door opened. Sancia slipped through and slowly shut it behind her. She crouched behind the wall, listening. Her ankles ached, her feet ached, her hands ached, her back ached – but at least for once her head didn't hurt much.

<*Thanks, Clef,*> she said.

<*Don't mention it. Let's hope that worked.*>

She heard footsteps on the other side, someone walking, slowing down . . . and then they tried the handle of the iron door.

Sancia stared at the handle, fervently praying that the handle didn't keep moving – but it didn't. It moved just a tiny, tiny bit – and then it stopped.

The person on the other side grunted. Then they walked away.

Sancia waited for a long time. Then she let out a slow breath, and turned to face the grey spires and domes and smokestacks of the Michiel campo.

<*We made it!*> said Clef. <*We got away!*>

<*Sure,*> said Sancia. <*Only now we're unarmed, and stuck in hostile territory.*>

<*Oh. Right. Well. What do we do?*>

Sancia rubbed her eyes. She had to get out of the city, but this presented a familiar problem.

She needed money. She always needed money. Money to bribe someone, money to buy tools to get more money, money to get a safe place to store her damned money. Life was cheap, and cash, as ever, remained dauntingly expensive.

Her normal source of money had been Sark. But Sark wasn't an option anymore.

Then she had an idea, and slowly cocked her head. *But his house – that might be a different case.*

<*Sark always kept a panic kit,*> she said to Clef. <*An emergency bag to help him run, just in case someone really heavy came after him again. With*

money, and forged papers from the merchant houses that could let us get on any ship.>

<*So?*>

<*So, if we get it, we'll be set! God knows Sark would have overprepared for something like this!*>

<*For something like* this?>

<*Well. Maybe not something like this. But it's a lot better than all the nothing we have.*>

<*How are we going to get to it? You're beat to shit, kid, and your own kit's completely gone. And if these guys were following Sark to your meeting place – don't you think they at least know where he lives?*>

<*Yeah . . .* >

<*So you're going to need more than a charming smile and me in your pocket to get in there.*>

She sighed and rubbed her eyes. <*Well. I guess I could go to the Scrappers. There's a shortcut over the Michiel foundries, then through Foundryside to Old Ditch. They'll have something that could help . . .* >

<*For free?*>

<*No. But you can maybe help me get some quick cash, Clef. I know some easy targets. Not enough to get out of the city – but maybe enough to pay for some of the Scrappers' tools.*>

<*Is a bad plan better than no plan? I'm not sure.*>

<*Sometimes you're tons of help, and other times you're no help at all.*> She turned left, through the foundry yards. <*Hey, Clef?*>

<*Yeah?*>

Sancia tried to think about how to phrase these words, as they were essentially incomprehensible to any Tevanni. <*Have . . . have you ever heard of something that can, like, turn off scrivings?*>

<*What? Why? Is . . . Wait, is* that *what you think happened back there?*>

<*Pretty sure.*>

<*Oh, hell. Well. No.*>

Sancia grimaced. <*Yeah.*>

<*That's . . . really concerning.*>

<*Yeah.*>

She glanced to the east, where the giant cloud of dust was drifting toward the moon.

<*So is that,*> said Clef.

<*Yeah.*>

Sancia kept to the rooftops as she made her way through Foundryside to Old Ditch. Her hands hurt like hell and her head wasn't much better, but she had to make do. Every once in a while she'd peer down into the warrens and spy someone who looked large, well fed, well armed, and quite mean – and she'd know she wasn't out of danger yet.

She briefly stopped in Old Ditch to hit up a once-favourite stop of hers: the Bibbona Wine Brewery. Everyone said the cane wine made there was atrocious, but they still did a brisk business – brisk enough to be worth her robbing the place every once in a while, back in the day. But then some clever bastard had not only installed a reinforced door in the brewery, but they'd also rigged up a timing system: three Miranda Brass locks that had to be unlocked within twenty seconds of each other – otherwise, they'd all re-lock. Even with Sancia's talents, the hassle hadn't been worth the payout.

But with Clef, it was easy – one, two, three, and suddenly she had two hundred duvots in her pocket.

<*I guess this is the life we'd lead if a whole army wasn't looking to cut you to ribbons, huh?*> asked Clef as she crept away.

She quickly scaled the side of a rookery and scrambled onto the rooftop. <*Something like that.*>

Luckily, the Scrappers were in the first place she looked – an abandoned loft in Old Ditch. To her surprise, they weren't in their workshop, but were instead standing on the balcony, staring out at the distant chaos in Foundryside. Sancia peered over the rooftop at them, then carefully started climbing down.

Giovanni screamed in surprise and fell backward into the other Scrappers as Sancia dropped down to the balcony. 'For the love of God!' she said, standing. 'Could you keep it down!'

'San?' said Claudia. 'What the *hell* are you doing here?' She looked up along the wall. 'Why were you on the roof?'

'I'm here to buy,' said Sancia. 'And buy fast. And I had to take a safe route.' She glanced at the street below. 'Can we go indoors?'

'No,' said Claudia. 'All our lights are off. Nothing works, that's why we're out here.'

'Have you checked recently?' asked Sancia.

'Why?' said Giovanni suspiciously.

'We haven't,' said Claudia. 'Because the second we came outside, some scrumming buildings started falling down! The whole neighbourhood's gone mad!'

'Oh,' said Sancia. She coughed. 'Ah. Very strange, that. But – can we, uh, light a candle, and go inside anyway?'

Giovanni narrowed his eyes at her. 'Sancia . . . I suddenly feel that your arrival, and all these disasters, seems terribly coincidental.'

Sancia spied someone in a steel cap walking down the alley below. 'Can we *please* just go *inside*?' she begged.

Claudia and Giovanni exchanged a glance. Then Claudia said to the rest of the Scrappers, 'Stay out here. Let me know if anything . . . I don't know, explodes or something.'

Inside, Sancia quickly told them what had happened – or tried to. The more she talked, the madder it all felt. As she spoke, she washed her hands in the candlelight and wrapped her palms and wrists in chalk cloth. She didn't like it much – she didn't like any new clothing – but she knew she had to do a lot more climbing soon.

Claudia stared at her in disbelief. 'You've got a whole goddamn campo army out looking for you?'

'Pretty much,' said Sancia.

'And . . . and Sark's *dead*?' asked Giovanni.

'Yes,' she said quietly. 'Almost certainly.'

'And . . .' Claudia looked at her, frightened. 'You say some campo lordling is running around . . . with some rig that can turn scrivings *off*?'

'It all happened fast,' said Sancia. 'So I'm not positive. But . . . that seems to be what I saw. He hit a button, and everything just *stopped*. I'm guessing those buildings fell down because they were being supported by scrivings, in some fashion or another. And his soldiers expected it – that was why they switched to regular espringals, rather than scrived ones.'

'Shit,' said Claudia weakly.

'You really think this was all about your key?' said Giovanni.

'That I'm sure of.'

'Where did you hide it?' he asked. 'Did you bury it, or put it in a safe drop, or just throw it away?'

Sancia thought about what to say. 'Ah . . .'

Giovanni went white. 'You don't still have it, do you? You didn't bring it *here*?'

Sancia's hand guiltily crept up to her chest, where Clef was hanging from her neck. 'At this point, bringing Clef here isn't any more dangerous than *my* being here.'

'Oh my Lord,' whispered Giovanni.

'Goddamn it, Sancia!' said Claudia, furious. 'I . . . I *told* you to stop taking house jobs! You're going to get us all killed just by our knowing you!'

'Then get me out of here fast,' said Sancia. 'I need to get to Sark's and grab his emergency kit. I get that, and I can get out of Tevanne, and you'll never know me again.' She took what she'd stolen from the brewery and dropped it on the table. 'There's two hundred here. You said I'd get a fifty per cent discount next time. I'm calling it in. Now.'

Claudia and Giovanni looked at each other. Then Claudia sighed deeply, took the candle to a cupboard, and started pulling out a box. 'You want dolorspina darts again – yes?'

'Yeah. These are trained soldiers. A one-shot stop would be damned handy. But do you have anything else? I need any fight to be as unfair as it can get.'

'There's . . . something new I cooked up,' said Giovanni. 'But it's not totally ready yet.' He opened a drawer and pulled out what looked like a small black wooden ball.

<Neat!> said Clef in her head. *<It's . . . I don't know, it's like some kind of screwed-up lamp that pops . . . >*

Sancia tried to ignore him. 'What is it?'

'I rigged it up so it uses multiple lighting scrivings from the four houses,' he said. 'In other words, you hit the button, throw it, and it makes an ungodly amount of light, flashing bright. Enough to blind someone. Then . . .'

'Then what?' said Sancia.

'Well, this is the part I'm not so sure about,' said Giovanni. 'There's a charge inside – no more than a firecracker. But I've made its chamber sensitive to vibrations so it *feels* like it's playing host to a much, much larger combustion. It amplifies the noise, in other words . . .'

'So it makes a really, really loud bang,' said Claudia.

'That,' said Giovanni, 'or it might *actually* explode. It's hard to test things like this. So I'm not sure yet.'

<*I am,*> said Clef. <*And it won't.*>

'I'll take as many of those as I can buy,' she said.

Giovanni took out three more of the black balls and popped them in a sack for her. 'Sancia . . . you ought to know that Sark's apartments likely aren't safe, either.'

'I know that,' she said. 'That's why I'm here!'

'No, listen,' said Claudia. 'Some big thug walked into The Perch and Lark just a handful of hours ago and beat every single one of Antonin di Nove's men half to death – as well as Antonin himself – all while asking for information about the waterfront job.'

Sancia stared at her. 'One guy? *One* guy fought all of Antonin's crew, single-handedly, and *won*?'

'Yes,' said Claudia. 'I've no doubt Antonin told him everything he knew about Sark – which was probably a lot. Seems you've called all kinds of devils out of the dark with your antics.'

'And now you, Sancia Grado,' said Giovanni, tying up the sack, 'at all of five foot no inches, and a hundred and nothing pounds, are going to take them all on.' He held it out to her, grinning. 'Good luck.'

9

Gregor Dandolo stood below the Selvo Building and looked up. It was large, dark, and crumbling – in other words, it looked much like the sort of place where a thief's fence would reside. Each room had a short balcony, though few looked sturdy.

He glanced back at the plume of dust rising from Foundryside. Something bad had happened back there – likely a building had collapsed, if not several. Every instinct of his told him to run to the site and help, but he realised that his previous actions tonight made that unwise. There was now an entire criminal organisation that wanted him dead, and this Sark would surely soon catch word that Gregor was looking for him, and go to ground.

The one night I have business in the Commons, he thought to himself, *is, of course, the one night the entire place falls apart.*

He checked to make sure Whip was working. His weapon seemed to be all in order – he had no idea what that odd bit of business had been about back there. Grimacing, he walked inside the Selvo and found a few residents anxiously wandering the halls, wondering what the crash was.

Sark's door was easy to find – it was the one with eight locks on it. He listened for a bit but heard nothing inside. He walked down the rooms on Sark's side of the building and quietly tried all the doorknobs. One was open on the very far end. The room within was empty – for sale or abandoned, he supposed.

Gregor stumbled through the dark room. He fumbled with the door on the far end and walked out onto the balcony that dangled on the side of the building. Then he looked down the face of the building at all the balconies, all lined up close together.

An idea occurred to him. *I must try my hardest,* he thought, straddling the baluster, *not to look down.*

With slow, careful movements, Gregor Dandolo vaulted from balcony to balcony toward Sark's rooms. There wasn't much of a gap between the balconies, only about three feet or so, so his primary concern was that the balconies might not be able to support his weight. But despite a few creaks and cracks, they held.

Finally he came to Sark's rooms. The door leading in was locked, but this lock was far weaker than the ones in the front door. He wedged the bottom of Whip's handle into the crack and tugged at it. The lock popped free easily.

He was about to go in when he paused . . . He thought for just one moment, just a split second, that he'd seen someone on the rooftop across the alley. But now that he looked there didn't seem to be anyone. He grunted and slipped inside.

It took a moment for his eyes to adjust. Gregor took out a match, struck it, and lit a candle.

Now. What's to find here?

What he found made his heart sink: this Sark had at least ten safes, all of them lined up along the walls, all of them locked and, to Gregor, impenetrable.

He sighed. *If there is evidence in there,* he thought, *I can't get to it. So I must find any evidence outside of the safes, then.*

He searched the rooms. The space looked like something adapted for an invalid: lots of canes, lots of handles, lots of low seats. He also found Sark had little in the way of crockery and cutlery and pans. He apparently did not make his own food much at all, which was not terribly unusual. Few Commoners could afford all the materials that went into the preparation of food.

Gregor was about to move past the cooking stove and into the living room when he paused.

'If he doesn't have plates or spoons,' he said aloud, looking down, 'and if he doesn't eat at home . . . then why does he have a stove?'

Certainly not for heat – Tevanne had no shortage of that: the city's two seasons were hot and wet, or unbelievably hot and unbelievably wet.

Gregor squatted before the stove. There was no wood ash inside – which was odd.

Grunting, Gregor reached down and felt the back of the stove, until he found a small switch.

He turned it, and the back of the stove popped open. 'Oho,' said Gregor. Inside were four small shelves, and on those shelves were many precious items.

He looked at the safes around him. *These are just a distraction, aren't they? Make any interlopers focus on them, while the real safe sits hidden right in front of you . . .* He suddenly thought this Sark a very clever man.

There was a small bag on the top shelf, and he opened it and carefully looked through it. 'My goodness,' he murmured.

Inside were four thousand duvots – paper duvots, no less – and multiple documents, almost certainly forged, that would allow the holder to secure quick passage on any number of ships. One of them even granted the bearer the powers of a minor ambassador from Dandolo Chartered – and even though Gregor had little to do with his family's house, he couldn't help but feel insulted by that.

He looked through the rest of the bag, and found a knife, lockpicks, and other unseemly tools. *He's definitely the fence,* he thought. *And the man was ready to run in a heartbeat.*

He searched the rest of the hidden safe. It contained small sacks of gemstones, jewellery, and the like. On the bottom shelf was a small book. Gregor grabbed it and flipped through it, and found it was full of dates, plans, and tactics for Sark's many jobs.

At first the notes were extremely detailed – methods of entry and escape, tools required for breaking a specific lock or safe – but at one point, about two years ago, the jobs suddenly got a lot more frequent and the payouts a lot higher, but the notes became far sparser. Gregor got the impression that Sark had made a connection with someone good enough that they didn't need much of his help.

He flipped to the last entry and found Sark's notes on the waterfront job. He felt a bit pleased to see that his defences had frustrated this Sark immensely – one scribbled line read: *This bastard Dandolo is going to make S work double-time!!*

Gregor made a note of that – 'S'. He doubted it stood for 'Sark'. *That must be the thief – whoever they are.*

But there was another note at the end that he found deeply curious – scrawled in the margins of the paper were two words: *Dandolo Hyp??*

Gregor stared at the words.

He knew that they did not refer to him – they had to be shorthand for 'Dandolo Hypatus.' And that was very, very troubling.

A hypatus was a merchant house officer who acted as something akin to a head of research, experimenting with sigillums to dream up new methods, techniques, and tools. Most hypati were madder than a speared striper, mostly because they often didn't survive long – experimental scrivings had a tendency to inflict gruesome death on anyone involved with them. And then there was the backstabbing the position attracted: since every scriver on a campo wanted to be a hypatus, betrayals and even assassinations were common hazards of the job.

But the Dandolo Chartered hypatus was Orso Ignacio – and Orso Ignacio was notorious, if not legendary, for being an amoral, arrogant, duplicitous, and fiendishly clever campo operator. He'd lasted nearly a decade as hypatus, which had to be a record in Tevanne. And he hadn't risen from within the ranks of Dandolo Chartered – he'd originally been employed at Company Candiano, though Gregor had heard rumours he'd departed that house under leery terms. It was a known fact that the whole damned merchant house had almost collapsed mere weeks after his departure.

Yet as unsavoury as Orso Ignacio's reputation might be – would he be willing to hire an independent thief to rob Gregor's waterfront? Since Gregor was the son of Ofelia Dandolo – the head of the entire Dandolo Chartered merchant house – this seemed totally insane. But then, hypati were generally agreed to be insane, or close enough to it.

Gregor considered what he knew. Only one thing had been stolen that night – a box, entered into the safes under the name of 'Berenice'. Which could have been a false name, for all Gregor knew.

So – was Orso Ignacio the buyer? Or was he the one being robbed? Or is this small note here just nonsense, a complete coincidence?

He wasn't sure. But he now intended to find out.

Gregor heard something, and sat up. There were footfalls in the hallway – all heavy boots. And it sounded like there were a lot of them.

He didn't wait to listen and see if the new arrivals came to Sark's door. Instead he took Whip out and walked quietly into the bedroom, where he hid behind the open door, peering through the crack in the hinge at the living room beyond.

Could this be Sark? Has he returned?

There was a tremendous *crack* as someone kicked the door down.

Ah, no, he thought. *Probably not Sark.*

Gregor watched as two men in dark-brown clothing and black cloth masks walked into Sark's rooms. But what really caught Gregor's eye were their weapons.

One bore a stiletto, the other a rapier – and both were scrived. He could see the sigils running along the lengths of the blades, even from where he was.

He sighed inwardly. *Well. That's going to be a problem.*

Gregor was familiar with scrived weapons. Scrived armaments, though prohibitively expensive, were the primary reason why the city of Tevanne had been so successful in warfare. But you couldn't just glance at a scrived weapon and know what it was scrived to do. It could be anything.

For example, the common blades used in the Enlightenment Wars were scrived so that they'd automatically target the weakest part of whatever they were swung at, and then target the weakest part of that weakest part, and then to target the weakest part of *that* weakest part of the weakest part, and then strike that *exact* area. Operating off of these commands, the blades would be able to cut through a solid oak beam with little force.

But that was just one possibility. Other scrivings convinced the blades they were hurtling through the air with amplified gravity –

this was what Whip's head was scrived to do, for example. Others had been scrived specifically to break down and destroy other metals, like armour and weapons. And still others burned incredibly hot when whirled through the air, giving them the possibility of setting one's opponent alight.

All of these possibilities ran through Gregor's head as the two thugs stalked through Sark's rooms. *So what I need to do,* he thought, *is make sure they never get to use them.*

He watched as the two men examined the open back of the stove. They crouched and peered in, then exchanged a glance, perhaps worried.

They turned and approached the balcony door. One gestured to the other, silently pointing out that the lock had been broken in. Then they started walking toward the bedroom, with the one with the rapier in the lead.

Still hidden behind the door, Gregor waited until the first of his opponents had stepped into the bedroom, with the second one right behind him. Then he kicked the door as hard as he could.

The door hurled shut, smashing the second thug in the face. Gregor could feel the wood resonate with the blow, and felt satisfied with the damage done. The thug with the rapier turned around, raising his weapon, but Gregor snapped Whip forward and cracked him in the face.

But the man did not crumple, whimpering, as Gregor had been expecting. Instead the thug stumbled back, shook himself, and charged forward again.

The man's mask, thought Gregor. *It must be scrived to deflect strikes. Maybe all of his scrumming clothing's scrived!*

Gregor dove to the side as the man's rapier slashed through the wall like it was made of warm cheese. Though it was dark in the rooms, he could tell that the rapier was, like Whip's head, scrived to amplify its gravity, crashing through the air like a man ten times as strong had swung it. Which, Gregor knew from experience, was a dangerous weapon to face – but also a dangerous weapon to wield.

Gregor rose and flicked Whip out. The truncheon's head flew forward and smashed the man on his knee, hard enough to knock him over – but he stayed standing. *Not good,* thought Gregor. *Their outfits must have cost a fortune . . .*

He did not have time to reflect on the cost of their armaments, though, because then the second thug barged in, almost knocking the door off its hinges. The thug with the rapier then pivoted, sword in his hand, trying to pin Gregor into the corner.

Gregor grabbed the mattress on Sark's bed and flung it at his two assailants. The man with the rapier slashed it in two, sending feathers flying everywhere. Gregor used this momentary distraction to hurl yet more furniture at them – a chair, a small desk – though his goal was not to harm them, but to clutter the room, making it harder to move.

The man with the rapier hacked his way through, cursing. But now the space was too small for them both to confront him – only the one with the rapier could engage.

He led the man back, toward the window of the bedroom, and got in position. His attacker gave a rough shout, and thrust forward with the rapier, aiming for Gregor's heart.

Gregor fell to the side and sent Whip's head flying at the man's feet.

His attacker tripped. And ordinarily this would not have meant much – but Gregor's attacker had just thrust his rapier forward, expecting to plunge it into Gregor's chest, and the weapon accelerated as it flew; and now that there was nothing to stop it, it just kept hurtling forward, pulling the man along like someone trying to walk a large dog that's just seen a rat and bolted after it.

The sword plunged right through the window behind Gregor – and took its owner with it. Gregor stood and watched with grim pleasure as the thug sailed down three floors and crashed onto the wooden sidewalk.

Scrived defences or not, he thought, *the man's brain is soup now.*

'Son of a bitch,' snarled the second attacker. 'You . . . You son of a *bitch*!' He did something to his stiletto – adjusted some lever or button – and the blade started vibrating hard and fast. This augmentation was new to Gregor, and he did not like it: that blade wouldn't make a nice puncture hole, but instead would tear him to pieces.

The man advanced on him. Gregor flicked Whip forward, and the man ducked – but the man had not been his target. Rather, Gregor had been aiming at the bedroom door, which was barely hanging on to the doorframe after its ill treatment. The truncheon's head punched through the door and even part of the wall, and the impact finally severed the door from its frame.

The man glanced back at it, then rose and growled as he started to advance on Gregor.

But then Gregor hit the switch on the side of Whip, and it started to retract the truncheon's head.

And, as Gregor had hoped, it hauled the bedroom door along with it. The door crashed into the man's back, and Gregor leapt aside just in time as the sheer momentum carried his attacker forward and into the wall.

Gregor stood, ripped Whip free of the shattered remains of the door, and started bashing the back of the prone man's head. Gregor was not the sort of person to beat a fallen man to death, but he had to make sure the man stayed down, as his opponent's defences likely dulled the impact of anything that hit him.

After seven or so strikes, Gregor paused, chest heaving, and kicked the thug over. He realised he might have inadvertently overwhelmed the scrived defences of the man's clothing. A pool of blood was slowly spreading out into a gruesome halo around his head.

Gregor sighed. He did not like killing.

He looked out the window. The man with the rapier was still lying on the broken wooden sidewalk. He hadn't moved.

This is not how I wanted the evening to go, thought Gregor. He didn't even know who these men had been coming for. Were they Sark's men, responding to his break-in? Or had they been looking for Sark? Or was it something else entirely?

'Let's at least find out who you are,' he said. He knelt and started to pull the man's mask off.

But before he could, the wall behind him exploded.

The second the wall erupted, two thoughts entered Gregor's mind.

The first was that he had really been quite stupid: he'd heard the number of footsteps outside Sark's door, and he'd *known* there had been more than two men who'd come to the room. He'd just forgotten it in the melee – a very stupid move.

The second thought was: *I cannot be hearing this right now. It is impossible.*

Because as the wall exploded, sending shattered wood and stone flying through the room, there was a sound over the fracas that was distinct: a high-pitched, wailing shriek. And Gregor had not heard that sound since the Enlightenment Wars.

He dove to the ground as dust and debris showered over him. He looked up just in time to see it – a large, thick, iron arrow hurtling through the far wall of the bedroom, flying just over him, and punching out the other wall as if it were made of paper. The arrow was burning hot, bright and red, leaving a trail of fire in its wake, and he knew that eventually it would erupt into a shower of hot, flaming metal.

He sat up, dust pouring off of him, and watched in horror as the burning-hot missile shrieked out over the Greens before exploding. Bright sparks and flaming shrapnel danced down to the buildings below.

No! he thought. *No, no! There are civilians, there are* civilians*!*

Before he could think further on it, the wall erupted again in a different place, and another shrieker punched through the walls of Sark's bedroom, showering Gregor with stones and smoking splinters and passing just overhead.

Gregor lay on the ground, stunned. *How is this happening? How do they have shriekers?*

The Tevanni military had always used altered weaponry to terrific results. There were the swords, certainly, but its bolts and arrows were also scrived, much like Whip, to believe that they were not being flung forward but were instead falling down, obeying gravity. Thus they were able to fly perfectly straight, reach a high velocity, and go much farther than conventional ranged weapons could.

There were some downsides, however. The military had to lug

around miniature lexicons specifically built to power such scrivings, and once the projectiles reached the limit of that lexicon's range, the scrivings failed and the bolts began to descend as any normal projectile would.

So the Tevanni scrivers experimented. Their eventual inspiration came from the release scrivings on common bolts – for Tevanni bolts were not *just* scrived to believe that they were falling, since a bolt travelling the distance of, say, fifty feet at the constant acceleration of a free-falling object would not do much damage at all.

Instead, the release scrivings on the bolts worked so that the instant the bolts were released, they suddenly believed that they had been falling straight down for around seven thousand feet, give or take. This produced an initial release velocity of over six hundred feet per second, which everyone found satisfyingly lethal.

So, when pressed to develop an armament with a longer range, the scrivers had simply upped the distance. A lot. They'd developed a projectile that, when released from its caster, did not simply believe it'd been falling for a few thousand feet, but rather that it'd been plummeting toward the earth for *thousands and thousands of miles*. The second you released it, it'd suddenly roar forward, plunging through the air at a phenomenal speed like a black bolt of lightning. Usually the projectile would get so hot from sheer friction that it would abruptly explode in midair. Even if it didn't, the damage it did was nothing short of catastrophic.

The name for this projectile had been easy to choose. Because as the projectile gained heat and boiled the air around it, it tended to create a high-pitched, terrifying roaring sound.

Gasping, Gregor started crawling toward the living room. He blinked blood out of his eyes. A stone or piece of wood had struck him on the head, and the room was now so smoky it was hard to breathe.

He tried not to think of Dantua, with its tattered walls and smoke, its streets echoing with moans, and the sound of the army laying waste to the countryside beyond . . .

Stay here, he pleaded with his mind. *Stay with me . . .*

Another shrieker ripped through the walls of the living room as Gregor crawled forward. Hot ash and smoking debris rained over him once more. He knew now that there was a third man in the hallway, armed with a shrieker, and he must have decided to use it when he heard the fight and his two compatriots did not emerge.

But this should have been impossible. For a shrieker to work, you had to have a nearby lexicon that would permit it. And that was strictly outlawed in Tevanne. A shrieker brought within Tevanne should have been just another piece of dumb metal.

What is going on? How is any of this happening right now?

Gregor finally made it into the living room, exhausted and battered, still crawling forward with Whip in one hand. He got to the centre and looked out the front door.

At first, the way out was clear. But then a man stepped into the doorway, dressed in black. Balanced on one of his arms was a huge device made of metal and wood, like a monstrous, handheld ballista. Nestled in the pocket of the ballista was a long, slender iron arrow. It seemed to be quivering slightly, like a furious animal on a leash.

The man pointed the shrieker at Gregor. Gregor, coughing and disoriented, stared at him.

In a low, growling voice, the man asked, 'Is the thief here?'

Gregor stared back, unsure what to say.

But then something flew in through the open balcony door. It was small and round, and it flew over Gregor's head and landed just before the man with the shrieker.

Then the world lit up.

It was like someone had turned on a thousand lights at once, a sort of brightness Gregor had not known was even possible – and then there was a tremendous, earsplitting, earth-shattering *bang*.

Gregor almost lost consciousness from sheer oversensation – or perhaps that was due to the blow to the head he'd taken.

The light and sound faded. Gregor's ears were still ringing, but his eyesight returned. He could see the man with the shrieker was still in the hallway, but he'd dropped his weapon and was rubbing his eyes, evidently as blinded as Gregor had been.

Gregor rolled over and looked at the balcony door, just in time to see a very short girl dressed in black drop in out of nowhere, stand on the balcony, lift a pipe to her lips, and blow.

A dart flew out of the pipe, zipped across the room, and hit the man with the shrieker in the neck. His eyes went wide. He pawed at his throat, trying to pull it out, but then he turned a dull shade of green and toppled over.

Gregor's saviour put away the pipe and ran over to him. She looked at his Waterwatch sash, sighed, grabbed him by the arm, and hauled him up. Even though his hearing was still scrambled, he could hear what she said: 'Come on, arsehole! Run! *Run!*'

✣

Gregor staggered through the alleys of the Greens, one arm thrown on the shoulders of his small but surprisingly strong rescuer. If anyone saw them they'd have assumed it was a friend helping a drunk get home.

Once they were safe, she stopped and shoved him to the ground. Gregor tumbled over and crashed into the mud.

'You,' said the girl, 'are *scrumming lucky* I happened to be watching! What the hell is the matter with you? You and those other fools practically blew up the whole building!'

Gregor blinked and rubbed the side of his head. 'Whu . . . What's going on? What *was* that back there?'

'It was a stun bomb,' said the girl. 'And it was damned valuable. I'd barely had it for more than an hour too. And a fat lot of good it's done for me, after you've scrummed everything up!' She began pacing around the alley. 'Now where am I going to get money? Now how am I going to get out of the city? Now what do I do!'

'Who . . . Who are you?' asked Gregor. 'Why did you save me?'

'I wasn't even sure I was going to,' she said. 'I saw those three bastards watching the room and decided to hold off. Then I see *you* come and jump from balcony to balcony like a damned fool and break in. And then *they* see *you* and try to blow you to smithereens! I think I mostly did it so that one mad bastard would stop shooting up the Greens!'

Gregor frowned. 'Wait. What was it you said? Where are you going to get money? You . . . You mean you came to Sark's for . . .'

He stared at the young woman in black, and slowly realised that this person, despite having saved him, was likely one of Sark's thieves.

And, knowing it was Sark, it was suddenly likely that this young woman was the person who had robbed the Waterwatch and burned down the waterfront.

Without another word, Gregor rose and tried to dive at her – but between her stun bomb and the damage the shrieker had done to him, he could barely walk in a straight line.

The young woman danced aside and kicked his feet out from under him. Gregor tumbled down into the mud, cursing. He tried to stand up, but she put a boot in his back and shoved him down. Again, he was surprised at how strong she was – or maybe he was just that weakened.

'You burned down the waterfront!' he said.

'That was an accident,' she said.

'You robbed my damned safes!'

'Okay, well, *that* wasn't. What did you find in Sark's?'

Gregor said nothing.

'I saw you reading. I know you found something. What?'

He considered what to say – and then he considered her behaviour: how she'd acted, and what she'd done, why she was here. And he started to develop an idea of her circumstances.

'What I found,' he said, 'is that you have either stolen from, or stolen for, some of the most powerful, merciless people in the city of Tevanne. But I think you knew that. And I think your arrangement has gone quite wrong, and you are now desperate to escape. But you won't. They will find you, and kill you.'

She pressed harder into his back and crouched down. He couldn't see her face – yet he could smell her.

And strangely, her smell was . . . familiar.

I know that scent, he thought. *How odd* . . .

He felt something sharp being drawn along the side of his neck. She showed it to him – another dart. 'Know what this is?' she asked.

He looked at it, then looked her in the eye. 'I am not afraid to die,' he said. 'If that is your intent, I suggest you hurry it along.'

She paused at that, clearly surprised. She tried to gather herself. 'Goddamn it, tell me what you fo—'

'You are no killer,' said Gregor. 'No soldier. That I can see. The wisest course of action here is to surrender now and come with me.'

'What, so you can have me harpered?' asked the girl. 'This is some shit negotiation you're trying.'

'If you surrender,' said Gregor, 'I will plead mercy for you personally. And I will do everything I can to prevent your death.'

'You're lying.'

He looked over his shoulder at her. 'I do not lie,' he said quietly.

She squinted at him, surprised by his tone.

'Nor do I kill anymore,' said Gregor, 'unless I have to. I have had enough of that for one life. Surrender. Now. I will protect you. And though I will see justice done, I will not allow them to kill you. But if you do not surrender – I will not stop coming for you. And either I will catch you, or they will kill you.'

She seemed to be considering it. 'I believe you,' she said. She leaned close. 'But I'm still willing to take my chances, Captain.'

There was a sharp pain in his neck. Then everything went dark.

When Gregor Dandolo awoke, he was no longer convinced that consciousness was the best choice for him. It felt as if some foundryman had swung by, opened up his head, and filled it with smelted metals. He groaned and rolled over, and realised he'd been lying facedown in the mud for what must have been hours, since the sun was now out. It was a miracle someone hadn't cut his throat and robbed him blind.

But then, it did look as if the young woman had covered him in trash and refuse so no one could see him. Which he supposed was a generous gesture – even if it made him smell like a canal.

He sat up, whimpering and rubbing his skull. Then his thoughts turned to the young woman, and he remembered how she'd smelled.

Her odour had been distinct. Because it had smelled like she'd been in a Tevanni foundry, or near a foundry's smokestacks.

And as Ofelia Dandolo's child, Gregor knew a great deal about Tevanni foundries.

He laughed to himself in disbelief, and stood and hobbled away.

10

The next morning, Gregor held his head high as he walked through the southern gates of the outermost Dandolo Chartered wall. As he moved from Commons to campo, the change was abrupt, and severe: from muddy pathways to clean cobblestone; from the odour of smoke and dung and rot to the faint aroma of spiced meat being grilled nearby; and then, of course, there were the people in the streets, whose clothing changed to being clean and colourful, whose skin became clear and unblemished, who suddenly moved without any ailment or deformity or drunkenness or exhaustion.

It never failed to amaze him: you walked exactly one dozen feet, and fell out of one civilisation and into another. This was the outer campo too, not even one of the nicer parts. *Behind each door*, he thought, *another world waits. And another and another and another . . .*

He counted his steps as he walked across the threshold. 'One,' he said. 'Two . . . Three and four . . .'

The guardhouse door popped open, and a Dandolo house guard in full scrived armour trotted up to keep pace with him. 'Morning, sir!' called the guard.

'Good morning,' said Gregor. *Four steps – they're getting slow.*

'Going far, Founder?' asked the guard. 'Would you like me to call you a carriage?'

'My formal title, Lieutenant,' he said, glancing at the guard's helm for his rank, 'is *Captain*. Not Founder.'

'I see, Foun . . . I mean, I see, sir.' He coughed nervously. 'But the sachet you carry, ah, it notified us tha—'

'Yes,' said Gregor. 'I know what my sachet told you. Either way, there's no need for a carriage, lieutenant. I am content to walk.' He bowed to the man, touching his brow with two fingers. 'Good morning!'

The guard, confused, stopped and watched Gregor leave. 'Good day, sir . . .'

Gregor Dandolo walked from the outer campo wall to the second wall gates. And, again, he had to turn down another offer of a carriage – as he did at the third wall, and the fourth, penetrating deeper and deeper into the Dandolo Chartered campo. The guards offered the carriages with a nervous eagerness, because Gregor's sachet was flagged as founder lineage – and the idea of founderkin just walking around the campo on their own two feet was unthinkable to most Tevannis.

The truth of it was, he would have loved a carriage ride – his head still ached from that poison that girl had put in him, and he'd already walked damn near across Tevanne the night before, looking for Sark. But Gregor ignored all offers. He ignored them just as he ignored the flocks of floating lanterns that coiled above the Dandolo campo streets, and the bubbling fountains, and the tall, white stone towers, and the beautiful women picking their way through the campo parks, adorned in silk robes and sporting faces painted with intricate, curling patterns.

This could have been his – as the son of Ofelia Dandolo, he could have lived in these gleaming streets like the most pampered princeling in all the world. And maybe, once, he would have.

But then Dantua had happened. And Gregor, and perhaps the world, had changed.

Though from the way everyone on the Dandolo campo was acting, maybe the world had changed again, just last night. People looked grave, solemn, and shaken, and they talked quietly, in hushed, anxious tones.

Gregor understood how they felt all too well. Scriving was the foundation of their entire society. After the blackouts last night, they were no doubt worrying their entire way of life could crumble to pieces, much like the Zoagli block, and take them with it.

Finally he came to the campo illustris – the administrative facility, where the elites governed all merchant house duties. It was a massive, white structure, with a huge, vaulted ceiling supported by a curling vanguard of riblike buttresses. Countless officials trotted up and down the clean white steps at the front, gathering in clumps to discuss business in hushed tones. They stared at Gregor as he walked by, tall and only somewhat washed and wearing his leather armour and Waterwatch sash. He gave them no notice, leapt up the steps, and strode into the building.

As Gregor paced through the illustris, he reflected that the whole place felt more like a temple than an administrative building: too many columns, too much stained glass, too many floating lanterns drifting amongst the vaulted ceilings, suggesting a divine light above. But perhaps that was the intended effect: perhaps it made those employed here believe they worked the very will of God, rather than the will of Gregor's mother.

It could be worse, he thought. *It could be like the Mountain of the Candianos, which is practically its own damn city, if not its own nation.*

He trotted up the back spiral staircase until he came to the fourth floor, where he took a winding hallway to a huge, imposing wooden door. Gregor hauled it open and walked in.

The room within was long, ornate, and it ended in a huge, grand desk that sat before an undistinguished door. A man sat at the desk, small and plump and bald, and he looked up as Gregor entered. Even though Gregor was quite far away, he could hear the man's miserable sigh at the sight of him: 'Oh, for God's sake . . .'

Gregor walked across the room to the desk, glancing to either side as he did. The walls were covered with paintings, and he knew most of them by heart, especially the more recent ones. He eyed them as he walked through the room – he'd been so distracted with his case, he'd forgotten to prepare himself for this.

The painting he most dreaded sat at the end of the room, behind the desk. It showed a man, nobly built, nobly arraigned, and nobly positioned, standing behind a chair with his chin and chest thrust out. In the chair sat a tall, handsome, dark-skinned woman with curling black hair. Beside her stood a young boy of about five, dressed in black velvet, and sitting in her lap was a fat infant, wrapped in gold robes.

Gregor stared at the painting – especially at the woman in the chair, and the fat infant. His gaze lingered on the baby. *That is how she still thinks of me,* he thought. *Despite all my deeds and scars and accomplishments, I am still a fat, gurgling infant to her, bouncing in her lap.*

His eyes moved to the boy in black velvet – his brother, Domenico. He looked at the face of the painted boy, so earnest and hopeful, and felt a shard of sorrow somewhere within him. The child that had posed for this painting could never have known he'd die in less than ten years alongside his father in a carriage crash.

The bald man at the desk cleared his throat, and said, 'I . . . assume . . . that . . .' The words seemed to reluctantly drip out of him, like poison from a wound. 'That you wish to . . . *see* her.'

Gregor turned to him. 'If I could, sir,' he said chipperly.

'Now. You want to see her . . . now? Of all times?'

'If I could,' said Gregor again. 'Sir.'

The bald man considered it. 'You are aware,' he said, 'that we have had a major scriving incident just last night. One we are still recovering from.'

'I did hear rumour of that, sir.' Gregor smiled at him. He kept smiling, showing all of his large white teeth, while the bald man glowered back.

'Fine,' said the bald man, exasperated. 'Fine, fine . . .' He sat forward and rang a bell. The door behind him opened, and a young man of about twelve dressed in Dandolo house colours popped out.

The bald man opened his mouth, but struggled with what to say. He gestured to Gregor, then at the door, and, seeming to surrender, wearily said, 'You see?'

The boy nodded and ducked back into the doorway. They waited.

The bald man glared at Gregor. Gregor smiled back at the bald man. Then, after what felt like hours, the boy popped back out again.

'She will see you, Founder,' he said, his voice low and passive – the tone of someone used to being spoken over.

'Thank you,' said Gregor. He bowed to the man, and followed the boy into the sanctum beyond.

To be the descendant of a merchant house founder was to wield an almost incomprehensible degree of wealth, power, and resources in Tevanne. One of the Morsini sons only took meetings in his private gardens, while mounted atop a giraffe bedecked in a jewelled saddle cover and bridle. Tribuno Candiano's sister had apparently had a silk dress designed for each day of the year: each gown was laboured over by dozens of seamstresses, worn once, and then promptly disposed of.

So it was probably inevitable that Ofelia Dandolo, as not only of founder lineage but also head of the house itself, was a supremely impressive person. But what Gregor found most impressive about his mother was that she actually *worked.*

She was not like Torino Morsini, head of Morsini House, who was hugely fat and often hugely drunk, and usually spent his time trying to stuff his aged candle into every nubile girl on his campo. Nor was she like Eferizo Michiel, who had retired from the burdensome life of responsibility to pass his days painting portraits, landscapes, and nudes – quite a *lot* of nudes, actually, Gregor had heard, chiefly of young men.

No – Ofelia Dandolo passed her days, and indeed most of her nights, behind desks: she read and wrote letters behind desks, sat through meetings behind desks, and listened to her countless advisers prattle on and on from behind desks. And since that madness in Foundryside and the Greens last night, Gregor was not at all surprised to find her seated behind her desk in her personal office, reviewing reports.

She did not look up as he walked in. He stood before her, hands clasped behind his back, and waited for her to finish. He eyed her as she read a report: she was wearing evening attire, and her face was painted in an ornate pattern, with a red bar across her eyes and blue curls emanating from her blue lips. Her hair was also done up in an elaborate bun. He suspected she'd received news of the Foundryside blackout during a party of some sort, and had been working ever since.

She was still grand, and beautiful, and strong. But she was also looking her age, he thought. Perhaps it was the job. She'd taken over for the merchant house after Gregor's father had died in the carriage accident, and that had been, what, twenty-three years ago? Twenty-four? He'd assumed she'd eventually start relinquishing duties, but his mother had not – instead, she'd taken on more and more responsibilities until she practically *was* Dandolo Chartered, and all of its policies and decisions emanated solely from her person.

Ten years of that would kill a normal person. Ofelia Dandolo had managed two decades – but he wasn't sure she had a full third in her.

'Your brow is damp,' she said quietly – without looking up.

'Pardon?' he said, surprised.

'Your brow is damp, my dear.' She scratched out a response to the report, and set it aside. 'With sweat, I assume. You must have walked a long way. I will assume you refused a carriage from all the house guards? Again?'

'I did.'

She looked at him, and a lesser person would have winced: Ofelia Dandolo's amber eyes shone bright against her dark skin, and they had the curious power of making her will feel almost palpable. A glare from her felt like a slap. 'And I will assume you took smug delight in confusing and disappointing them?'

Gregor opened his mouth, unsure what to say.

'Oh, never mind,' she said, setting her report aside. She looked him over. 'I *hope*, Gregor, that you've come to offer aid to your campo. I *hope* that you heard about the disasters in Foundryside, about how all the scrivings failed in what seems to have been a half-mile radius across the Commons, and came straight here to see how you could assist. I hope these things – but I do not *expect* these things. Because I doubt if even this disaster could make you come back to us, Gregor.'

'Was Dandolo Chartered really affected by the blackout?'

She laughed lowly. 'Was it affected? A foundry lexicon failed in the Spinola site, right next to the Greens. We were lucky we had two others in the region to keep everything running smoothly. Otherwise things would have graduated from disaster to outright *catastrophe*.'

This was startling. A foundry lexicon was an intricate, bafflingly complicated, and stupendously expensive device that essentially made all scrived devices work on the campo. 'Do you suspect sabotage?'

'Possibly,' she said reluctantly. 'Yet whatever happened to us also hit the Michiel campo bordering Foundryside. It doesn't seem to have discriminated much. But you're not really here to talk about that – are you, Gregor?'

'No, Mother,' he said. 'I'm afraid I am not.'

'Then . . . what *are* you interrupting me for, at this worst of all moments?'

'The fire.'

At first she looked surprised, then furious. 'Really.'

'Really,' he said.

'Our entire civilisation has just been gravely threatened,' she said, 'and yet you want to talk about your little project? About resuscitating your . . . *municipal militia*?'

'City police,' said Gregor quickly.

She sighed. 'Ah, Gregor . . . I know you were worried the fire had ruined your project, but trust me, that's the *last* thing on everyone's minds right now. Everyone's probably forgotten all about it! I know *I* did.'

'I wanted to make you aware, Mother,' said Gregor, stung, 'that I believe I am mere moments away from catching the saboteur that set the fire. I was in the Commons last night.'

Her mouth fell open. 'You were in the Commons? Last *night*? When—'

'Yes. When all hell broke loose. I was making inquiries at the time – and was quite successful, if I might say so. I have located the thief, and will almost certainly capture them tonight. When I do so, I would like to bring them before the Tevanni council.'

'Ahhh,' she said. 'You want a big, showy, public trial – to clear your name.'

'To make it clear that the Waterwatch project is sustainable,' said Gregor. 'Yes. So . . . if you would begin clearing the way for that process . . .'

She smirked. 'I thought, my dear, that you didn't like using your family access,' she said.

This was true. His mother was one of the major committee chairs for the Council of Tevanne. The council was entirely populated by merchant-house elites, and generally ensured that the houses didn't *excessively* sabotage or plagiarise one another – though the definition of 'excessively' was getting more nebulous these days. It was the closest thing the city of Tevanne had to a real government, though in Gregor's opinion, it was not that close at all.

As such, Gregor could have used his mother's position to press all kinds of advantages – yet he'd always refrained, thus far. But not today.

'If it is to advance the greater good of Tevanne,' said Gregor, 'then I will use any means necessary.'

'Yes, yes. Gregor Dandolo, friend of the common man.' She sighed. 'Odd that your solution is to start chucking so many common men in jail.'

Gregor's natural response would have been – *It is not just common men that I wish to jail.* But he wasn't so stupid as to come out and say that.

She considered it. A handful of moths flitted down out of the ceiling to rotate around her head in a drunken halo. She waved a hand at them. 'Shoo, now. Damn things . . . We can't even keep our offices clean.' She glared at Gregor. 'Fine. I will initiate the proceedings – but the blackout takes precedence. Once that's resolved, we will move on to your Waterwatches and your thieves and scoundrels. All right?'

'And . . . how long will that take?'

'How in the hell should I know, Gregor?' she snapped. 'We don't even know what happened, let alone what to do next!'

'I see,' he said.

'Are you satisfied?' she asked, picking up her quill.

'Almost,' he said. 'I had one last request . . .'

She sighed and put her quill back down.

'Would it be possible for me to consult with the Dandolo hypatus?' he said. 'I had some questions I wanted to ask him.'

She stared at him. 'With . . . with *Orso*?' she said, incredulous. 'Whatever do you want to do *that* for?'

'I had some scriving questions related to the theft.'

'But . . . but you could go to any scriver for that!'

'I could go to ten different scrivers and get ten different answers,' said Gregor. 'Or I could go to the smartest scriver in Tevanne and get the right one.'

'At the moment, I doubt if he could give it to you,' said Ofelia.

'Not only is he occupied with the blackout, but I've recently come to wonder if he's even more insane than I'd previously thought.'

That piqued Gregor's interest. 'Oh? Why would that be, Mother?'

She seemed to debate whether to answer, then sighed. 'Because he's screwed up. Considerably. When they found the ruins in Vialto, Orso lobbied me *heavily* to try to secure some of the items before they were snatched up by our competitors. I consented – reluctantly – and Orso did his utmost to acquire one curious relic. It was an old, cracked stone box, but it had some similarities to a lexicon. Orso spent a fortune getting it – but then, while in transit between Vialto and here, it . . . vanished.'

'It was lost at sea?' said Gregor. 'Or was it stolen?'

'No one can say,' said Ofelia. 'But the loss was significant. I have seen the numbers in the balance books. They are large, and *not* positive. I forbade any future efforts. He didn't take it well.'

So . . . Orso Ignacio might have been robbed before, thought Gregor. He made a note of it.

'If you really want to talk to Orso Ignacio,' she said, 'you'll need to go to the Spinola Foundry – the one bordering the Greens. That's where the lexicon failed – so that, of course, is where Orso is, trying to figure out what the hell happened.' She looked at him sharply. Gregor suppressed a wince at the sight of it. 'I know I can't tell you what to do, Gregor. You've always made that clear. But I strongly suggest you consider going elsewhere with your questions. Orso is not someone to trifle with – and after the blackouts, I've no doubt he'll be in the foulest of foul moods.'

He smiled politely. 'I have dealt with worse people,' he said. 'I believe I can handle myself, Mother.'

She smiled. 'I'm sure you think so.'

'Son of a scrumming bitch!' echoed the voice up the stairs. *'Son of a worthless, toothless, shitting whore!'*

Gregor paused at the top of the Spinola Foundry stairs and glanced at the foundry guard, who gave him a nervous shrug. The voice continued screaming.

'What do you mean, you think *the records are accurate? How do you shitting* think *records are accurate? Accuracy is a binary scrumming state – they either* are *accurate, or they ARE! NOT!'* These last two words were screamed so loud, they genuinely hurt Gregor's ears, even from here. *'Are you married, man? Do you have children? If so, I'm stunned, I'm just flummoxed, because I'd have thought you were so damned stupid you wouldn't know how to stick your candle in your wife! Maybe check around and see if there are any other slack-jawed idiots about with a strong resemblance to your grubby spawn! I swear to God, if you aren't back here in one hour with records that are genuinely, unimpeachably, undeniably accurate, I'll personally paint your balls with fig jelly and toss you stark naked into a hog pit! Now, get out of my goddamn sight!'*

There was the sound of frantic footfalls below. Then silence.

'It's been like that all morning,' said the foundry guard quietly. 'I'd have thought his voice would've given out by now.'

'I see,' said Gregor. 'Thank you.' He started off down the stairs to the lexicon chamber below.

The stairs went down, and down, and down, into the dark.

As Gregor descended, things began to feel . . . different.

They felt heavier. Slower. Denser. Like he was walking not through dank, musty air but was instead at the bottom of the sea, with miles and miles of water pressing down on him.

How I hate getting near lexicons, thought Gregor.

Like most people, Gregor did not understand the mechanics of scriving. He could not tell one sigillum from another. In fact, he couldn't even differentiate one house's scriving language from another, which was even more fundamental. But he knew how scriving worked, in broad terms.

The basic sigillums were symbols that naturally occurred within the world. No one knew exactly where the base sigils came from. Some said the Occidentals had invented them. Others said that the symbols were written into the world by the Creator, by God Himself, that He had defined reality by encoding it with these sigillums, forging the world much as the foundries forged scrived rigs. No one was sure.

Each basic sigillum referenced specific things: there were symbols for stone, wind, air, fire, growth, leaves, and even ones for more abstract phenomena, for 'change' or 'stop' or 'start' or 'sharp'. There were millions, if not billions, of them. If you knew these symbols – though few did – then there was nothing stopping you from using them. Even in the most primitive settlement out in the middle of nowhere, if you were trying to carve wood into some intricate shape, you could inscribe it with the base sigil for 'clay' or 'mud,' and this tiny alteration would make the wood slightly, slightly more malleable.

But despite all the legends around its origins, basic scriving was very restricted. To start with, its effects were minor, no more than a slight nudge. But worse, if you wanted to tell an axe, 'You are very durable, very sharp, very light, and you part the wood of the cedar tree as if it were water' – something much more complicated than just 'sharp' or 'hard', in other words – such a command would be fifty or sixty sigils long. You'd run out of room on the axe blade – and you'd also have to get the sigil logic *just right* so the axe blade would understand what it was supposed to be. You had to be specific, and definite – and this was hard.

But then the city of Tevanne had discovered an old cache of Occidental records in a cave down the coast. And in those records they'd discovered something crucial.

The sigil for 'meaning'. And then some cunning Tevanni had got a brilliant idea.

They'd figured out that you could take a blank slate of iron, write out that extensive, complicated scriving command; but then, you could follow it with the sigil for 'meaning', and next write *a completely new sigil,* one you yourself just made up. Then that new sigil would essentially mean 'You are very durable, very sharp, very light, and you part the wood of the cedar tree as if it were water' – and then you'd just have to write that *one sigil* on your axe blade.

Or on a dozen blades. Or a thousand. It didn't matter. Every blade would do the same thing.

After that discovery, much more complicated scriving commands were suddenly possible – yet even this was *still* quite limited.

For one thing, you had to stay close to whichever slate of iron had the commands written on it. If you walked too far away, then the axe blade essentially forgot what that new sigil was supposed to mean, and it stopped working. It no longer had a reference point, in a way.

The other problem was that if you wrote too many complicated scriving definitions on one slate of metal, it had a tendency to burst into flames. A common object such as an iron plate, it seemed, could only bear so much meaning.

So the city of Tevanne, and its many nascent scriving houses, then had a problem to solve: how were they to house all the definitions and meanings for these complicated scrivings without having everything burst into flames and melt?

Which was why they'd invented lexicons.

Lexicons were huge, complicated, durable machines built to store and maintain thousands and thousands of incredibly complex scriving definitions, and bear the burden of all of that concentrated meaning. With a lexicon, you didn't have to worry about wandering a dozen feet too far and suddenly having all your scrived devices fail on you: lexicons could amplify and project the meaning of those definitions for great distances in all directions – enough to cover part of a campo, if not more. The closer you were to a lexicon, though, the better your scrivings worked – which was why a lexicon was always the beating heart of any foundry. You wanted all of your biggest, most intricate rigs to work at peak efficiency.

And since lexicons were the beating heart of foundries, they were, in effect, the beating heart of all of Tevanne.

But they were complicated. Incredibly complicated. *Astoundingly* complicated. Only geniuses and madmen, everyone agreed, could truly understand a lexicon, and the difference between the two was almost nil.

So it probably said something that out of all the hypati in the entire history of Tevanne, Orso Ignacio understood lexicons better than anybody. After all, Orso had been the one to invent the combat lexicon – a smaller version of the regular kind, which ships and teams of oxen could haul around. That device was still quite large, complicated, and improbably expensive, and it could only manage to power a cohort's armaments – but without that contribution, Tevanne would have never captured the Durazzo Sea, and all the cities around it.

Gregor knew quite a bit about combat lexicons. He'd had one at the siege of Dantua – right up until he didn't. So he also knew quite a bit about what it was like to *lose* a lexicon. And he thought he could understand how Orso Ignacio felt right now. Perhaps he would be able to work the man from that angle.

He found himself promptly disabused of these notions when he entered the lexicon chamber and instantly heard the words, 'Who the *shit* are you?'

Gregor blinked in the dim light while his eyes adjusted. The lexicon chamber was wide, dark, and mostly empty. There was a thick glass wall at the back with an open door set in its centre, and a tall, thin man stood in the doorway, staring at Gregor. He wore a thick apron, thick gloves, and a pair of thick, dark goggles. He held in his hands a threatening-looking tool, some kind of bendy, looped metal wand with a lot of sharp teeth.

'P–pardon?' said Gregor.

The man tossed the wand away, lifted his goggles, and a pair of pale, deep-set, harsh eyes stared at him. 'I said, who. The shit. Are *you*?' asked Orso Ignacio, this time much louder.

Orso had the look of an artist or sculptor who'd just stepped away from his studio, wearing a stained, beige shirt and off-white hose under his apron, and his beaked shoes – customary for the highest echelons – were ratty and had holes in the toes. His white hair rose up in a wild, unkempt shock, and his once-handsome face was dark and lined and skeletally thin, as if the man had sat for too long in a fish curer's shed.

Gregor cleared his throat. 'I apologise. Good morning, Hypatus. I'm terribly sorry to interrupt you during this most diffic—'

Orso rolled his eyes and looked across the room. 'Who is he?'

Gregor peered through the shadows, and saw that there was someone else at the back of the room, someone he'd missed: a tall, rather pretty girl with a still, closed face. She was sitting on the floor before a tray of scriving blocks – an abacus-like device that scrivers used to test scriving strings – and she was popping the blocks in and out with a frightening speed, like a professional scivoli player moving their pieces across the board, creating a steady *clackclackclack* sound.

The girl paused and glanced at Gregor, her face immaculately inscrutable. 'I believe,' she said, in a quiet, even voice, 'that that is Captain Gregor Dandolo.'

Gregor frowned at her, surprised. He'd never met this girl in his life. The girl calmly resumed slotting the blocks in and out of the tray.

'Oh,' said Orso. 'Ofelia's boy?' He peered at Gregor. 'My *God*, you've gained weight.'

The girl – Gregor suspected she was Orso's assistant of some kind – cringed ever so slightly.

But Gregor was not insulted. The last time Orso had glimpsed him he'd probably just returned from the wars. 'Yes,' said Gregor. 'That tends to happen when a person goes from a place that has no food at all to a place that has some.'

'Fascinating,' said Orso. 'So. What the hell are you doing down here, Captain?'

'Yes, I—'

'You're still slumming it down at the waterfront, right?' His eyes suddenly burned with a strange fury. 'If there *is* still a waterfront to slum in, that is.'

'Yes, and in fact I—'

'Well, as you may notice, Captain . . .' He held his hands out and gestured to the large, dark, empty room. 'Our current environs are bereft of waters, as well as fronts of all kinds. Not much for you to do here, it seems. Got plenty of doors, though. Loads of 'em.' Orso turned to examine something behind him. 'I advise you scrumming make use of one. Any one. I frankly don't care.'

Gregor strode forward into the chamber, and said in a slightly louder voice, 'I am here to ask you, Hypatus . . .' Then he stopped, wincing as a headache pulsed through his skull, and rubbed his forehead.

Orso looked at him. 'Yes?' he said.

Gregor took a deep breath. 'I'm sorry.'

'Take your time.'

He swallowed and tried to collect himself – but the headache persisted. 'Does that . . . does that go away?'

'No.' Orso was smiling unpleasantly. 'Never been near a lexicon before?'

'I have, but this one seems very . . .'

'Big?'

'Yes. Big. The machine is off, isn't it? I mean – that's the problem, correct?'

Orso scoffed and turned to stare at the device behind him. 'Right now, it is not "off", as you put it – the more accurate term is *reduced*.

It's difficult to turn a lexicon just *off* – it's not a damned windmill, it's a collection of assertions about physics and reality. Turning it off would be like, oh, converting a striper into all the carbon and calcium and nitrogen and whatever else makes it up – conceptually feasible? Sure, why not. Practically possible? Not scrumming likely.'

'I . . . see,' said Gregor. Though in truth he was nowhere close to seeing.

Orso's assistant exhaled softly, as if to say – *Here he goes again.*

Orso grinned at Gregor over his shoulder. 'Want to come closer? Take a look?'

Gregor knew Orso was goading him – the closer you got to a lexicon, the more uncomfortable it felt. But Gregor wanted to put Orso's guard down, however he could – and allowing himself to be toyed with was one option.

Squinting in pain, he walked over to the glass wall and looked in at the lexicon. It resembled a huge metal can lying on its side, only the can had been cut into tiny slivers or discs – thousands of them, or maybe even millions. He knew in vague terms that each disc was full of scriving definitions – the instructions or arguments that convinced scrived devices to work the way they ought to – though he was aware that he understood this to about the same degree that he understood that his brain was what did all his thinking for him.

'I've never seen one this close before,' said Gregor.

'Almost no one has,' said Orso. 'The stress of all that meaning, forcing reality to comply with so many arguments – it makes the thing hot as hell, and damned difficult to be around. And yet, last night this device – all its assertions about reality – went *poof*, and turned off. Like blowing out a damned candle. Which, as I have just generously described to you, ought to be impossible.'

'How?' asked Gregor.

'Beats the ever-living shit out of me!' said Orso with savage cheer. He joined the girl at the scriving blocks and watched as she plugged in strings one after the other, the tiny metal cubes flying in and out as her fingers danced over the tray with blinding speed. Each time, a tiny glass at the top of the tiles would glow softly. 'Now all kinds of goddamn strings work!' he said. 'They work perfectly, implacably, and inarguably! How comforting. It's like the whole thing never happened.'

'I see,' said Gregor. 'And, may I ask – who is this, exactly?' He nodded at the girl.

'Her?' Orso seemed surprised by the question. 'She's my fab.'

Gregor did not know what a 'fab' was, and the girl seemed uninterested in answering, ignoring them as she tested string after string of sigils. He decided to move on.

'Was it sabotage?' he asked. 'Another merchant house?'

'Again – beats the *ever-living shit* out of me,' said Orso. 'I've checked all the infrastructural scrivings that keep the thing afloat, and those strings are all working away, cheery as can be. The lexicon itself doesn't show any damage. It shows no sign of having been properly *or* improperly reduced. If the dumb piece of *shit* who's in charge of maintenance could *confirm* the thing's regularly scheduled checkups, I could rule that out. And the tiles are all arranged in some pretty basic, boring, conventional configurations. Right?'

His assistant nodded. 'Correct, sir.' She gestured to the walls behind her. 'Manufacturing, security, lighting, and transport. That's the extent of the wall's load.'

Gregor looked at the walls and slowly realised what she meant. 'The wall' was the industry term for a tremendous wall of thousands of white tiles, covered in sigils, which slid up or down on a short track. Each tile represented a scriving definition: if the tile was in the up position, the definition was inactive, and thus did not work; if it was in the down position, then it did.

This sounded simple, but only a scriver with decades of high-level training could look at a wall and tell exactly what was going on. A lexicon's wall, of course, was carefully watched and maintained: if someone slid the wrong tile up, and deactivated a crucial definition, it could, say, render all the scrived carriages in the Dandolo campo suddenly unable to stop. Which would be bad.

Or, if someone slid several critical tiles down, and activated some extremely complicated definitions, then it could overload the lexicon, and then . . .

Well. That would be much, much worse.

Because a lexicon was essentially a giant violation of reality – that was why it was so unpleasant to be close to one. The consequences of a lexicon going haywire were too horrific to contemplate. And this was the chief reason that the city of Tevanne, with all of its power, corruption, and fractious merchant houses, had yet to experience much deliberate turmoil: as the entire city was essentially maintained by a system of huge bombs, that tended to make people cautious.

'How troublesome,' said Gregor.

'Yes. Isn't it?' Orso peered at him suspiciously. 'Doesn't your mother know all this? I thought I'd been a good boy and properly kept her up to date.'

'I cannot speak to my mother's knowledge regarding your situation here, Hypatus,' said Gregor. 'I'm not here about the blackouts. Rather, I had a question for you regarding the waterfront.'

'The *waterfront*?' said Orso, irritated. 'Why the hell would you bother me about that?'

'I wanted to ask you about the theft that took place.'

'What a waste of time! You can't expect me to . . .' He paused. 'Wait. Theft? You mean the fire.'

'No, no,' said Gregor politely. 'I mean the theft. Our investigations suggest that the fire was set as a distraction to allow a thief to get at our safes.'

'How do you know that?' he demanded.

'Because we have looked in our safes,' said Gregor. 'And found something missing.'

Orso blinked, very slowly. 'Ah,' he said. He was quiet for a moment. 'I . . . had thought the safes burned down along with the Waterwatch headquarters. I thought they were destroyed.'

'That was nearly the case,' said Gregor. 'But when it became clear that the fire would spread, I had all of our safes loaded on carts and removed to safety.'

Again, Orso blinked. 'Really.'

'Yes,' said Gregor. 'And we found something was stolen. A small, plain, wooden box, from safe 23D.'

Orso and his assistant had gone very, very still. Gregor could not help but feel pleased.

It's nice to be right, sometimes.

'Odd . . .' said Orso carefully. 'But you said you had a question for me – and I've yet to hear a question, Captain.'

'Well, I did some follow-ups in the Commons last night, trying to track down the thief. I located their fence – the person who sells the things a thief steals – and found a note in their belongings referencing the Dandolo hypatus, in relation to this theft, and fire. My question, Hypatus, would be – why do you think that is?'

'I've no idea.' The man's face – which had previously been riddled with contempt, impatience, and suspicion – was now perfectly bereft of almost all emotion. 'You think I commissioned the theft, Captain?'

'I think little so far, because I know little so far, sir. You could have been the person who was robbed.'

Orso smirked. 'You think someone stole scriving definitions from me?'

A diversion. But Gregor was willing to be diverted for a bit. 'Well . . . they are the most valuable thing in Tevanne, usually. And they can be quite small, sir.'

'They *can* be. That's true.' Orso stood, walked over to a shelf, pulled out three huge tomes, each about seven inches thick, and walked back over to Gregor. 'Do you see these, Captain?'

'I do.'

Orso dropped one on the ground, and it made a large *thud*. 'That is the opening definition for reducing a lexicon.' Then the second – which also made a huge *thud*. 'This is a *continuation* of that definition.' He dropped the third. 'And that is the closing definition for reducing a lexicon. Do you know how I know that?'

'I . . .'

'Because I wrote them, Captain. I wrote every sigil and every string in those big goddamn books.' He stepped closer. 'A scriving definition *might* have fit in a small box. But not one of *mine*.'

It was a good performance. Gregor was almost impressed. 'I see, sir. And nothing else was stolen from you?'

'Not that I'm aware of.'

'Well, then. I suppose the fence made the note concerning you by accident, perhaps.'

'Or you misread it,' said Orso.

Gregor nodded. 'Or that. We shall find out soon, I believe.'

'Soon? Why?'

'Well . . . I *think* I am close to catching the thief. And unless my instincts are incorrect, I think that their arrangements to sell what was stolen have gone quite wrong. Which means they *might* still have what was stolen. So we might soon find it, and get to the bottom of all this.' He smiled broadly at Orso. 'Which I'm sure we all find reassuring.'

Orso was perfectly frozen now – the man was barely breathing. Then he said, 'Yes. We certainly do, I'm sure.'

'Yes.' Gregor looked at the grand machine behind him. 'Is it true what they say about lexicons, and the hierophants, sir?'

'What?' said Orso, startled.

'About the hierophants. I've heard old stories about how when people were close to a true hierophant – like Crasedes the Great himself – they suffered from powerful migraines. Much like how one feels these days, when close to a lexicon. Is that true, sir?'

'How should I know?'

'I understand that you're interested in the Occidentals yourself, yes?' asked Gregor. 'Or you were, once.'

Orso glared at him, and the severity of his harsh, pale eyes rivalled Ofelia Dandolo's stare. 'Once. Yes. But no longer.'

For a moment the two men just stared at each other, Gregor smiling placidly, Orso's face fixed in a furious glare.

'Now,' said Orso. 'If you will excuse us, Captain.'

'Of course. I will let you get back to your business, sir,' said Gregor. 'Sorry to trouble you.' He started toward the steps, but paused. 'Oh, I'm sorry, but – young lady?'

The girl looked up. 'Yes?'

'I apologise, but I believe I have been quite rude. I don't think I ever learned your name.'

'Oh. It's Grimaldi.'

'Thank you – but I meant your first name?'

She glanced at Orso, but he still had his back to her. 'Berenice,' she said.

Gregor smiled. 'Thank you. It was nice meeting you both.' Then he turned and trotted up the stairs.

⊹

Orso Ignacio listened as the captain's footfalls faded. Then he and Berenice turned to look at each other.

'Sir . . .' said Berenice.

Orso shook his head and lifted a finger to his lips. He pointed at the various hallways and doors leading out of the lexicon chamber, then pointed to his ears: *Could be people listening.*

She nodded. 'Workshop?' she asked.

'Workshop,' he said.

They exited the lexicon chamber, called a carriage, and rode back to the Hypatus Department of the inner Dandolo enclaves, a sprawling, rambling structure that somewhat resembled a university. Orso and Berenice walked in, then silently climbed the stairs to Orso's workshop. The thick, heavy wooden door felt Orso coming, and began opening. He'd scrived it to sense his blood – a deviously difficult trick – but he was impatient, and shoved it open the rest of the way.

He waited for the door to shut after him. Then he exploded.

'Shit. Shit! *Shit!*' he screamed.

'Ah,' said Berenice. 'Yes. I agree, sir.'

'I . . . I thought the goddamn thing had been *destroyed*!' cried Orso. 'Along with the rest of the goddamn waterfront! But . . . It was stolen? Again? I've been robbed *again*?'

'It would seem so, sir,' said Berenice.

'But *how*? We kept it between us, Berenice! We only discussed it in this room! How did someone find out *again*?'

'That *is* concerning, sir,' said Berenice.

'Concerning! It's a hell of a lot more than conce—'

'True, sir. But the larger question is . . .' She glanced at him, anxious. 'What happens if Captain Dandolo does as he suggested, and catches this thief tonight – and they still have the item in their possession?'

Orso went pale. 'Then when he brings the thief back . . . Ofelia will find out.'

'Yes, sir.'

'She'll find out that I paid for another expedition, another artefact.'

'Yes, sir.'

'And . . . and she'll find out how I paid for it! And how *much*.'

Orso grabbed the sides of his head. 'Oh, God! All the thousands of duvots I took, all that *money* I took, all that money I arranged in the ledgers *just* right!'

She nodded. 'That is my concern, sir.'

'Shit,' said Orso, pacing. 'Shit! *Shit!* We have to . . . We have to . . .' He looked at her. 'You have to follow him.'

'I beg your pardon, sir?'

'Follow him!' said Orso. 'You have to follow him, Berenice!'

'*Me*, sir?'

'Yes!' He ran to a cabinet and grabbed a small box. 'He can't have left yet. Gregor Dandolo *walks* all over the campo, like an idiot! Ofelia complains about it all the time! Grab a carriage, go to the southern gates, wait for him, and *follow* him! And . . .' He fumbled with the box, frantic, and snatched something out of it. 'Take this.'

He shoved what appeared to be a small, scrived strip of tin into her hands, with small tabs at the top and the bottom. 'A twinned plate, sir?' she asked.

'Yes!' he said. 'I'll keep its pair. Ah, let's see – snap off the top tab if Gregor catches the thief. Snap off the bottom if he doesn't. And snap off *both* if he catches them *and* they still have the artefact! If the thief gets away, follow them if you can, and find out where they are. Whatever you do, the same thing will happen to my plate, so I'll know exactly what's happened.'

'And you will stay here and do what, exactly, sir?'

'There are favours I can call in,' said Orso. 'Debts people owe me, so that I can maybe cover up my *own* debts to the goddamn company! If Gregor Dandolo comes back here with that key, I need to make it look like I put just a *toe* out of line, not my whole damn body and *thirty thousand scrumming duvots* of Dandolo Chartered money!'

'And you plan to arrange all that in . . .' She glanced out the open workshop window at the Michiel clock tower. 'Eight hours?'

'Yes!' he said. 'But it would certainly be *nice* if Gregor Dandolo didn't bring the thief back here, so then I'd never have to do this at all!'

'I hesitate to say this, sir,' she said. 'But I'm surprised that you aren't asking me to interfere with the captain's efforts, and make sure the thief gets away. Then Ofelia would never know.'

He paused. 'Gets away? Gets *away*? Berenice – that key could change everything, *everything* we know about scriving. There's almost nothing I wouldn't do to get it. If I've got to let Ofelia Dandolo cane me raw, so be it! I just don't want her tossing me in the campo prison and keeping it for herself! And . . .' His face slowly twisted into an expression of pure, murderous rage. 'And I certainly wouldn't mind getting ahold of that damned thief – who has humiliated me not once, but *twice* – and seeing them dismembered right in front of my scrumming *nose*, either.'

11

So now what?> asked Clef.

Seated on the edge of a Michiel rooftop, just downwind from the foundries, Sancia tried to shrug, and found she didn't have the spirit. *<I don't know. Survive, I suppose. Maybe steal some food out of a campo's trash for dinner.>*

<You'd eat out of the trash?>

<Yeah. Have before. Probably will again.>

<The jungles to the west look very tropical. Maybe you could hide out there for a while?>

<There are wild pigs as tall as a man's eye. Apparently they enjoy killing people for sport. Not sure a magic key could be of much help there.>

<Okay, but . . . but this is a giant city, right? You can't find anywhere to hide? Anywhere?>

<Foundryside and the Greens aren't safe. Maybe I could go to the Commons in the north, away from the channel. But the Commons only occupies about a tenth of Tevanne's land. The rest of the city is campo – and it's damn hard to hide there.>

<We're pulling it off now,> said Clef.

<*For now. On a rooftop. Yes. But this isn't exactly a sustainable arrangement.*>

<*Okay . . . so what? What's the plan?*>

Sancia thought about it. <*Claudia and Giovanni mentioned that the Candianos changed up their sachets . . .* >

<*The who?*>

<*The Candianos. One of the four merchant houses.*> She pointed north. <*See that big dome out there?*>

<*Like, the really, really,* really *big one?*>

<*Yes. That's the Mountain of the Candianos. They used to be the most powerful merchant house in the world, until Tribuno Candiano went insane.*>

<*Oh yeah, you mentioned him. They locked him in a tower, right?*>

<*Supposedly. Anyways, Claudia said they changed their entire sachets up overnight, and no one does that unless something's gone really wrong. It means chaos and confusion somewhere on the campo, and it's easiest to steal things during chaos and confusion.*> She sighed. <*But it'd need to be something big to get us the cash we need.*>

<*Why not rob that Mountain place? It looks like it's full of valuable stuff.*>

She laughed lowly. <*Yeah, no. No one – and I mean* no one *– has ever broken into the Mountain. You couldn't break into that place even if you had the wand of Crasedes himself. I hear weird rumours about the Mountain – that it's haunted or . . . well. Something worse.*>

<*So what are you going to do?*>

<*Figure it out. However I can.*> She yawned, stretched out, and lay down on the flat stone roof. <*We have a few hours until sunset. I'm going to rest until then.*>

<*What, you're going to sleep on a stone roof?*>

<*Yeah? What's wrong with that?*>

Clef paused. <*I get the sense, kid, that you've lived in some rough places.*>

Sancia lay on the roof, staring up at the sky. She thought about Sark, about her apartment – which, as barren as it was, now seemed like a paradise to her.

<*Talk to me, Clef,*> she said.

<*Huh? About what?*>

<*Anything. Anything besides what's going on right now.*>

<*I see.*> He thought about it. <*Hmm. Well. There are thirty-seven*

scrivings currently active within a thousand-foot radius of us. Fourteen of those are interrelated, actively engaged with each other, feeding information or heat or energy back and forth.> His voice grew soft, and a singsong cadence crept into it. <*I wish you could see them as I see them. The ones below us are dancing, in a way, seesawing back and forth ever so gently as one hands off heat into a giant block of dense stone, storing it deep in its bones, while another scriving scoops it up and spills the heat across a plate of glass beads, softening them, melting them, until they form a plate of clearest glass . . . There's a scrived light on in a bedroom across the street from us. Its light is rosy and soft. Its scrivings stored up all this old candlelight and now they're slowly letting it leak out a dribble at a time . . . The light is bouncing, very softly, something's jostling it. I think a couple is making love on a nearby bed, perhaps . . . Imagine it – these people sharing their love in light that could be days, weeks, even years old . . . It's like making love under starlight, isn't it?*>

Sancia listened to his voice, her eyelids growing heavy.

She was glad to have him here. He was a friend when she had none.

<*I wish you could see them as I do, Sancia,*> he whispered. <*To me, they're like stars in my mind . . .* >

She slept.

Sancia did not dream anymore, after the operation. Yet sometimes when she slept her memories returned to her, like bones bubbling up from the depths of a tar pit.

There on the roof, Sancia slept, and remembered.

She remembered the hot sun of the plantations, the bite and slash of the sugarcane leaves. She remembered the taste of old bread and the swarms of stinging flies and the tiny, hard cots in the shoddy huts.

She remembered the smell of shit and urine, festering in an open pit mere yards from where they slept. The sound of whimpering and weeping at night. The panicked cries from the woods as the guards hauled away a woman, or sometimes a man, and did as they pleased with them.

And she remembered the house on the hill, behind the plantation house, where the fancy men from Tevanne had worked.

She remembered the wagon that had trundled away from the house on the hill every day at dusk. And she remembered how the flies had followed that wagon so closely, its contents hidden beneath a thick tarp.

It hadn't taken long for everyone to realise what was happening. One night, a slave would simply vanish – the next day, the wagon would trundle away from the house on the hill, a horrid reek following it.

Some had whispered that the missing slaves had escaped, but everyone had known this was a lie. Everyone had understood what was happening. Everyone knew about the screams they heard from the house on the hill, always at midnight. Always, always, always at midnight, every night.

Yet they'd been voiceless and helpless. Though they'd outnumbered the Tevannis eight to one on the island, the Tevannis bore armaments of terrifying power. They'd seen what happened when a slave raised a hand against their master, and wanted no part of it.

One night she'd tried to run away. They'd caught her easily. And perhaps because she'd tried to run away, they'd decided that she would be next.

Sancia remembered how the house had smelled. Alcohol and preservatives and putrefaction.

She remembered the white marble table in the middle of the basement, its shackles for her wrists and ankles. The thin, metal plates on the walls, covered with strange symbols, and the bright, sharp screws paired with them.

And she remembered the man down in that basement, short and thin and one eye just a blank socket, and she remembered how he was always dabbing at his brow, wiping away sweat.

She remembered how he'd looked at her, and smiled, and wearily said, 'Well. Let's see if this one works, then.'

That had been the first scriver Sancia had ever met.

She often remembered these things when she slept. And whenever she did, two things happened.

The first was that the scar on the side of her head would ache as if it were not a scar, but a brand.

And the second was that she forced herself to remember the one memory that made her feel safe.

Sancia remembered how everything had burned.

It was dark when she awoke. The first thing she did was slip her fingers out of her glove and touch the roof of the foundry.

The roof lit up in her mind. She felt the smoke coiling across it, felt the rain puddling at the base of the stacks, felt her own body, tiny and insignificant, pressing against its huge, stone skin. But most important, she felt she was alone. No one up here but her and Clef.

She started moving. She stood up, yawned, and rubbed her eyes.

<*Morning,*> said Clef. <*Or should I say good eveni—*>

There was a sharp crack from somewhere in the distance. Then something slammed into her knees, hard.

Sancia toppled over, crying out in surprise. As she did, she looked down and saw a strange, silvery rope was looping around her shins like a snare. She dimly realised that someone out on the rooftops across from her had hurled or fired this rope at her – whatever it was.

She crashed onto the stone roof. <*Damn!*> said Clef. <*We've been spotted!*>

<*No shit!*> said Sancia. She tried to start crawling away, but found she couldn't. The rope suddenly seemed impossibly heavy, as if it were not made of fibres but rather lead, and no matter how she heaved she could barely drag the coil of rope any farther than half an inch.

<*It's scrived to think it's denser than it actually is!*> said Clef. <*The more someone tries to move it, the denser it gets!*>

<*So can we break i—*>

She never finished, because then there was a second *crack*. She looked up in time to see a silvery rope hurtling toward her from a rooftop nearly a block away. It stretched out like someone opening their arms for an embrace before slamming into her chest, knocking her back onto the roof.

She started to heave at it, but stopped. <*Wait. Clef, can I accidentally make it so dense that it could crush my chest?*>

<*It's a loop, so it'll distribute the force – somewhat. You* could *make it so dense that you fall through the roof, though.*>

<*Shit!*> she said. She looked down at the cords – there seemed to be a locking mechanism on the side, awaiting a scrived key. <*Do something! Unlock me!*>

<*I can't! I'd have to be touching it!*>

Sancia tried to pull him out of her shirt, but the second rope kept her arms tied fast to her body. <*I can't reach you!*>

<*What do we do, what do we do?*>

Sancia stared up at the night sky. <*I . . . I don't . . . I don't know.*>

They waited there, looking up, the chants of the scrived ropes echoing in Sancia's ears. Then, after a long while, she heard footsteps coming close. Heavy ones.

The bruised, scratched face of Captain Gregor Dandolo leaned overhead, a huge espringal on his back. He smiled politely. 'Good evening again.'

Apparently Captain Dandolo had the control for the ropes: after adjusting something on his espringal, he was able to reduce their density enough that he could flip her over. He kept her bound, of course. 'Something we used back in the wars, when capturing trespassers,' he said merrily. He grabbed the ropes with each hand, and picked her up much as one would a bound pig. 'I'd know the smell of the Michiel foundry smoke like I would the scent of jasmine. I had to come here all the time to commission armaments. Flame and heat, as one would expect, are useful when making war.'

'Let me go, you dumb bastard!' she said. 'Let me go!'

'No.' He somehow packed an infuriating amount of cheer into that one word.

'You put me in prison and they'll kill me!'

'Who, your client?' he said, making his way for the stairs down. 'They won't be able to get at you. We'll put you in the Dandolo jailhouse, which is quite safe. Your only concern will be me, young lady.'

Sancia bucked and kicked and snarled, but Dandolo was quite

strong, and seemingly indifferent to her countless swears. He hummed happily as they started down the stairs.

He exited the stairs and hauled her across the street to a scrived carriage bearing the Dandolo loggotipo – the quill and the gear. 'Our chariot awaits!' he said. He opened up the back, set her down on the floor, and reactivated the scrivings on the rope – there was some kind of dial on the side of the espringal – until she was pinned to the floor. 'I hope this will be comfortable during our short ride.' Then he looked her over, took a breath, and said, 'But first, I must ask . . . where is it?'

'Where's what?'

'The item you stole,' he said. 'The box.'

<*Oh, shit,*> said Clef. <*This guy isn't as stupid as he looks.*>

'*I* don't have it!' said Sancia, inventing a story as fast as she could. 'I gave it over to my client!'

'Did you,' he said flatly.

<*I don't think he believes you,*> said Clef.

<*I know that! Shut the hell up, Clef!*>

'Yes!' she said.

'Then why is your client trying to kill you, if you did as they asked? That is why you're trying to escape the city – yes?'

'Yes,' said Sancia honestly. 'And I don't *know* why they're out for me, or why they killed Sark.'

That gave him pause. 'Sark is dead?'

'Yes.'

'Your client killed him?'

'Yes. Yes!'

He scratched his beard at his chin. 'And I suppose you don't know who your client is.'

'No. We were never to know names, and never to look in the box.'

'What did you do with it, then?'

Sancia decided on a story that was close to the truth. 'Sark and I took the box to an appointed place and time – an abandoned fishery in the Greens. Four men showed up. Well-fed, campo sort. One took the box away and said he wanted to confirm it. Left us with the other three. Then there was some signal, and they stabbed Sark, and nearly killed me.'

'And you . . . fought your way out?'

She narrowed her eyes at him. 'Yes,' she said defensively.

His large, dark eyes flicked over her small frame. 'All by yourself?'

'I'm decent enough in a fight.'

'What fishery was this?'

'By the Anafesto Channel.'

He nodded, thinking about this. 'Anafesto, eh. Well then,' he said. 'Let's go have a look, then!' He shut the door and climbed into the pilot's seat.

'Look where?' said Sancia, startled.

'To the Greens,' said the captain. 'To this fishery of which you speak. Presumably there will be dead bodies inside – yes? Bodies that might suggest exactly who paid you to rob my waterfront?'

'Wait! You . . . you can't take me there!' she cried. 'Just hours ago there were dozens of big bastards walking around there, looking to gut me!'

'Then you had better stay quiet, hadn't you?'

Sancia lay perfectly still as the carriage rattled over the muddy Commons lanes to the Greens. This was possibly the worst outcome for her: she'd intended to never return to the Greens, let alone trussed up in Captain Gregor Dandolo's carriage. *<You tell me the second you sense something big coming at me, okay?>* she said.

<Why, so you can sit and watch your death approach?> said Clef.

<Just do it, all right?>

Finally the carriage rolled to a stop. There was darkness outside the windows, but she could tell they were at the fisheries by the smell. Dread bloomed in her stomach as she remembered that night – just last night, though it seemed so long ago now.

For a long time, Dandolo said nothing. She imagined him sitting hunched in the cockpit, watching the streets and the fisheries. Then she heard his voice, quiet but confident: 'Won't be a moment.'

The carriage rocked slightly as he climbed out and slammed the door.

Sancia sat there, and waited. And waited.

<How the hell are we going to get out of this?> asked Clef.

<*No idea yet.*>

<*If he searches you . . . I mean, I'm just on a string around your neck!*>

<*Gregor Dandolo is a campo gentleman,*> said Sancia. <*He might also be a veteran, but deep down, all good campo boys have absolutely no desire to touch a Commons person, let alone feel up a Commons girl's chest.*>

<*I think you've misjudged hi . . . Wait.*>

<*What?*>

<*There . . . there is something scrived nearby.*>

<*Oh God . . .* >

<*No, no, it's small.* Really *small. Tiny, even, easy to miss. It's . . . like a dot, stuck to the outside of the carriage, in the back.*>

<*What's it doing?*>

<*It's . . . trying to join something else? Kind of like your construction scrivings, I guess. It's like a magnet, it's pulling really hard toward something that must be . . . kind of close . . .* >

Sancia tensed up. She realised what must be happening. <*Shit!*> she said. <*He's been followed!*>

<*What do you mea—*>

The cockpit door opened, and someone climbed in – presumably Gregor Dandolo, but she couldn't see. Then she heard his voice quietly saying, 'No bodies. None.'

Sancia blinked in shock. 'But . . . That's impossible.'

'Is it?'

'Yes. Yes!'

'Where ought there have been bodies, young miss?'

'Upstairs, and on the stairs!'

He looked over the back of the seat at her. 'Are you sure? Positive?'

She glared at him. 'Yes, damn it!'

He sighed. 'I see. Well. I *did* find quite a bit of blood in both of those locations – so I must grudgingly admit that *some* aspect of your story appears to be at least *somewhat* true.'

She stared at the ceiling, outraged. 'You were testing me!'

He nodded. 'I was testing you.'

'You . . . You . . .'

'Do you know what was in the box?' he demanded suddenly.

Surprised, Sancia tried to recover. 'I told you. No.'

He stared off into the distance, thinking. 'And . . . I suppose you don't know anything about the hierophants?' he said softly.

Her skin went cold, but she said nothing.

'Do you?' he asked.

'Beyond that they were magic giants?' said Sancia. 'No.'

'I think you're lying. I think you're lying to me about something – about what was in the box, about how your deal went down, about how that blood got there.'

<*Goddamn,*> said Clef. <*This guy is terrifying.*>

<*Are you sure that thing's on the back of the carriage?*>

<*Yeah. Bottom right if you're facing it.*>

'And I think I'm about to save your life,' she said. 'Again.'

'Beg pardon?'

'Walk around to the back of your carriage and look for something. It'll be stuck on the bottom right. Looks like a button, one that shouldn't be there.'

He narrowed his eyes at her. 'What kind of ploy is this?'

'It's not a ploy at all. Go on,' she said. 'I'll wait.'

He looked at her for a moment. Then he reached down and pulled at her ropes, confirming they were secure. Satisfied, he opened the door again and climbed out.

She listened to the crunch of his feet outside. He stopped somewhere behind the carriage.

<*He got it,*> said Clef. <*Pried it off.*>

Gregor walked around and looked through the back passenger window at her. 'What's this?' he asked, slightly outraged. He held it up – it looked like a big brass tack. 'It's scrived, on the bottom. What *is* this?'

'It's like a construction scriving,' said Sancia. 'It pulls at its twin, like a magnet.'

'And why,' he said, 'would someone want to stick a construction scriving to *my* carriage?'

'Think for a second,' said Sancia. 'They stick one half to your carriage. Then they tie another to a string. Then the string will act like a needle in a compass, always pointing to you like you're true north.'

He stared at her. Then he looked around, peering at the streets behind him.

'Now you're figuring it out,' asked Sancia. 'See anyone?'

He was silent. Then he thrust his head back through the window. 'How did you know it was there?' he demanded. 'How did you know what it *was*?'

'Intuition,' she said.

'Nonsense,' he said. 'Did you put it there?'

'When could I have done that? When I was sleeping on the roof, or tied up with your ropes? You need to let me go, Captain. They didn't put it on there to track you – they put it on there to find *me*. They're coming for me. They figured out you knew where I was, so they just followed you. And now you're right here in it with me. Let me go, and maybe you can survive this.'

He was quiet for a while. It strangely pleased her – for so long it'd seemed like the captain had ice in his veins, so it was nice to see him sweat.

'Hm. No,' he said finally.

'What?' she said, surprised. 'No?'

He dropped the button on the ground and stomped on it. 'No.' He climbed back into the cockpit.

'Just . . . Just no?'

'Just no.' The carriage started off again.

'You . . . You goddamn fool!' she shouted at him. 'You're going to get us both killed!'

'You have damaged lives and careers through your actions,' said the captain. 'Not just mine, but those of my officers. You harm those around you without reflection or compunction. I am obligated to amend that. And I will not permit any threat, any lie, or any attack to dissuade me from my path.'

Sancia stared at the ceiling, stunned. 'You . . . You smug idiot!' she said. 'What right do you have to speak such flowery words with the Dandolo name hanging over you?'

'What does that have to do with it?'

'Harming people, using people, damaging lives – that's all the merchant houses ever do!' she said. 'You people are every bit as dirty as I am!'

'That may be so,' said Dandolo with infuriating serenity. 'This place has a tainted heart. That I've seen up-close. But I have also seen horrors out in the world, young lady. I learned to tame some of them. And I have come home to bring to this city the very thing I am delivering you to.'

'And what's that?'

'Justice,' he said simply.

Her mouth fell open. 'What? Are you *serious*?'

'As serious,' he said as the carriage turned, 'as the grave.'

Sancia laughed, incredulous. 'Oh, as simple as that? Just like dropping off a package? "Here, friends – have some justice!" That's the dumbest damned thing I ever heard!'

'All great things must start somewhere,' he said. 'I started with the waterfront. Which you burned down. By capturing you, I can continue.'

She kept laughing. 'You know, I almost believe you, you and your holy-crusade talk. But if you really are as noble and honest as you sound, Captain Dandolo, you won't live long. If there's one thing this city can't tolerate, it's honesty.'

'Let them try,' he said. 'Many already have. I nearly died once. I can afford to do so agai—'

But he never finished his statement. Because then the carriage went careening out of control.

Gregor Dandolo had piloted scrived carriages many times before, so he was well acquainted with how to manoeuvre such a vehicle – but he had never piloted one that suddenly had only one front wheel.

And that seemed to have been what had happened, in the blink of an eye: at first they'd been rolling along – and then, suddenly, the driver's front wheel had simply exploded.

He shoved down the deceleration lever while also spinning the pilot wheel away from the damaged carriage wheel – but this proved unwise, because then the carriage jumped a wooden walkway, which snapped the other front wheel, which meant he no longer had any control over the carriage's direction at all as it hurtled across the muddy lanes.

The world was rattling and quaking around him, but Gregor had sense enough to decipher where the carriage was now headed – and he saw that that space was occupied by a tall, stone building. One that looked well built.

'Oh dear,' he said. He leapt through into the back of the carriage, where the girl was stuck to the floor.

'What did you do, you big idiot?' she cried at him.

Gregor grabbed his espringal and turned the density of her bonds down – otherwise they could fly around throughout the carriage and crush him, and certainly her. 'Hold on, please,' he said. 'We're about t—'

Then the world leapt around them, and Gregor Dandolo remembered.

He remembered the carriage crash from long ago. The way the vehicle tipped, the way the world tumbled, the sprinkle of glass and the creak of wood.

And he remembered the whimpering in the dark and the glimmer of torchlight from outside. How the light caught the ruined form of Gregor's father, crumpled in the seat, and the face of the young man beside him in the ruined carriage, weeping as his blood poured out of his body.

Domenico. He'd died terrified and whimpering in the dark for their mother. The way many young men in this world died, Gregor would later find.

Gregor heard whimpering again, and had to tell himself: *No. No. That is the past. That all happened long ago.*

Then his mother's voice in his ear: *Wake up, my love . . .*

The muddy world congealed around him, and reality returned.

Gregor groaned and looked up. It seemed the carriage had flipped over, so one passenger window was now pointed at the sky while the other was stuck in the mud. The young woman lay in a heap next to him. 'Are you alive?' he asked.

She coughed. 'Why do you give a damn?'

'I am not in the business of killing captured people, even accidentally.'

'Are you so sure that was an accident?' she said, her voice rasping. 'I told you. They followed you. They're coming for me.'

Gregor glared at her, then pulled out Whip and climbed up through the cab of the carriage. He crawled through the window of the passenger door, which now faced the night sky.

He sat on the edge of the tipped-over carriage and looked at the front axle. A large, thick, metal espringal bolt was sticking out of it right where the wheel had been.

It must have gone right through the spokes of the wheel – and as the wheel spun around it, it shredded the damned thing . . .

It was an impressive shot. He looked around, but he could see no assailants. They were in one of the larger fairways in Foundryside, but the street was empty – after the building collapse and the shriekers last night, odds were the residents thought if they poked their heads out to see what the commotion was, they'd lose them.

The young woman cried: 'Ah, shit. *Shit!* Hey, Captain!'

'What now?' sighed Gregor.

'I'm going to say something else you're not going to believe. But I'm still going to say it.'

'You are, of course, free to say what you like, miss.'

She hesitated. 'I . . . I can hear scrivings.'

'You . . . You what?'

'I can hear scrivings,' she said again. 'That's how I knew about the thing on your carriage.'

He tried to understand what she was implying. 'That's impossible!' he said. 'No one can jus—'

'Yeah, yeah, yeah,' said the young woman. 'But listen – you need to know this because right now, *right now*, a number of *very loud* scrived rigs are converging on us. I know because I can hear them. And if they're really loud, that means they must be really powerful.'

He scoffed. 'I know you think I'm stupid – after all, you have said so both loudly and repeatedly – but it is biologically impossible that someone could be stupid enough to believe *that*.' He looked around.

'I don't see anyone walking down the street toward us carrying, say, a shrieker.'

'I don't hear them on the street. Look up. They're above us.'

Rolling his eyes, Gregor looked up. And then he froze.

On the side of the building façade above him, four stories up, was a masked person, dressed all in black. They were standing on the building façade as if it were not the side of a building but was actually the floor – in full defiance of all known laws of physics – and they were pointing an espringal at him.

Gregor dove down into the upended carriage. The next thing he knew there were a lot of loud *thunks*. He shook his head and looked up.

Five espringal bolts were now poking in through the side of the carriage. They had almost punched straight through – and since the walls and floors of this carriage were reinforced, that meant their attackers were using scrived weapons.

More than one of them, he thought. *At least five.*

'Impossible,' said Gregor. 'That *can't* be.'

'What?' said the young woman. 'What's out there?'

'There . . . there was a man standing on the building's side!' said Gregor. 'Standing there like gravity doesn't work at all!'

He looked up through the open window on the side of the carriage, and watched in shock as a figure in black appeared to gracefully float over the carriage like a bizarre cloud. Then he pointed an espringal down, and fired.

Gregor hugged the wall of the carriage as the bolt came hurtling down. The young woman screamed as it thudded into the mud below them.

Gregor and the young woman looked at it, then stared at each other.

'I scrumming hate being right,' she said.

12

The entire theory of scriving relied on the idea that you could convince an object to behave like something that it wasn't. But the early Tevanni scrivers figured out pretty quick that it was a lot easier to convince an object it was something it was *similar* to, rather than something it was not similar to at all.

In other words, it would not take much effort to scrive a block of copper into thinking it was a block of iron. However, it would take an *impossible* amount of effort to convince the block of copper that it was actually, say, a block of ice, or a pile of pudding, or a fish. The more convincing an object needed, the more complicated the scriving definitions became, and the more of a lexicon they'd take up, until finally you were using a whole lexicon or even multiple lexicons to make one scriving work.

The first scrivers hit this wall pretty quickly. Because one of the initial things they tried to alter was an object's gravity – and gravity proved to be a deeply stubborn bastard that simply *could not* be convinced to do things it didn't believe it ought to.

The first efforts to scrive objects to sort of gently, casually step around the laws of gravity were utter disasters – explosions, mutilations, and maimings were common. This had been a great surprise to the scrivers, since they knew from the old stories that the hierophants had been able to make objects float across the room, and some hierophants were recorded as flying nearly all the time. The hierophant Pharnakes was even said to have crushed an entire army with boulders from a mountaintop.

But eventually, after an untold number of deaths, the Tevanni scrivers came up with a somewhat decent solution.

The laws of gravity would not be outright denied. But it was possible to obey the laws of gravity in very *unusual* ways. Like scrived bolts – they were convinced they were just obeying gravity; they just had some interesting new ideas about where the ground was, and how long they'd been falling for. Or floating lanterns, which believed they contained a sack full of gas that was lighter than air, though they did not. All these designs *acknowledged* the laws of gravity. They just obeyed the letter of the laws, rather than the spirit.

But despite these successes, the dream stayed alive: Tevanni scrivers kept trying to find ways to truly *defy* gravity – to make people float, or fly, just like the hierophants of old. Even though such efforts almost always had lethal side effects.

For example, some scrivers accidentally adjusted their gravity so that two different portions of themselves recognised two different directions of pull, causing their limbs to stretch or simply get ripped clean off their bodies. Others accidentally crushed themselves into a bloody, flat disc, or a ball, or a cube, depending on their methodology. Others gravely underestimated the amount of gravity they should have, and they wound up floating away into the ether until they reached the limits of their lexicon, at which point they rather anticlimactically smashed into the surface of the earth.

This was considered a pleasant way to go. You had something to bury that way.

Many of these attempts had coincided with a larger effort to scrive the human body – and these experiments had been *far* more horrific than tinkering with gravity.

Unimaginably worse. Unspeakably worse.

And so, after they'd cleaned up all the bloodstains from the umpteenth disaster, the merchant houses had made a rare, diplomatic agreement: they'd all decided that trying to scrive a body or its gravity was to be banned, and never trifled with. Humans had enough danger just handling altered items – they didn't need to worry about their own limbs or torsos going haywire on them too.

And that was why Gregor Dandolo simply could not believe what he was seeing as he peeked out the top of the carriage: nine men, all dressed in black, running across the building faces with impossibly balletic grace. Some even ran upside down along the overhangs of roofs.

Such a thing was not only illegal, as much as anything could be in Tevanne – it was also, as far as he was aware, technologically impossible.

Three of the men stopped and pointed their espringals at him. Gregor ducked back down as bolts punched into the carriage just where he'd been peeking out.

'They're good shots too,' he muttered. 'Of course.' He considered what to do – but there was little he could accomplish, being stuck in a box in the middle of the road.

'Do you want to live?' asked the girl.

'What?' he said, irritated.

'Do you want to live?' she said again. 'Because if you do, you should let me go.'

'Why would I do that?'

'Because I can help you get out of this.'

'If I let you go, you'll run off the first second you can get! Or you'll stab me in the back and leave me to get shot full of bolts.'

'Maybe,' she said. 'But they're here for me, not you. It wouldn't hurt my feelings if you put those bastards in the ground, Captain. I'd be happy to help you do that.'

'And what could you do to help me?'

'Something. Which is better than nothing. Besides, Captain, you owe me one – I saved your life, remember?'

Scowling, Gregor rubbed his mouth. He hated this. He'd worked ceaselessly to get here, to capture this girl who'd been the source of all his problems, and now he was either going to die for having her, or have to let her go.

But then, slowly, Gregor's priorities shifted.

The men flying around up there almost certainly worked for a merchant house – only a house could have outfitted them with such rigs.

A merchant house is trying to kill me to get the girl, he thought. *So they almost certainly also commissioned the theft, of course.*

And it was one thing to catch a grubby thief and make a show of her as the cause of great evils in Tevanne – but it was quite another to expose massive misconduct, conspiracy, and death being perpetrated by a merchant house faction right here in the city. The merchant houses did conduct espionage and sabotage against one another, everyone knew that – but there was a bright, unspoken line they did not cross.

They did not make war upon one another. War in Tevanne would be disastrous, everyone knew that.

But a bunch of flying assassins, Gregor thought, *certainly looks a lot like war.*

He reached into the front seat, rummaged around, and brought back a thick metal cord. He quickly fastened it to the girl's left foot with a small, scrived key, which had a dial on the head.

'I said to let me go!' she said. 'Not tie me up *more.*'

'This thing works the same way as the cords on you right now.' He held up the key and pointed to it. 'I turn up the dial, and it gets heavier, and heavier. You try to run or kill me, and you'll find yourself stuck in one spot out in the open. Or it could crush your foot. So I recommend you behave.'

To his frustration, this didn't seem to intimidate her much. 'Yeah, yeah. Just get the rest of these things off me, all right?'

Gregor glared at her. Then he pulled the release key out of the stock of his espringal and used it to free her. 'I assume you haven't ever dealt with assailants such as this before,' he said as she shook off the cords.

'No. No, I have not tangled with a bunch of flying arseholes before. How many of them are there?'

'I counted nine.'

She peered up as another assassin danced over the carriage. There was a *thunk* as the bolt struck the door above. Gregor noticed the girl did not flinch. 'They like us out in the open,' she said softly. 'Where we're exposed.'

'So how do we get to someplace confined where their tools will offer less advantage?'

The girl cocked her head, thought, and then scrambled up to the top window, gripping the edges of the seat. She readied herself, then leapt up with a swift, measured grace, popping up through the window before falling back down to the mud. A chorus of *thunks* echoed throughout the carriage as she landed.

'Shit,' she said. 'They're fast. But at least I know where we are now. You drove the carriage into the Zorzi Building, which is lucky.'

'I did not *drive* it into the building,' he said, indignant. 'We crashed.'

'Whatever. It used to be a paper mill or something. It stretches across the whole block. A bunch of vagrants live there now, but the top floor is big and open, with lots of windows – and the street on the other side is pretty narrow.'

'How does that help us?'

'It doesn't help *us*,' said Sancia. 'It helps me, though.'

He frowned at her. 'What exactly are you planning, here?'

She explained. And Gregor listened.

When she was done, he considered what she was asking of him. It was not a bad plan. He'd heard worse ones.

'Think you can do it?' she asked.

'I know I can,' said Gregor. 'Do you think you can get into the building?'

'That won't be a problem,' she said. 'Just give me that big goddamn crossbow.' He handed it over, and she slung it across her back. 'I just point and shoot like a normal espringal, right?'

'Essentially. The cords will wrap around their target, and then they should start amplifying their densities – the more the target moves, of course.'

'Terrific.' She pulled two small, black balls out of a pocket on her side. 'You ready?'

He climbed up to the open window, looked down, and nodded.

'Here we go.' She took one of the balls in her hand and pressed a small plate on its side. Then she threw one of the balls out the window, waited a beat, and then threw the other. The instant the streets lit up with that incredible, bright flashing light, Gregor leapt out of the carriage and made a run for it.

Despite the fact that he'd witnessed this phenomenon before, the flash and sound of the stun bombs was no less stupefying for Gregor. He caught the barest glimpse of the Foundryside street, and then it was all wiped away in a flash of illumination brighter than a lightning strike, followed by a tooth-rattling *bang.* He staggered blindly for the alley ahead, hands outstretched. He tripped on a porch, crashed into the wooden slats, and crawled forward until he felt a corner of wood.

He crawled around the corner, shakily stood, and pressed his back to the wall. *There. I'm there.*

He stood up and began to wobble down the alley, one hand on the wall, the other outstretched before him, the sounds of the stun bombs still ringing in his ears.

Eventually the world took shape around him. He was stumbling down a dark, decrepit alley, lined with refuse and rags. He looked over his shoulder and saw the lights of the stun bombs were fading. Then six silhouettes emerged in between the building faces of the alley – and, bizarrely, began bounding back and forth among the shop fronts like leaves on the wind.

Gregor stepped into a shadowed doorway. *Remarkably odd to see,* he thought, watching them drift gracefully through the air like acrobats on wires. After a moment, a seventh man joined them.

That's two of them unaccounted for, thought Gregor. Then he took Whip out. *Still. Time to test the limits of gravity.*

He watched their progression, calculated their arcs, and flicked Whip forward.

His shot was true. The truncheon's head caught the man directly in the chest – and, since the man's reality had apparently been rearranged to believe he was as light as a feather, he went hurtling off into the sky like he'd been fired out of a cannon.

His comrades paused on a linen shop's roof to watch him sail off into the night sky. Then they raised their espringals and fired.

Gregor leapt back into the doorway as the bolts thudded around him. Whip came zipping back to its shaft. He waited a beat, then dashed out and started running.

One down, he thought. *Eight to go.*

Sancia waited quietly underneath the carriage, the big espringal on her back. She tried to ignore her rapid heartbeat and the trembling in her hands. When the stun bombs had gone off, she'd leapt out and hidden in the gap between the carriage and the base of the building. She could hear one of the assassins standing on the top of the carriage, peering down into the empty vehicle. Then she watched, relieved, as he joined his comrades in chasing Gregor down the side alley.

<*You think he's gonna make it?*> asked Clef.

There was a *thud*, a cry of pain, and then one of the men came rocketing out of the alley, tumbling arse-over-head.

<*I think he'll be fine,*> said Sancia. <*Any more of those rigs nearby?*>

<*Not that I can tell. I think you're clear.*>

She wormed her way out from underneath the carriage, pulled Clef off her neck, and stuck him in the side door to the Zorzi Building. There was the usual *click*, and Sancia darted inside.

The place reeked of sulfur and whatever other chemicals they'd used to make paper back in the day – as well as a variety of other, more human smells, because the bottom floor appeared to have been totally taken over by vagrants. Piles of rags and straw and refuse were everywhere. A few of the occupants cried out at the sight of her, a huge espringal slung over her shoulder.

Sancia knelt, touched a bare finger to the ground, and let the layout of the building unscroll in her mind. Once she felt the stairs, she popped up, leapt over one of the shrieking vagrants, and darted over to the hallway that led to the stairs. <*I hope I make it up in time,*> she thought.

Gregor turned the corner on the fairway, then turned again, until he was headed toward the other side of the Zorzi Building – but hopefully his attackers didn't realise that. He looked ahead and saw a welcome sight: there were dozens of clotheslines strung up over the narrow fairway beside the old paper mill, running about four stories up, old dresses and grey undergarments and bedsheets drifting in the night breeze.

Ah, he thought. *Cover. That should do nicely.*

He ran to the left, finding shelter under a thick set of off-white bedsheets, and looked up. With the clotheslines above, he was much less exposed.

And hopefully, he thought, glancing up, *the girl will be getting into position sometime soon . . .*

He saw an iron baluster on a balcony across the street, which gave him an idea. He took Whip out, aimed carefully, and flicked it at the baluster . . .

With a loud *clang*, Whip's head caught on the iron railing. Gregor pulled the cable taut, hid in a doorway, and waited.

He couldn't see them coming through the clothes above. He could only hear the soft scrape of their boots on the building fronts, echoing all around him. He imagined them dancing from rooftop to rooftop, weaving through the hanging clothes, drifting like dust motes on a gentle breeze. But then, as if he were fishing, his line suddenly gave a great leap . . .

There was a gagging sound, and a cough. Gregor peeked around the corner and saw one of their attackers spinning wildly through the air, having apparently been caught on Whip's cable. The man sailed through the clotheslines, flying end-over-end, the lines and clothes wrapping around his form as he coughed. Finally he crashed into the street below, trailing tangles of clothing like some kind of bizarre kite, and was still.

Gregor nodded, pleased. *That worked nicely.* He hit the switch to retract Whip's head from the baluster. It took a jerk or two from him, but soon the truncheon's head came zipping down – and accidentally pulled a string of clothes with it.

Which, he realised, told his attackers exactly where he was.

He looked up as a black-clad man did a flip over the clotheslines, tumbling like an acrobat. Then the man adjusted something on his stomach, which caused him to fall rapidly back toward the building face opposite Gregor. Once the man's feet were steady, he looked up at Gregor, and raised his espringal.

Gregor started to flick Whip forward, but he knew it was too late. He could see it happening, see the bolt whipping down at him, see its black tip glinting in the moonlight. He tried to withdraw farther into the doorway, but then his arm lit up with pain.

He cried out and looked at his left arm. He immediately saw that he'd been lucky: the bolt had caught him on the inside bottom of his forearm, slashing it open. The unnatural momentum of the bolt meant it'd shredded his flesh as it passed directly through, but it had not speared his arm, or hit the bone. Scrived bolts did tremendous damage to the human body.

Cursing, Gregor looked up just in time to see a second assassin join the one who'd just fired – and this one, he suspected, would not miss.

Gregor fumbled to get Whip ready.

The attacker raised his espringal . . .

But then a silvery, strange rope came hurtling from above to wrap itself around the second man's legs.

The second attacker staggered as the ropes struck him – at least, he staggered as much as anyone could while defying gravity and standing on a wall.

Praise God, thought Gregor. *The girl came through.* He looked up, but the windows above were lost in the fluttering storm of laundry. Presumably she was somewhere up there, firing away.

The bound man tried to leap off the building front – but this quickly proved to have been a bad idea: the density cords wrapped around the man's shins believed that, as long as the target they were bound to was not at rest, they would keep increasing their density until it was.

However, the man's gravity rig – whatever it was – allowed him to circumnavigate gravity itself: the one force that allowed objects to come to a resting state.

So, because of his rig, he could not be at rest. And because he could not be at rest, the bonds got denser, and denser . . .

The man started shrieking in surprise and pain, and he slapped at something on his chest, some kind of control mechanism for his gravity rig, probably. This caused him to just float in the middle of the air over the street – but that did not amend his situation, it seemed.

His shrieking got higher-pitched, and louder . . .

There was a sound like a tree root cracking in half, or fabric being torn. Then came a horrific spray of blood – and then the man's legs separated from the rest of his body at the knees.

Sancia stared over the sights of her espringal as the man screamed in agony, floating above the street, pouring blood from his knees. She was crouched on the remnants of a wooden walkway that ran the perimeter of the Zorzi's upstairs, peering through the old windows. She'd assumed that shooting the flying men with the espringal would just weigh them down until they couldn't fly anymore – she certainly hadn't thought it would do *that*.

<*Oh God,*> said Clef, disgusted. <*Did you mean for that to happen, kid?*>

She swallowed her nausea. <*You keep asking me that, Clef,*> she said. She started reloading. <*No. I never meant for any of this to happen.*>

Gregor watched in dull surprise as the man's feet and calves crashed into the earth, still wearing the density bonds. Then the man just hung there in the air, screaming as blood poured out of him onto the ground like a horrific water feature of the neighbourhood . . .

And that, thought Gregor, *is why scrivers so rarely fool with gravity.*

Understandably, such a phenomenon got one's attention. It certainly seemed to have distracted the man who'd injured Gregor – he was still standing on the building face across the fairway, staring at the sight, having seemingly forgotten all about Gregor.

Narrowing his eyes, Gregor took aim with Whip and flung the truncheon's head forward at the man. There was a dull *plonk!* sound, and the thick weight cleanly connected with the man's left temple.

The man's body went slack and he dropped the espringal. Then, slowly, his legs slipped off the wall and his unconscious body started drifting over the street. It seemed his rig was set to keep him at a specific level – he neither rose nor fell. It looked like he was slowly skating over an invisible ice pond.

Gregor peered at the espringal lying in the mud. Then he got an idea. It was one of his favourite tactics: when outnumbered and outmatched, clutter up the battlefield as much as you can. *Only this battlefield*, he thought, *is the very air above our heads.*

He took aim at the unconscious, floating man, and hurled Whip forward. The truncheon's head caught the man's body in the chest and – just as Gregor had hoped – the momentum sent the man ricocheting off the building fronts, hurtling through hanging clothes, bouncing off his dying colleague, and generally wreaking havoc.

Gregor watched, satisfied, as the chaos unfolded. One of the men tried to get out of the way and leap across the alley, but the growing tangle of clotheslines caught him like a fish in a net.

Gregor scrambled forward, grabbed the espringal, raised it, and shot the tangled man, all in one smooth motion. The man cried out and went still.

Five down, said Gregor. *Four left*.

He looked up, reloaded, and saw two attackers flit across the street and twirl in midair. Gregor tried to draw a bead on one of them – but then both of them gracefully tumbled through the upstairs windows of the Zorzi Building.

Gregor lowered the espringal. 'Oh hell,' he sighed.

Sancia saw them coming. She pointed the big espringal at one of the attackers just as they passed through the windows, and fired. But the shot went wide, and the density cords tangled around a rafter – which was, of course, already at rest, so that didn't do much.

'Shit!' she cried. She leapt forward as a scrived bolt hurtled toward her. As she fell she reached into her pocket, grabbed a stun bomb, pressed its plate, and tossed it into the rafters.

She knew, of course, that in this terribly dark place it would blind her as well, along with whichever vagrants were still in there with her. But Sancia was pretty good at getting around without seeing.

The flash of the bomb was tremendous, as was the *pop* from its charge. For a moment she just lay there on the walkway, her head ringing and her eyes aching. Clef's voice cut through all her sensory overload.

<There's two of them in here with you,> he said. *<Up in the rafters, hiding. They can't see you now – but I'm guessing you can't see them either.>*

Sancia was keenly aware that wouldn't last forever – though the effects might likely last unusually long, given the dark environment. Yet she found she could hear her attackers, or at least their rigs – there was a faint chanting in the blistering, flashing darkness, from their gravity rigs. *I guess I don't hear scrivings with my ears,* she thought, which was a curious revelation. She also realised that these rigs must be terribly powerful for her to be able to hear them from so far away.

That gave her an idea. She slipped out her bamboo pipe, which was loaded with a single dolorspina dart. *<Clef – can you see in here?>*

<Sure. Why wouldn't I?>

Clef seemed to not understand this was disturbing, since it suggested his method of seeing things was different from human eyes. She lifted the pipe to her lips. *<Tell me if I'm pointing this thing at one of their rigs.>*

<What? Are you serious? This has to be the worst way t—>

<Just do it, damn it, before they can see again!>

<Fine . . . Walk down the walkway about five feet . . . Wait, no, four feet – just stop. Stop! Okay. Now. They're on your right. No, God, your other right! Okay . . . Now, keep turning. That's it. Stop. All right. Put the pipe thing in your mouth. Point it up . . . Up more . . . Too far, back down. Down more. That's it! Now to your right just a little – okay. Now. Hard.>

Sancia took a deep breath in through her nose and blew as hard as she could.

She had no idea what happened – she still couldn't see or hear much. It was like firing the dart into the blackest of nights in here. But then Clef said, *<He . . . He moved! Just a touch . . . And now it . . . it looks like he's drifting, maybe? I think you got him, kid! I can't believe it!>*

She could see blurs in the darkness – her vision was coming back, but only slightly. *<Let's assume I did,>* she said. *<Where's the other one?>*

<On the far wall, to your right. You don't have a shot.>

<I don't need a shot.> She touched her bare hand to the wall beside her, then the rafter above her, and she listened to both of them. She let all the rafters and the supports and the beams overhead pour into her.

It was too much, far, far, too much. Her head felt like it was going to break open. *I'm going to pay for this later,* she thought. But she kept going until every inch of the ceiling had made an impression in her thoughts, every beam of wood and every brick fixed in her mind.

Then, still mostly blind and deaf, Sancia leapt up, grabbed a rafter, lifted herself up, and started crawling through the rafters of the Zorzi Building with her eyes closed.

She couldn't see any of the dangers underneath her, but Clef could. *<Oh my God,>* he said. *<Ohhhh my God . . . >*

<It would really help,> she said as she blindly leapt from one rafter to another, *<if you would shut up, Clef.>*

She kept going, hopping from rafter to rafter, beam to beam, until she felt like she was getting close. *<Are we almost there?>* she asked.

<I thought you wanted me to shut up.>

<Clef.>

<Yeah, we're almost there. Reach out with your left hand after this next jump . . . You should feel the wall.>

She did so, and found he was right. And as she touched the wall, she felt him.

A tight, warm bundle of a person, pressed up in the crevice between the wall and the ceiling, like a bat in its roost. Waiting for his vision to return, probably. But the second she felt him . . .

He moved. Fast. Speeding down.

He must have felt me coming! she thought. *I hit the damned rafter too hard!*

But she still felt what the wall felt – and the wall had felt him push off, including how hard and which direction he was going.

Sancia gauged his likely position and blindly jumped into open space.

For a moment she just fell, and she was sure she'd cocked it up, sure she'd missed him, sure she would just plummet three stories down into the vagrants' nest, where she'd break a leg, or her skull, and then she'd just die there.

But then she hit him. Hard.

Sancia instinctively threw her arms around the man and clung tightly to him. Her hearing was coming back, and she heard him scream in surprise and anger. They were still falling, but as someone who was somewhat used to falling in space, the way they were falling was so *strange*: they suddenly, rapidly decelerated to a curiously steady rate, like they were trapped in a floating bubble, twisting through the air.

Until they hit the ground. Then the man shoved off, hard, and they went rocketing throughout the old paper mill.

The man smashed Sancia into walls, into rafters, and, once, into what she guessed was his floating, unconscious comrade. He hurtled back and forth throughout the building, trying to shake her off and struggling with her grasp.

But Sancia was strong, and she held fast. The world was tumbling and twirling about them, the vagrants were screaming and shrieking, and her sight was slowly, slowly coming back to her . . .

She saw the fourth-floor windows flying at them, and realised what was going to happen.

'Ah, shit!' she cried.

They crashed through a pair of shutters, and then they were outside, flying through the open night air, still tumbling over and over and over. Now he could fly up a mile and dump her off, or have one of his comrades pry her off and slit her throat, or . . .

<*The controls for his rig are on his stomach!*> Clef shouted at her.

Sancia clung tighter to him, gritted her teeth, and started swatting at the man's stomach with her hand, clawing and tearing at anything she could find there.

Then her hand felt a small wheel – which she managed to turn.

They froze, hanging in midair.

'*No!*' screamed the man.

And then he seemed to explode.

It was as if someone had filled a huge water skin with hot blood and jumped on it. The spray of gore was unspeakably tremendous, and totally shocking to Sancia.

More concerning, though, was that the man she'd leapt on was no longer . . . well, *there*. It was as if he'd simply disappeared, leaving only the scrived gravity device behind.

Which meant Sancia was now falling.

She tried to grab at something, anything. The only thing to hold on to was the dead man's device, which was covered in blood. She grabbed it purely out of instinct, yet this did nothing. Everything seemed to slow down as she fell to the fairway below.

<*Bad!*> cried Clef. <*This is real bad!*>

Sancia had no mind to answer. The world was sliding by her, every ripple of the bedsheets and twist of the undergarments frozen in space . . .

And then Gregor Dandolo was there, beneath her.

He cried out in pain as Sancia landed in his arms. Sancia herself was still dumbfounded, her mind reeling as she tried to understand what had just happened. Then he dumped her in the mud, cursing and rubbing his lower vertebrae.

'You . . . you caught me?' she said aloud, still stunned.

He groaned and fell to his knees. 'My scrumming back . . . Consider my debt repaid,' he snarled.

She looked at herself. She was trembling, absolutely covered in blood, and she still clutched the gravity device in her hands. It looked like two plates connected with cloth bands – one for your belly, one for your back – and one plate had a series of little dials on it.

She stammered out, 'I . . . I . . .'

'You must have sabotaged the device he was using to float,' said Gregor. He looked up at the bedsheets above, which were all spattered with gore. 'Causing his gravity to collapse, crushing him. Somewhere in the street is probably a fleshy marble that was once the whole of that man's body.' He looked around. 'Help me up. Now!'

'Why? That's all of them, right?'

'No, that was just seven! There were nine in tota—'

Gregor never got the chance to finish. Because then the remaining two attackers crested the peaks of the roofs on one side of the street, and fired.

Sancia's adrenaline was still running strong, so the world still seemed terribly slow and clear, every second sliding by like the slice of a razor.

She watched the two men take positions on the roof, her eyes catching every gesture and movement. She knew there was no running from them, no shelter, no trick up her sleeve. She and Gregor were exposed in the alley, unarmed, with nowhere to run.

Clef's voice roared in her ear: *<TOUCH ME TO THE GRAVITY RIG! NOW, NOW, NOW!>*

Sancia didn't stop to think. She ripped Clef off the string around her neck and stabbed him down to the bloody plates in her lap.

Their attackers loosed their bolts. She watched helplessly as the scrived bolts leapt forth from their espringal pockets like fish jumping out of the water to catch an unsuspecting fly.

She felt metal strike metal as Clef touched the gravity plate. And then . . .

A curious pressure fell across Sancia's body, and her stomach fluttered unpleasantly, like she was falling again – but she was standing still. Wasn't she?

But then, *everything* seemed to be standing still. The bolts weren't flying forward anymore – they hung limply in the air. The attackers were like statues stuck to the walls. The hanging clothes were barely rippling anymore – a curl of a bedsheet hanging above the alley almost perfectly still, like icing on a cake.

Sancia looked around at the drifting world, dazed. 'What the hell . . .'

She was still touching Clef, and he was still stuck to the gravity plate, and she heard his voice whispering, speaking, chanting. She couldn't understand what he was saying, but she could tell he was doing . . . *something* to the device.

Then she and Gregor slowly started to float off the ground, rising up as if they had no weight at all.

She heard Gregor crying out, '*What the devil?*'

Clef's chanting filled her ears. She dimly realised he was making the rig work for him, making it do something it was not meant to do, something it should have *never* been able to do.

Because from what she'd seen that night, these gravity rigs only affected the gravity of the person wearing them – yet Clef was now somehow using this rig to control the gravity of *everything around them.*

Other objects began to float into the air, barrels and bags and firebaskets and the body of one of their attackers, festooned with laundry. The two attackers on the walls began screaming in terror as they helplessly floated off the building fronts, slowly turning end over end.

Clef's voice overpowered her thoughts, filling her mind. His strange chanting grew louder.

How is he doing this? she thought. *How can he possibly be doing this?*

Then her scar grew hot, and she heard something, smelled something, saw something . . .

A vision.

A vast, sandy plain. Tiny stars twinkling above. The sky at dusk, dark and purpled at the horizon.

There was a man on the plain, wearing robes. And in his hand, a wink of gold.

He raised the golden thing, and then . . .

The stars began dying, one by one. Snuffed out as if they were but candle flames.

Darkness fell.

Sancia heard herself screaming in terror. The vision bled out of her mind and the world returned to her, with Gregor and all the random objects floating in the muddy fairway, the barrels and the firebaskets and the bolts.

She watched as the two bolts slowly, slowly flipped in midair, changing direction so they pointed not at Sancia and Gregor but rather at the men who had fired them.

The bolts trembled with pent-up energy. The men, realising what was about to happen, shrieked in naked terror.

Clef said a single word, and the bolts hurtled forward. They flew so fast they almost fell apart in the air. When the bolts struck the men, they punched through their bodies as if their ribs and stomachs were made of soft gelatin, shredding them effortlessly, like scythes parting soft, green grasses.

Clef's chanting halted. Instantly, Gregor, Sancia, the floating corpses, and all the other levitating things in the fairway crashed to the ground.

For a moment they just lay there. Then Gregor sat up and peered at the bodies lying in the mud.

'They're . . . They're dead.' He looked at Sancia. 'How . . . How did you do that?'

Sancia's mind was still whirling, but she had wit enough to slip Clef up her sleeve before Gregor could see him. *<Was that . . . Was that you, Clef?>* she asked him.

Clef was silent.

<Clef? Clef, are you there?>

Nothing. She looked at the gravity plates, and saw the device was now melted and smeared, like Clef's manipulations had burned the thing out.

'How did you *do* that?' demanded Gregor again. For once, the captain looked genuinely shaken.

'I don't know,' she said.

'You don't know?'

'No!' she shouted. 'No, no! I don't even know if I *did* do that!'

She sat there in the fairway, bewildered and exhausted. Gregor watched her, wary.

'We've got to get out of here,' she said wearily. 'There could be more of them. Last time they called in a whole damn army! There could b—'

She stopped talking as a black, unmarked carriage rattled into the fairway.

'Shit,' she sighed.

Gregor scrambled through the mud, grabbed his espringal, and pointed it at the carriage – but then he lowered it, surprised.

The carriage pulled up in front of them. A young, rather pretty girl wearing white-and-yellow robes peered out of the cockpit window. 'Get in, Captain,' she said. 'Now.' She looked at Sancia. 'You too.'

'Miss Berenice?' said the captain, astonished.

'Now means *now*,' she said.

The captain hobbled around and started climbing in on the other side of the cockpit. 'I'm not going to have to make you get in this thing, am I?' he asked Sancia.

Sancia briefly calculated the risks. She had absolutely no idea who in the hell this girl was. But with the captain's bond still on her ankle, Clef suddenly dead and silent, and the whole of the Commons suddenly deeply unsafe for her, she had few choices.

She climbed in the back, and the carriage took off toward the Dandolo Chartered campo.

13

Sancia sat huddled in the passenger seat, gripping her wrist where she'd hidden Clef. She stayed quiet. Her skull was pounding terribly, and she had no idea what in hell was going on. For all she knew this girl was the queen of Tevanne, and could have her head lopped off with but a word.

She tugged at the bond on her ankle. It held fast, of course. She'd considered using Clef to undo it during the fight – but that would have tipped off the captain to the fact that she possessed something that could break scrived locks, so she'd refrained. She bitterly regretted the choice now.

Gregor sat in the cockpit with the girl, wrapping up his injured arm. He peered up at the rooftops outside. 'You saw them?' he asked. 'The flying men?'

'I saw them,' said the girl. Her voice was oddly calm.

'They have spies everywhere,' he said. 'Eyes everywhere.' Then he sat up. 'Did . . . Did you check this carriage? They put this thing on mine, this scrived button so they could follow me! You should pull over, now, and we should—'

'That won't be necessary, Captain,' she said.

'I am deadly serious, Miss Berenice!' said Gregor. 'We should pull over now and look over every inch of this carriage!'

'That is not necessary, Captain,' she said again. 'Please calm down.'

Gregor slowly turned to look at her. 'Why?'

She said nothing.

'How . . . How did you happen upon us, anyway?' he asked, suspicious.

Silence.

'They weren't the ones who put that button on my carriage at all, were they?' he asked. 'It was you. *You* put it there.'

She glanced at him as she piloted the carriage through the Dandolo southern gates. 'Yes,' she said reluctantly.

'Orso sent you to follow me,' he said. 'As I went to catch the thief.'

The girl took a long breath in, and let it out. 'It has been,' she said with a touch of fatigue, 'a very eventful evening.'

Sancia listened closely. She still didn't understand what the hell they were talking about, but now it seemed to involve her. That was bad.

She considered her options. <*Goddamn it, Clef, wake up!*> she said. But Clef was silent. If he was awake, she could pop the bond off her ankle and jump out of the carriage the first chance she got. She supposed she could dart Dandolo, or both of them, and steal the key to the bond. But she'd been in an out-of-control carriage once tonight, and had no desire to repeat the experience. And either way, both options left her abandoned on the Dandolo campo – and without Clef, her life there wasn't worth a copper duvot.

So she stayed put, and waited. An opportunity would present itself eventually. Provided they all stayed alive.

'So it *was* Orso's box,' he said, triumphant. 'Wasn't it? I was right! He had you ship it into my waterfront, under your name, didn't he? And he . . .' He stopped. 'Wait. So if *you* put the scrived button on my carriage instead of our attackers . . . how did our attackers find us at all?'

'That's simple,' said the girl. 'They found you because they were following me.'

He stared at her. 'You, Miss Berenice? What makes you say that?'

She pointed up. Gregor and Sancia slowly looked up at the ceiling. 'Oh,' said Gregor quietly.

The roof of the carriage sported three large, ragged holes, and one bolt point was lodged in it as well. 'I assume you wondered why two of them split off from the main attack force,' said Berenice. 'They chased me for a block or so, but left when they heard the screaming.' She glanced backward at Sancia. 'There was a *lot* of screaming, it seemed.'

'What makes you so sure they were following you?' said Gregor.

'They certainly knew which carriage to shoot at,' said Berenice.

'I see. But how did they know to follow you to begin with? Certainly they couldn't have followed you all the way from the inner Dandolo enclaves.'

'I'm not sure yet,' said Berenice. 'But this was planned. They intended to kill all of us at once, I suspect. Everyone involved . . .' She trailed off.

'Involved with me,' said Sancia quietly. 'With the box.'

'Yes.'

'Everyone involved . . .' said Gregor. 'Orso's back at the campo?'

'Yes,' said the girl. 'So he should be safe.'

Gregor peered out the window. 'But if you go high enough over a campo wall,' he said, 'you don't trigger any of its warding scrivings – do you?' He looked back at Sancia. 'That's what you did at the waterfront, correct?'

She shrugged. 'Basically?'

He looked at Berenice. 'So if you have a rig that can allow you to fly, you can sail right over all the campo walls – and no one would ever know you'd done it.'

'Damn,' Berenice said quietly. She pressed the accelerating lever farther forward. The carriage sped up. Then she cleared her throat. 'You back there,' she said.

'Me?' said Sancia.

'Yes. There's a bag at your feet. Inside is a strip of metal with two tabs at the ends. Let me know when you find it.'

Sancia rummaged around in the satchel in the passenger seat. She found the strip of metal quickly, and recognised a few of the sigils on the back.

'Got it,' she said. 'It's twinned, isn't it?'

'It is,' said Berenice.

'How'd you know that?' asked Gregor.

'I, uh, used a scriving like this to blow up your waterfront,' said Sancia.

Gregor scowled and shook his head.

'I need you to tear off both tabs,' said the girl. 'And then I need you to scratch a word on the back of it – *not* the side with the scrivings, that'll ruin the rig.'

Sancia tore the tabs off. 'Scratch something in it? With, like, a knife?'

'Yes,' said Berenice.

Gregor handed Sancia his stiletto. 'What word?' he asked.

'*Run.*'

Alone in his workshop, Orso Ignacio reviewed the ledger page he'd hidden among his scriving materials.

He'd concealed it quite cleverly, he thought. Much like his door, he'd scrived the book to sense his blood, so that only he (or someone with a lot of his blood) could read it. The instant he touched a hand to the covers, a slot in the spine opened up, and he could slip out the page hidden inside.

A page that was covered with figures. Extremely *bad* figures, he now thought as he reviewed it. Amounts he'd pilfered from this department or that department, jobs and tasks that had been paid for but did not really exist. Discovering any one of these figures would lead to serious charges. But discovering all of them . . .

I got stupid, he thought, sighing. *The idea of that key was too good. And now . . .*

Then there was a tinny *ping!* noise from his desk.

He sat up, dug through the papers, and found the twinned plate.

One tab had popped off. He stared at it. *That means Dandolo has found the thief.*

He watched the plate closely. Then, to his dismay, there was another *ping!* The second tab popped off.

'Oh shit,' he moaned. 'Oh *God*.' This meant that Dandolo had the thief – and the thief had the key.

Which meant he was going to have to start calling in favours. Favours he desperately did not wish to call in.

But before he could move, something strange happened.

The plate twitched. He turned it over, and saw that something was happening to the back.

Someone was writing there, gouging letters deep into the metal, and it was *not* Berenice's clear, perfect script. This was harsh and jagged, and it spelled out one word.

RUN.

'Run?' said Orso, perplexed. He scratched his head. Why would Berenice message him to run?

He looked around his workshop, and he didn't see anything he needed to run from. There were his definition tomes, his scriving blocks, his test lexicon, and the open window on the far wall . . .

He paused.

He didn't remember opening the window.

There was a creak from somewhere in his workshop. It was something akin to the creak of a floorboard as you walk across the room – but this did not come from the floor. It came from the ceiling.

Orso slowly looked up.

A man was crouched on his ceiling, in full defiance of gravity, dressed in black, wearing a black cloth mask.

Orso's mouth dropped open. 'What in he—'

The man fell on him, knocking Orso to the floor.

Cursing, Orso struggled to get up. As he did, the man calmly walked over to Orso's desk, snatched up his page of secret accounts, walked back, and kicked Orso in the stomach. Hard.

Orso collapsed again, coughing. Then his attacker slipped a loop over his head, and pulled it tight around his neck. He gagged and his eyes watered. The man hauled him to his feet, the cord cutting into his windpipe, and whispered in his ear, 'Now, now, poppy. Don't struggle too much, eh?' He jerked the cord back, and Orso nearly blacked out. 'Just come along, then. Come along!'

His attacker shoved him toward the window, then ripped the cord hard, pulling Orso along like a dog on a leash. Orso clawed at the cord, coughing, but it was tight and ferociously strong. The man glanced out the window. 'Not quite high enough, is it?' he mused aloud. 'We do want to make *sure*. Come along, poppy!'

Then – unbelievably – the man slipped out the window and stood on the side of the building as if it were the ground. He adjusted something on his stomach, nodded, and ripped Orso out after him.

Sancia stared as the carriage hurtled through the gates, one after the other. She realised, to her alarm, that they were careening into the deepest enclaves of the Dandolo campo, where the richest, most powerful people resided. She'd never even dreamed she'd get into such areas – especially not under these circumstances.

'There,' said Berenice. 'The Hypatus Building is just ahead.'

They peered through the front window of the carriage. A sprawling, elaborate, three-storey structure emerged from the rosy glow of the streets. It looked dark yet peaceful, as most buildings would in the middle of the night.

'It . . . doesn't look like anything's wrong,' said Gregor slowly.

Then something moved in the window on the third floor, and they watched, horrified, as a man in black climbed out the window, stood on the side of the wall, and hauled out a struggling human form, dangling from a rope of some kind by the neck.

'Oh dear,' said Gregor.

Berenice shoved the acceleration lever forward, but it was too late – the man in black hopped up the wall and tugged the helpless person onto the roof.

'No,' said Berenice. '*No!*'

'What can we do?' asked Gregor.

'The way up onto the roof is the south tower! It'll take forever to get there!'

Sancia looked at the side of the building, thinking. Perhaps this was the opportunity she'd been waiting for – she was well aware she was now dealing with some powerful people, and she was at their mercy.

Which she did not like one bit. It would be handy to put them in her debt.

'So, that's your guy, right?' she asked. 'Orso, or whatever?'

'Yes!' said Berenice.

'The guy whose box I stole?'

'Yes!' said Gregor.

'And . . . you want him to live?'

'*Yes!*' said Gregor and Berenice at the same time.

Sancia stuck Gregor's stiletto into her belt and tugged off both her gloves. 'Pull up close to the corner of the building there,' she said.

'What are you going to do?' asked Gregor.

Grimacing, Sancia rubbed her temple with two fingers. This would be too much, she knew. 'Something real dumb.' She sighed. 'I sure hope this arsehole is rich.'

'Up, up, up we go!' said the man. He hauled Orso up over the edge of the roof, adjusting the device on his belly as he did. Then he dragged Orso across the roof to the east side of the building, which overlooked the square.

The man dropped Orso and turned around. 'Now, don't get testy, poppy!' he said. He kicked Orso in the stomach again. Orso curled up, whimpering, and barely noticed as the man slipped the loop off of his head. 'Can't leave any evidence, dearie. You must be *immaculate.* Simply sparkling.' He walked around and kicked Orso again, rolling him toward the edge of the roof.

'This will be handy,' said the man, pocketing Orso's page of accounts. 'All your pilfered money, all for a key. Once everyone finds this, no one will suspect a thing.' He gave Orso another brutal kick, again pushing him toward the edge.

No, Orso thought. *No!* He tried to fight, to grab hold of the roof, to push back against his attacker, but the blows kept coming, landing on his shoulder, his fingers, his stomach. Orso watched through teary eyes as the edge of the roof came closer and closer.

'A bitter, old screw,' said the attacker with savage relish. 'Deep in debt.' Another kick. 'In over his head.' Another kick. 'A dumb bastard who has thoroughly shat where he ate.' He paused to position the final blow. 'Who'd be surprised to think you'd go and kill yourse—'

Then someone small and dressed in black came sprinting down the edge of the rooftop and tackled the man, knocking him to the ground.

Gasping, Orso looked up and watched as the two people in black wrestled. He had no idea who this new arrival was – it appeared to be a small, bloody, and somewhat dirty-looking young woman – but she tore into the man with savage intensity, slashing at him with a stiletto.

Yet the man was far more skilled in combat. He rebounded quickly, dodging her attacks and managing to land a fierce blow on her chin, knocking her to the side. She coughed and cried, '*Dandolo! Are you scrumming coming or not?*'

Orso's attacker dove at the woman hard enough that the two rolled over and over again, tumbling right toward . . .

Orso watched as they rolled close. 'Oh no,' he whispered.

The two combatants knocked him toward the edge. He felt numb and slow and stupid as his body tipped over. He reached out frantically, scrabbling for a handhold, and then his fingers finally found purchase on the edge . . .

Orso let out a rather undignified shriek as he dangled from the edge of the roof. The man and the young woman were just above him, almost on top of his fingers, wrestling and clawing at each other. Orso's attacker finally overpowered the young woman and climbed on top, fingers around her throat, clearly intending to choke her to death, or throw her off the roof, or both.

'Stupid little whore,' the man whispered. He leaned down on her throat. 'Just a bit more, just a *bit* more . . .'

The young woman, gagging, clawed at the device on his stomach, twisting and turning it.

Then something on the device slid into place.

The man froze, horrified, let her go, and looked down.

And then he simply . . . erupted.

Orso nearly let go of the roof in shock as the blood rained down on him in a hot wave. It stung his eyes and spattered into his mouth, a coppery, saline taste. If he had not been terrified, he would have been unspeakably disgusted.

'Ah, *shit*,' said the young woman, sputtering and coughing. She tossed away some remnant of the dead man – something akin to two plates held together with cloth. 'Not *again*!'

'H-help?' stammered Orso. 'Help. *Help!*'

'Hold on, hold on!' she said. The young woman rolled over, wiped her hands on the roof – her clothing was not an option, as it was just as bloody as her palms – and grabbed his wrists. With surprising strength, she hauled him up and dumped him onto the roof.

Orso lay on the roof, gasping in pain and horror and confusion and staring up at the night sky. 'What . . . What . . . What was . . .'

The young woman sat next to him, heaving with exhaustion. She looked terribly ill. 'Captain Dandolo's on his way up. Idiot is probably still looking for the stairs. You're Orso, right?'

He looked at her, still shocked. 'What . . . Who . . .'

She nodded at him, panting. 'I'm Sancia.' Her face went slack, and she suddenly vomited onto the side of the roof. She coughed and wiped her mouth. 'I'm the one who stole your shit.'

Sancia turned her head and vomited again. It felt like her brain was burning up. She'd pushed herself much too far tonight, and her body was breaking down.

She lugged the man to his feet and limped with him across the roof. He was shaking, blood-spattered, and he kept coughing and gagging after what the cord had done to his throat – but he still looked better than she felt. Her skull was fire and her bones were lead. If she managed to stay conscious, she'd count herself lucky.

She felt herself getting weaker as they hobbled over the peaks. The door to the south tower opened, and light spilled across the red-tile rooftop. The blade of light was a golden, buttery smear in the dark, and no matter how hard she blinked, she couldn't focus on it.

She realised her vision was blurred, like a drunk's. The man – Orso – seemed to be saying something to her, but she couldn't understand it.

This startled her. She knew she was doing bad, but not *that* bad.

'I'm sorry,' she mumbled. 'My head . . . It . . . My head really . . .'

She felt herself listing to the side, and knew that she needed to get the man away from one of the peaks – because she was about to collapse.

She got him to a decently flat part, then let go of him and knelt on the ground. She knew she didn't have long.

She fumbled for Clef, slipped him out of her sleeve, and stuffed him deep into her boot.

Maybe they wouldn't think to look there. Maybe.

Then she leaned forward until her forehead touched the roof. Things went dark.

14

'. . . say we just haul her out and dump her somewhere. She might have done us all a favour and up and died.'

'She's not dead. And she saved your life.'

'So what! She also robbed me and burned down your damned waterfront! God, I'd never have imagined the fabled lone survivor of Dantua could be so *soft*.'

'She is the only person who could possibly know who's behind all this. I doubt if *you* know much, Orso. From the looks of things, you've just been up here panicking.'

'I don't need this shit. She's a blood-spattered, grimy girl in *my* office! I could have the house guard come in and arrest her if I wanted!'

'If that happened, then they would ask me questions. And I would be obliged to answer them, Hypatus.'

'Oh, son of a bitch . . .'

Sancia felt consciousness flickering somewhere in the hollows of her head. She was lying on something soft, with a pillow under her head. People were talking around her, but she couldn't make sense of it. The fight on the rooftop was a handful of broken moments scattered through her mind. She picked through each one, trying to fit them together.

There was a man on the roof of a campo building, she thought. *About to be killed . . .*

Then she heard them: thousands and thousands and thousands of hushed, chattering voices.

Scrivings. More scrivings than I've ever been around. Where the hell am I?

She cracked an eye and saw a ceiling above her. It was an odd thing to think, but it was undoubtedly the most ornate ceiling she'd ever seen in her life, made of tiny green tiles and golden plaster.

She glimpsed movement nearby and shut her eye all the way again. Then she felt a cold rag being pressed against her head. She felt the rag speak to her, the cool swirl of water, the twist of so many fibres . . . It pained her greatly in her weakened state, but she managed not to flinch.

'She's got scars,' said a voice nearby – a girl's. Berenice's? 'Lots of them.'

'She's a thief,' said a raspy man's voice. She'd heard it on the rooftop, she remembered – that must be Orso. 'Probably a hazard of the damned job.'

'No, sir. This looks more like surgery. On her skull.'

There was a silence.

'She climbed the side of this building like a monkey in the canopies,' said Gregor's voice quietly. 'I've never seen anything like it. And she says she can hear scrivings.'

'She said she *what*?' said Orso. 'What rot! That's like saying you can taste a goddamn sonata! The girl must be a raving loon.'

'Maybe. But she knew where those men in the gravity rigs were. And there was something she did, with one of the rigs . . . I doubt if even you've ever seen anything like it. She made it—'

Sancia realised she needed to stop this line of discussion. Gregor was about to describe Clef's trick with the gravity plates; and Orso, apparently, was the man who'd owned or at least tried to own Clef, so he might be able to identify what he could do – which meant he might hear Gregor's story and realise Sancia was still walking around with him.

She sucked in a breath, coughed, and started to sit up.

'She wakes,' said Orso's voice sourly. 'Oh goody.'

Sancia looked around. She was lying on a sofa in a large and dazzlingly sumptuous office: rosy scrived lights flickered along the walls, a huge wooden desk stretched along one half of the room, and every inch of the walls was covered in shelves and books.

Sitting behind the desk was the man she'd saved – Orso – still stained with blood, though his throat was black and blue under the dried gore. He was glaring at her over a glass of bubble rum – an outrageously expensive liquor she'd stolen and sold before, but never tried. The gravity plates from the man who'd exploded on the roof sat on the desk before him, crusted with blood. Gregor Dandolo stood next to him, arms crossed, one forearm wrapped in bandages. And beside her, on the sofa, sat the girl, Berenice, who watched everything with a calm look of detached bemusement, as if this were all a birthday party entertainment gone thoroughly awry.

'Where the hell am I?' asked Sancia.

'You're in the Dandolo campo inner enclaves,' said Gregor. 'In the Hypatus Building. It's a sort of research buildi—'

'I know what the goddamn hypatus does,' said Sancia. 'I'm not an idiot.'

'Mm, no,' said Orso. 'Stealing my box was very much an idiot thing to do. That was you, yes? Can we cop to that?'

'I stole *a* box,' said Sancia. 'In *a* safe. I'm only just now figuring out who you are.'

Orso scoffed. 'You're either ignorant or a liar. So. It's Sancia, is it?'

'Yeah.'

'Never heard of you. Are you a canal operator?' asked Orso. 'What house do you work for?'

'None.'

'An independent, eh?' He poured another glass of bubble rum and tossed it back quickly. 'I never did much canal work on other houses, but I understood the independents didn't last long. About as reusable as a wooden knife. So. You must be good, if you're still breathing. Who was it? Who hired you to steal from me?'

'She said she doesn't know,' said Gregor.

'Can't she speak for herself?' said Orso.

Gregor glanced at Orso, then Sancia. 'Let's find out. Sancia – do *you* know what was in the box?'

At that, Orso froze. He glanced at Berenice, then stared resolutely at the floor.

'Go on,' said Gregor.

'I already told you,' said Sancia. 'My client said not to open the box.'

'That is not an answer,' said Gregor.

'It's what they said.'

'I don't doubt that.' He turned back to Orso. 'I doubt if you find that odd either, Hypatus. Because these criminals knew, just as you did, that its contents were Occidental – weren't they?'

Even though he was covered in blood, Sancia could see Orso going pale. 'What . . . What do you mean, Captain?' he asked.

'I will dispense with all pretences,' said Gregor, sighing. 'I've neither the time nor the energy for them.' He sat in a chair opposite Orso. 'You broke my mother's ban on the purchase of Occidental items. You tried to buy something valuable. This item was stored at my waterfront, for it could not be stored at the Dandolo campo. While it was there, young Sancia here was hired to steal it. Her partner, Sark, dutifully passed it along to their client – and was murdered for his troubles. And since then, this person has tried to kill anyone who's had the remotest of interactions with that item – Sancia, you, Berenice, and me. And I suspect that such efforts will not end tonight – because the item must be incredibly important. As Occidental tools generally are. After all, they say Crasedes built his own god out of metals and stones – and a tool that could do *that* would be beyond value. Yes?'

Orso started rocking back and forth.

'What was in the box, Orso?' asked Gregor. 'You need to tell me. It appears our lives depend on it.'

Orso rubbed his mouth, then suddenly turned to Sancia and spat, 'Where is it now? What did you *do* with it, damn you?'

'No,' said Gregor. 'First tell me what could be so valuable that it drove someone to try to kill us all tonight.'

Orso grumbled for a moment. Then he said, 'It was . . . It was a key.'

Sancia did her utmost not to emote, but her heart was suddenly thrumming. Or maybe she *should* emote, she thought. She tried her best to look confused.

Gregor raised an eyebrow. 'A key?'

'Yes. A key. Just a key. A golden key.'

'And did this key do anything?' asked Gregor.

'No one knew for certain. Grave robbers tend to lack the proper testing experience, you see. They found it in some giant, musty, collapsed fortress in Vialto. It was one of several Occidental tools they and the pirates and all the rest discovered.'

'You'd already tried to purchase one such tool, hadn't you?' asked Gregor.

'Yes,' said Orso through gritted teeth. 'I assume your mother told you about that. It was something like a lexicon. A big, ancient box. We paid dearly for it, and it vanished between Vialto and here.'

'How dear is dearly?' asked Gregor.

'A lot.'

Gregor rolled his eyes and looked at Berenice.

'Sixty thousand duvots,' said Berenice quietly.

Sancia coughed. 'Holy shit.'

'Yes,' said Orso. 'Hence Ofelia Dandolo's frustration. But the key . . . It was *worth* trying again. There are all kinds of stories about the hierophants using scrived tools to navigate the barriers of reality – barriers we ourselves barely understand!'

'So you just wanted to make more powerful tools,' said Gregor.

'No,' said Orso. 'Not just. Listen – when we inscribe an item with sigillums, we alter its reality, as anyone knows. But if you wipe the sigillums away or move beyond a lexicon, then those alterations vanish. The Occidentals not only developed tools that didn't need lexicons – when the Occidentals altered reality, it was *permanent*.'

'Permanent?' said Sancia.

'Yes. So, say you have a scrived hierophantic tool that, oh, can make a stream burble up from the ground. Sure, you'd need sigillums to make the tool – but if you use the tool on the ground, then that water is there *forever*. It will have edited reality in a direct, instantaneous, and *everlasting* fashion. Supposedly the wand of Crasedes could unthread reality and tie it all back together again, if the stories are to be believed.'

'Whoa,' said Sancia quietly.

'Whoa is right,' said Orso.

'How is that possible?' asked Gregor.

'That's one of the giant goddamn mysteries I was trying to solve!' said Orso. 'There are *some* theories. A few hierophantic texts call the basic sigils we use the *lingai terrora* – the language of the earth, of creation. But the Occidental sigils were the *lingai divina* – the language of God.'

'Meaning?' said Sancia.

'Meaning our sigils are the language of reality, of trees and grass and, hell, I don't know, fish. But Occidental sigils are the language God used to *fashion* that reality. So – use God's coded commands, and reality is your plaything. Still, just a theory. The key would have helped me figure out how true all that was.'

<*Clef,*> said Sancia. <*Are you hearing this?*> But Clef remained silent, stuffed down the side of her boot. She wondered if his efforts had broken him, just as her own had almost broken her tonight.

'But the key was stolen as well . . .' said Gregor.

'Well, originally I thought the damned thing had got burned to bits in the waterfront fire.' He scowled at Sancia. 'But the fire was you as well?'

Sancia shrugged. 'Shit got out of hand.'

'I'll say,' said Orso. 'But what happened next? What did you *do* with it?'

Sancia then reiterated the story she'd told Gregor – bringing it to the fishery, Sark's death, the fight, the escape.

'So you gave it over,' said Orso.

'I did,' she said.

'And your Sark said he suspected founder lineage behind this.'

'It's what he said.'

Orso looked at Gregor.

'*I* might be founder lineage,' said Gregor, 'but I think we can count me out, yes?'

'That's not what I was looking at you for, idiot!' snapped Orso. 'Do you believe her or not?'

Gregor thought about it. 'No,' he said. 'I don't. Not entirely. I think there's something she's not telling us.'

Shit, thought Sancia.

'Have you searched her?' said Orso.

Sancia's heart leapt in her chest. *Shit!*

'I've not had the time,' said Gregor. 'Nor am I, ah, willing to submit a woman to my touch without her conse—'

Orso rolled his eyes. 'Oh, for the love of God . . . Berenice! Would you *please* search Miss Sancia here for us?'

Berenice hesitated. 'Uh. Really, sir?'

'You've already been shot at,' said Orso, 'so you know this won't be the *worst* thing to have happened to you tonight. Just wash your hands well afterwards.' He nodded at Sancia. 'Go on. Stand up.'

Sighing, Sancia stood and raised her arms above her head. Berenice quickly patted her down. She was about a head taller than Sancia, so she had to stoop to do it. She paused at Sancia's hips, and pulled out the last remaining stun bomb, a handful of old lockpicks, and nothing else.

Sancia tried to suppress the relief in her face. *Thank God she didn't make me take my scrumming boots off.*

'That's it,' said Berenice as she stood. The girl turned away quickly, but oddly enough, she was blushing.

Gregor looked at Sancia hard. 'Really,' he said.

'Really,' said Sancia with as much defiance as she could muster.

'Terrific,' said Orso. 'So we have a thief with a dull story, and no treasure. Is there anything else? *Anything* else?'

Sancia thought rapidly. She knew there was quite a lot more. The problem was what to keep, and what to give up.

Her current problem was that despite saving Orso's life, her own still offered no value to these men. One bore the authorities assigned to him by the city, the other carried with him all the privileges of the merchant houses – and she was just a Commons thief who, as far as they were aware, no longer possessed the treasure everyone was seeking. Either one of them could have her killed, if they wished.

But she knew things they didn't. And that was worth something.

'There's more,' she said.

'Is there?' asked Gregor. 'You omitted something from what you told me?'

'Yeah,' she said. 'I didn't tell you the part about how my client is the one who shut down all the scrivings in the Commons.'

The room fell silent. Everyone stared at her.

'*What?*' sputtered Orso. 'What do you mean?'

'Your client?' said Gregor.

'Yeah,' said Sancia.

'One man did all that?' asked Gregor.

'Yeah,' said Sancia.

'*Yeah?*' said Orso, exasperated. 'You can't say something like that and then just keep saying *yeah*!'

'Yes. Please explain yourself,' said Gregor.

She told them about the escape, how she'd fled the fisheries and hidden in the Greens – omitting, of course, the bit about how Clef had helped her – and then she told them about the campo man, and his odd golden pocket watch.

Orso raised his hands, shaking his head. 'Stop. Stop! This is *insane*. You're telling me your client used one device, just *one*, and it somehow dampened or negated all the scrivings in the Greens, and Foundryside, and half a dozen other places to boot?'

'Basically,' said Sancia.

'One button, and all the commands and all the bindings and all the etchings just *stopped*?'

'Basically.'

He laughed. 'It's madness. It's idiotic! It's . . .'

'It's like the Battle of Armiedes,' said Berenice suddenly.

'Eh?' said Orso. 'What? What's that?'

She cleared her throat. 'The Battle of Armiedes, from the Occidental Empire. Long, long ago. There was a giant fleet of scrived ships, threatening to overthrow the empire. The hierophants met the fleet with but one boat – but that boat had a weapon on it, and when this weapon was used, all the ships . . .'

'Simply sank to the bottom,' said Orso slowly. 'That's right. I remember now. When did you learn about that, Berenice?'

'When you made me read those eighteen tomes of hierophantic history while we were negotiating with our people in Vialto.'

'Ah. Now that I think about it, it seems a bit cruel that I made you do that, Berenice.'

'That is because it was, sir.' She turned, looked at a bookcase behind her, and found one huge tome. She hauled it out, flipped it open, and scanned the lines. 'Here's the passage. "*. . . but by focusing the influences of the imperiat, the hierophants were able to wrest control of all the sigillums of their foes, and discard them as if they were chaff among the wheat. And so the king of Cambysius and all his men sank to the bottom of the bay, and drowned, and were never heard from again.*"' She looked around at them. 'That description always puzzled me . . . but if they were describing an actual tool, it might make sense.'

Orso cocked his head and half closed his eyes. 'By focusing the influences of the imperiat . . . Hm.'

'So it doesn't say if it looked like a big, weird pocket watch?' asked Sancia. 'Because what I saw looked like a big, weird pocket watch.'

'It doesn't,' said Berenice. 'But if the key survived, then I suppose other tools could have as well.'

'How does knowing this help us?' asked Gregor.

'It doesn't,' said Sancia. 'But I *saw* him. I saw his face. And he's got to be the man running the whole crew, from the men who ambushed me at the fishery to the ones who tried to kill us just tonight. If this gold pocket watch – this imperiat, if that's the word for it – if it's anything like the key, he probably spent fortunes getting it. You don't hand that off to your lieutenant. You keep it in your own damn pocket. So that must have been him.'

'What did he look like, Sancia?' asked Gregor.

'Like campo sort,' said Sancia. 'Clean. Clean skin. Clean clothes. Proper clothes. Like you, I guess,' she said, pointing at Berenice. 'Not like you,' she said to Orso.

'Hey,' said Orso, offended.

'What else?' said Gregor.

'Tall,' she said. 'Curly hair. Stooped posture. An indoor man for indoor work. Measly beard. But he didn't have a loggotipo, or crest, or anything so simple.'

'That is a *vague* description,' said Gregor. 'I suspect you will now say that if you saw him, you'd recognise him. Which would be useful for you – since we'd then need to look after you.'

'If I had more, I'd tell you more,' said Sancia.

'But it could be anyone!' said Orso. 'Any house! Morsini, Michiel,

Candiano – or even our own, I suppose! And we've no way of winnowing down our options!'

'The gravity rig doesn't tell you anything, Orso?' asked Gregor.

'No,' said Orso. 'Because *that* thing is some unprecedented, groundbreaking work! It's some truly genius shit, of a kind I've never seen before. Whoever's made this rig has been keeping their talent a dead secret, it seems.'

At that, Berenice cleared her throat. 'There is another unanswered question, sir. Whoever this man is – how did he find out about the Occidental lexicon? About the key? About Captain Dandolo going to capture Sancia, and my following them? How did he know all that?'

'That's, like, *six* unanswered questions!' said Orso. 'And the answer is simple! There's a leak, or a mole, or a spy somewhere here on the campo!'

Berenice shook her head. 'We only talked about the key to each other, sir. And there was no one around when you told me to follow Captain Dandolo, just today. But there *is* a commonality, sir.'

'There is?' said Gregor.

'There is. They all took place in the same location – your workshop.'

'So?' said Orso.

Berenice sighed. She then reached into a desk, produced a large sheaf of paper, dipped a pen in some ink, and then drew at least twenty elaborate, complicated, beautiful symbols onto the paper, dazzlingly, *dazzlingly* fast. It was like a party trick, effortlessly creating these gorgeous designs in the blink of an eye.

Berenice showed the piece of paper to Orso. They had no meaning to Sancia – but he gasped at the sight of it. 'No!' he said.

'I think so, sir,' she said.

He turned and stared at his workshop door, his jaw slack. 'It couldn't be . . .'

'What just happened?' asked Gregor. 'What is that you drew there, Berenice?'

'An old scriving problem,' said Berenice. 'An incomplete design, created to make students wonder – how do you make a rig that captures sounds of the air?'

'Someone's solved it,' said Orso faintly. 'It's a rig. A rig! It's all just a rig, isn't it?'

'I suspect so, sir,' said Berenice. 'A device, a secret one, planted in your workshop that somehow reports our conversations.'

For once, Gregor and Sancia seemed to be on the same side – both of them glanced at each other, bewildered.

'You think a *rig* is spying on you?' said Sancia.

'Isn't that impossible?' said Gregor. 'I thought scriving mostly moved things around or made them light or heavy.'

'That's true,' said Berenice. 'Scriving is good at big, simple processes, huge exchanges done on a grand scale. It makes things get fast, get hot, get cold. But little things, delicate things, complicated things . . . those are trickier.'

'Trickier,' said Orso. 'But not impossible. A sound rig – one that makes or captures noise – is a favourite theory problem for scrivers to toy with. But no one's ever actually *done* it.'

'But if these people have scrived gravity,' said Berenice, looking at the plates on Orso's desk, 'who knows what other barriers they've broken?'

'Assuming they could make such a rig – how could they get it in there?' asked Gregor.

'They can fly, arsehole,' said Sancia. 'And this place has windows.'

'Oh,' said Gregor. 'Right.'

'Still,' said Berenice. 'This is all just a theory I have. I could be totally wrong.'

'But if my client *did* put that thing in there,' said Sancia, 'now we just go in and get it – right? And then, I don't know, smash it or something, yeah?'

'Think,' said Orso. 'If the rig were obvious, we'd have already spotted the damn thing!'

'We've no idea how such a rig would even look,' said Berenice. 'It could look like anything. A plate. A pencil. A coin. Or it could be hidden in the walls, or floor, or ceiling.'

'And if we go digging around for it, and they *hear* us,' said Orso, 'then we'll have given the game away.'

Gregor looked at Sancia. 'But Sancia – you can hear scrivings, can't you?'

The room went quiet.

'Uh,' said Sancia. 'Y–yeah.' Of course, it'd been Clef who'd heard the gravity rigs converging on them before. Sancia had just told him a half truth. It was getting hard to keep up with all her lies.

'So you can just go in to the workshop and listen for it, yes?' said Gregor.

'Yes, can't you?' said Orso, sitting forward. He was looking at her a little too intensely.

'I can try,' said Sancia. 'But there's a lot of noise around here . . .' This was true. The campo was echoing with whispered commands, muttered scripts, quiet chanting. Every once in a while they would spike, growing loud as some vast, invisible infrastructure performed some task, and her brain could hardly bear it.

'Is there?' demanded Orso. 'And how can you hear this noise? How does this process work?'

'It just does. You want my help or not?'

'That depends on whether you can actually give it.'

Sancia didn't move.

'What's the problem here?' asked Orso. 'You go look, you find, that's it, right?'

Sancia looked around at them. 'If I do this . . . I'm not going to do it for free.'

'Oh, fine,' said Orso dismissively. 'You want money? I'm sure we can work out some kind of arrangement. Especially because I'm convinced you'll fail.'

'No,' said Gregor. 'Orso can promise you money all he likes. But he is not the person you are bargaining with. That would be me.' He held up the key to her bond.

'Son of a bitch,' snapped Sancia. 'I'm not your hostage! I'm not doing this for nothing!'

'You would be doing it because you owe it to me. And for the good of the city.'

'It's not my damned city! It's yours! I just live here, or try to! But you people are making it goddamn hard!'

He looked surprised by her ferocity. He considered it. 'Find the rig, if you can,' he said. 'Then we'll talk. I am not unreasonable when it comes to these things.'

'Could have scrumming fooled me,' said Sancia. She stood, opened the door to the workshop, and walked inside.

'Hey,' Orso called after her. 'Hey – *don't touch anything in there, all right?*'

Walking into Orso Ignacio's workshop would have been startling to anyone. The amount of stuff – the sheer, ungodly avalanche of so many *things* – was awe-inspiring.

The workshop was a large room, containing six long tables piled up with bowls of cooled metals, as well as styli, wooden buttons, and dozens and dozens of machines, devices, contraptions – or parts of them. Some of the rigs were *moving*, twirling ever so slowly or arrhythmically clunking away. Where the walls weren't covered with bookcases, they were covered with papers, drawings, engravings, sigil strings, and maps. The oddest device sat in the back, some kind of giant metal can full of discs covered in scrivings. It sat on rails that would slide it back into what appeared to be some kind of oven set in the wall, like the one they made pies in at the Greens. She supposed it was a test lexicon – a tiny version of the real thing. She'd heard of them from the Scrappers, but she'd certainly never seen one before.

It was a lot to see. But to Sancia, it was deafening.

The room echoed and swarmed with quiet chanting, all these scrived devices muttering like a rookery of uneasy crows. Sancia's mind was still weak after saving Orso, so it was like rubbing sand on a sunburn.

One thing's for sure, she thought. *These people are doing a hell of a lot more than the Scrappers ever were.*

She started stalking through the room, listening carefully. She walked past the innards of some component, dissected and laid out on a piece of linen; then a set of bizarre, scrived tools, which all seemed to be vibrating softly; then rows and rows of blank black boxes that were curiously veiled in shadow, as if they sucked up light itself.

If something in here is a traitor, she thought, *I don't know how I'm going to identify it.* She wished Clef were awake. He'd sniff it out right away.

Then she glimpsed something on the wall, and stopped.

Hanging on the wall between two bookcases was a large charcoal sketch of Clef. It wasn't perfect – the tooth was all wrong – but the head, with its odd butterfly-shaped hole, was perfect.

Sancia walked closer to it, and saw there was a handwritten note scrawled at the bottom:

What could it open?

For what grand lock was this designed??

This guy has been thinking about Clef for a lot longer than I have, she thought. *Maybe he knows more than he's letting on – just as I do.*

Then she saw there was a smudge at the bottom of the sketch, at the bottom, where the paper was crinkled. Someone must have pinched the paper there repeatedly.

She reached out, grabbed the paper, and lifted it – and saw there was something behind the sketch of Clef.

It was a large engraving. And the sight disturbed her.

The engraving depicted a group of men standing in a hall. They looked like monks, wearing plain robes, though each robe bore a curious insignia – perhaps the outline of a butterfly, she couldn't quite tell. She found she did not like the sight of the hall: it was a massive, ornate stone chamber, huge and blocky with angles in all the wrong places. It felt like light bent in the wrong ways in that room.

At the end of the hall was a box, like a giant casket or treasure chest. The group looked on as one man stood before the box, raised his hands, and seemed to open it by will alone. Emerging from this open box was . . .

Something. A person, perhaps. Perhaps a woman, or perhaps a statue, though there was something indistinct about the figure, like the artist had not been sure what they were depicting.

Sancia looked at the print at the bottom of the engraving. It read:

> CRASEDES THE GREAT IN THE CHAMBER AT THE CENTRE OF THE WORLD: The hierophants are recorded as believing the world is a machine, wrought by God, and somewhere at its heart is a chamber which was once His seat. Crasedes, finding the seat of God vacant,

> attempted to install a god of his own making in the chamber to oversee the world. This engraving, like so many sources, suggests he was successful. But if he was, it does not explain why his grand empire fell to ash and ruin.

She shivered, looking at the engraving. She remembered what Claudia and Giovanni had said the hierophants could do. Then she remembered what Clef did to the gravity rig – the vision of the man in the desert, turning out the stars.

She imagined what a man like Orso Ignacio could do with Clef, and shivered again.

Then she heard it – a chattering, a murmuring. But this one was louder than the others.

That's . . . unusual.

She shut her eyes, listening to it, and walked to the back of the room. The sound was much louder here.

Just like the gravity plates, she thought. *So maybe . . . it's either really powerful, or made by the same person?*

She realised the noise was coming from a desk at the back, some kind of drafting table where Orso scrawled out strings of sigils. She tilted her head to it, listening to the pencils, the inkpots, the blocks of stone, and then . . .

A small, golden statue of a bird sat on the corner of the desk. Sweating, Sancia picked it up and held it up to her ear. The sound of it was almost deafening to her.

If it's anything in this room, she thought, *it's this.* She set it back down, feeling quite pleased. She'd never used her talents like this before. As she walked back to the office, she wondered – ever so briefly – what else she could do.

Ten minutes later they all huddled around a table in Orso's workshop, watching as he turned the golden statue over. There was a small, copper plate on the bottom with a large screw in the centre. Orso glanced around at them, held a finger to his lips, picked up a screwdriver, and began to unscrew it. He gently, gently plucked the screw out, and then, with a tiny, flat tool, pried out the plate.

Orso's mouth fell open in a silent gasp. Inside the statue was a device – but a device so tiny, so fragile, it was like it was made of spider webs and mouse bones.

He grabbed a light and a magnifying glass and peered carefully at it. His eyes shot wide, and he gestured to Berenice, who also took a look. She blinked, startled, and glanced at Orso, who nodded, his face serious.

Finally the inspection was finished. Orso gingerly placed the device on the table, and they all crept back into the office.

Orso shut the door to his workshop – and then he erupted. 'I've been a goddamn fool!' he shouted. 'I've been a slack-jawed, crotch-pawing *fool*!'

'So . . . it seems your suspicion was correct?' asked Gregor.

'Of course!' cried Orso. 'God, we're in a state. Who knows what they've heard? What have I said in front of that stupid little bird? And I never, never, never would have known!'

'You're welcome,' said Sancia.

'That statue is an exact copy of one that once sat on my desk,' he continued, ignoring her. 'I suppose they must have replaced it long ago with an altered version.'

'By flying up using those rigs,' said Gregor.

'Yes,' said Berenice, shaken. 'And whoever made that thing is . . . good.'

'Damned good,' said Orso. '*Amazingly* good. That's top-rate work, there! I feel sure if someone was *that* good in this city, we'd all know about it. Everyone would be lining up to lick his candle, I've no doubt!'

Gregor pulled a face. 'Thank you for that elaboration.'

'Have you ever seen anything like it, Captain?' asked Orso. 'You're more well travelled than I am, and the houses have used a lot of experimental stuff during the wars. Have you seen any military faction using rigs like *this*?'

He shook his head. 'No. And the only thing I've ever seen that was similar to the gravity rigs is a lorica – and those rigs far outclassed any lorica.'

'What's a lorica?' asked Sancia.

'It's a scrived suit of armour,' said Gregor. 'But unlike the armour we have here in Tevanne, which is scrived to be both preternaturally light and preternaturally strong, a lorica also augments the movements of the person within it. It amplifies their gravity, in other words, making them faster and stronger than a normal person.'

'I thought scriving gravity was illegal,' said Sancia.

'It is,' said Gregor. 'Which is why loricas are only used abroad in the wars, and in limited numbers, at that.' He rubbed his face. 'Now. Can we focus on the consequential conclusions, please?'

'Yeah,' said Sancia. 'What the hell do we do about this? Can't you look at that thing and figure out . . . I don't know, something?'

Berenice took a breath. 'Well. What I believe we saw in there was an advanced version of twinning.'

'What, like the explosive I used at the waterfront? And that plate of yours?' asked Sancia.

'Exactly. But what's been twinned is a tiny, tiny, *tiny* needle, in the centre of the device. A delicate one that's somehow terribly sensitive to noise.'

'How is a needle sensitive to noise?' asked Gregor.

'Because sound travels through the air,' said Berenice. 'In waves.'

Sancia and Gregor stared at her.

'It does?' said Sancia.

'Like . . . the ocean?' said Gregor.

'We don't have time to amend your dogshit educations!' said Orso. 'Assume that *yes*, it does! The sound hits the needle, and it shakes it. The needle vibrates. But it's twinned, so there's another needle that vibrates with it – somewhere.'

'And that's the tricky part,' said Berenice. 'What then? This second needle vibrates, and then . . .'

'Oh, come on, Berenice,' said Orso. 'It's obvious! The second needle scratches its vibrations into a soft surface – tar, or rubber, or wax of some kind. Then that surface hardens . . .'

Her eyes grew wide. 'Then you can run another needle through the surface, through all the scratches . . . and it'll duplicate the noise.'

'Right. It'd be a shitty rendition, but it'd be enough to catch words.'

'Wait,' said Gregor, holding up a hand. 'Are you really saying someone has come up with a scrived method of capturing sounds out of the *air*?'

'That's crazy,' said Sancia. 'So you could make the same sound or conversation over and over and over again?'

'You just used some magic-ear bullshit to find that damn thing!' said Orso angrily, pointing at the door. 'And a flying man just tried to throw me off the roof! Our idea of "crazy" is obviously in need of some updates!'

'But this is some delicate twinning,' said Berenice.

'How is that significant?' asked Gregor.

'Twinning is a proximal effect,' she said. 'Usually the two twinned items don't have to be *too* close, since the effects you want to twin often aren't complicated. Like a detonator – it's motion, friction, and heat. You can twin those effects over miles. But *this* . . . This is much more complicated.'

Orso stopped pacing. 'So the second needle has to be very close!' he said. 'You're right, Berenice! The apparatus that writes down the sound, that engraves the vibrations in wax – it has to be somewhere near for it to accurately capture *all* the sounds!'

'Somewhere on the property, sir,' said Berenice. 'Probably somewhere in this very building. That's the only way to make it work properly.'

'You!' Orso pointed at Sancia. 'Do the thing again and *find* it!'

Sancia froze. That was far, far beyond her talents. Hearing a powerful device in a single room was one thing – but combing an entire building to find a specific rig was quite another. She'd need Clef for that – if he ever spoke again.

To her relief, Gregor cleared his throat. 'That will have to wait,' he said.

'What!' said Orso. 'Why, damn it?'

Gregor nodded to the window. 'Because the sun is rising. People will be coming here soon. And when they do, it would probably be best if they did not find a blood-spattered girl wandering the halls with a blood-spattered hypatus.'

Orso sighed. 'Goddamn it. We're running out of time.'

'What do you mean?' said Gregor.

'I have a Tevanni council meeting tomorrow about the Commons blackouts. Tons of merchant-house officers from all four houses will be there, along with me and Ofelia. I'll be seen by loads of people.'

'So word'll get out that you're not dead,' said Sancia. 'Which will tip off whoever sent these assassins.'

'And they'll come for the captured sounds, to see what happened,' said Berenice.

'Right,' said Orso. 'We've got to get to it before them.'

'We'll return as soon as we can,' said Gregor. 'But for now, we need a place to clean up.'

Orso thought about it. Then he turned to Berenice and said, 'Check out a carriage again, and take them to my house. Get them bathed and cleaned up. They can spend the day there. But this is *not* a permanent fix. Even the inner enclaves aren't safe.'

15

Berenice checked out a small passenger carriage and drove them north, grumbling a touch about 'not being a damned house servant.' Sancia stared out the windows as they drove. She hadn't really been paying attention before, but now she couldn't stop staring at the inner Dandolo enclaves.

The strangest thing about them was that almost all of them *glowed*. The enclaves glowed a soft, warm, rosy colour that seemed to emanate from the corners of the huge towers, or from the bases, perhaps – it was hard to tell. She suspected that scrived lights had been built into the façades, lights that had been designed to cast indirect luminescence so no beams of light shone into anyone's windows at night.

There were other wonders, of course. There were floating lanterns, like the ones her client had used to search for her: they drifted in flocks above the main fairways like schools of jellyfish. There were also many narrow canals, full of needle-shaped boats with reclining seats. She imagined residents hopping in a boat and being zipped off across the waters to their destination.

It was unreal. To imagine that people lived in muddy alleys mere miles from here, that she herself had lived in a squalid rookery that shared the same rain clouds as this place . . . She glanced at Berenice and Gregor. Berenice was totally indifferent to it all. Gregor, on the other hand, had a faint scowl on his face.

Finally they came to a tall, gated mansion, the sort of place for a prestigious campo official. It was impossible to imagine Orso Ignacio living here – yet the copper gates silently parted before them.

'The hypatus bound them to respond to my blood,' said Berenice. She didn't sound too happy about it. 'Along with his own, of course. It's a favourite trick of his. He rarely comes here.'

'Why wouldn't he come to the goddamn mansion he owns?' asked Sancia.

'He gets the house as a condition of his position – he didn't go out and buy the place. I don't think he actually cares about it at all.'

This became apparent when they walked inside: the carpets, tables, and lanterns all bore a faint coating of dust. 'Where does he sleep?' asked Sancia.

'In his office,' said Berenice, 'I think. I've never actually seen him sleep.' She gestured to the stairs. 'The bedrooms are upstairs on the fourth floor, as are the bathing facilities. I suggest you both use them if you're going to be on the campo, in case someone spots you – it would be wise if you looked the part.' She looked at them and wrinkled her nose. 'And you don't, right now.'

Gregor thanked her and Berenice departed. Sancia wandered upstairs to the third floor, where she found an immense set of windowed doors that opened onto the balcony. She opened them, stepped out, and looked.

The Dandolo inner enclaves curled out before her, bright and creamy and pink as a rose. There was a park across the cobblestone fairway, with a hedge maze and bursting flowers. People were walking the paths together. It was a stupefying idea to Sancia – in the Commons, if you were outdoors at night, there was a decent chance you'd die.

'They went a bit overboard, didn't they,' said Gregor's voice behind her.

'Eh?' said Sancia.

He stood beside her. 'With the lights. The Daulos call us the glow-men, in their language, because we tend to put lights on everything.'

'Something you picked up in the Enlightenment Wars?'

'Yes.' He turned to her, leaning up against the balcony. 'Now. Our deal.'

'You want my client,' said Sancia.

'I want your client,' he said. 'Very much so. If you can give him to me.'

'In what condition? You want his name, his head, or what?'

'No, no,' said Gregor. 'No heads. These are the stakes of our deal – you not only help me find him, but also get the evidence I need to *expose* him. I don't want his name, his money, his company, or his blood. I want *ramifications*. I want *consequences*.'

'You want justice,' she said, sighing.

'I want justice. Yes.'

'And why do you think I can help you get it?'

'Because you have evaded nearly every effort to kill you or seize you. And you stole from me. You are – and this is *not* a compliment, mind – a very accomplished sneak. And I suspect we will need someone with your talents if we are to succeed.'

'But this is a tall goddamn order!' said Sancia. 'Sark said he thought our client was founder lineage, just like you, or someone close to it. That means me working in places like this.' She nodded at the city below. 'In the enclaves. The places that are basically designed to make sure people like me die the second I step foot in them.'

'I'll help you. And Orso will too.'

'Why would Orso help me?'

'To get back his key, of course,' said Gregor. 'Along with any other Occidental treasures the man's been hoarding. Our opponent has stolen two items from Orso, and seems to have acquired a third – this imperiat. No doubt there's more.'

'No doubt.' She suppressed the flicker of anxiety in her belly. She wasn't sure what seemed harder – delivering founderkin to Gregor, or returning a treasure she wasn't supposed to have. 'So I help you get this . . . this justice of yours, and then you let me go?'

'In essence.'

She shook her head. 'Justice . . . God. Why are you doing all this?

Why are you out here risking your life?'

'Is justice such an odd thing to desire?'

'Justice is a luxury.'

'No,' said Gregor. 'It is not. It is a right. And it is a right that has long been denied.' He stared out at the city. 'The chance for reform . . . for real, genuine reform for this city . . . I would shed every drop of blood in my body for such a thing. And then, of course, there is the fact that if we fail, then a vicious person will possess tools of near-divine power. Which I, personally, would find quite bad.' He took out the key to her bond and held it out. 'You can do the honours yourself, I believe.'

'I thought Orso was crazy,' she said, unlocking the bond. 'But you're *really* crazy.'

'I'd thought you would be more amenable to the idea than others,' he said lightly.

'And why's that?'

'For the same reason I think wearing that bond irked you so, Sancia,' he said. 'And the same reason you conceal the scars on your back.'

She froze and slowly turned to stare at him. 'What?' she said softly.

'I am a travelled man, Sancia,' he said. 'I know the look of you. I have seen such things before. Though I hope I never will agai—'

She stepped forward, sticking her finger in his face. 'No,' she said fiercely. '*No.*'

He drew back, startled.

'I am *not* having this conversation with you,' she said. 'Not now. Maybe not ever.'

He blinked. 'All right.'

She slowly lowered her finger. 'You don't know a goddamn thing about me,' she said. Then she walked back indoors.

She stalked upstairs, found a bedroom, and shut and locked the door. She stood there in the darkened room, breathing hard.

Then a voice spoke up in her mind: <*That was a bit of an overreac-*

tion, wasn't it, kid?>

<*Clef!*> she said. <*Holy shit! You're alive!*>

<*As much as a key could be, yeah.*>

<*How long have you been . . . I don't know, there?*>

<*Just now. That was the first time I've seen the captain look scared of anyone. How about getting me the hell out of your shoe?*>

She sat down in the middle of the floor, hauled her boot off, and held him in her bare hands. Then she pummelled him with questions. <*Where did you go, Clef? How did you do that thing with the gravity rig? Are you hurt? Are you all right?*>

He was silent for a long time. <*No,*> he said in a quiet voice. <*No, I'm not all right. But . . . we'll get to that. First – where are we? Are we in, like, a mansion?*>

She tried to catch him up as fast as she could.

<*So,*> he said. <*You're . . . working for the captain now?*>

<*Kind of. I like to think it's more of a partner thing, personally.*>

<*He can still kill you at any time, right?*>

<*Well. Yeah?*>

<*Then you're not partners. You're also working for this Orso guy? The guy who tried to buy me? And you're going to steal, uh, me back for him?*>

<*I think I vaguely agreed to that.*>

<*How's that going to work?*>

<*If you haven't figured out yet that I'm making this up as I go, Clef, I don't know what to tell you.*>

Clef said nothing for a bit. A flock of floating lanterns trickled through the street below, casting pulsing pink light on the ceiling.

<*How did you do that thing with the gravity rig, Clef?*> she asked. <*How did you make it control the gravity of . . . of everything? And what happened to you?*>

<*It's . . . hard for me to explain,*> he said, sighing. <*It's all a matter of boundaries. I can't make a scrived device do anything beyond its own boundaries. I can't make a rig that heats up iron then turn that iron into clay or snow or whatever, in other words.*>

<*So?*>

<*So, with the gravity rig, its boundaries were really, really big, and really, really* vague. *It gave me a lot to work with. Even though the device itself couldn't stand the strain – because the more a rig pushes against its boundaries, the more it falls apart. And when I made it do that, I . . . I remembered some-*

thing. And then I fell asleep, and dreamed.>

<*You fell . . . asleep? What did you remember?*>

<*I remembered . . . someone else who'd been able to manipulate gravity. Someone from long ago . . . A shadow of a person to me now.*> His voice took on a dreamy cadence. <*He could make anything float . . . and whenever he wished, he could fly through the air, like a sparrow in the night . . .* >

Sancia's skin crawled. <*But . . . Clef, the only people who've ever been able to fly were the hierophants.*>

<*Yeah. I know. I think . . . I think I was remembering the person who made me, Sancia.*>

She didn't know what to say to that.

<*The hierophants are all dead, aren't they?*> he asked.

<*Yes.*>

<*That makes me feel . . . alone,*> he said quietly. <*And frightened.*>

<*Why frightened?*>

<*Because when I dreamed, I . . . I remembered my making. I can show you, if you like.*>

<*What do you mean, show me?*>

<*Here. I'm going to put something into your mind now. Something small. Think of it like you're in the water, swimming, and I'm going to throw you a line. Focus, and grab on to it.*>

<*O . . . Okay?*>

There was a pause. And then . . . she felt it.

Or, rather, she heard it: it was a quiet, rhythmic *tap-tap, tap, tap* – a soft series of beats and pulses, echoing through her mind. She listened to it, reached out, grasped it, and then . . .

The beats unfolded, expanded, and enveloped her, filling her thoughts.

And then the memory took her.

Sand. Darkness. Quiet, anxious mutterings from somewhere nearby. She was lying on a stone surface, staring up into the darkness.

Midnight, she thought to herself. *When the world grinds to a stop, and then restarts.* She knew that – but she didn't know how she knew it.

Then a flame, bright and hot, molten metal glowing in the shadows. She felt pain, fierce and terrible, piercing her, running her through, and she heard herself cry out – but it wasn't her, she was someone else, she knew that – and then, suddenly, she felt herself fill this form, this function, this design.

She felt her mind flooding into the shaft, the teeth, the notches, the tip. She became the key, became this thing, this apparatus. Yet she now understood that she was to be much, *much* more than a key.

A compendium, a compilation. A device filled with so, *so* much knowledge of scrivings, of sigils, of the language and makeup of the world. A tool, bright and terrible. Just like a blade is meant to part wood or flesh, she was meant to part . . .

Sancia gasped and the memory released her. It was too much, too much. She was back in the bedroom, yet she was so stunned she nearly collapsed.

<*Did you see?*> Clef asked.

She tried to catch her breath. <*That was you? That . . . That happened to you?*>

<*This is a memory I have. I'm not sure if it's mine or someone else's . . . because I'm not totally sure it happened to me. It's all I know.*>

<*But . . . But if that's how you were made, Clef . . . it seems like you weren't always a key. It seemed like, for a second there, you used to be a person.*>

More silence. Then: <*Yeah. Weird, right? I'm not sure what to think of that. Perhaps that's why I remember the taste of wine, and what it feels like to sleep, and the smell of the desert at night . . .* > He laughed sadly. <*I don't think I was supposed to know.*>

<*Know what?*>

<*To know myself. I'm a device, Sancia. They took me and they put me inside this thing, and rigs aren't supposed to be self-aware. It's like you said when we first met. I sat in the dark for so long. I wasn't supposed to wait that long.*> A pause. <*You know what that means, don't you? I'm a machine that's falling apart. And eventually, I won't work. I'm . . . I think I'm dying. Do you see?*>

She sat there for a moment, stunned. <*What? Clef . . . Are you . . . Are you sure?*>

<*I can feel it happening. Me, being sentient . . . I'm like a tumour inside the key. I grow and I grow, but I'm not what was intended. I'm an error. And it's breaking the rest of me apart. And the people who could fix me . . . they're all dead. They died hundreds if not thousands of years ago.*>

Sancia swallowed. She'd imagined many horrors when it came to Clef – mostly that he might fall into the wrong hands, or she might lose him – but the idea of him dying had never occurred to her. *<How long do you have?>*

<I'm not sure. It's a . . . process. The more I do, the more I break down. So it could be months. Or it could be weeks.>

<So I can't . . . I can't use y—>

<No,> he said firmly. *<I want you to use me, Sancia. I want to . . . to do things with you. To be alive with you, to help you. You're the only person I can remember ever truly knowing. I'm not even sure if I want to be fixed, to be honest, even if someone could fix me – because then I'd go back to my original state. A device with no mind at all.>*

She sat there, trying to process this. *<I don't know what to think about this.>*

<Then don't. I think you need rest. I also think you need a bath.>

<People keep telling me that.>

<That's because you do.>

<I can't bathe. I can't sit in water. That's too much contact – it'll kill me.>

<Well. Try something at least. It'll make you feel better.>

She hesitated, then walked into the bathing room. It was all marble and metal with a huge porcelain tub, and it had mirrors – something she'd seen only rarely in her life. She looked around for a place to hide Clef in case someone walked in, and settled on a cabinet.

<Don't hate Captain Dandolo,> said Clef as she set him down. *<I think he's broken, just like you and me. He's just trying to fix the world because it's the only way he knows to fix himself.>*

Sancia shut the cabinet.

Alone in the bathing room, Sancia stripped down. Then she looked at herself in the mirrors.

Her arms and thighs and shoulders, strong and rippling and wiry. Her belly and breasts, covered in rashes and bites and filth.

She turned around, and saw her back. She took a sharp breath in.

She'd thought they'd have gone away by now, or shrunk, but they seemed just as huge as ever, the bright, shiny strips of scars that ran from her shoulders down to her buttocks. She stared at them, transfixed. It had been so long since she'd last seen them, for mirrors were rare in the Commons.

They'd told stories of slaves that had bravely borne countless whippings, stoically taking lash after lash. But the instant she'd been whipped, Sancia had realised it'd all been a lie. The second the lash had touched her, all her pride and fury and hope had been dashed away. It was surprising, how fragile your idea of yourself was.

Sancia stood in the tub, soaked a cloth in hot water, and scrubbed herself clean. As she did, she told herself she was not a slave anymore. She told herself she was free, and strong, that she'd been alone for years, and she'd be alone again one day, and she would, as always, survive. Because surviving was what Sancia did best. And as she scrubbed at her filthy, scarred skin, she tried to tell herself that the drops on her cheeks were just water from the spigots, and nothing more.

II

CAMPO

And so great Crasedes came to the city of Apamea, on the edge of the Sea of Ephios, and though no text survives of what he said to the kings of this city, it is clear from secondhand sources that he brought his usual message: of co-option, of integration into their empire, and urgings of surrender. By now word had spread of the hierophants' arrival in the region, and many were fearful – but the kings and wealthy landowners of Apamea refused him, and rudely rebuffed great Crasedes.

Crasedes did not respond with any wrath, as some had feared. Instead he simply walked to the city square, where he sat in the dust and began to build a cairn out of grey stones.

The legend goes that Crasedes built the cairn from noon to sunset, and the height of the construct grew to be extraordinary. Exact accounts differ regarding the height – some say a hundred feet tall, others hundreds of feet. However, every version of the story omits two critical parts: if the cairn of stones was extraordinarily tall, how did Crasedes, an average man in height, manage to keep stacking the stones on the top? It was said Crasedes could make many things float, and could fly himself – but this is not noted in this story. So – how?

And secondly, where did all these stones come from?

Some sources suggest that Crasedes had assistance in the

construction of the cairn. These renditions claim that before he began, Crasedes took out a small metal box, and opened it – though the box appeared to be empty to onlookers. However, the stories say that the people of Apamea then saw footprints forming in the dust around the cairn, footprints far larger than a person's. These versions would suggest that Crasedes had held some kind of invisible sprite or entity within the box, which he released to aid him. Yet such tales hew close to some of the more fantastical stories regarding the hierophants – fables of Crasedes making the stars dance with his magic wand, and so on – and thus must be treated with skepticism.

Regardless of the particulars, Crasedes began to build the cairn, and did not stop. And as night fell, and as they watched this curious display, the people of Apamea suddenly grew fearful, and left.

In the morning, when they returned to the city square, Crasedes was seated in the dust, still waiting patiently, and the cairn was gone – as were, the people later discovered, all the kings and wealthy landowners of Apamea, along with their families, old and young, and all their livestock, and the very buildings they'd lived and worked in. All had vanished overnight without a sound – perhaps taken to the place that the cairn had also gone.

The purpose of the cairn remains unknown, as does the final destination of those who resisted Crasedes in Apamea, who are still lost to history. Apamea, of course, no longer resisted Crasedes, and submitted to the rule of the hierophants – though it, like all of the lands of the Occidental Empire, was eventually totally destroyed. As is well documented, it is unknown if a civil war was the source of this conflict, or if, perhaps, the hierophants battled against another, greater force.

Such an idea troubles me – and yet, it must be considered.

– GIANCAMO ADORNI, DEPUTY HYPATUS OF THE HOUSE OF GUARCO, *COLLECTED TALES OF THE OCCIDENTAL EMPIRE*

16

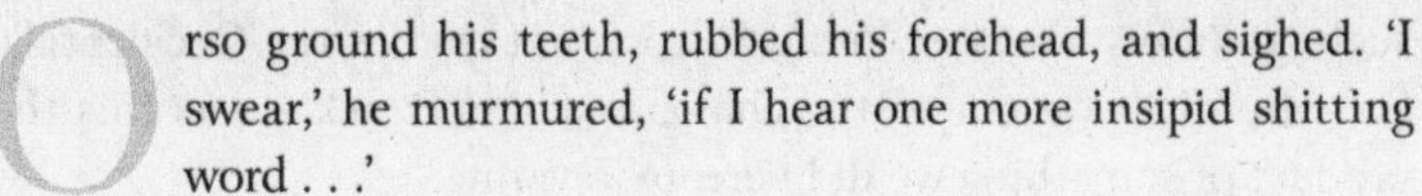

Orso ground his teeth, rubbed his forehead, and sighed. 'I swear,' he murmured, 'if I hear one more insipid shitting word . . .'

'Quiet,' whispered Ofelia Dandolo.

Orso rested his head on the table before him. He was talented at putting abstract concepts together. That was essentially his entire profession: he wrote essays and arguments that convinced reality to do some new and interesting things.

So if there was one thing he truly despised – one thing that absolutely, positively drove him mad – it was when someone just could not get to the scrumming point. To observe someone fumbling around with words and ideas like a schoolboy trying to navigate a woman's under-robes was akin to swallowing shards of glass.

'The point is thusly,' said the speaker – a Morsini deputy hypatus, some overdressed arsehole whose name Orso couldn't be bothered to remember. 'The point is – is it possible to develop criteria by which we can measure, analyse, and establish the possibility that the Commons blackouts were a natural occurrence – by which I mean some by-product of a storm or meteorological fluctuation in the atmosphere – as opposed to being *anthropological* – by which I mean, human-caused?'

'Little shit probably just learned the word,' growled Orso. Ofelia Dandolo glanced at him. Orso cleared his throat as if the comment had been a cough.

This was now hour four of this Tevanni council meeting on the blackouts. To his surprise, they'd somehow managed to drag both Eferizo Michiel and Torino Morsini out of their campo cradles. You almost never saw either house head at all, let alone in the same place. Eferizo was trying to sit up and look nobly concerned, whereas Torino was nakedly emanating boredom. Ofelia, as always, comported herself quite well, in Orso's opinion – but he could see even her stamina was flagging.

Yet Orso was quite alert. He kept looking from face to face, thinking. This room contained some of the most powerful men in the city – and many of them were founder lineage. If anyone acted surprised to see him alive – well. That would be a helpful indication.

Ofelia cleared her throat. 'There is no recorded *natural* occurrence of scriving blackouts,' she said. 'Not like a typhoon or some such, anyways – neither in our history, nor that of the Occidentals. So, why don't we cut to the chase, and simply ask – was this the product of something we did here, in Tevanne?'

The room swelled up with muttering.

'Are you accusing another merchant house of this act, Founder?' demanded a Morsini representative.

'I accuse no one,' said Ofelia, 'for I understand nothing. Could it not have been an *accidental* effect of some research endeavour?'

The muttering grew louder. 'Ridiculous,' someone said.

'Preposterous.'

'Outrageous.'

'If Dandolo Chartered is willing to make such a supposition,' said one of the Michiel deputies, 'perhaps the Dandolo hypatus can provide us with some supporting research?'

All eyes turned to look at Orso.

Great, he thought.

He cleared his throat and stood. 'I must *slightly* correct my founder's testimony,' he said. 'There is, in hierophantic history, one obscure legend in which the phenomenon we witnessed possibly appears – the Battle of Armiedes.' He coolly looked around at the gathered crowd. *Come on, you bastard,* he thought. *Break for me. Show yourself.* 'Such methodologies remain beyond the abilities of Tevanne, of course,' he said. 'But if we trust our histories, then it is possible.'

One of the Morsinis sighed, exasperated. 'More hierophants, more magicians! What more could we expect from a disciple of Tribuno Candiano?'

The room went silent at that. Everyone stared at the Morsini representative, who slowly grew aware that he had greatly overstepped.

'I, ah, apologise,' he said. He turned toward a part of the room that had hitherto remained quiet. 'I misspoke, sirs.'

Everyone slowly turned to look at the portion of the room dominated by Company Candiano representatives. There were far fewer of them than the other houses. Sitting in the founder's seat was a young man of about thirty, pale and clean-shaven, wearing dark-green robes and an ornate flat cap trimmed with a large emerald. He was an oddity in many ways: for one, he was about a third of the age of the other three founders – and he was not, as everyone knew, an actual founder, or indeed a blood relation to the Candiano family at all.

Orso narrowed his eyes at the young man. For though Orso hated many people in Tevanne, he especially loathed Tomas Ziani, the chief officer of Company Candiano.

Tomas Ziani cleared his throat and stood. 'You did not misspeak, sir,' he said. 'My predecessor, Tribuno Candiano, brought great ruin to our noble house with his Occidental fascinations.'

Our noble house? thought Orso. *You married into it, you little shit!*

Tomas nodded at Orso. 'An experience that the Dandolo hypatus, of course, is keenly aware of.'

Orso gave him the thinnest of smiles, bowed, and sat.

'It is, of course, preposterous to imagine that any Tevanni merchant house is capable of reproducing any hierophantic effects,' said Tomas Ziani, 'let alone one that could have accomplished the blackouts, to say nothing of the moral implications. But I regret to say that Founder Dandolo has not truly cut to the quick of the question – what I think we all want to know is, if we want to find out if any merchant house is behind the blackouts . . . how shall we institute this authority? What body shall have this oversight? And who shall make up this body?'

The room practically exploded with discontented mutterings.

And with that, Orso thought with a sigh, *young Tomas delivers the killing blow to this idiot meeting.* For this notion was heresy in Tevanne – the idea of some kind of municipal or governmental authority that could inspect the business of the merchant houses? They would genuinely rather fail and die than submit to that.

Ofelia sighed. A handful of tiny, white moths flitted around her head. 'What a waste of time,' she said softly, waving them away.

Orso glanced at Tomas, and found, to his surprise, that the young man was watching him. Specifically, he was looking at Orso's scarf – very, very hard.

'Maybe not entirely,' he said.

When the meeting closed, Orso and Ofelia held a brief conference in the cloisters. 'To confirm,' she said quietly. 'You do not think this is sabotage?'

'No, Founder,' he said.

'Why are you so certain?'

Because I have a grubby thief who says she saw it happen, he thought. But he said, 'If it was sabotage, they could have done a hell of a better job. Why target the Commons? Why only glancingly affect the campos?'

Ofelia Dandolo nodded.

'Is there a . . . *reason* to suspect sabotage, Founder?' he asked.

She gave him a piercing look. 'Let's just say,' she said reluctantly, 'that your recent work on light could attract . . . attention.'

This was interesting to him. Orso had been fooling around with scrived lights for decades, but it was only at Dandolo Chartered, with its superior lexicon architecture, that he'd started trying to engineer the reverse: scriving something so it *absorbed* light, rather than emitting it, producing a halo of perpetual shadow, even in the day.

So the suggestion that Ofelia Dandolo might worry about other houses fearing this technology . . . that was curious.

What exactly, he wondered, *is she planning to veil in shadow?*

'As in all things,' she said, 'I expect your secrecy, Orso. But especially there.'

'Certainly, Founder.'

'Now . . . if you will excuse me, I've a meeting shortly.'

'I as well,' he said. 'Good day, Founder.'

He watched her go, then turned and swept out to the hallways around the council building, where the legions of attendants and administrators and servants hovered to assist the throngs of great and noble men within. Among them was Berenice, yawning and rubbing her puffy eyes. 'Just four hours?' she said. 'That was quick, sir.'

'Was it,' said Orso, rushing past her. He walked through the crowd of people dressed in white and yellow – Dandolo Chartered colours – and moved on to the red-and-blue crowd – Morsini House – and then the purple-and-gold crowd – which was, of course, Michiel Body Corporate.

'Ah,' said Berenice. 'Where are we going, sir?'

'You are going somewhere to sleep,' said Orso. 'You'll need it tonight.'

'And when will you sleep, sir?'

'When do I ever sleep, Berenice?'

'Ah. I see, sir.'

He stopped at the crowd of people dressed in dark green and black – Company Candiano colours. This crowd was much smaller, and much less refined. The effects of the Candiano bankruptcy still lingered, it seemed.

'Uh . . . what would you be planning to do here, sir?' asked Berenice with a touch of anxiety.

'Ask questions,' he said. He peered through the crowd. At first he wasn't sure she'd be there and thought himself absurd for even imagining it. But then he saw her: one woman, standing apart from the group, her posture tall and noble.

Orso stared at her, and instantly regretted this idea. The woman wore a bewilderingly complicated dress, with puffs on her upper sleeves and her hair twisted up in an intricate brooch that was covered in pearls and ribbons. Her face was painted white, with the now-fashionable blue bar across her eyes.

'My God,' said Orso quietly. 'She went in for all that aristocratic fluffery. I can't believe it.'

Berenice glanced at the woman. Her eyes grew wide, and she stared at Orso in naked terror. 'Don't, sir.'

He flapped a hand at her. 'Go home, Berenice.'

'Don't . . . Don't go talk to her. That would be *deeply* unwise.'

He understood her fear perfectly: the idea of approaching the daughter of the founder of a competing merchant house was mad. *Especially* if she was also the wife of the chief officer of that same house. But Orso had built a career on bad choices. 'Enough,' he said.

'It would be *outrageously* inappropriate for you to approach her,' she said, 'whatever your . . .'

He looked at her. 'Whatever my what?'

Berenice glared at him. 'Whatever your history with her, sir.'

'My own affairs,' said Orso, 'are just that – *my own*. And unless you want to get tangled up in them, I suggest you leave now, Berenice.'

She looked at him for a moment longer. Then, sighing, she walked away.

Orso watched her go. He swallowed and tried to compose himself. *Am I doing this for good reason*, he wondered, *or just to talk to her?* He decided not to dither on it anymore. He pivoted on his heel and marched up to the woman.

'That dress,' he said, 'looks absurd on you.'

The woman did a double take, her mouth open in outrage. Then she saw him, and the surprise evaporated from her face. 'Ah. Of course. Good afternoon, Orso.' She glanced around nervously. Many of the Candiano Company servants were either staring or trying hard not to stare. 'This is . . . very inappropriate, you know.'

'I guess I forget what "appropriate" means these days, Estelle.'

'My experience, Orso, suggests you never knew in the first place.'

He grinned. 'Does it? It is good to see you, Estelle. Even if you are stuffed into the back halls like a damned valet.'

She smiled back, or at least tried to. It was not the smile he was familiar with. When he'd known her years ago, Estelle Candiano's eyes had been bright and alive, and her gaze had been sharper than a stiletto. Now there was something . . . dull to them.

She looked tired. Even though she was still twelve years his junior, Estelle now looked old.

She gestured ahead, and they moved out of earshot from the rest of the group. 'Was it you who killed the meeting?' she asked. 'Four hours is a little short, yes?'

'Not I. That would have been your husband.'

'Ah. What did Tomas say?'

'Some rather disparaging things about your father.'

'I see.' An awkward pause. 'Were they *true* things, though?'

'Well, yes. But they still pissed me off.'

'Why? I thought you hated him. When you left Company Candiano, Orso, there was a lot of bad blood between you and my father.'

'Bad blood,' he said, 'is still blood. How is Tribuno these days?'

'Still dying,' Estelle said curtly. 'And still mad. So. About as bad as one can get.'

'I . . . see,' he said quietly.

She peered at him. 'My God,' she said. 'My God! Could that be pity crossing the once-handsome face of the infamous Orso Ignacio? Could it be *regret*? Could it be *sorrow*? I'd never have believed it!'

'Stop.'

'I never saw this tenderness when you were with us, Orso.'

'That isn't true,' said Orso sharply.

'I . . . apologise. I meant tenderness for *him*.'

'That isn't true, either.' Orso thought carefully about what to say. 'Your father was and probably still is the most brilliant scriver in all the history of Tevanne. He practically built this damned city. A lot of his designs are still keeping everything standing. That means something, even if the man himself changed a lot.'

'Changed . . .' she said. 'Is that the word for it? To watch him decay . . . To watch him rot, and corrupt himself, chasing after these Occidental vanities, spending hundreds of thousands of duvots on decadent fantasy . . . I am not sure I'd just call that *change*. We still haven't recovered, you know.' She glanced at the crowd behind her. 'Look at us. Just a handful of servants, dressed like clerks. We used to practically own the council. We'd walk through these halls like gods and angels. How far we've fallen.'

'I know. And you're not scriving anymore. Are you?'

Estelle seemed to deflate. 'N . . . no. How did you know?'

'Because you were a damn clever scriver back when I knew you.'

They exchanged a look, and both understood there were unspoken words there – *Even if your father never recognised it.* For though Tribuno Candiano had been a wildly brilliant man, he'd been supremely disinterested in his daughter, and had made it well known that he'd have preferred a son.

And perhaps that was why he'd treated her as he had. For when Tribuno Candiano's Occidental obsessions had bankrupted his merchant house, he'd essentially auctioned off his daughter's hand in marriage to pay off his debts – and young Tomas Ziani, scion of the outrageously wealthy Ziani family, had been only too keen to buy the rights.

'What do you mean?' she asked.

'If Tomas was letting you work,' said Orso, 'you'd have turned Company Candiano around, I bet. You were good. Damned good.'

'That's not the place of a chief officer's wife, though.'

'No. Seems like an officer's wife's place is here, waiting in the halls, and being seen waiting in the halls, meek and obedient.'

She glared at him. 'Why did you come talk to me, Orso? Just to dig your fingers in old wounds?'

'No.'

'Then what?'

He took a breath. 'Listen, Estelle . . . there's some shit going on.'

'Are you sure you can talk about this? Or will Ofelia Dandolo have your balls braised for it?'

'She probably would,' he said, 'but I'm going to say it anyway. Regarding your father's materials . . . His Occidental collection, I mean, all that stuff he bought. Are those still at Company Candiano? Or were those auctioned away?'

'Why?' she demanded.

He remembered how Tomas Ziani had looked at him, smirking. 'Just curious.'

'I don't know,' she said. 'All of that is under Tomas's control now. I'm nowhere close to management, Orso.'

He thought about this. Tomas Ziani was sinfully rich, and had a reputation as a cunning merchant – but a scriver he wasn't. When it came to sigils, he probably couldn't tell his arse from a hole in the ground. The idea of him making something as powerful as the listening rig or the gravity plates was laughable.

But Tomas had resources, and ambition. What he couldn't make himself, he could perhaps buy.

And he might still have access, thought Orso, *to the smartest scriver in all of Tevanne.*

'Does Tomas ever see Tribuno?' he asked.

'Sometimes,' said Estelle, now deeply suspicious.

'Does he talk to him? And, if so, what about?'

'This is now thoroughly out of line,' she said. 'What's going on, Orso?'

'I told you. There's some shit going on in the city. Estelle . . . If Tomas was going to . . . to make a play at me, to come at me – you'd tell me, wouldn't you?'

'What do you mean, come at you?'

Orso pulled down the edge of his scarf with a finger and allowed her a glimpse of his bruised neck.

Her eyes opened wide. 'My God, Orso . . . Who . . . who *did* that to you?'

'That's what I'm trying to find out. So. If Tomas was going to make a play like this for me – would you warn me?'

'Do . . . do you really think *Tomas* could have done that?'

'I've had some civilised and proper people try to kill me over the years. Do you know anything, Estelle? And, again, if you did – would you tell me?'

She stared at him, and a mixture of expressions passed over her face: surprise, anger, resentment, then sadness. 'Do I owe you that?'

'I think so,' said Orso. 'I never asked you for much.'

She was silent for a long while. 'That's not true,' she said. 'You . . . you did ask me to marry you. But after that . . . no, you never asked me for anything else again.'

They stood in the hallway, surrounded by servants, not knowing what to say.

Estelle blinked rapidly. 'If I thought Tomas was a threat to you, I would tell you, Orso.'

'Even if it betrayed Candiano interests to do so?'

'Even if it did that.'

'Thank you.' He bowed deeply to her. 'I . . . I appreciate your time, Lady Ziani.' He turned and walked away.

He kept his head level and his arms stiff as he moved. Once he was about a few hundred feet down the hall, he ducked beside a column and watched the Company Candiano crowd.

He could tell when Tomas Ziani and the others emerged – the servants all sat up straight, keenly aware that their masters were now here. But not Estelle. She stood seemingly frozen, staring into space. And when her husband came and took her hand and led her away, she barely seemed to notice.

17

Sancia was still asleep when there was a knock at the door. 'Sun is setting,' Gregor's voice said. 'Our chariot shall be here soon.'

Sancia groaned, hauled herself off the sheetless bed, and staggered downstairs. All the injuries and scrapes from the past two days felt like they'd grown until her whole body was a bruise. When she saw Gregor she realised he must feel the same way: he was standing crooked, so as to not put pressure on his back, and he had his bandaged arm pulled close to his chest.

After a while, the front door opened and Berenice walked in. She looked at the two of them. 'Good God,' she said. 'I've seen cheerier faces in a mausoleum. Come on. The carriage is ready. I'll warn you, though – he's in a foul mood.'

'He doesn't seem like the kind of guy who has good moods,' said Sancia, following her.

'Then this is a *worse* mood,' said Berenice.

She drove them back to the hypatus department just as the sun slipped behind the clouds.

<Are you ready for this, Clef?> Sancia asked.

<Sure,> he said. He sounded chipper and cheerful again.

<And . . . you feel all right?>

<I feel great. Really great. That's kind of the problem, kid.>

She tried not to let her concern show in her face.

<Cheer up,> said Clef. *<I'll get you out of this jam, at the least. I promise.>*

The hypatus offices were still and dark. They used a back entrance to a small, forgotten staircase, and they climbed until they found Orso waiting at the top, next to his workshop.

<So that's the guy who bought me, huh?> asked Clef.

<Yeah.>

<What's he like?>

'Took you damned long enough!' snapped Orso. 'God, I thought I'd die of scrumming old age up here!'

<Never mind, I think I got it.>

'Good evening, Orso,' said Gregor. 'How was the committee meeting?'

'Dull and short,' said Orso. 'But not . . . entirely useless. I had some ideas – and if we can find that damn rig, I can confirm if those ideas are right.' He stood and pointed at Sancia. 'You. Are you ready to do this again?'

'Sure,' said Sancia.

'Then please,' he said. 'Astound us.'

'All right. Give me a second.' She looked down the stairs. To her, it was all just a sea of noise, of whispers and chanting. *<Clef?>*

<Yeah?>

<So, ah, you hear anything?>

<Oh, lots of stuff. But here. Let me focus.>

There was a silence. She assumed he was searching, and would answer her after he found something.

But then things . . . changed.

The murmurings and chanting grew louder, and then the sounds seemed to stretch . . . And bubble . . . And blur . . .

Then words emerged among them – words she could *hear*.

< . . . bring heat, bring it up, bubble it up, and store it away, there it goes, keep the heat there, oh, please, how I love to make the tank hot . . . >

< *. . . will NOT let anyone in, absolutely NO ONE, they CANNOT enter unless they possess KEY, key is VERY IMPORTANT, and I . . .* >

< *. . . rigid form, rigid form, rigid form, pressure at the corners, I am like the stone in the depths of the earth . . .* >

Sancia realised she could hear the scrivings, that she could understand them – *without* touching them. She nearly fell over from shock. She was fairly sure she'd just heard some kind of water tank, a lock, and a scrived support structure, all from somewhere in the building.

<*Holy . . . holy shit!*> she said.

The voices returned to quiet chanting. <*What?*> said Clef. <*What is it?*>

<*I . . . I could hear them! I could hear what they were saying, Clef! All the devices, all of them!*>

<*Huh,*> said Clef. There was a pause. <*Yeahhhh, I was worried that might happen.*>

<*That what might happen?*>

<*As I grow stronger, more of my thoughts may leak into you. Into your brain, your mind. I'm, uh, overpowering you a little, I think.*>

<*You mean I'm hearing what you hear?*>

<*And feeling what I feel, yeah. So.*> Clef coughed. <*I guess this could get weird.*>

She noticed Orso glaring at her impatiently. <*Is it dangerous?*>

<*I don't* think *so . . .*>

<*Then let's just ignore it for now. Find the recording rig before these bastards start worrying, and we'll figure this out later!*>

<*All right, all right . . . It's, like, a thing that captures sound, right?*>

<*I guess! I barely understand any of this shit!*>

<*Hm. Okay.*>

There was another pause . . . and then the voices flooded back into her head, an avalanche of words and desires and anxious fears.

Except some of the voices grew louder or softer, rapidly, one after another. It was as if Clef were sorting through a stack of papers, looking at each one before passing on to the next – except it was happening inside her brain. The sensation was profoundly disorienting.

Then one voice arose from the chaos: < *. . . I am a reed in the wind, dancing with my partner, my mate, my love . . . I dance as they dance, I move as they move, I trace our dance within the clay . . .* >

<*That's it,*> said Clef. <*That's the one. Hear it?*>

<*Dancing? Clay? Love? What the hell?*>

<*That's how they think, how they work,*> said Clef. <*These rigs are made by people. And people make things that work kind of like people – if you want a device to do something, you build the desire into the device, see? It's in the basement, I think. Come on.*>

'I've got it, I think,' said Sancia.

'Then lead the way,' said Gregor.

Listening to the whispering device, Sancia wandered through workshops filled with half-built devices, rows of cold furnaces, wall after wall of bookshelves. Clef led her down the stairs, across the mezzanine, and then to a side hall, which then led to another stairway. Then he led her down flight after flight of stairs, to the basement, which seemed to double as a library. Orso, Berenice, and Gregor followed, bearing small, scrived lights, not speaking – but Sancia's head was filled up with words.

She was still getting used to this. For so long she'd been accustomed to scrivings being nothing more than murmurings in the back of her head. To have Clef clarify them was like having someone wipe away a layer of sand to reveal words written on the path before you.

But if I'm hearing this from him, wondered Sancia, *what else am I picking up? And what's he picking up from me?* She wondered if she would start to think like Clef, to act like him, and never even notice it.

They entered the basement. And then, abruptly, the trail ended before a blank wall.

<*Now what?*> asked Sancia.

<*It's, uh, back there.*>

<*What do you mean, back there? Behind the wall?*>

<*Seems to be. I can show you where it is, but I can't tell you how to get to it. Listen . . .* >

Another pause, and then she heard it, mumbling behind the walls: < *. . . still no dance . . . still no sounds. Silence. Nothing to dance to, no steps and twirls to scrawl in the clay . . .* >

<*Yeah,*> said Sancia. She stepped back and looked at the wall. <*It's back there. Shit.*> She sighed, and said, 'Anyone know what's behind this wall?'

'More wall, I would assume,' said Orso.

'It's not. The thing's back there.'

'You found the rig?' Gregor asked. 'You're sure?'

'Yes. Now we just have to figure out how they access it.' She grimaced, then pulled off her gloves. 'Hold on a second.' She took a breath, focused, shut her eyes, and placed her palms against the wall.

Instantly, the wall bloomed inside her mind, all those old, pale stones and layers of plaster leaping into her thoughts. The wall told her of age and pressure, decades spent bearing all the weight of the building above and transferring it to the foundation below. Except . . .

In one place, the foundation wasn't there.

A passageway, she thought.

Keeping her eyes shut, she walked along the wall, bare palm pressed to its surface. Finally she came to it – the gap in the foundation was just below her. She opened her eyes, knelt, and pressed her palms to the floor.

The floorboards crackled to life inside of her, creaking and groaning, telling her of thousands of footfalls, leather soles and wooden soles and, sometimes, bare feet. Her skull tickled as termites and ants and other tiny insects roved through her splintering bones.

But one part of the floor was different – it was separate, and it had something screwed into it.

Hinges, thought Sancia. *A door.* She followed the feeling in her mind until she came to the far corner of a dusty blue rug. She pulled it aside. Underneath was an old and scarred trapdoor.

'A basement?' said Gregor.

'When the hell did we get a basement?' asked Orso.

'The scriving library was renovated years ago,' said Berenice. 'Much of the old walls were torn down and built over. Artefacts are still around – doors that go nowhere, things like that.'

'Well, this goes somewhere,' said Sancia. She wedged her fingers underneath it and lifted the trapdoor up.

Below was a short flight of musty stairs, which ended in a small tunnel that ran behind the wall. It was completely dark at the bottom.

'Here,' said Berenice, holding out her light to Sancia.

Sancia put her glove back on – aware, suddenly, of Orso's careful gaze – and took it from her. 'Thanks,' she said, and she dropped down, holding the scrived light.

She touched a bare hand to the wall. The tunnel spoke to her, darkness and dust and cool, stale moisture. She followed its path to a small, rickety ladder, which led to an old crawlspace, an interstitial segment of an older floor plan, walled off and forgotten. And at the far back was . . .

<*. . . await to trace my path in the pool of clay and wax . . . When will my mate begin to dance again? When shall we move, when shall we sway?*>

<*There it is,*> said Sancia. <*Finally. I'll crawl up and swipe the thing.*> She crawled forward.

<*Wait,*> said Clef. <*Stop.*>

She stopped. <*What?*>

<*Move forward . . . just a bit. A foot. No more.*>

She did so.

<*Shit,*> said Clef. <*There's something else. It's almost overpowered by the listening rig. Hear it?*>

Again, a voice emerged from the mutterings – but this one was not the recording rig.

<*. . . I wait. I wait for the signal, for the token, for the sign,*> said this new rig. <*How I long to see the sign, how I long to feel it press upon me. But if not . . . If my lands are broached by those who do not bear the sign, oh, oh, the spark I shall make, bright and flashing, hot and sizzling, a brief, wondrous star . . .*>

<*What the hell is that?*> asked Sancia.

<*I don't know,*> said Clef. <*It's back there with the recording rig, though. Right next to it. I can't show you what it is, though – only what the scrivings do.*>

Sancia held the scrived light up, but she couldn't see that far back into the crawlspace. She thought about it, then pressed a bare hand into the wood.

She felt wood, and nails, and dust, and termites . . . and she felt the rig back there, or what she thought was the rig. It was some kind of iron stand that was quite heavy – she guessed the roll of wax or clay or whatever it wrote on was big.

But beside it was something else quite heavy. A barrel, she thought . . . Wooden and round and filled with something . . .

She smelled the air, and thought she smelled something sulfurous.

She froze. <*Clef – so . . . this thing . . . if someone gets close to it without the right, uh, signal or whatever . . .*>

<*Then it makes a spark,*> said Clef.

There was a pause.

<*Wait,*> said Clef.

<*Yeah,*> said Sancia.

<*It's a bomb, isn't it.*>

<*Yeah. It's a goddamn bomb. A big goddamn bomb.*>

Another pause.

<*I'm, uh, going to walk away slowly,*> said Sancia. <*Really slowly.*>

<*Good idea,*> said Clef. <*Great idea. I like this idea.*>

She slowly withdrew back down the passageway. <*I guess there's no way to break the scrivings,*> she said.

<*Not without touching it,*> said Clef. <*I can see what it is, learn a bit about what it does, and I can show you – but I can't tamper with it without contact.*>

<*So. We're scrummed.*>

<*Unless you want to risk being blown into pudding, then yeah, basically.*>

She sighed. <*Well. Let's go tell the others, then.*>

'So we can't get close to it,' said Gregor. 'We're stuck here.'

'Right,' said Sancia, sitting on the floor in the dark, brushing dust off of her arms and knees.

Orso stood in silence, staring down into the dark passageway. Ever since she'd returned, he hadn't said a word.

'Surely there must be a way around the device?' said Berenice.

Gregor shook his head. 'I've dealt with scrived mines in the wars. Unless you have the right signalling device on you, you'll be pulped.'

'So we can't get to the listening rig,' said Berenice. 'But that can't be *that* critical, yes? I mean, we generally know all the things we've divulged to these people, right, sir?'

Orso didn't answer. He just kept staring down into the passageway.

<*I don't like that,*> said Clef.

<*Me neither.*>

'Uh,' said Berenice, disconcerted. 'Well. I meant we *could* try to look at the rig itself to identify the person who made it – but I've been working on the gravity plates all afternoon, and I still have nothing.'

'Then we focus on what we know,' said Sancia. 'We know the rig's down there. We know it's working. We know everyone got to see Orso at this damn meeting, and they know he's alive now. So someone will be coming. Soon.'

'And when they come,' said Gregor, 'we either capture them or follow them. Following them is my preference – it can reveal so many more things . . .' He sighed. 'But I suppose capturing and questioning them is our only choice. We've no idea what campo this agent of theirs would return to, nor which enclave within the campo itself! We'd need sachets and keys and all sorts of credentials . . .'

<*Sounds like fun to me,*> said Clef.

<*You sure you want to do that, Clef? We don't know what kind of obstacles we'd run into.*>

<*I told you. I don't want to sit uselessly in your pocket all day, kid.*>

'I . . . I can talk to my black market contacts,' said Sancia. 'I can get sachets to get into the campos.'

'You can get *that* many sachets?' asked Gregor, surprised.

The idea was preposterous. But maybe they didn't know that. 'Yeah.'

'And credentials?' asked Berenice.

'If you pay me enough,' said Sancia, 'I can get you into the campos.'

Clef laughed. <*That's an easy profit.*>

'Then I think it's settled,' said Gregor. 'You get your sachets, we set our trap, and wait. Right?'

'Right,' said Berenice.

'Right,' said Sancia.

They all waited, and turned to Orso.

'Sir?' asked Berenice.

Finally, Orso moved, turning to look at Sancia. 'That was . . . quite some performance,' he said quietly.

'Thanks?' she said.

He looked her over. 'There's a simple way to stay alive as a hypatus, you know – never include a scriving in your designs that you don't completely understand. And, girl . . . I must admit, I don't understand you at all.'

'You don't need to,' said Sancia. 'You just need to understand the results I get you,'

'No,' said Orso. 'I need a lot more than that. For example – how do I know you're telling the truth about any of this?'

'Huh?' she said.

'You go into the dark, say you found the rig, but we can't get close to it. If we go down there and look ourselves, we die. There's no way to check. That all seems convenient to me.'

'I've helped you before,' she said. 'I found the damn rig in the statue!'

'But how did you do *that*? You never told us. You haven't told us a damned thing!'

'Orso,' said Gregor. 'I believe we can trust her.'

'How can we trust her if we don't know how she's doing what she's doing? Finding a rig is one thing, but seeing through walls, finding the trapdoor . . . I mean, she went straight to it like a dog on the hunt!'

<*Uh oh,*> said Clef.

Orso turned to her. 'You figured all this out just by *listening*?'

'Yeah?'

'And touching the walls?'

'Yeah? What of it?'

He stared at her for a long, long time. 'Where are you from, Sancia?' he demanded.

'Foundryside,' she said defiantly.

'But where originally?'

'Back east.'

'But where east?'

'Go east enough and you'll find it.'

'Why are you so evasive?'

'Because it's none of your damn business.'

'But it *is* my business. You made yourself my business when you stole my key.' He stepped closer, squinting at her, his eye tracing over the scar on the side of her head. 'I don't need you to tell me,' he said quietly. 'I don't need you to tell me anything. I already know.'

She tensed up. Her heart was beating so fast it felt like a murmur.

'Silicio,' said Orso. 'The Silicio Plantation. That's where you're from, isn't it?'

The next thing she knew, Sancia had her hands around his throat.

She hadn't meant to do it. She'd barely even understood what was happening. One moment, she'd been sitting on the floor. Then Orso spoke that name, and suddenly she smelled the sting of alcohol, heard the whine of flies, and the side of her head was bright with pain – and then she was screaming and throttling a terrified Orso Ignacio, trying to crush his already-bruised windpipe with her bare hands.

She was screaming something, over and over again. It took her a moment to realise she was saying, '*Was it you? Was it you? Was it, was it?*'

Berenice was suddenly on top of her, trying to haul her off of him, with little success. Then Gregor was there, and since he was two if not three times Sancia's size, he had much more success.

Gregor Dandolo hugged Sancia tight to his body, his big arms holding her still.

'*Let me go!*' she screamed. '*Let me go, let me go, let me go!*'

'Sancia,' said Gregor, surprisingly calm. 'Stop. Be still.'

Orso was coughing and gagging and trying to sit up. 'What in all the damned *world* . . .'

'*I'll kill him!*' screamed Sancia. '*I'll kill you, you scrumming bastard!*'

'Sancia,' said Gregor. 'You are not where you think you are.'

'What's the matter with her?' said Berenice, terrified.

'She's having a reaction,' said Gregor. 'I've seen this among veterans, and experienced it myself.'

'*He did it!*' shrieked Sancia. She kicked uselessly at Gregor's legs. '*It was him, it was him, it was him!*'

'She's reliving a memory,' he said, grunting slightly. 'A bad one.'

'It was *him*!' she screamed. She felt the blood vessels standing out on her forehead, felt the hot, muggy air on her skin, heard the songs in the fields, the whimpering in the dark. 'It was, it *was*!'

Orso coughed, shook himself, and shouted, 'It *wasn't me*!'

Sancia struggled against Gregor's arms. Her back and neck burned with fatigue, but still she struggled.

<*Kid,*> said Clef in her ear. <*Kid! Are you listening? He said it wasn't him! Come back to me! Wherever you are, come back,* please!>

Sancia slowed as she heard Clef's words. The many sensations of the plantation retreated from her mind. Then she went limp, exhausted.

Orso sat on the ground, panting, and then said, 'It was *not* me, Sancia. I had nothing to do with Silicio. Nothing! I swear!'

Sancia said nothing. Her breath was ragged, and she was spent.

Gregor slowly lowered her to sit on the floor. Then he cleared his throat like they'd all had a loud disagreement at the breakfast table. 'I must ask – what is this Silicio?'

Orso looked at Sancia. Sancia glared back, but did not speak.

'To me, it was no more than a rumour,' said Orso. 'A rumour of a slave plantation where . . . where scrivers practised the one art we are strictly forbidden to pursue.'

Berenice turned to stare at him, horrified. Gregor said, 'You mean . . .'

'Yes,' said Orso, sighing. 'The scriving of human beings. And to look at Sancia . . . it seems like it worked, at least once.'

'Barely anyone remembers the first days, when they tried scriving humans,' Orso said darkly, sitting at the head of one of the big wooden tables in the scriving library. 'Nor would they wish to. I was hardly out of school when they outlawed it. But I saw the cases. I know what happened. I know why they abandoned it.'

Sancia sat silent at the other end of the table, gently rocking back and forth. Gregor and Berenice glanced between her and Orso, waiting to hear more.

'We know how to change an object's reality,' said Orso carefully. 'We speak the language of objects. To speak this language to people, to try to command our bodies with our sigils . . . It doesn't work.'

'Why?' asked Gregor.

'On one level, it's because we're just not good enough,' said Orso.

'It's kind of like safely scriving gravity, only worse. It would take a *huge* amount of effort to do – three, four, five lexicons, all to alter one person.'

'But on another level?'

'On another level, it doesn't work because objects are *dumb*,' said Orso. 'Scriving is all about careful, precise definition, and objects are easy there. Iron is iron. Stone is stone. Wood is wood. Objects have an uncomplicated sense of self, so to speak. People, though, and living things . . . their sense of self is . . . complicated. Mutable. It *changes*. People don't think of themselves as just a bag of flesh and blood and bones, even if that's what they basically are. They think of themselves as soldiers, as kings, as wives and husbands and children . . . People can convince themselves to be anything, and because of that, the scrivings you bind them with can't stay anchored. To try to bind a person is like writing in the ocean.'

'So what happened to the people the scrivers tried to alter?' asked Gregor.

Orso was quiet for a long while. 'Even I won't speak of such things. Not now. Not ever, if I can help it.'

'Then where did this Silicio come from, sir?' asked Berenice.

'The practice is illegal in *Tevanne*,' said Orso. 'But the laws of Tevanne, as we are all well aware, are weak and restricted. Intentionally so. None of them extend to the plantations. The policy of Tevanne has always been that, provided we get our sugar, coffee, and whatever else on time, we couldn't care less about what goes on out there. So . . . if it was communicated to a plantation that, if they accommodated a handful of scrivers from Tevanne, and supplied them with . . . *specimens* to experiment on . . .'

'Then they would receive a bonus, or an amenable contract, or some kind of lucrative reward,' said Gregor dourly, 'from one of the merchant houses.'

'On matters completely unrelated to these visiting scrivers,' said Orso. 'It all looks aboveboard, from a distance.'

'But why?' said Berenice. 'Why experiment on humans at all, sir? We're successful with our devices – why not focus on those?'

'Think, Berenice,' said Orso. 'Imagine if you'd lost an arm, or a leg, or were dying from some plague. Imagine if someone could develop a sigil string that could *cure* you, or regrow a limb, or . . .'

'Or keep you alive for much, much longer,' said Berenice softly. 'They could scrive you so that you could cheat death itself.'

'Or they could scrive a soldier's mind,' said Gregor. 'Make them fearless. Make it so they don't value their own lives. Make them do despicable things, and then forget they'd ever done them. Or make them bigger, stronger, faster than all other soldiers . . .'

'Or scrive slaves to thoughtlessly do their masters' bidding,' said Berenice, glancing at Sancia.

'The possibilities,' said Orso, 'are beyond count.'

'And this is what Silicio was?' asked Gregor. 'An experiment run by a merchant house?'

'I'd only heard rumors of it. Some plantation, out in the Durazzo, where people were still attempting the forbidden arts. I heard it moved around, from island to island to make it harder to trace. But a few years ago, news came of a disaster on the island of Silicio. A whole plantation house burned to the ground. All the slaves were running wild. And among those killed in the blaze were a number of Tevanni scrivers, though no one could *quite* explain what they'd been doing there.'

They looked at Sancia, who was sitting completely still now, her face totally blank of all expression.

'Which house was behind this experiment?' Gregor asked.

'Oh, it probably wasn't just one merchant house,' said Orso. 'If one was trying to scrive humans, they all were. It might still be going on, for all I know. Or perhaps Silicio scared them all off.'

'Even . . .' Gregor furrowed his brow. 'Even Dandolo Chartered?'

'Oh, Captain . . . How many merchant houses have been doomed because they were too slow to bring a new design to market? How many careers have ended because a competitor found a way to make better wares?'

'But to do *that* . . .' said Berenice. 'To . . . to *people* . . .'

Suddenly Sancia laughed. 'God. God! As if that was any worse! As if *that* was any worse than the other things happening out there!'

They looked at her, uneasy.

'What do you mean?' asked Berenice.

'Don't . . . don't you understand what the plantations *are*?' said Sancia. 'Think of it. Think of trying to control an island where the slaves outnumber you eight to one. How would you keep them in line? What would you do to keep them docile? What sort of tortures would you apply to those who lashed out? If . . . If *any* of you could understand the things I've seen . . .'

'Do they really?' said Berenice. 'Then . . . then why do we allow the plantations to exist?'

Orso shrugged. 'Because we're stupid, and lazy. After the first stage of the Enlightenment Wars – which was what, twenty or thirty years ago? – Tevanne had expanded and exhausted itself. It needed cheap grain, cheap resources, and it had a lot of captives on hand. It was to be a short-term fix – but then we got dependent on it. And it just keeps getting worse and worse.'

Sancia shook her head. 'Scriving the human body . . . those horrors are nothing, *nothing*, compared to all the other horrors that make the islands run. And if I had the chance, I'd . . . I'd do it all over again.'

Gregor looked at her. 'Sancia . . . How did Silicio burn?'

She was silent for a long while. 'It . . . it burned,' she said, 'because I set it alight.'

⁂

She started speaking.

They'd brought her to the big house behind the plantation, then down to the basement, down to where that . . . *place* was. She hadn't even known the word for it. Mortuary? Laboratory? Some cross in between? Sancia hadn't understood. She'd just smelled the alcohol, looked at the drawings and illustrations on the wall, and all those plates with the strange signs written on them; and she'd remembered the wagon that left the house every morning, reeking and followed by flies; and she'd known in an instant that she wasn't getting out of there alive.

They'd forced her to drink a sedative – a powerful brandy of some kind, awful and putrid. It'd made her brain muddy and slow, but it didn't kill the pain that would come later. Not really.

They'd cut off all her hair and shaved her pate with a razor. She remembered blinking blood out of her eyes. Then they'd dropped her down on the table, tied her down, and the one-eyed scriver had wiped her skull with alcohol – how it burned, how it *burned* – and then . . .

'Desperate times,' the one-eyed scriver had sighed, picking up a knife, 'do call for desperate measures. But don't we have the right to be unorthodox, my dear?' He'd smiled at her, a simpering expression. 'Don't we?'

And then he'd cut her head open.

Sancia had no words for the sensation. No words for the feeling of having your scalp slashed open and peeled back like the skin of an orange. No words for feeling him measure the bend of your skull, and listening to him *tap-tap* the plate into shape. No words for suddenly feeling those screws, those horrid screws *biting* into you, the gritty, grinding feeling as they bored into your skull, and then, and then . . .

Things had gone black.

She'd died. She'd been sure of it, at the time. There'd been just nothing. But then she'd felt someone . . .

Someone lying on top of her. Felt their warmth. Felt them bleeding.

It'd taken her a long time to realise she was feeling herself.

She'd been feeling her own body, lying on a dark stone floor. Only she'd been feeling herself from the perspective of the floor. She'd *become* the floor, just by touching it.

In the dark, alone, young Sancia had awoken and done her best to re-collect her sanity. Her skull had screamed and shrieked with pain – one whole side was swollen and sticky and bristly with stitches – but she'd realised then, alone, blind, that she was perhaps becoming something *else,* like a moth struggling to fight its way out of its pupa.

There had been chains around her wrists. A lock. And because of what she'd become, she'd felt she *was* the chains, she *was* the lock – and so she'd known how to pick it, of course, using a shred of wood she'd pulled off the wall.

They hadn't intended this, surely. They hadn't planned for her to become this thing. If they had, they would have tied her up better. And they wouldn't have sent the one-eyed scriver alone to check on her in the night.

The creak of the door, the spear of light stabbing into the shadows.

'Are you awake, poppet?' he'd called sweetly. 'I doubt it . . .'

He'd probably thought she'd be dead. He certainly hadn't expected her to be hiding in the corner, lock and chain in hand.

She'd waited until he'd stepped inside. Then she'd sprung.

Oh . . . Oh, to hear the sound of the thick, heavy lock striking his skull. Oh, to hear him crumple to the ground, gagging, shocked. Then she was on him, wrapping the chain around his throat and pulling it taut, tighter, and tighter, and tighter.

Wild, agonised, and covered in blood, she'd slipped out and roved through the darkened house, feeling the boards beneath her, the walls on either side of her, feeling all these things, feeling everyone in the house all at once . . .

The house had become her weapon. And she'd used it against them.

She'd locked their bedroom doors, one by one. Locked everything as they slept, except one way out. And then she'd gone downstairs to where they'd kept the alcohol, and the kerosene, and all those reeking fluids, and found a match . . .

A struck match sounds like a kiss in the dark, sometimes. She remembered thinking that, watching the flame crack to life and then flutter down to the pools of alcohol running across the floor.

No one had made it out. And as she'd sat and watched, she'd realised – master or slave, all screams sounded alike.

Silence filled the library. Nobody moved.

'How did you come to Tevanne?' asked Gregor.

'Snuck aboard a ship,' Sancia said softly. 'Easy to stow away when you have the floorboards and the walls to tell you who's coming and going. When I got off, I stole the name "Grado" from a winery sign I saw, since everyone just expected me to have a last name. Hardest thing was figuring out the limits of what I could do. Touching everything, being everything . . . it nearly killed me.'

'What's the nature of your augmentation?' asked Orso.

She tried to describe it – knowing what objects were feeling, what they'd felt, the sheer avalanche of sensation that she constantly fought to keep at bay. 'I try to . . . to touch as few things as possible,' she said. 'I can't touch people. That's too much. And if the scrivings in my skull get overtaxed, they burn, just burn, like hot lead in my bones. When I first came to Tevanne, I had to wrap myself in rags like a leper. It didn't take me long to realise that what had been done to me was some kind of scriving. So I tried to find out how to get fixed. How to make me human again. But nothing in Tevanne is cheap.'

'That was why you stole the key?' asked Berenice. 'To pay for a physiquere?'

'A physiquere who wouldn't turn and sell me out to a merchant house,' said Sancia. 'Yeah.'

'What?' said Orso, startled. 'A what?'

'A . . . a physiquere,' she said. 'One that can fix me.'

'A physiquere . . . who can *fix* you?' he said faintly. 'Sancia . . . My God. You are aware that you are probably the only one of your kind *alive*, yes? I know I've never seen a scrumming scrived human in my life, and I've seen boatloads of mad shit! The idea of a physiquere who can just, I don't know, patch you up – it's preposterous!'

She stared at him. 'But . . . but I'd been told that . . . that they'd found a physiquere who knew what to do.'

'Then either they were lying,' said Orso, 'or being lied to. No one knows how to do what was done to you, let alone reverse it! They were probably going to either take your money and cut your throat, or take your money and sell you to the closest house!'

<*Shit,*> said Clef, dismayed.

Sancia was trembling. 'So . . . so what are you saying? Are you saying I'm stuck like this . . . forever?'

'How should I know?' said Orso. 'I told you, I've never even *seen* this before.'

'Sir,' hissed Berenice. 'Some . . . tact? Please?'

Orso looked at her, and then Sancia, who was now white and quivering. 'Oh, hell . . . Listen. After all this, you can stay here. With me, and Berenice. And *maaaybe* I try to figure out how in the hell they made you, and how to reverse it.'

'Really?' said Gregor. 'That's charitable of you, Orso.'

'It damned well isn't!' he said. 'The girl's a goddamn marvel, who knows what kind of secrets she's literally carrying around in her head!'

Gregor rolled his eyes. 'Of course.'

'Do you think you could actually figure it out?' said Sancia.

'I think I have a better chance than every other dumb bastard in this city,' said Orso.

Sancia considered it. *<What do you think, Clef?>*

<I think this nutter doesn't care about money – and someone who doesn't care about money is less likely to sell you out.>

'I'll consider it,' she said.

'Terrific,' said Orso. 'But let's not get too tickled over the idea yet. There's some devilish arsehole out there who wants us all dead. Let's make sure we're going to *have* a future before we start planning for one.'

'Right,' said Sancia. 'Do you think you can rig up another tailing scriving?' she asked Berenice. 'Like the one you used on Gregor?'

'Of course,' she said. 'Those aren't tricky at all.'

'Good.' She looked at Gregor. 'And you – are you able to come with me to follow this bastard?'

To her surprise, Gregor looked uncertain. 'Uh . . . Well. That is . . . unlikely.'

'Why?'

'Probably for the same reason Orso can't assist either.' Gregor cleared his throat. 'Because I am moderately recognisable.'

'He means he's famous,' said Orso, 'because he's Ofelia Dandolo's scrumming son.'

'Yes. And if I were to be seen strolling around the other campos – that would raise alarms.'

'But I'm going to need someone with me,' said Sancia. 'I've been shot at by these arseholes so many times, it'd be nice to have someone to shoot back for a change.'

Gregor and Orso looked at each other, then at Berenice. She sighed deeply. '*Ugh.* Fine. Fine! I don't know why I'm always the one following people around the city, but . . . I suppose I can assist.'

'But . . .' said Sancia. 'I mean, I'm sure Berenice is very organised and helpful, but I was hoping for someone a bit more . . . robust?'

'Although Captain Dandolo is admirably large of arm,' said Orso, 'the nice thing about scriving is that it makes *this*' – he tapped his head – 'a much more tangibly dangerous weapon. And in that regard, young Berenice has little competition. I've seen the things she can make. Now. Shut up and get to work.'

18

Sancia sat alone in the library broom cupboard and dozed.

It was not sleep – sleeping now, while she waited for the spy, would be disastrous. Rather, it was a kind of meditation she'd taught herself long ago, slumbering while alert and aware. It was not as restful as actually sleeping – but it didn't leave her as vulnerable.

There was the sound of footfalls somewhere upstairs.

<*It's not them,*> said Clef.

Sancia took a breath and resumed resting.

Minutes ticked by in the dark. Then there was the sound of a door closing somewhere.

<*Not them, either,*> said Clef.

<*Okay. Thanks.*>

She tried to return to her dozing. This moment alone in the cupboard was invaluable to Sancia, who desperately needed rest, and also frankly needed some time without any stimulation at all: being immersed in so many scrivings was deeply wearying for her.

Clef was doing her a favour, of course, or at least trying to – since the spy would have to be carrying a scrived signal to access the rig, that made it easy for him to identify them. But it didn't help that he kept telling her all the ones that *weren't* the spy.

The sound of footsteps echoed above her.

<*Not them,*> said Clef.

<*Clef, goddamn it! You don't need to tell me all the times it's not them! Just tell me when it* is *them!*>

<*Okay. Well . . . I'm pretty sure this next one is them.*>

<*Huh?*>

A door opened somewhere in the basement.

<*Yeah, that's them,*> said Clef. <*They've got the signal. Listen . . .* >

There was a silence, and then the chanting and whispering peaked, and she heard a voice among them: < *. . . I am given rights, given forbearance, because I am chosen, I am allowed, because I am awaited, I am expected, I am NEEDED . . .* >

<*God,*> said Sancia. <*Are all scrivings so neurotic?*>

<*They're compelled to act in one specific fashion,*> said Clef. <*Which is basically the definition of neurotic, if that helps.*>

Sancia reached out and touched the floor with a bare hand. The wooden boards crackled to life in her mind, one by one – and, eventually, she felt someone slowly walking across them.

A woman – Sancia could tell by the size of the feet, the build of the shoe, the gait. Walking very . . . cautiously.

<*She's spooked,*> said Clef.

<*This is an emergency pickup. I'd be spooked too.*>

The woman walked by the broom cupboard – and even tried the knob, though it was locked. *Must be checking everything,* thought Sancia. Then, finally, she went to the trapdoor to the rig.

Sancia waited, and waited, and waited, one finger pressed to the floor. Then she felt the reverberations in the wood as the trapdoor shut, then footsteps as she came back – and these footsteps were slightly heavier.

<*She's got it,*> said Sancia.

Sancia waited until the woman had passed, turned the corner, and started up the stairs. Then she silently unlocked and opened the broom cupboard door, and chased after her.

She caught up with the woman on the main floor of the Hypatus Building, exiting through the lobby. It was late afternoon, and the building was quite busy – though Sancia was wearing Dandolo Chartered colours, so she drew no attention. Sancia spied the woman immediately: she was young, hardly older than Sancia herself, a skinny, dark-skinned thing dressed in formal yellow-and-white robes and bearing a large, leather bag.

She was a secretary or assistant, it seemed – and, as such, no one paid any attention at all to her.

<*That's her, right?*> said Sancia.

<*That's her. But if she gets past fifty or so yards, I can't keep up with her. So stay close, or tag her with Berenice's scriving.*>

<*Yeah, yeah.*>

Sancia exited the building after the woman and kept her in eyesight, pacing across the Hypatus Building's front steps and down into the streets. It was dreadfully hot, and foggy and rainy – not the best conditions to be following someone. Most of the streets were too empty for Sancia to feel comfortable making a play for the woman, but when they approached a busy carriage fairway ahead, she saw her chance.

The woman waited along with a small crowd of campo denizens as a train of carriages thundered past. Sancia sidled up, got close, and in a smooth, quick motion that resembled waving away a fly, she dropped the tailing scriving in the woman's bag.

The carriage train tapered off. The woman, perhaps sensing something, turned to look around, but Sancia was already gone.

Sancia reached into her pocket, grabbed Berenice's twinned plate, and snapped it in half – her signal that the tag had taken place. Then she pulled out her half of the trailing scriving – a small wooden dowel with a wire tied to it, and a scrived button tied to the end of the wire. The wire was pointing straight at the woman.

<*It's on,*> said Sancia.

Sancia was following the woman to the south gates when she saw the carriage – unmarked, stationed about twenty feet away from the gates, with a single figure in the front. She walked up to it, keeping an eye as the woman passed through the gates to the Commons.

Berenice nodded at her from the carriage's front window. The girl's face was unpainted, but she was, rather frustratingly, still quite pretty. 'That's her,' Sancia said. 'Let's go.'

'We're not taking this gate,' said Berenice. 'We'll go to the east gate and loop back around.'

'What! Why the hell would we do that? We don't want to lose her!'

'The rig you put on her should give us a mile range to work with,' said Berenice. 'But more to the point – we're assuming that girl's employer is the one who paid for all those flying assassins, yes? Well, if she's as valuable as we think she is, they'll likely pay to give her a few guardian angels – who will be *quite* interested in anyone who comes out the gates directly after her.'

<*Good point,*> said Clef. <*And as a heads-up, kid – your friend is loaded up something fierce.*>

<*What do you mean, loaded up?*>

<*I mean she's like a walking goody bag of rigs. You don't hear them all?*>

<*I've been on the campos too long. It's tough for me to hear anything specific anymore, unless it's powerful.*> She looked Berenice over. <*She really is?*>

<*Yeah. She's come prepared – but for what, I don't know. Stay on your guard.*>

'Hurry up and get in,' said Berenice. 'Change clothes. And stop arguing.'

Sancia did as she asked, climbing into the back. There was a set of clothes more suitable to the Commons laid there. Sighing – she hated changing clothes – Sancia crouched down and started putting them on.

The carriage took off, speeding down the campo wall to the east gate. 'Hold on,' said Berenice, spinning the wheel and sending it hurtling through the gates. Then she took a hard right and sped back toward the south gates.

'Could you scrumming slow down?' shouted Sancia, who'd tumbled over in the back, her head stuck in a light coat.

'No,' said Berenice. She held up the tailing wire, which, rather alarmingly, had gone slack. Then, abruptly, the button shot up and pointed off into the Commons. 'There,' she said. 'We're in range.' She brought the carriage skidding to a halt, grabbed a pack from the floor, and jumped out. 'Come on, grab the clothes. We'll go on foot. A carriage would stand out here.'

Sancia was tangled in a set of breeches. 'Give me a damn second!' She struggled into the clothes, buttoned them up, and jumped out of the carriage.

The two of them started off into the Commons. 'Keep your tailing wire in your breast pocket,' Berenice said quietly. 'You can feel it tug in the right direction without having to look at it.' She eyed the streets and the windows. 'I assume you can spot someone who means us ill?'

'Yeah, look for someone big and ugly with a knife,' said Sancia.

They closed in on their mark, and found the woman seated in a taverna at the edge of Old Ditch. She'd bought a mug of cane wine, but she wasn't drinking from it.

Sancia peered at the streets around the taverna. 'It's a handoff. Someone else will take it the rest of the way.'

'What makes you so sure?'

'Well, I'm not totally sure,' said Sancia. Then she spotted him: a man, standing on the corner dressed as a Commoner. He kept glancing at the woman with the bag with an anxious, wary stare. 'But that guy looks like a likely candidate, yeah?'

The man looked around at the street for a while before he finally moved, stalking into the taverna and up to the bar. He ordered and, as he waited, the woman stood and left without a word – leaving the bag behind. When the man got his drink, he walked over to her table, sat, drank his wine in no fewer than five gulps – staring anxiously out at the street – picked up the bag, and left.

He turned east, walking quickly with the bag over his shoulder. Sancia felt the tailing wire twitching in her pocket as he moved. Yet as he walked, Sancia noticed that more people were walking with him, trickling after the man one by one from doorways and alleys. They were all large, and though they were dressed like Commoners, there was an undeniable heft and professionalism to them.

'We'll keep our distance,' said Berenice quietly.

'Yeah,' said Sancia. 'As much of it as we can.'

The group of men kept going east, through Old Ditch, then through Foundryside, until they came to the Michiel campo walls.

'The Michiels?' said Berenice, surprised. 'Really? I didn't think they had the guts. They're more artisans, focusing on heat and light and glass and—'

'And they're not going in,' said Sancia. 'They're still moving. So cut the speculation.'

They kept following, lagging behind a bit to give the men some breathing room. Sancia felt the tailing wire in her pocket twitch as the men moved – and, now that they were away from the campos, she could hear the multitude of mutterings emanating from Berenice's person, many of them quite powerful, by the sound of it.

Sancia glanced sideways at her and cleared her throat. 'So – what's your relationship to Orso?'

'Our relationship?' said Berenice. 'You want to talk about that now?'

'A natural conversation would be a good cover.'

'I suppose that's so. I'm his fab.'

Sancia had no idea what that was. 'So . . . does that mean you and he are, uh . . . I mean, you know . . .'

Berenice looked at her, disgusted. 'What? No! God, why does *everyone* always think a fab is a sex thing when *I* say it? Plenty of men are fabs and no one ever gets that impression about them!' She sighed. 'Fab is short for *fabricator*.'

'Still not following you.'

She sighed again, deeper. 'You know how sigils rely on definitions? Discs of thousands and thousands of other sigils that define what that one new sigil means?'

'Vaguely.'

'A fabricator is the person who makes those definitions. Every elite scriver has one, if not several. It's like architects and builders – the architect dreams up these vast, grand plans, but they still need an engineer to actually make the damned thing.'

'Sounds complicated. How'd you get into that line of work?'

'I've a head for remembering things. My father used to make money off me. I'd memorise all the hundreds and thousands of scivoli moves – the game with the checked board and the beads on strings? – and he'd take me around the city and bet against my opponents. Scivoli is a favourite among fabricators, and it became something of a competition to see which one could beat me. But since they all played among themselves, they all basically had the same moves – so it was pretty easy to memorise their games as I went along. So I won.'

'How'd that get you to working for Orso?'

'Because the hypatus found out his fabricator got beat by a seventeen-year-old girl,' said Berenice. 'And he called me in. Looked at me. Then he fired his old fabricator and hired me on the spot.'

Sancia whistled. 'I guess you traded up pretty quick. That's lucky.'

'It was lucky twice over,' she said. 'Not only was I plucked out at random to become a scriver, but women are rarely admitted to scriving academies these days. It's become a more masculine pursuit, after the wars.'

'What happened to your old man?'

'He was . . . less lucky. He kept coming around to the office and demanding more money. Then the hypatus sent some people to talk to him, and he never came back.' Her words had a forced lightness to them, as if describing a half-remembered dream. 'Whenever I go into the Commons, I wonder if I'll see him. I never do.'

The men began walking northeast. Then they turned a corner, and Berenice sucked in a breath. 'Ohhh, *shit*.'

'What's wrong?' asked Sancia.

'I . . . think I know where they're going,' she said.

'And where's that?'

Then she saw it: five blocks down the muddy fairway from them was a campo gate, lit with flickering torches. Set in the dark stone arch above the gate was a familiar loggotipo: the hammer and the chisel, crossed before the stone. The men appeared to be heading straight for it.

'The Candianos,' sighed Berenice. She watched as the men trickled through the gates. The Candiano house guards nodded to them. 'He knew . . .' she said quietly. 'That's why he talked to her. Because he'd already suspected.'

'What?' said Sancia. 'What are you talking about?'

'Never mind,' said Berenice. 'You said you can get us in there?'

'Yeah. Come on.' Sancia trotted down the Candiano campo wall until she found a small steel, altered door.

'This is a security door,' said Berenice. 'What the guards use when they need to infiltrate the Commons. You really got a key to here?'

Sancia shushed her. <*Clef – can you break this thing* without *blowing it off its hinges?*>

<*Ehh, yeah. Shouldn't be hard. Listen to it . . .* >

A swell of whispering, and the voice emerged: < *. . . strong and firm and hard and true, I await . . . I await the key, the key of light and crystal to shine stars within my depths . . .* >

<*What the hell is it saying?*> asked Sancia.

<*It's kind of clever,*> said Clef. <*The lock is waiting for a key to go into its housing and shine light in a few places. Then it'll unlock and open.*>

<*How are you going to make light?*>

<*I'm not going to make light. I'm just going to trick the door into* thinking *it's had light shone in all the right places. Or maybe I'll make the door forget which places need light . . . and instead make it think the whole front of the door is that specific place . . . Yeah, that should be easy!*>

<*Whatever. And it won't set off the alarms if we go through without sachets?*>

<*I can make this entry forget what human bodies feel like when they pass through it, so it won't know to perform a check – but it'll only last for a few seconds.*>

<*Fine. Just do it fast.*> She looked at Berenice. 'Keep watch. We can't get caught doing this.'

'What are you going to do?'

'Use a stolen key,' said Sancia. She approached the door, and, making sure Clef wasn't visible and that Berenice's back was turned, she stuck him into the lock.

She'd expected the exchange from before – the bellowing voice, the dozens of questions – but it didn't come. Rather, the exchange happened so much . . . *faster.* It was more like when Clef had picked the mechanical locks, popping the Miranda Brass in the blink of an eye, only she felt a burst of information exchanged between Clef and the door.

He really is getting stronger. The thought filled her with dread.

She pulled the door open. 'Come on,' she said to Berenice. 'Hurry!'

Inside, they had to change topclothes again – this time into Candiano colours, the black and the emerald. As they dressed, Sancia glanced sideways at Berenice and caught a glimpse of a smooth, pale shoulder dappled with freckles, and tawny, moist hair clinging to her long neck.

Sancia looked away. *No,* she thought. *Stop. Not today.*

Berenice pulled on a coat. 'Your contacts are good,' she said, 'if they were able to get a security key.'

Sancia thought quickly for an excuse. 'Something's up with the Candiano campo,' she said. 'They're mixing up all their security procedures. They even changed over all their sachets. Change makes for a lot of opportunities.' Then she had an idea – because this was all true. 'You don't think that has anything to do with whatever is going on?'

Berenice thought about it, her cool, grey eyes fixed on the Mountain of the Candianos in the distance. 'Possibly,' she said.

Once they were changed, they started off into the Candiano campo. And as they walked, Sancia realised something.

She looked at all the houses and streets and shops – these done in a darker shade of moss clay than the rest of the campos she'd seen. And she found none of them familiar.

'I've . . . never worked here before,' she said.

'What?' said Berenice.

'I've done jobs on the other campos before,' she said. 'Filching this or that. But . . . never the Candiano campo.'

'You wouldn't have. You know Company Candiano almost fell apart about ten years ago, right?'

'No. I've barely lived here three years, and I've mostly been trying to survive, not sharing work gossip.'

'Tribuno Candiano was like a god in this city,' said Berenice, 'He was probably the greatest scriver of our era. But then they found out he'd been doctoring the financials, spending fortunes on archaeological digs and supposedly hierophantic artefacts. Then the company came crashing down. They lost a huge amount of talent after that,' said Berenice. 'Including the hypatus.'

'You can just call him Orso, you know.'

'Thank you. I am well aware of that. Anyway, nearly everything got bought up by the Ziani family, but not many people stuck around to make sure the ship would still float. That tremendous exodus was a great boon to the other merchant houses, but Company Candiano has never really recovered.'

Sancia looked around. There were a lot fewer lights here, no floating lanterns, and almost no scrived carriages. The only impressive thing in sight was the Mountain of the Candianos, which loomed in the distance like a vast whale parting the seas. 'No shit.'

Berenice watched the group of men skulking through the streets of the campo. They seemed to be following the outer wall. 'Why aren't they going deeper in? If this is as secretive as it's supposed to be – why aren't they headed straight for the Mountain?'

'You either hide secrets close to your heart,' said Sancia, 'or out in the hinterlands. It must be somewhere close, though – otherwise they'd have grabbed a carriage, yes?'

They followed the men along the campo wall. Evening was coming on now, and the mist thickened as the sun withdrew. The pale lights of the Candiano campo were a brittle white – not at all the pleasant rosy or yellow hues of the other campos. They looked spectral and strange in the fog.

Then a constellation of lights emerged ahead – a tall, sprawling construct that Sancia had trouble making out. 'Is that a . . .'

'Yes,' said Berenice quietly. 'It's a foundry.'

Finally the man came to the foundry gates. Sancia could read the stone sign above – CATTANEO FOUNDRY. Yet unlike most of the foundries she'd encountered in her life, this one did not seem to be operating: there was no stream of smoke, no quiet roar of equipment, no chatter or cries from the yards beyond.

They watched as the men entered through the gates. The guards out front were heavily armoured, and heavily armed – yet they also seemed to be the only people around.

'The Cattaneo Foundry . . .' said Berenice. 'I thought that one was closed when the house went bankrupt. What in hell is going on?'

Sancia spied a tall townhouse next to the foundry walls. 'I'll get a better look.'

'You'll get a . . . Wait!' said Berenice.

Sancia trotted over, took off her gloves, and slowly scaled the side of the townhouse. As she climbed, Sancia could hear Berenice fretting down below, muttering, 'Oh my God . . . Oh my *God* . . .'

Sancia nimbly pulled herself up onto the slate roof. From here she could see the whole of the foundry yards . . . and they were empty. Just yards and yards of blank mud or stone. It was a queer sight. Yet she could spy the men in the distance, filing into the foundry main facilities ahead, a huge, fortresslike structure of dark stone, with tiny windows, a copper roof, and dozens and dozens of smokestacks – though only one seemed to be operating, a small one on the west side, which sighed a narrow thread of grey smoke.

So the question is, thought Sancia, *what are they making?*

She watched the walls and yards of the foundry, and saw that although the facility appeared empty, it was not deserted. There were a handful of men standing along the walls or the ramparts of the foundry, and though it was hard to make out from this distance, she could see the gleam of scrived armour on their shoulders.

<*This place gives me the creeps,*> said Clef.

<*Me too,*> said Sancia. She took stock of the defences, counting the guards, their positions, and the doors and gates throughout the facility. Then she looked at the main building, and she saw a handful of windows had light in them – there, in the corner rooms, on the third floor on the northwestern side. <*But I think we need to get in there.*>

Clef sighed. <*I was worried you were going to say that.*>

Sancia carefully climbed back down to the street level, where Berenice stood fuming. 'Next time, at least consider asking me before you do that!'

'It's not shut down,' said Sancia.

'What?'

'The foundry's not shut down. There's smoke or steam coming from some of the stacks. So it's still forging something. Do you have any idea what?'

'Not at all. But the hypatus might. We can go back and consult with him, and then perhaps we can come up with a plan to—'

'No,' said Sancia. 'There are twelve guards patrolling the foundry walls tonight. If this bastard listens to the captured sounds from the workshop and gets spooked, there could be fifty tomorrow – or they could move out altogether.'

'So what? Wait . . .' Berenice stared at her. 'You surely aren't proposing what I think you are – are you?'

'We've caught him unawares,' said Sancia. 'We take advantage of the opportunity, or we lose it.'

'You want to break into a foundry? Right *now*? We don't even know if anything's going on in there!'

'There is. There are lights on the third floor in the northwest corner.'

Berenice narrowed her eyes. 'The third floor . . . then the administrative offices, possibly?'

'So you know something about foundries. Do you know how to get *into* a foundry?'

'Well, certainly, but there are countless sachets required,' said Berenice. 'But worse, there are only a few ways in, and even a skeleton crew can watch them all, unless you can . . .' Then she trailed off, staring into the distance.

'Unless you can what?'

Berenice glowered like she'd just had a thought she dearly didn't want to have.

'Does this have anything to do with all the rigs you're carrying with you?' asked Sancia.

Her mouth fell open. 'How did you know about those?' Then a sheepish look crossed her face. 'Oh. Right. You can, uh, hear them. I was going to say – unless you can make your *own* door somewhere.'

'And . . . can you do that?'

She squirmed. 'I . . . Well. It's all, ah . . . very *experimental*. And it will depend on finding the right bit of stone wall.'

19

Berenice led Sancia down to the canal running along the foundry. There they came upon a clutch of huge tunnels and pipes sticking out of the canal walls.

'Intake,' muttered Berenice as they reviewed them. 'Outtake . . . Intake, intake, intake . . . and outtake.'

'These all look like iron,' said Sancia. 'Not stone wall.'

'Yes, thank you, that's clear.' She pointed at one, a huge, gaping iron pipe with a thick grate across its mouth. 'That's it. That's the one – the metallurgical outtake pipe.'

'What are we going to do about the grate?'

'Go through it,' said Berenice. She walked to the closest tunnel and tried to climb onto its top, but, despite her height, she rather pathetically slid back down the side. 'Ah – little help?'

Sancia shook her head and gave her a boost. 'I guess fabs and scrivers don't get out much,' she muttered.

Together they crawled across the tunnel tops to the big outtake pipe. Berenice sat and took out a case of what appeared to be a dozen small, scrived components, and many small plates covered with complicated sigils. She selected one component – a slim metal wand whose rounded, bulbous tip looked like molten glass – and looked it over.

'What's that?' asked Sancia.

'I'd made it to be a small spotlight, but we obviously need something a bit more now. Hmm.' She reviewed her components, selected a rounded handle with a bronze knob on the side, and slid the small end of the wand inside until there was a *click*. Then she took a long, thin plate, and slotted it into the side of the handle. 'There. A heating element. That should do.'

'Do what?'

'Help me down. I'm going to get the grate out of the way.'

Sancia lowered Berenice down until the girl delicately balanced on the lip of the pipe. Then she lifted the wand to one of the big rivets holding up the grate, adjusted the knob on the side, and . . .

<*Crap!*> said Clef. <*Shut your eyes, kid.*>

<*Why?*>

The tip of the wand flared bright hot, like a shooting star had plummeted down to land in the scummy pipe. Sancia cringed and looked away, eyes watering. There was a loud, furious hissing sound. She looked back when it stopped, and saw the rivet was now a glowing blob of smoking, molten metal.

Berenice coughed and waved her hand in front of her face. 'I'll do the sides and the tops, and leave one rivet on the bottom. Then you pull me back up and I'll attach an anchor to the top – like the one the captain used to weigh you down. This should pry the grate open, and we can slip inside.'

'Shit,' said Sancia. 'Why did you bring all this?'

Berenice touched the wand to another rivet. 'I got shot at the other night. Rather a lot. I came prepared to prevent such a thing from happening again. A lot of components that can do a lot of different things – when combined the right way, that is.' The wand flared bright.

When Berenice was finished, Sancia hauled her back up. Berenice took out the anchor – a small bronze ball that was covered in shiny brass sigils, with a shiny latch on its side – and chained it to the top of the grate. She slid the latch aside, revealing a wooden button, and touched it. Suddenly the grate groaned and creaked, until it slowly fell open, like a drawbridge.

'Inside,' said Berenice. 'Quick.'

They dropped down into the mouth of the pipe and ran into the darkness. Sancia was about to touch a hand to the wall to see, but there was a *click*, and Berenice's wand glowed bright again – yet she'd apparently removed whatever component made it capable of burning through iron, and it now only gave out light. 'Keep your eyes out for any stone,' she said. She adjusted the light, turning down the brightness.

'Where the hell are we, again?'

'We're in the metallurgical outtake tunnel of the foundry. Processing so much metal – iron, brass, bronze, lead – it takes a lot of water, which gets tainted and rendered unusable after the forging's done. So they dump it all out into the canals. It's a big pipe that runs through a lot of the foundry – and if we see any brick, I should be able to get you in.'

'How?'

'I'll tell you once we find it.'

They kept walking, and walking, until finally Sancia saw it. 'There. On the side.' She pointed. The iron walls of the pipe stopped short about ten feet ahead, and from there on out the walls were stone and brick, like an old sewer.

Berenice reviewed the stone wall and glanced back at the mouth of the tunnel. 'Hum. This could work. I *think* we're next to the storage bays. But I'm not sure – and I would really prefer to be sure.'

'Why?'

'Well, we could be next to the water reservoirs – which means the tunnel would flood and we'd drown.'

'Crap. Hold on.' Sancia slid off a glove, placed her hand to the bricks, and shut her eyes.

The wall was thick, at least two to three feet. She kept letting it pour into her mind, telling her what it felt, or at least what was on the other side . . .

She opened her eyes. 'It's just wall,' she said. 'Nothing on the other side.'

'Is it thick?'

'Yeah. At least two feet.'

Berenice grimaced. 'Well. Maybe it will still work, then . . .'

'Maybe what will work?'

She didn't answer. She reached into her pocket and pulled out what looked like four small bronze spheres with sharp steel screws on their ends. She examined the wall, sucked her teeth, and started screwing the bronze spheres into the wall in the shape of a square, with one ball at each corner.

'Can you please just tell me what this is?' asked Sancia impatiently.

'You know about construction scrivings, right?' said Berenice, adjusting the bronze spheres.

'Yeah. They glue bricks together to make them think they're all one thing instead of separate things.'

'Yes. But lots of foundries use the *same kind* of stone, or something close to it – which makes it a lot easier to twin.'

'Twin with . . . what?' asked Sancia.

'With a section of stone wall that's back in my office,' said Berenice, standing up. 'One that has a big hole in the middle.'

Sancia stared at the wall, then at Berenice. 'What? Really?'

'Yes,' said Berenice. She scrunched her nose, reviewing her handiwork. 'If it works, it should convince this section of wall that it's the same as the one in my office. That'd then weaken all the Candiano construction scrivings in a circle, and basically carve a hole for you. But . . . I've really never tested this in the field before. Especially not on a wall this *thick*.'

'And if it doesn't work?'

'Frankly, I don't have a damned clue what will happen if it goes wrong.' She glanced at Sancia. 'Still feeling experimental?'

'I've done dumber shit in the past few days.'

Berenice took a breath, and twisted the tops of all four brass spheres, one after another. Then she stepped back and slowly moved away, like she was preparing to run.

For a moment, nothing happened. Then the colour of the brick changed, ever so slightly, growing just a tiny bit darker. Then came a creaking sound. The bricks shuddered and rippled – and then, suddenly, the wall fractured in the middle in a perfect circle, like someone had carved it with a saw.

'It works,' said Berenice. 'It works!'

'Great,' said Sancia. 'Now, how the hell do we get that big plug of stone out of the way?'

'Oh. Right.' Berenice pulled out yet another trinket from her pockets: this one appeared to be just a small iron handle with a button on the side. 'Just a construction scriving. It'll stick to the plug's centre.' She placed the handle in the centre of the stone plug, confirmed it was stuck, and gave a mighty heave.

Nothing happened. She tugged again, her face turning pink, and stopped, gasping. 'Well,' she said. 'I didn't *quite* anticipate this.'

'Here,' said Sancia. She knelt, gripped the handle, placed one foot against the wall, and pulled.

Slowly, with a low grinding noise, the short stone column slid a few inches out of the wall. Sancia took a breath and pulled again, and it finally fell to the tunnel floor with a *plunk*, leaving about a two-foot-wide hole in the wall.

'Good,' said Berenice, miffed. 'Well done. Can you fit?'

'Keep your voice down. Yeah, I can fit.' She crouched and peered into the hole. The room on the other side was dark. 'Do you know what that is over there?' she whispered.

Berenice turned up her scrived light and stuck it through the hole. They glimpsed a wide room with a steel walkway running around the edges, and a huge heap of twisted metals in the centre. 'It's the waste bin, essentially – all the castoff bits of metals go here to be melted down and reused.'

'But I'll really be inside the foundry – yes?'

'Yes?'

She shook her head. 'Goddamn. I can't believe we just broke into a foundry just with some random shit in your pockets.'

'I'll take that as a compliment. But we're not there yet. This is the basement. The administrative offices are on the third floor. If you want to find out what's going on here, that's the place to look.'

'Any advice for how to get up there?'

'No. I've no idea what doors will be locked or what passages will be blocked or guarded. You'll be on your own. I . . . assume you don't want me to come with you?'

'Two house-breakers makes for a quick trip to the loop,' said Sancia. 'It'd be better if you kept a lookout.'

'Fine with me. I can go back to the streets outside, and if I see something I'll try to think of some way to warn you.'

Sancia slipped her feet into the hole. 'You wouldn't happen to have any more useful rigs, would you?'

'I do. But they are destructive, and foundries are delicate – meaning if you cut through or break the wrong thing, you would die and probably take a lot of people with you.'

'Great. I sure as shit hope we get something out of this,' said Sancia, sliding forward.

'Me too,' said Berenice. 'Good luck.' Then she trotted back down the tunnel.

Sancia slipped through the hole in the wall, stood up, and tried to get her bearings. It was pitch-black in there now, and she was reluctant to use up her talents just to get around a room.

<*Scrived lock on the door on your left,*> said Clef. <*Up the steps. I can sense it. All the pipes and walls are crawling with sigils. The entire place is a device that makes other devices . . . Wow.*>

<*And it's a headache to be inside it,*> said Sancia, stumbling over to the door. She fumbled for the lock, stuffed Clef inside, and opened it. She was relieved to see weak light filtering through the hallway on the other side,

Using Clef, Sancia unlocked door after door as she penetrated the depths of the foundry. She was astounded by the sheer density of the thing, all tiny passageways that led to huge, complicated processing bays, full of giant loomlike devices or cranes that perched over tables or lathes like spiders weaving cocoons about their prey. The heat within the foundry was immense, but there was a constant wind in every hall and passage, carrying the hot air out to – well, somewhere, she assumed. It was like being trapped in the innards of some kind of giant, mindless creature.

Most of it was deserted. Which made sense, since only a portion of it was being used now. But then . . .

<*Three guards up ahead,*> said Clef. <*Heavily armed.*>

Sancia looked ahead. The passageway ended in a closed wooden door. Presumably there was some kind of hallway being guarded beyond it.

<*What floor are we on?*> she asked.

<*Still on the ground floor, I think.*>

<*Ugh.*>

She took off a glove and felt the wall, then the ceiling. The foundry was so alive with scrivings that this felt like walking under a powerful waterfall – the sudden pressure almost knocked her over. But she held on, walking along the walls, her bare fingers trailing over the stone and the metal, until she felt a long, narrow, vertical cavity just ahead . . .

A hatch. A shaft.

She took her hand away, shook herself, and withdrew back down the hallway until she found a small door. A sign on the front read: LEXICON MAINTENANCE ACCESS. The lock on the front was deeply forbidding.

She took Clef out and stuck him in the keyhole. There was a burst of information, and Clef batted the lock's defences away like it was a wall of straw.

<*That seemed easy,*> she said, opening the door. The shaft within was narrow and ran perfectly straight, up and down, with ladder bars on the opposite side. It was dark within, so she couldn't see what was above or below.

<*It was. But . . .* >

<*But what?*>

<*There's . . . something down there.*>

<*Yeah. The lexicon.*> She reached out and started climbing up.

<*Right. But it feels . . . familiar.*>

<*How do you mean?*>

<*I don't know. It's like . . . if you smelled the perfume of someone you hadn't smelled in a long, long time. It's weird. I'm not sure why.*>

Sancia climbed until she came to the third floor. She turned until she was facing the door, and blindly found the handle. <*Anyone out there?*>

<*Oh, hell yeah. This place is crawling with armed men. Go to the fourth floor. It's deserted.*>

She did as he asked, came to the fourth floor, and opened the hatch. This floor, unlike the others, had windows. Slashes of moonlight lay scattered across the blank stone floor. It looked like this area was mostly storage – lots of boxes, but not much else.

She glanced out a nearby window, got her bearings, and started off toward the administrative offices. <*I'm guessing there aren't any other unguarded passageways down to the next floor.*>

<*None.*>

<*Great. How secure are the windows?*>

<*Well . . . They're basically scrived to be unbreakable, so no one, you know, tries to shoot bolts into the foundry. But it looks like they do swing open, at the tops, to let out heat or smoke.*> There was a pause. <*Uh, before you ask, they do open wide enough to let you in or out, probably.*>

She smiled. <*Excellent.*>

Berenice huddled in a doorway beyond the foundry walls, squinting at the windows through a spyglass. She found it hard to focus. Despite her occasional dabbling in campo intrigue, she was not at all accustomed to such high-stakes trickery. She certainly hadn't expected anyone to climb any buildings tonight, let alone break into a damned foundry.

Still, it seemed Sancia was right: something *was* going on, there on the third floor. She could make out a handful of people inside – but they seemed to be slowly gravitating toward the administrative offices.

That's less than optimal, she thought. *How will Sancia manage to get i* –

She stopped.

Was that a window opening? There on the dark fourth floor?

She watched, openmouthed, as a small figure in black slipped out of the fourth-floor window and clung to the corner of the building.

'Ohhh my God,' said Berenice.

Sancia hung tight to the corner of the foundry, her fingers digging into the narrow gaps in the stones. She'd held on to trickier places in her time – but not many.

She slipped down inch by inch to the next floor. She found a dark window, which meant no one would be inside, hopefully. She wedged her boots into the stone, then reached out with her stiletto and inserted its tip into the gap at the top of the closed window. She gently pushed the handle of the blade until she'd got it open a crack, she pulled back until it was wide open. Then she climbed up and lowered herself down into the gap.

Clef said, <*That was . . .* >

<*Amazing?*> She was hanging by the inside lip of the window – she suddenly felt grateful about them being unbreakable – and she lowered herself until she stood on a desk.

<*Amazingly stupid, maybe. Watch out, now. There are guards almost all around you, in the big area outside the door.*>

She slipped off the desk and got her bearings. This seemed to be a large, empty meeting room, one that hadn't been used in some time. She walked over to the door opposite the window and squinted through the keyhole. There was some kind of a wide, open area beyond, with four armoured Candiano guards standing around, looking bored and tired.

'Whoof,' she said quietly. She stepped back and looked around. There were two other doors on the left and right, presumably leading to adjoining offices.

She walked over to the door on the right and tried the handle. It was unlocked. She silently opened it and looked in. Another office, empty and dark.

She closed it and went to the final door. Yet as she approached . . .

She stopped. <*Was that a moan I just heard?*> she said.

<*Yeah,*> said Clef. <*And . . . it sure sounded to me like the fun kind of moan.*>

Sancia got close to the door, knelt, and pressed a hand to the floor. She let the floor pour into her mind – a difficult thing, since there were so many scrivings wearing her stamina thin. Yet soon she felt it . . .

A bare foot. Just one, the ball of the foot pressed into the floor. And it was pumping, up and down.

<*Yep,*> said Clef. <*Yep, yep. What I thought.*>

Sancia peered through the keyhole. This office was somewhat grand. There were scrived lanterns inside, a long desk covered with old, wrinkled papers, and a set of wooden boxes. There was also a bed in the far corner, and there were two people on the bed, a man and a woman – and they were quite naked and obviously coupling, the man keeping one foot on the floor and his other knee on the bed.

Due to her condition, Sancia did not know a great deal about sex, but she got the impression that this was not particularly good sex. The woman was quite young, about her own age, and terribly pretty, and though her face was fixed in an expression of pleasure there was something anxious and artificial about it, like she was dreading the displeasure of the man more than she was enjoying the experience. And though the man had his back turned to her – his skinny, pale back – there was a mechanical and determined quality to his thrusting, like he'd set his mind to do a job and was hell-bent on doing it.

Sancia watched them, wondering what to do now. She didn't think she could sneak out and snatch the papers off the desk. The girl kept looking around, anxious and yet bored, like she'd prefer to look at anything else than what was being done to her.

Then there was a knock from somewhere within the office – there must be another door there, she guessed, also leading to the open area beyond.

'Just a minute!' shouted the man, somewhat angrily. He doubled the pace of his thrusting. The girl cringed.

Another knock. 'Sir?' said a muffled voice. 'Mr Ziani? It's done.'

The man continued his endeavours.

'You said to notify you immediately,' said the voice.

The man stopped and bowed his head in frustration. The girl watched him warily.

<*So . . . that's Tomas Ziani?*> said Sancia. <*The guy who bought out all of Company Candiano?*>

<*I guess,*> said Clef.

'Just a second!' shouted the man, louder. Then he turned and dug around on the floor for his clothes.

Sancia's eyes shot wide. Though it wasn't particularly bright in the room, she knew that face – the curls, the scraggly beard, the narrow cheeks.

It was her client. The man who'd turned on the imperiat that night in the Greens, and caused the blackouts – and the man who'd almost certainly had Sark killed.

She stared at him, trying not to move.

<*Holy hell!*> said Clef. <*That . . . That's the guy, isn't it?*>

<*Yeah. That's the guy,*> she thought. The sight of him filled her with a raging mix of terror, fury, and confusion. She briefly considered leaping in and planting her stiletto in his gut. That seemed an appropriate way for him to die, naked and confused and sexually frustrated. But then she remembered the guards mere feet away from them, and thought better of it.

<*So . . . this Ziani guy is who's behind all this?*> asked Clef.

<*Shut up and let's listen, Clef!*>

Ziani pulled on a pair of hose. Then he sighed and barked, 'Come in!'

A door opened somewhere in the office, and bright light spilled in. The nude girl in the bed pulled the sheets up to cover herself, glaring at them sullenly.

'Ignore her,' snapped Ziani. 'And come *in*.'

A man entered the room and shut the door behind him. He appeared to be a clerk of some sorts, dressed in Candiano colours, and he carried a small wooden box with him.

'I assume if it was a success,' said Ziani, sitting at the desk, 'you'd be looking much happier.'

'Did you expect a success, sir?' said the clerk, surprised.

Ziani impatiently waved a hand. 'Just bring it over.'

The clerk approached and held out the box. Ziani took it, glaring at him, and opened it.

Sancia almost gasped. Inside the box was another imperiat – but this one appeared to be made of bronze, not the gleaming gold she'd seen before.

<*What in hell?*> said Clef.

Ziani examined it. 'It's shit,' he said. 'It's *shit*, is what it is. What happened?'

'The . . . the same thing that's always happened, sir,' said the clerk. He was obviously uncomfortable having this conversation with a nude girl in the room. 'We forged the device to your specifications. Then we attempted the exchange . . . and, ah, well. Nothing happened. The device remained as you see it now.'

Ziani sighed and pawed through the notes on the desk. He pulled out one browned, wrinkled sheet of parchment and examined it.

'Perhaps . . .' said the clerk. Then he stopped.

'Perhaps?' said Ziani.

'Perhaps, sir, since Tribuno has been of such great help on the other devices . . . Perhaps you could also discuss his notes with him, regarding this subject?'

Ziani tossed the papers back onto the desk. Sancia watched the page fall. *Tribuno Candiano's notes? On what?*

'Tribuno is still mad as a tick on a burning hare's arse,' Ziani said. 'And he's only been *somewhat* useful. About once a month, we find something scrawled in his cell that, yes, is useful – like the strings for the gravity plates – but it's not like we can *control* that. And he's written shit-all about the hierophants.'

There was a silence. Both the girl and the clerk watched Ziani anxiously, wondering what he'd make them do next.

'The problem is with the shell itself,' said Ziani, looking at the bronze imperiat. 'Not the ritual. We're following the ritual's instructions *exactly.* So there must be some sigil we're missing . . . Some component of the original we either don't have or aren't using right.'

'Do you think we need to reexamine the other artefacts, sir?'

'Absolutely not. It took a lot of work to move the trove out of the Mountain. I wouldn't want to lead Ignacio or any other of these slippery bastards to it just because I wanted to check notes.' He tapped the bronze imperiat before him. 'We're doing something wrong. Something on these is being made improperly . . .'

'So . . . what would you suggest we do, sir?'

'Experiment.' Ziani stood and started getting dressed. 'I want a hundred of the shells made before morning and sent to the Mountain,' he said. 'Enough for us to experiment on and adjust, comparing it with the original.'

The clerk stared at him. 'A hundred? Before *morning*? But . . . sir, the Cattaneo's lexicon is at a reduced state right now. To produce that many, we'd have to spin it up quickly.'

'So?'

'So . . . the lexicon will spike. It will definitely cause nausea for all of us, I expect.'

Ziani was still. 'Do you think I'm stupid?' he asked.

The room grew tense. The girl shrank down below the sheets.

'C–certainly not, sir,' said the clerk.

'Because it feels like you might,' said Ziani. He turned to look at him. 'Just because I'm not a scriver. Just because I don't have as many certifications as you. Because of *that* – you think I don't know these things?'

'Sir, I just . . .'

'It's a risk,' said Ziani. 'And an acceptable one. Do it. I'll supervise the fabrication.' He pointed at the girl. 'You stay there. It's far too long since I waxed an agreeable cunny, and I won't have this dull bit of business delay that, either.' He buttoned up his shirt, his face twisted in faint disdain. 'I certainly won't deign to go pawing around Estelle's musty skirts for a bit of push.'

'And . . . sir?'

'Yes?' snapped Ziani.

'What should we do with the corpse?'

'The same thing we've done with all the others? I mean, why should *I* know? We have people for that, don't we?'

Ziani and the clerk left the office and shut the door behind them. The girl slowly shut her eyes, sighing half in relief, half in dismay.

Sancia silently slid out her bamboo pipe and loaded it with a dart.

<*I can't tell if this girl's night is about to get better or worse,*> said Clef.

<*Better, I think,*> said Sancia.

Sancia waited for a few minutes, making sure they were really gone. Then she silently opened the door a crack, trained the pipe on the girl's neck, and blew.

The girl made a soft, 'Ah!' as the dart struck her neck. She tensed, drunkenly slapped at her neck, fell back, and was still.

Sancia slipped into the room and went to the other office door.

She peered through the keyhole and confirmed no one was approaching. Then she looked at the papers and boxes on the desk.

She picked up the thing Ziani had called the 'shell' – his term for the bronze imperiat, which apparently did not work. She found he was right: it was little more than a curiosity, a dull, dead hunk of metal. Though it bore many strange sigils, it was not a true scrived device.

<*So . . . that's what they're making here,*> said Clef. He sounded genuinely frightened. <*They're . . . They're making more imperiats. Or trying to.*>

<*Yeah.*>

<*A hundred of them. A* hundred *imperiats . . . God, can you scrumming imagine?*>

She tried to, and shivered.

<*That guy could wipe out all the other merchant houses,*> said Clef. <*He could destroy every army and every fleet in the Durazzo!*>

<*I need to focus, Clef. What else is here?*> She looked at the papers on the desk, and saw most were yellow with age, and written in a strange, spidery hand, like the hand of someone who was either old, infirm, or both.

She looked at the top of one paper:

THEORIES ON THE INTENT OF HIEROPHANTIC TOOLS

The notes of Tribuno Candiano, she thought. *The greatest scriver of our age . . .* There were a lot of them, and she understood few at a glance.

But some of the papers were different. They appeared to be wax rubbings of stone engravings or tables or bas-reliefs . . . But what they depicted was confusing.

Each one showed an altar, always an altar, positioned at the centre of each paper. Floating above the altar was the image of a prone, sexless human body – perhaps it was an artistic rendition of someone lying on the altar's surface. Floating above the human body was always an oversized sword or blade, several times the size of the altar or the person. Written inside the blade were any number of complicated sigils, which varied from engraving to engraving, but all of them had these three things in common: the body, the altar, and the blade.

There was something gruesomely clinical to it all. They did not depict some religious rite, it felt. Instead, they seemed like . . .

<*Instructions,*> she thought. <*But instructions for what?*>

<*Maybe Orso knows?*>

<*Maybe.*> She scooped up all the papers, folded them, and stuffed them into her pockets. <*We got what we came here for, I think. Let's get the hell out of—*>

Clef moaned, a sound suggesting both pain and epiphany. <*Ohh . . . San. Do you . . . do you feel that?*>

<*Feel what?*>

<*There's . . . there's someone here. There's a mind down there . . .* >

<*Huh? Down where?*>

<*Down in the ground. It's waking, thinking, pulling . . . It's waking up, San,*> he said dreamily.

<*The . . . the lexicon, you mean?*>

<*I hadn't realised, you see . . . The lexicon is a mind, a clever one, one whose arguments are so convincing that all of reality has to listen. Do you know what that feels li—*>

Then her head lit up with agony.

It was like the world was dissolving, like a meteor had struck the earth, like the walls had been turned to ash and cinder . . . She was still in the office, still standing next to that sleeping girl, but there was a hot coal in her brain, burning it away, scorching the walls of her skull. She opened her mouth in silent pain and was surprised when smoke didn't come pouring out.

Sancia fell to her knees and vomited. *It's the lexicon spiking,* she tried to tell herself. *That's all it is . . . You're just . . . sensitive to it . . .*

Clef cried out joyously: <*Do you feel it waking up? I hadn't realised how beautiful they were!*>

She felt warmth running down her face, and saw drops of blood on the floor below her.

<I . . . I remember someone like that!> said Clef. *<I remember . . . I* remember *him, Sancia . . . >*

Images leaked into her mind. The dusty smell of the office faded, and she smelled . . .

Desert hills. Cool night breezes.

Then she heard the hiss of sand, and the sound of millions of wings, and she was gone.

Berenice peered through the spyglass, watching for Sancia. The girl had abruptly sunk to the ground and fallen out of view – which seemed odd.

What is she doing? Why isn't she getting out of there?

Then nausea hit her – a familiar sensation for her.

They're spinning up the lexicon, she thought. *Activating more scrivings. And maybe it's done something to Sancia.*

She watched for a moment, then glassed the big, open area beyond the office. She saw glints of metal, and realised guards in scrived armour were walking at a quick pace – not on patrol, then. They were looking for something. And they seemed to be heading straight for Sancia.

'Shit,' she whispered. She looked back at the office. She still couldn't see Sancia. 'Oh, *shit*.'

Sancia was no longer in the office, no longer in the foundry or the campo or even in Tevanne. She was gone from that place.

Now she stood atop creamy yellow sand dunes, the pale-pink moon hanging fat and heavy in the sky. And standing on the dune across from her was . . .

A man. Or something man-shaped, facing away from her.

He was wrapped in black cloth, every inch of his body, his neck and face and feet. He wore a short black cloak that went down to about mid-thigh, and his arms and hands were lost in its folds. Next to the man-thing was a curious, ornate golden box, about three feet high and four feet long.

She knew this thing, she knew the box. She recognised them.

I can't let him see me, she thought.

She heard a sound coming from somewhere in the sky . . . the sound of so many wings, tiny and delicate, like a giant flock of butterflies.

The man-thing's head twitched ever so slightly, like he'd heard something. The sound of flapping wings grew louder.

No, she thought. *No, no . . .*

Then the man-thing rose up, just a touch, floating a foot above the dunes, and hung there, suspended in the night air.

Berenice stared through the spyglass as the guards got closer and closer. She had to do something, to warn Sancia or wake her somehow, or at least distract the guards.

She looked around. She had quite a few more rigs on her person, of course – when Berenice Grimaldi prepared, she did so with enthusiasm – but she'd never have imagined preparing for this.

Then she spied a possibility: there was a massive globe light just outside the southwest corner of the foundry, standing on a tall, iron pole, about forty feet high. It probably lit up the main entrance when the foundry was running.

She did some calculations. Then she pulled out her fusing wand and ran over to it.

I scrumming hope this works.

The man-thing hung in the air above the dunes across from Sancia, silent and still. Then the sands started to swirl around him, undulating in smooth rings as if being whipped about by a storm – but there was no wind, at least not that strong.

Please, no, thought Sancia. *Not him. Anyone but him.*

The man-thing slowly started to rotate to face her. The sound of flapping wings was deafening now, as if the night sky were thick with invisible butterflies.

Terror filled her, wordless and shrieking and mad. *No! No, I can't! I can't let him see me, I can't LET HIM SEE ME!*

The thing raised a black hand, fingers extended to the sky. The air quaked, and the sky shuddered.

Then there was a tremendous *crack* sound, and the vision faded.

She was back in the office, on her knees. Her stomach was boiling with nausea, and there was vomit on the floor – but she was back in her own body.

<*What was that?*> she thought – though she already suspected. <*Clef . . . was that a memory? A memory of yours?*>

He didn't answer.

'What the *hell* was that sound?' said a voice beyond the office door.

She froze, listening.

'The damn lamp column fell over outside! It fell over the walls and into the yard!'

<*Clef?*> she asked. <*Clef. Are you there?*>

<*Yes,*> he said, though his voice was very small.

<*What's going on? Are there guards out there?*>

<*Yes. And they're coming straight for you.*>

Sancia stumbled forward and slipped through the door to the empty adjoining office. She climbed up onto the desk just as she heard a knock. 'Miss?' called a voice. 'Miss? We need to come in and get something off the desk. Don't be alarmed, please.'

'Shit,' muttered Sancia. She leapt up, grabbed the window, and hauled herself through the top. Then she slipped out, gripped the edge of the building, and started to climb up to the fourth floor.

She heard a voice cry, 'What in *hell*? What happened here! Wake the girl up, now, *now*!'

She crawled through the fourth-floor window and started

sprinting back toward the maintenance shaft. About halfway there she heard the floor below erupt in shouting.

<*They've sent the alarm out,*> said Clef quietly. <*They're looking for you now.*>

<*Yeah,*> she said, leaping into the shaft. <*I gathered.*>

Berenice exhaled with relief as she watched Sancia clamber back through the fourth-floor window. The half-melted base of the lamp tower was still glowing a cheerful red before her. She'd never intended to use the wand for this, and scrupulously made a note of this new application.

Then she heard the shouts from over the walls – guards, probably. And soon they'd be coming out to see what had happened.

'Shit,' said Berenice. She ran for the canal.

Sancia dropped down the lexicon shaft as fast as she could, leaping from rung to rung until she came to the ground floor. Then she staggered back down the passageways, heading to the rubbish room in the basement, where Berenice had so adeptly carved the hole in the wall.

She could hear footsteps in the hallways behind her and above her, men shouting and doors flying open. She ran as fast as she could, but her head felt slow and sluggish. She tasted blood in her mouth and realised her nose was bleeding quite a lot.

I hope I don't goddamn bleed out before I make it out of here, she thought wearily. *Not after all this work.*

Then she heard a voice far behind her: '*Stop! Stop, you!*'

She looked over her shoulder and saw an armoured guard behind her, standing far down at the end of the passageway. She saw him lift his espringal, and leapt behind a corner just as a scrived bolt shrieked down the hallway, cracking into the wall on the far end. *Scrumming terrible place to dodge shots*, she thought. But she had no choice: she flung herself back around the corner and sprinted for the door to the rubbish bin.

'*She's here, she's here!*' screamed the guard.

She reached the metal door, threw it open, and leapt into the darkness, slamming the door behind her. She fumbled down the dark steps to the hole in the wall, half-worried she'd fall off the walkway into the piles of scrap metal below. Then there was a harsh *crack-crack-crack*, and the room filled with weak light. She looked back to see the door behind now had three large holes in it, undoubtedly put there by scrived bolts.

God, they'll tear through that in a second! she thought.

'Come on!' hissed a voice in the darkness. 'Come *on*!'

She turned and saw a light on the far wall – Berenice's scrived light, shining through the hole she'd made. Sancia leapt down the steps and threw herself through the breach.

'We won't run far!' she gasped as she emerged. 'They're right behind me!'

'I am aware of that.' Berenice had her back to her, and she seemed to be fiddling with something in the roof of the tunnel. 'There,' she said, stepping back. Sancia saw it was the anchor she'd used to open the grate of the pipe, but now it was attached to the end of a spike that looked like it'd been stabbed up into the bricks. 'Come on. Now we *really* need to run.'

Sancia staggered to her feet and limped down the tunnel. There was a faint crackling sound behind them.

'No, faster,' said Berenice, anxious. 'Like, *much* faster.' She grabbed Sancia, threw her arm over her shoulder, and hauled her forward just as the crackling grew to a rumble.

Sancia looked back to see the brick section of the tunnel suddenly collapse, sending a wall of dust flying at them. 'Holy hell,' she said.

'I don't think it should bring down the metal parts of the pipe,' said Berenice as they hobbled up to the grate. 'But I would prefer not to find out so – up! Up and out, now!'

Sancia wiped blood from her face, grabbed the rungs, and started to climb.

20

'I . . . I thought I told you just to *follow* them!' said Orso, aghast.

'Well, we did that,' croaked Sancia. She spat another mouthful of blood into a bucket. 'You didn't say *not* to do all the other stuff.'

'To break into a foundry?' he squawked. 'And . . . and to *collapse* its metallurgical outtake piping? I had thought such things would have easily been beyond the pale of common sense – or am I mad, Berenice?'

He glared at Berenice, who was sitting in the corner of his office, sorting through the notes Sancia had stolen. Gregor leaned over her shoulder, idly reviewing them with his hands clasped behind his back. 'I was merely confirming a suspicion you had articulated, sir,' she said.

'And which one was that?'

She looked up. 'That it was Tomas Ziani who's behind all this. That *is* why you spoke to Estelle at the meeting yesterday – correct, sir?'

Gregor blinked and stood. 'Estelle Ziani? Wait – the *daughter* of Tribuno Candiano? Orso talked to *her*?'

'You sure are telling a hell of a lot of tales out of school!' Orso snarled at her.

'Why did you suspect Ziani, Orso?' asked Gregor.

Orso scowled at Berenice, then tried to think of what to say. 'When I was at the council meeting, with everyone talking about the blackout, none of the house leaders seemed to act odd – except *possibly* Ziani. He looked at me, at my neck, and he went out of his way to dig at me on the hierophants. There was something to that that just . . . bothered me. Just a hunch.'

'A good hunch,' said Sancia. She blew her nose into a rag. 'I mean, I saw him – *all* of him. He's behind this. All of it. And he's trying to build dozens, if not hundreds, of his own imperiats.'

There was a silence as they all considered this.

'Which means that, if Tomas Ziani figures this process out,' said Gregor quietly, 'he can essentially hold the civilised world hostage.'

'I . . . I still can't believe it's Ziani,' said Orso. 'I asked Estelle if she would tell me if Ziani was coming after me, and she said she would.'

'You trusted the man's wife to betray him?' asked Gregor.

'Well, yes? But it sounds like Tomas Ziani is basically keeping her locked in the Mountain, much like her father. So although she might have a reason to betray him, I don't know how much she could actually know.'

'Uh, I don't know who this Estelle person is,' said Sancia, 'but I just assume it's someone Orso is scrumming?'

They all stared at her, scandalised.

'Okay,' said Sancia, 'someone you *were* scrumming then?'

Orso's face worked as he tried to figure out how offended he was. 'I was . . . *acquainted* with her, once. When I worked for Tribuno Candiano.'

'You were scrumming your boss's daughter?' said Sancia, impressed. 'Wow. Gutsy.'

'As entertaining as Orso's personal life is,' said Gregor loudly, 'we should return to the issue at hand. How can we prevent Tomas Ziani from building up an arsenal of hierophantic weapons?'

'And how does he even plan to make them?' asked Berenice, paging through Tribuno's notes. 'It seems to be going wrong for him somehow . . .'

'Please, Sancia, go over what Ziani said,' said Orso. 'Line by line.'

She did so, describing every word of the conversation she'd heard.

'So,' said Orso when she was finished. 'He called it a shell. And described some . . . some kind of failed exchange?'

'Yeah,' said Sancia. 'He also mentioned a ritual. I don't know why he called it a *shell*, though – shells have something inside them, usually.'

'And he thought the shell itself was the problem,' said Berenice. 'The imperiats they'd made somehow weren't *exactly* like the original imperiat.'

'Yeah. That seemed to be it.'

There was a pause. Then Berenice and Orso looked at each other in horror.

'It's the Occidental alphabet,' Berenice said. 'The *lingai divina*.'

'Yes,' said Orso faintly.

'He's . . . he's missing a piece. A sigil, or more. That's got to be it!'

'Yes.' Orso heaved a deep sigh. 'That's why he's been stealing Occidental artefacts. That's why he stole my scrumming key! Of course. He wants to complete the alphabet. Or at least get enough of it to make a functional imperiat.'

'I'm lost,' said Gregor. 'Alphabets?'

'We only have *pieces* of the Occidental alphabet of sigils,' said Berenice. 'A handful here, a handful there. It's the biggest obstacle to Occidental research. It's like trying to solve a riddle in a foreign language where you only know the vowels.'

'I see,' said Gregor. 'But if you steal enough samples – the bits and pieces and fragments that have the right sigils on them . . .'

'Then you can complete the alphabet,' said Orso. 'You can finally speak the language to command your tools to have hierophantic capabilities. Theoretically. Though it sounds like that greasy bastard Ziani is having a time of it.'

'But he *is* getting help,' said Berenice. 'It *is* Tribuno Candiano who's writing the sigil strings to make rigs like the gravity plates, and the listening device. Only he's doing it thoughtlessly, mindlessly, in his madness.'

'But that still doesn't hang together for me,' said Orso. 'The Tribuno I knew didn't bother with the usual gravity bullshit so many scrivers wasted their lives on. His interests were far . . . grander.' He pulled a face, like remembering Tribuno's interests disturbed him. 'I feel like it just *can't* be him.'

'The Tribuno you knew was sane,' said Gregor.

'True,' admitted Orso. 'Either way, it sounds like Ziani does have all of Tribuno's Occidental collection – that would be the trove that he'd moved out of the Mountain, right?'

'Yeah,' said Sancia. 'He mentioned some other artefacts he'd hidden away somewhere – mostly to hide it from you, Orso.'

Orso smirked. 'Well. At least we've got the scrummer rattled. I suspect he's been stealing Occidental artifacts from all kinds of people. He must have quite the hoard. And . . . there was that last bit . . . the one I find most confusing. They had to dispose of a *body*?'

'Yeah,' said Sancia. 'He made it sound like they'd been disposing of bodies for some time. Didn't seem to matter whose bodies they were. I get the impression it had something to do with this ritual – but I don't understand any of that.'

Gregor held up his hands. 'We're getting off track. Alphabets, hierophants, bodies – yes, all that is troubling. But the core issue is that Tomas Ziani intends to manufacture devices that can annihilate scriving on a *mass scale*. They would be as bolts in a vast quiver to him and his forces. But his entire strategy rests upon one item – the original imperiat. That's the key to all of his ambitions.' He looked around at them. 'So. If he were to lose that . . .'

'Then that would be a massive setback,' said Berenice.

'Yes,' said Gregor. 'Lose the original, and he'll have nothing to copy.'

'And if Sancia is right, Tomas flat-out said where he was keeping it,' said Orso thoughtfully. He turned in his chair to look out the window.

Sancia followed his gaze. There, huddled in the distant cityscape of Tevanne, was a vast, arching dome, like a smooth, black growth in the centre of the city: the Mountain of the Candianos.

'Ah, hell,' she sighed.

⸻

'It's insane,' said Sancia, pacing. 'The damned idea is insane!'

'Breaking into a foundry on a whim was pretty goddamn insane,' said Orso. 'But you seemed game about that!'

'We caught them with their hose down,' said Sancia, 'in an abandoned foundry in the middle of nowhere. That's different from trying to break into the scrumming Mountain, maybe *the* most guarded place in the damned city, if not the world! I doubt if Berenice has some delightful trinket in her pockets that could help us get into there.'

'It *is* insane,' said Gregor. 'But it is, regrettably, our only option. I doubt if Ziani can be lured out of the Mountain with the original imperiat. So we must go in.'

'You mean *me*,' said Sancia. 'I doubt if your dumb arses will be the ones being dropped in there.'

'Let's not get ahead of ourselves,' said Gregor. 'But I admit, I've no idea how to break into such a place. Orso – did you live there ever?'

'I did once,' said Orso. 'When it was freshly built. That was a hell of a long time ago, it seems now.'

'You did?' asked Sancia. 'Are the rumours true? Is it really . . . haunted?'

She half expected Orso to burst out laughing at the notion, but he didn't. Instead he leaned back in his chair and said, 'You know, I'm not sure. It's . . . difficult to describe. It's big, for one thing. The sheer size of the thing is a feat in and of itself. It's like a city in there. But that wasn't the oddest thing. The oddest thing about the Mountain was that it *remembered*.'

'Remembered what?' asked Sancia.

'What you did,' said Orso. 'What you'd done. Who you were. You'd walk into a bathing room at the same time every day and find a bath already drawn for you, piping hot. Or you'd walk down the hall to your lift at the usual time and find it waiting for you. The changes would be subtle, and slow, just incremental adjustments – but, slowly, slowly, people got used to the Mountain knowing what they were doing inside of it, and adjusting for them. They got used to this . . . this *place* predicting what they'd do.'

'It learned?' said Gregor. 'A scrived structure *learned*, like it had a mind of its own?'

'That I don't know. It seemed to. Tribuno designed the thing in his later years, when he'd got strange, and he never shared his methods with me. He'd grown hugely secretive by then.'

'How could it know where people were, sir?' asked Berenice.

A guilty look came over Orso's face. 'Okay, well, I *did* have something to do with that . . . You know the trick with my workshop door?'

'It's scrived to sense your blood . . . Wait. That's how the Mountain keeps track of everyone inside? It senses *every* resident's blood?'

'Essentially,' said Orso. 'Every new resident has to log a drop of blood with the Mountain's core. Otherwise it won't let them into where they need to go. Your blood is your sachet, getting you in and out. Visitors are either restricted to visitor areas, or they have to carry around sachets of their own.'

'That's why the Mountain is so secure,' said Sancia quietly. 'It knows who's supposed to be there.'

'How could it do all that?' asked Gregor. 'How could a device be so powerful?'

'Hell, I don't know. But I did once see a specification list for the Mountain's core – and it included cradles for six full-capacity lexicons.'

Berenice stared at him. '*Six* lexicons? For *one* building?'

'Why go to all that effort?' asked Gregor. 'Why do all this in secret, and never capitalise on it, never share it?'

'Tribuno's ambitions were vast,' said Orso. 'I don't think he wanted to mimic the hierophants – he wanted to *become* one. He grew obsessed with a specific Occidental myth. Probably the most famous one about the most famous hierophant.' He sat back. 'Besides his magic wand, what's the one thing everyone knows about Crasedes the Great?'

'He kept an angel in a box,' said Berenice.

'Or a genie in a bottle,' said Gregor.

'He built his own god,' said Sancia.

'They all amount to the same thing, don't they?' said Orso. 'A . . . a fabricated entity with unusual powers. An artificial entity with an *artificial mind*.'

'And so,' Gregor said slowly, 'you think that when he made the Mountain . . .'

'I think it was something of a test case,' said Orso. 'An experiment.

Could Tribuno Candiano make the ancestral home of the Candianos into an artificial entity? Could it act as a draft effort at an artificial god? It was a theory he'd mentioned to me before. Tribuno believed that the hierophants had once been *men* – ordinary human beings. They'd just altered themselves in unusual ways.'

'He thought they were people?' said Gregor. 'Like *us*?' This idea was utter nonsense to most Tevannis. To say that the hierophants were once men was akin to saying the sun used to be an orange, grown on a tree.

'Once,' said Orso. 'Long ago. But look around you. See how scriving has changed the world in a handful of decades. Now imagine that scriving could also change a *person*. Imagine how they could change over time. His suspicion, I think, was that their elevation came from this artificial being they'd made. The men built a god, and the god helped them become hierophants. He believed he could walk in their footsteps.'

'Creepy,' said Sancia. 'But none of this makes me any more eager to get in there. If we even can.'

Orso sucked his teeth. 'It seems insurmountable, but . . . There's always a way. A complicated design means more rules, and more rules mean more loopholes. We have a much more immediate problem, though. How fast are you these days, Berenice?'

'How fast, sir? I average thirty-four strings a minute,' she said.

'With successful articulation?'

'Of course.'

'Full strings, or partials?'

'Full. Inclusive up to tier four for all Dandolo language components.'

'Ah,' said Gregor. 'What are we, uh, talking about here?'

'If we're breaking into the Mountain, even Berenice can't handle all *that* work. And besides, she's no canal man. We'd need more scrivers. Or thieves. Or scrivers who are thieves.' Orso sighed. 'And we can't do it here. Not only will Gregor's mother notice us plotting treason right in her scrumming workshops, but this place isn't safe from the assassins. We'd need a full crew, and a new place to work. Without those, this whole thing is just a daydream.'

Sancia shook her head. *I'm going to regret this.* 'Orso – I need to know . . . how rich are you?'

'How *rich*? What, you want a number or something?'

'What I'm saying is, do you personally have access to large sums of cash you can quickly retrieve without raising eyebrows?'

'Oh. Well. Certainly.'

'Good. All right.' She stood. 'Then get up. We're all taking a trip.'

'Where to?' asked Gregor.

'Into the Commons,' said Sancia. 'And we're going to need to tread lightly.'

'Because there are still thugs out there who want us dead?' asked Berenice.

'There's that,' said Sancia. 'And we're going to bring a hell of a lot of money with us.'

Four lanterns – three blue, one red, hanging above a warehouse door. Sancia scurried up, looked around, and knocked.

A slot in the door opened and a pair of eyes peeked out. They looked at her and sprang wide. 'Oh God! You? Again? I just assumed you were dead.'

'You're not so lucky,' said Sancia. 'I've brought you a deal, girl.'

'What? You're not here to ask for a favour?' said Claudia from the other side of the door.

'Well. A deal and to ask for a favour.'

'Should have known,' said Claudia with a sigh. She opened the door. She was dressed in her usual leather apron and magnifying goggles. 'After all, how could you have the resources to offer us a deal?'

'They're not my resources.' She handed a leather satchel out to Claudia.

Claudia looked at it mistrustfully, then took it and looked inside. She stared. 'P–paper duvots?'

'Yeah.'

'This has to be . . . a thousand, at least!'

'Yeah.'

'What's it for?' asked Claudia.

'That bit there is to calm you down so you listen. I've got a job for you. A big one. And you need to hear me out.'

'What, are you playing at being Sark now?'

'Sark didn't ask for anything this big,' said Sancia. 'I need you and Gio to help on this job specifically, full-time, for a matter of days. And we also need a secure space to work in, and all kinds of scriving materials. If you can get me that, there's a hell of a lot more money where that came from.'

'That *is* a big ask.' Claudia turned the leather satchel over in her hands. 'So that's the job bit?'

'That's the job bit.'

'What's the favour bit?'

'The favour bit,' said Sancia, looking her hard in the eye, 'is you forget everything you ever heard about Clef. Ever. Now. This instant. You've never heard of him. I'm just some thief who comes to you to get tools and credentials to get into the campos, and nothing else. You do that, and you get your money.'

'Why?' asked Claudia.

'Never mind why,' said Sancia. 'Just erase all of that from your brain, get Gio to do the same, and you'll both be rich.'

'I'm not so sure I like this, San . . .'

'I'm going to make a signal now,' said Sancia, 'and they're going to walk up. When they do, don't start screaming.'

'Start screaming? Why would I . . .' She stopped as Sancia raised a hand, and Berenice, Gregor, and Orso emerged from the shadows and joined her at the door.

She stared in horror, mostly at Orso, who was cursing after having stepped in a puddle. 'Holy . . . holy *shit* . . .' she whispered.

Orso looked up at Claudia and the warehouse. He wrinkled his nose. 'Dear God,' he said. 'They work *here*?'

'You had better let us in,' said Sancia.

Orso paced around the Scrappers' workshop like a farmer buying chickens at a seedy market. He examined their scriving blocks, their sigil strings on the walls, their bubbling cauldrons full of lead or bronze, their air fans strapped to carriage wheels. Claudia had ushered all the other Scrappers out before letting them in, but now she and Giovanni sat there, watching Orso dart around their quarters with terrified looks, like a panther had broken into their home as they slept.

He walked over and looked at the sigils scrawled on a blackboard. 'You're . . . making a way to control carriages remotely,' he said slowly. It wasn't a question.

'Uh,' said Giovanni. 'Yes?'

Orso nodded. 'But it's not expressing right. Is it, Berenice?'

Berenice stood and joined him. 'The orientation's wrong.'

'Yes,' said Orso.

'Their calibration tools are far too complicated,' she said.

'Yes.'

'The rig probably gets confused, isn't sure which way it's facing. So it likely just shuts down after a couple dozen feet or so.'

'Yes.' Orso looked at Giovanni. 'Doesn't it?'

Gio looked at Claudia, who shrugged. 'Um. Yes. So far. More or less.'

Orso nodded again. 'But just because it doesn't work . . . that doesn't mean it's *bad*.'

Claudia and Gio blinked and looked at each other. They slowly realised that Orso Ignacio, legendary hypatus of Dandolo Chartered, had just given them a compliment.

'It's . . . something I've worked on for a long time,' said Gio.

'Yes,' said Orso. He looked around the room, taking it all in. 'Worked on with crude tools, secondhand knowledge, fragments of designs . . . You've improvised fixes to problems no campo scriver's ever had to deal with. You've had to reinvent fire every day.' He looked at Sancia. 'You were right.'

'Told you so,' said Sancia.

'Right about what?' said Claudia.

'She said you were good,' said Orso. 'And you might be good enough for this. Maybe. What did she tell you about the job?'

Claudia glanced at Sancia, and Sancia thought she could detect a hint of wrath there, which she couldn't blame her for. 'She said you needed us,' said Claudia. 'And a workshop of your own. And materials.'

'Good,' said Orso. 'Let's try to keep things that simple.'

'They can't possibly stay that simple,' said Claudia. 'You're disrupting everything we do here. We've got to know more to get on board with this!'

'Fine,' said Orso. 'We're going to break into the Mountain.'

They stared at him, incredulous.

'The *Mountain*?' Giovanni looked at Sancia. 'San, are you *mad*?'

'Yes,' said Orso. 'That's why we're here.'

'But . . . but why?' said Claudia.

'Doesn't matter,' said Orso. 'Just know that someone wants us dead – including, yes, me. The only way for us to stop them is to get into the Mountain. Help us, and you get paid.'

'And what's the payment?' said Claudia.

'Well, that depends,' said Orso. 'Originally I was going to pay you some huge sum of money . . . but having seen what you're doing here, some alternate options seem available. You're working with spotty, secondhand knowledge. So . . . perhaps some of the third- and fourth-tier sigil strings from Dandolo Chartered *and* Company Candiano would be more valuable to you.'

Sancia didn't understand what that meant, but both Claudia's and Giovanni's eyes shot wide. They froze, and both seemed to do some rapid calculations.

'We'd want fifth tier too,' said Claudia.

'Absolutely not,' said Orso.

'Half the Dandolo fourth-tier fundamentals are intended to function with fifth-tier strings,' said Giovanni. 'They'd be useless without them.'

Orso burst out laughing. 'Those combinations are all for massive designs! What are you trying to do, build a bridge across the Durazzo, or a ladder to the moon?'

'Not all of them,' said Giovanni, stung.

'I'll give you some Candiano fifth-tier strings,' said Orso. 'But none from Dandolo.'

'Any Candiano string from you is going to be outdated,' said Claudia. 'You haven't worked there in a decade.'

'Possibly. But it's all you're going to get,' said Orso. 'Select Candiano fifth-tier strings, and the fifty most-used third- and fourth-tier strings for both Dandolo and Candiano. Plus whatever proprietary knowledge you gain during the planning process, plus a sum to be agreed upon later.'

Claudia and Giovanni exchanged a glance. 'Deal,' they said at the same time.

Orso grinned. Sancia found it a distinctly unpleasant sight. 'Excellent. Now. Where the hell are we going to be headquartered?'

Most of the canals in Tevanne were either full or close to it most of the time – but not all.

Every fourth year in the Durazzo was a monsoon year, when the warm waters bred monstrous storms, and although Tevanne lacked any central authority, water cared not a whit about which campo it flowed into. So, eventually, the merchant houses had decided they were obliged to do something about it.

Their solution was 'the Gulf' – a massive, stone-lined flood reservoir in the north of the city, which could store and dump floodwater into the lower canals as needed. The Gulf was empty most of the time, essentially a mile-wide, artificial desert of grey, moulded stone, dotted with drains. Sancia knew it was prone to shantytowns and vagrants and stray dogs, but there were some parts of the Gulf that even they weren't desperate or stupid enough to inhabit.

Yet, to her concern, Claudia and Giovanni were leading them to exactly one such spot.

<We've been to some rough places, kid,> said Clef's voice suddenly in her ear, *<but this is the roughest yet.>*

Sancia was so surprised she almost leapt into the air. *<Clef! Holy shit! You haven't talked since that . . . that thing in the foundry!>*

<Yeah. I'm . . . I'm sorry about that, kid. I think I almost broke you.>

<Yeah, what was that? What was the thing wrapped in black? Was that . . . Was that who made you, Clef?>

There was a silence. *<I think . . . maybe. Being close to that lexicon, when it was spiking . . . I just remembered that was what it felt like to be . . . Well. To be around him.>*

<Who's him?>

<I don't know. It was just a flash – a picture of him atop the dunes – and no more. That's all I have.>

Her skin crawled. *<They say the way it feels to be close to a lexicon – the headaches, the nausea – that's what it was like to draw near to a hierophant.>*

<Do they,> said Clef quietly. *<After hearing what Orso said . . . maybe someone made me, and then he changed himself so much, he . . . he became that thing. I don't know.>*

She tried to keep the fear out of her face as she listened to this. *<God.>*

<Yeah. It's not comforting to think of Tomas Ziani trying to follow in such a thing's footsteps.>

'There it is!' said Giovanni, trotting along the west side of the slanted stone walls. He pointed ahead and, though it was now night, they could see he was pointing to a large, dripping tunnel, blocked off with thick, crisscrossing iron bars.

'That is a storm drain,' said Gregor.

'True,' said Gio. 'What marvellous eyes, you have, Captain.'

'Correct me if I'm wrong,' said Gregor, 'but the problem with working out of a storm drain is that, when there is a storm, it tends to fill with water – which I, personally, cannot breathe.'

'Did I say we were going to be working *in* a storm drain?' said Gio. He led them down a moulded stone path to the storm drain and took out a small, thin, scrived strip of iron. He examined the bars, tapped the strip to one section, and then gave the bars a tug. The bottom quarter of the bars swung open, like the gate of a garden fence.

'Clever,' said Orso, peering at the hinges. 'It's a weak door, and a weak lock – but you don't need it to be strong if no one knows it's there.'

'Exactly.' Gio bowed and extended an arm. 'After you, good sir. Mind the sewage.'

They entered the massive drain. 'I have to admit, I'm getting pretty goddamn tired of pipes,' said Sancia.

'Seconded,' said Berenice.

'We won't be here for long,' said Claudia. She and Giovanni produced a handful of scrived lights, slashing rosy hues across the rippled walls. They walked down the tunnel about three hundred feet or so. Then the two Scrappers started peering around them.

'Oh, goodness,' said Claudia. 'I haven't been here in ages . . . Where is it?'

Giovanni slapped his forehead. 'Damn! I'm being stupid, I forgot. Just a second.' He pulled out a small, scrived bead of metal, and seemed to twist it, like it was two rotating halves. Then he held it up and let go. The bead zipped over to one wall like it had been ripped along by a string. 'There!' said Gio.

'That's right,' said Claudia. 'I forgot you'd installed a flag.' She walked over to the bead – which was now stuck to the wall – and held up a light. Right below the bead was a tiny slot that was practically invisible if you didn't know to look for it. Gio took back out the scrived iron strip he'd used on the drainage bars and stuck it into the slot.

There was the sound of stone groaning on stone. Gio shoved at the wall with his shoulder, and suddenly a large segment pivoted inward, swinging like a large, circular stone door. 'Here we are!'

Sancia and the rest all peered into the rounded door. Inside was a long, tall, narrow passageway, with ornately wrought walls that were lined with what appeared to be some kind of cubbyholes, most of which were empty – but not all. In some of the cubbyholes, Sancia spied urns and . . .

'Skulls,' she said aloud. 'A . . . Uh, a crypt?'

'Precisely,' said Giovanni.

'What in the hell is a crypt doing in the Gulf?' asked Orso.

'Apparently there had been quite a few minor estates here before the merchant houses made the Gulf,' said Claudia, walking inside. 'The houses just tore them down and paved over them. No one thought much about what was underneath, until they started digging the tunnels. Most of the crypts and basements have got flooded out – but this one is in fairly good condition.'

Sancia followed her in. The crypt was large, with a big, round, central chamber, and several smaller, narrow wings splitting off from it. 'How'd you find it?'

'Someone once traded us jewellery for rigs,' said Claudia. 'The jewellery was old and branded with a family crest – and one of us realised it'd had to come from a family grave. We went looking, and found this.'

'We hole up here only when we've *really* pissed off a merchant house,' said Gio. 'And it sounds like you lot have done exactly that. So – this should work nicely.'

'So . . .' said Berenice, staring around. 'We're going to be scriving . . . and working . . . and, for a while, living . . . in a crypt. With . . . bones.'

'Well, if you're really going to try to break into the Mountain, then you're probably going to wind up dead anyway,' said Gio. 'Maybe this will help you get used to it.'

Orso had found a hole in the vaulted ceiling. 'Does this go up to the surface?'

'Yeah,' said Claudia. 'To let heat out if you're doing any minor forging or smelting.'

'Excellent. Then this should work quite well!' said Orso.

Gregor was leaning over a large stone sarcophagus with a caved-in lid. He peered through the gap at the remains below. 'Will it,' he said flatly.

'Yes,' said Orso. He rubbed his hands. 'Let's get to work!'

<*I hate this place,*> said Clef.

<*Why? It doesn't seem to have anyone in it trying to stab me, which makes me like it.*>

<*Because it makes me remember the dark,*> said Clef. <*Where I was for so long.*>

<*This isn't the same.*>

<*Sure it is,*> said Clef. <*This place is old and full of trapped ghosts, kid. Trust me. I used to be one. Maybe I still am.*>

Once they'd got the lay of things, Orso waited out in the tunnel, staring out at the shantytowns beyond. Greasy campfires and thick, black smoke crawled across the surface of the Gulf. The smoke turned the starlit sky into a dull smear.

Berenice emerged from the crypt and joined him. 'I'll make the requisitions now, sir,' she said. 'We should be able to move in and get everything ready to start work tomorrow night.'

Orso said nothing. He just stared out at the Gulf and the Commons beyond.

'Is something the matter, sir?' she asked.

'I didn't think it would be like this, you know,' he said. 'Twenty, thirty years ago, when I first started working for Tribuno . . . We all genuinely thought we were going to make the world a better place. End poverty. End slavery. We thought we could rise above all the ugly human things that held the world back, and . . . and . . . Well. Here I am. Standing in a sewer, paying a bunch of rogues and renegades to break into the place where I used to live.'

'Might I ask, sir,' said Berenice, 'if you could change anything – what would it be?'

'Hell, I don't know. I suppose if I thought I had a chance, I'd start my own merchant house.'

'Really, sir?' she said.

'Sure. It's not like there's any law forbidding it. You just have to file papers with the Tevanni council. But no one bothers anymore. Everyone knows the four prime houses would crush you instantly if you tried. There used to be dozens when I was young . . . and now, only four, and four forever, it seems.' He sighed. 'I'll be back tomorrow evening, Berenice. If I'm still alive, that is. Good night.'

She watched as he strolled down the tunnel and slipped out the iron grate. Her words echoed faintly after him: 'Good night, sir.'

'This is nuts,' whispered Claudia in the dark. 'It's insane. It's *madness*, Sancia!'

'It's lucrative,' said Sancia. 'And keep your voice down.'

Claudia peered down the warrens of the crypt, and confirmed they were alone. 'You've got him on you now, don't you?' she asked. 'Don't you?'

'I told you to forget about him,' said Sancia.

Claudia miserably rubbed her face. 'Even if you didn't have Clef, this is beyond foolish! How can you *trust* these people?'

'I don't,' said Sancia. 'Not Orso at least. Berenice is . . . well, normal, but she reports to Orso. And Gregor . . . Well, Gregor seems . . .' She struggled for the right word. She was unused to complimenting men of the law. 'Decent.'

'Decent? *Decent?* Don't you know who he is? And I don't mean him being Ofelia's son!'

'Then what?'

Claudia sighed. 'There was a fortress city in the Daulo states, called Dantua. Five years ago a Dandolo house mercenary army captured it – a big victory for the entire region. But something went wrong, and their scrived devices failed. They were helpless, trapped in the fortress. A siege followed, with the Dandolos inside. Things went from bad to worse – starvation and plague and fire. When the Morsinis sailed in to rescue them all, they found only one survivor – just one. Gregor Dandolo.'

Sancia stared at her as she listened to this. 'I . . . I don't believe you.'

'It's true. I swear to God, it's true.'

'How? How did he survive?'

'No one knows. But he did. The Revenant of Dantua, they call him. That's your decent man for you. You've gone and surrounded yourself with lunatics, Sancia. I hope you know what you're doing. Especially because you've got us mixed in with them too.'

21

The next night they stared at a map of the Candiano campo and brainstormed.

'You all only need to worry about getting Sancia to and from the Mountain,' said Orso. 'I've got my own ideas about manoeuvring through the thing itself.'

'There are always three ways,' Claudia said. 'You can go under, over, or through.'

'Over's not an option,' said Giovanni. 'She can't fly to the Mountain. To do that, she'd have to plant an anchor or a construction scriving that would pull her to it – and you'd have to get *in* to plant one.'

'And through is out,' said Gregor. He walked up to the map of the Candiano campo and traced the main road running up to the huge dome. 'There are eleven gates from the outer wall to the Mountain. The last two will be under constant watch, and you need all kinds of papers and scrived credentials to get through.'

Everyone stared at the map in silence.

'What's that?' asked Sancia. She pointed to a long, winding blue streak that led from the shipping channel to the Mountain.

'That's the delivery canal,' said Orso. 'It's used by barges full of wine and, hell, whatever else they need in the Mountain. It's got the exact same problem as the roads, though – the last two gates are intensely guarded. Every delivery is stopped and thoroughly searched before it's allowed to proceed.'

Sancia thought about it. 'Could I cling to the side of a barge? Just below the waterline? And you all could give me some way to breathe air?'

They all looked surprised by that idea.

'The canal gates check sachets just like the rest of the walls,' said Orso slowly. 'But . . . I believe they only pass things that go through them. Under them . . . that might be a different story.'

'I bet the underside of the barge would trigger the check too,' said Claudia. 'But if Sancia was walking along the bottom of the canal . . .'

'Whoa,' said Sancia. 'I didn't say that.'

'How deep are the canals?' asked Gregor.

'Forty, fifty feet?' said Gio. 'The walls definitely wouldn't check that far down.'

'I never suggested anything like *this*,' said Sancia, now alarmed.

'We can't scrive a way for a human to breathe air,' said Orso. 'That's impossible.'

Sancia sighed with relief, since it sounded like they were abandoning this train of thought.

'But . .' He glanced around, and laid one hand on a sarcophagus. 'There are other options.'

Claudia frowned at the sarcophagus for a moment. Then her mouth dropped open. 'A vessel. A casket!'

'Yes,' said Orso. 'One that's waterproof, and small, but capable of holding a person. We plant a weak anchor on one of the barges, and it drags the casket along the bottom of the canal behind it. Simple!'

'With . . . with me in it?' asked Sancia weakly. 'You're saying I'm in this casket? Being dragged along? Under the water?'

Orso waved a hand at her. 'Oh, we can make it safe. Probably.'

'Certainly safer than sneaking around the guards or whatever,' said Claudia. 'The barge would secret you up the entire length of the canal, and you wouldn't risk catching a bolt in the face this way.'

'No,' said Sancia. 'I'd just risk hitting a rock too hard and drowning.'

'I told you, we can make it safe!' insisted Orso. 'Probably!'

'Oh my God,' said Sancia. She buried her face in her hands.

'Is there any other proposed way of getting Sancia to the Mountain?' asked Gregor.

There was a long silence.

'Well,' said Gregor. 'It seems this is our choice, for now.'

Sancia sighed. 'Can we at least call it something besides a *casket*, then?'

'This just leaves the issue of the Mountain itself,' said Gregor. 'Getting Sancia up to Ziani's office.'

'I'm working on a way to give her access,' said Orso. 'But access doesn't mean there won't be obstacles. I haven't seen the inside of the Mountain in a decade, I've no idea what could have changed. And I understand very little about how the thing really works.'

Gregor turned to Berenice. 'There's nothing in Tribuno's notes about this? Nothing about how he designed the Mountain?'

She shook her head.

'What *is* in Tribuno Candiano's notes?' said Giovanni. 'I'd be curious to see the writings of our most acclaimed genius and madman.'

'Well,' said Berenice reluctantly, 'there's all these wax rubbings of what looks like human sacrifices – a body on an altar, and a dagger above – but as for Tribuno's notes . . .' She cleared her throat, and read aloud: '*I again return to the nature of this ritual. The hierophant Seleikos refers to a "collection of energies" or a "focusing of minds" and "thoughts all captured". The great Pharnakes refers to a "transaction" or "deliverance" or "transference" of sorts that must take place at "the world's newest hour". At other times he says it must be at "the darkest hour" or "the forgotten minute". Does he mean midnight? The winter solstice? Something else?*'

Giovanni stared at her blankly. 'What the hell is that?'

'Tribuno's efforts to determine the source of the hierophants' nature,' said Orso. 'In other words, a hell of a bigger problem than what we're trying to solve here.'

'It's not as useful as I hoped,' said Berenice. 'He just goes on and on about this transaction – the "filling of the pitchers" – though it's pretty clear Tribuno himself doesn't understand what he's talking about.'

'But obviously it was of great value to Tomas Ziani,' said Gregor.

'Or he just *thought* it was of value,' said Orso, 'and he's wasting blood and treasure on nonsense.'

At that comment, Gregor froze. 'Ahh,' he said softly.

'Ahh what?' said Sancia.

Gregor stared into the middle distance. 'Blood,' he said quietly. A look of horrible revelation entered his face. 'Tell me, Orso. Does . . . does Estelle Ziani ever see her father?'

'Estelle? Why?' asked Orso suspiciously.

'He's ill, isn't he?' He looked at Orso and narrowed his eyes. 'Surely she oversees his medical attention – yes, Orso?'

Orso was very still. 'Uh. Well . . .'

'The Mountain checks the blood of a person to make sure they're the right person,' Gregor said. 'You'd have to find a way to log your own blood with the Mountain in order to let you in.' He stepped closer to Orso. 'But . . . what if you had access to the blood of a resident? Like Estelle Ziani – or, better yet, her *father*? The man who made the Mountain itself? That's what you aim to do – isn't it, Orso? To use Tribuno Candiano's blood as a pass key for Sancia?'

Orso glared at him. 'Well. Aren't you a clever bastard, Captain.'

'Wait,' said Sancia. 'You're going to steal *Tribuno Candiano's* blood? Really?'

Everyone stared at Orso. Finally he sighed. 'I never said *steal*,' he said huffily. 'It would be voluntarily donated. I thought I'd just . . . you know, ask Estelle for it.'

'You can't be serious,' said Claudia.

'What?' he said. 'It's an opportunity we can't pass up! With his blood, the damned thing should open for her like a schoolgirl's legs! The Mountain's a kingdom, riddled with scrived guards, and no guard can turn away their king!'

'And, what, I cover myself with his blood?' asked Sancia. She pulled a face. 'That's not exactly stealthy.'

'I'm sure we can make some kind of container for it!' he said, exasperated.

'Assuming Estelle even consents,' said Berenice, 'surely the Candianos have rewritten all the permissions so Tribuno no longer has access, yes?'

'That would suggest there's someone on the Candiano campo who's a better scriver than Tribuno,' said Orso. 'Which is unlikely. If I'd scrived my own massive house, I'd have put in all kinds of permissions and goodies just for me.'

'And Ziani certainly isn't a scriver,' said Gio. 'But all this assumes our boy here can actually get the man's blood.'

'You really think that Estelle would do that for you, Orso?' asked Sancia.

'She might if I tell her you saw her husband kissing hips with some girl in a rundown foundry,' said Orso. 'Or maybe I don't even need to say that. Everyone knows Ziani is a privileged shit, and from the sound of it, he practically keeps her shackled up in the Mountain. I suspect she wouldn't turn down a way to stick a knife in Ziani's ribs.'

'True,' said Berenice. 'Maybe it's not as heavy an ask as we're all assuming. In a way, you'd be offering her freedom. And people risk many things for that.'

Then a curious thing happened: a deeply guilty look crossed Gregor's face, and he turned to Sancia and opened his mouth as if to say something. Then he seemed to think better of it, and he shut his mouth and was silent for the rest of the night.

Much later, they slept. And Sancia's dreams were filled with old memories.

She had never known her parents. Either she or they had been sold before she could know them, and instead she'd become, like so many slave children, a communal burden on the shifting assortment of women all crammed together in the quarters on the plantation. In some ways, Sancia'd had not one mother but thirty, all indistinct.

Except one. Ardita, a Gothian woman. She was a ghost to Sancia now, and all she retained were flashes of the woman's dark eyes, the wrinkles of her olive-coloured skin on her hard, scarred hands, her jet-black ringlets, and the way her smile showed the far back teeth in her wide mouth.

There are many dangers here, child, she'd said once. *Many. Many ugly things you're going to have to do. It will be a great contest for you. And you're going to think: how do I win? And the answer is – so long as you are alive, you are winning. The only hope you should ever have is to see the next day, and the next. Some here will whisper of liberty – but you can't be free if you aren't alive.*

And then, one day, Ardita had been gone. It had not been commented upon in the quarters. Perhaps because such things were common and forgettable, or perhaps because nothing needed to be said.

Sometime later, Sancia and the other children had been led to a new field to work, and they'd walked by a tree full of corpses hanging from ropes – slaves who had been executed for any number of crimes. The overseer called out, 'Look well, little ones! Look well, and see what's done to those who disobey.' And Sancia had looked up into the canopy of leaves and seen a woman suspended in the branches, her feet and hands hacked off, and Sancia had thought she'd spied jet-black ringlets on the corpse's shoulders, and a wide, toothy mouth.

In the darkness of the crypt, Sancia awoke. She heard snores and soft sighs from the others. She stared at the dark stone ceiling, and thought about what these people were proposing she do, the enormous risks they were asking her to take. *Is this survival? Is this liberty?*

<Beats the hell out of me, kid,> said Clef's voice, soft and sad.

22

Orso stood in front of the closed-down taverna and tried not to sweat. He had many reasons to – for one, he was wearing quite a lot of clothes, in a clumsy attempt to disguise himself. For another, he was on the Candiano campo using a false sachet that Claudia and Giovanni had supplied him with. And for another, there was a significant chance that none of this ploy could work. She might not come – and then they'd have wasted another day.

He turned around and looked at the taverna. It was old and crumbling, its moss clay cracking, its windows broken. The canal it overlooked was not the blossoming, picturesque stream Orso remembered, but a foetid, reeking mire. Nearly all of the balconies were gone, apparently fallen away – but one remained.

Orso stared at the balcony. He remembered how it had looked twenty years ago – the lights around it bright and beautiful, the smell of wine and flowers. And how beautiful she'd looked that night, until he'd spoken his heart.

That's not true, he thought. *She was still beautiful, even after that.*

He sighed and leaned against the fence.

She won't come, he thought. *Why would she come to this painful memory? Why am I even here?*

Then he heard footsteps in the alley behind.

He turned and saw a woman approaching, dressed like a house servant, wearing a muddy-coloured dress and a dull, unadorned wimple that covered most of her face. She walked right up to him, her eyes steady and still.

'The theatrics of youth,' she said, 'are unbecoming to aged folk such as we.'

'I'm a hell of a lot more aged than you are,' he said. 'I think I have more right to say what's unbecoming and what isn't. I'm amazed you're here. I can't believe you still had it, that it worked!'

'I kept the hand-harp for lots of reasons, Orso,' said Estelle. 'Some sentimental. But also because I made it, and I think I did a good job.' She was referring to the twinned hand-harps she'd scrived, back when she and Orso had been young and attempting to be surreptitious with their relationship. It had been their way of communicating: pluck a certain series of strings, and the other harp would make the same tune. Each note had been a code for where and when they should meet, and this taverna had once been a favourite of theirs.

Orso had always kept his harp, perhaps out of fondness – he'd had no idea he'd need it again one day, certainly not for this.

She peered at the taverna. 'So many things have dried up and faded away on the campo,' she said quietly, 'that it feels odd to mourn the loss of a single taverna. Yet I do.'

'If I could have got a message to you to meet somewhere else,' he said, 'I would have.'

'Shall we go inside?' said Estelle.

'Really? It looks like it's falling apart.'

'You're the one who started me reliving my memories, Orso, when you plucked the harp. I wish to continue.'

They walked up the steps and through the broken doors. The vaulted ceilings were still intact, as were the tiled floors, but that was about it. The tables were gone, the bar had fallen to pieces, and vines were erupting from the walls.

'I take it,' she said quietly as she walked through the ruins, 'that you're not here to whisk me away, and make me your own.'

'No,' said Orso. 'I have something to ask of you.'

'Of course. A sentimental tool, a sentimental place, used for unsentimental ends.'

'I need something from you, Estelle. Something mad.'

'How mad? And why?'

He told her only what she needed to know. She listened quietly.

'So,' she said. 'You . . . think my father was close to figuring out how the hierophants made their tools. And you think my husband is now trying to duplicate his efforts – and has killed many people in the process.'

'Yes.'

She stared out the windows at the one remaining balcony. 'And you need my father's blood. To make it through the Mountain, to steal this device from Tomas, and cripple his efforts.'

'Yes. Will you help us?'

She blinked slowly. 'That was the place, wasn't it?' she whispered.

He looked, and saw she meant the balcony before them. 'Yes,' he said. 'It was.'

'I want to see it.'

'It looks terribly unsafe.'

'I said *see,* not stand on.' She walked over to the doors, reached out to open them, and then winced and grabbed her side. 'Agh . . . I'm sorry. Orso – can you . . . ?'

'Certainly,' he said. He walked over to the doors and opened them for her.

'Thank you,' she said. She looked out at the balcony and the dreary sight of the canal below. She sighed, like the sight of it pained her.

'Are you hurt, Estelle?' he said.

'I fell recently. I hurt my elbow, I'm afraid.'

'You fell?'

'Yes. While climbing the stairs.'

He watched her for a long time, looking her over. Was he imagining it, or was she standing somewhat . . . crooked? As if walking on a ginger knee?

'You didn't fall, did you?' he said.

She said nothing.

'It was Tomas,' he said. 'He did this to you. Didn't he?'

She was still for a long time. 'Why did you leave, Orso? Why did you leave the house? Why did you leave me there, alone, with my father?'

Orso was silent as he thought about how to answer. 'I . . . I asked you to marry me,' he said.

'Yes.'

'On this very balcony.'

'Yes.'

'And . . . you said no. Because of the inheritance laws on the campo, everything you owned would go to me. You said you wanted to prove to your father that you could be as good as him, that you could be a scriver, a leader, someone who could guide the house. You thought he could change the rules for you. But . . . I knew he wouldn't ever do that. Tribuno was a foresighted man in many ways. But he was also terribly . . . traditional.'

'Traditional,' she echoed. 'What a curious word that is. So bland, and yet often so poisonous.'

'He mentioned it to me, once. Asked me why we weren't engaged yet. I told him you were considering your options. And he said, "If you want, Orso – I could just make her." As if I would ask for that. As if having you by force was the same as having you. So there I was. Stuck between two people I found increasingly unpleasant or . . . painful.'

'I see,' she said quietly.

'I'm . . . sorry,' said Orso. 'I'm sorry for all that's happened to you. If I'd known how things were going to go – if I'd known how deeply in debt Tribuno had gone, I'd . . .'

'You'd what?'

'Have tried to steal you away, I guess. Flee the city. Go somewhere new, and leave all this behind.'

She laughed quietly. 'Oh, Orso . . . I knew you were still a romantic, down underneath it all. Don't you see? I'd never have left. I'd have stayed and fought for what I felt I was due.' She grew solemn. 'I'll help you.'

'You . . . you will?'

'Yes. Father gets bled frequently for his condition. And I know a way into the Mountain. A way designed just for him, one Tomas has never known about.'

'Really?' said Orso, astonished.

'Yes. Father grew secretive in the later years, as you know. When he was buying up all that historical junk, spending thousands of duvots a day. He wanted to move freely, without anyone being aware of it.'

She told him when and where he could expect to receive Tribuno's blood, and where the secret entrance could be found. 'It'll open up for whoever's carrying the blood,' she said. 'Though you must keep the blood cooled – if it decays too much, it'll be useless. This means you'll have a short time period to get this done – you need to do it in three nights, essentially.'

'Three days to prepare?' he said. 'God . . .'

'It gets worse,' said Estelle. 'Because the Mountain will probably figure out that the person you've sent in is *not* my father – eventually. I doubt if they'll be able to leave the way they came in.'

Orso thought about it. 'We can fly her out, maybe. Use an anchor somewhere in the city, pull her to it – she's done such things before.'

'A dangerous flight. But it might be your only option.'

He glanced at her. 'And if we pull this off – what happens to you, Estelle?'

She smiled weakly and shrugged. 'Who knows? Maybe they'll let me take charge. Maybe I'll get a moment of freedom before they bring in another ruthless merchant to run things. Or maybe they'll suspect me immediately, and execute me.'

Orso swallowed. 'Please take care of yourself, Estelle.'

'Don't worry, Orso. I always do.'

23

For the next two days, they worked.

Sancia had seen the Scrappers scrive and alter devices before, but that was nothing compared to this. Berenice brought in raw iron ingots and, using the scrived cauldrons and devices they'd procured, they began to build the capsule from scratch, plate by plate and rib by rib. By the end of the first day it had started to resemble a huge metal seedpod, about six feet long and three feet in diameter, with a small hatch set in the centre. But though the sight of Berenice, Claudia, and Giovanni fabricating this thing out of raw metal was amazing, it didn't exactly make Sancia feel relaxed.

'Doesn't seem like there's a lot of breathing room in there,' she said.

'There will be,' said Berenice. 'And it will be quite safe. We'll apply bracing and durability sigils to the entirety of the capsule, along with waterproofing, of course.'

'How in the hell is this thing going to move around?' said Sancia.

'Well. That's been tricky. But your friends here have come up with a clever idea that might work.'

'Floating lanterns,' said Gio cheerfully.

'What do they have to do with this?' asked Sancia.

'Floating lanterns are scrived to believe they've got a big balloon in them,' explained Claudia, 'and then, on the campos, they follow guided paths along markers placed on the ground.'

'Only, this marker will be on the barge,' said Gio. 'It'll keep you a set distance below the water.'

'And . . . how do I get out of the water?'

'You hit this switch here.' Berenice pointed to the interior of the capsule. 'This will make the capsule float up and surface.'

'Then you climb out, shut the hatch,' said Gio, pointing to a button on the outside of the capsule, 'hit this, and it'll sink. Then you're all set. Somewhat. Except for the Mountain bit.'

'Orso's working on that,' said Berenice testily.

'One would hope,' said Gio.

Sancia stared at the capsule. She imagined being crammed inside the tiny thing. 'God. Now I sort of wish I'd let Gregor lock me up.'

'Speaking of which,' said Claudia, looking around, 'where is the captain?'

'He said he had business to attend to,' said Berenice. 'Back on the campo.'

'What business could possibly be more important than this?' asked Claudia.

Berenice shrugged. 'He mentioned putting a matter to rest – something that'd been bothering him. When I saw the look on his face, I didn't ask more.' She quickly scrawled out a line of sigils. 'Now. Let's make sure this thing is *really* waterproof.'

Gregor Dandolo was good at waiting. Most of military life was nothing but waiting: waiting for orders, waiting for supplies, waiting for the weather to change, or just trying to out-wait your opponent, baiting them into doing something.

Yet Gregor had been waiting in front of the Dandolo Chartered Vienzi site foundry for three hours now. And, since he had much better things to do that day, and since theoretically Tomas Ziani's thugs could try to kill him even there, this was really pushing it.

He looked back at the front gates of the Vienzi site foundry. He'd been told this was where he could find his mother, and this did not surprise him: the Vienzi was one of the newest Dandolo foundries, built to perform some of the company's most complicated production. He'd known that few were allowed inside, but he'd assumed that he, being Ofelia's son, would be granted entrance. And yet, he'd been simply told to wait.

I wonder what percentage of my life, he thought, *has been spent waiting for my mother's attentions. Five percent? Ten per cent? More?*

Finally there was a creak from the massive foundry gates, and the giant oak door began to swing open.

Ofelia Dandolo did not wait for the gate to fall completely open. She slipped through the crack, small and white and frail against the huge door, and calmly walked toward him.

'Good morning, Gregor,' she said. 'What a pleasure it is to see you so soon again. How is your investigation going? Have you found the perpetrator?'

'I have encountered, how shall I put this . . . more questions,' said Gregor. 'Some of which I've been turning over for some time. But I thought it was time to discuss a certain matter with you, personally.'

'A *matter,*' said Ofelia. 'What threateningly bland language. What would you like to talk to me about?'

He took a breath. 'I wanted to ask you . . . about the Silicio Plantation, Mother.'

Ofelia Dandolo slowly raised an eyebrow.

'Do you know . . . know anything about that, Mother?' asked Gregor. 'About what it is? What they did there?'

'What I've *heard*, Gregor,' she said, 'are mostly rumours that you've been involved, somehow, in some of the violence in the wake of the Foundryside blackout. Armed gangs fighting in the streets. Carriages crashing into walls. And somewhere, among it all, my son. Is this true, Gregor?'

'Please stop trying to change the subject.'

'Rumours of you and some street urchin,' said Ofelia, 'being shot at by a team of assassins. That must be fantasy, mustn't it?'

'Answer me.'

'Why are you asking me this, anyway? Who poured this poison in your ear, Gregor?'

'I will make my question clear beyond doubt,' said Gregor forcefully. 'Is Dandolo Chartered – my grandfather's company, my father's company, and *your* company, Mother – is it involved in the gruesome practice of attempting to scrive the human body and soul?'

She looked at him levelly. 'No. It is not.'

Gregor nodded. 'A second question,' he said. '*Was* it ever involved in such a practice?'

There was a soft hiss as Ofelia exhaled through her nose. 'Yes,' she said softly.

He stared at her. 'It was. It *was*?'

'Yes,' she said reluctantly. 'Once.'

Gregor tried to think, yet he found he could not. Orso had said as much, and the comment had slowly worked its way into Gregor's mind like a needle – yet he'd been unable to believe it. 'How could . . . How could you . . .'

'I did not know,' she said, shaken, 'until after your father died. Until after your accident, Gregor. When I took over the company.'

'You're saying father was the one involved in it? It was *his* program?'

'It was a different time, Gregor,' said Ofelia. 'The Enlightenment Wars were just beginning. We didn't understand what we were truly doing, neither as rulers of the Durazzo, nor as scrivers. And all of our competitors were doing the same. If we hadn't pursued this as well, we might have been ruined.'

'Such excuses,' said Gregor, 'all end the same way, Mother. With graves, and heartache.'

'I put a stop to it when I took charge!' she said fiercely. 'I killed the project. It was wrong. And we didn't need it anymore anyway!'

'Why not?'

She paused, as if she hadn't meant to say that. 'Be–because scriving had changed so much by then. Our lexicon technology had given us an impregnable position. The scriving of the body was no longer worth researching. It was impossible anyway.'

Gregor did not say, of course, that he was now acquainted with a living specimen that suggested otherwise. 'I . . . I just so *wish* that we had one good thing,' he said, '*one* good thing in Tevanne that was not born from ugliness.'

'Oh, spare me your righteousness,' she snapped. 'Your father did what was deemed *necessary*. He did his *duty*. And ever since Dantua, you, Gregor, have been fleeing your duties as a rat might a wildfire!'

He stared at her, scandalised. 'What . . . How can you say that? How can you—'

'Shut up,' she said. 'And come with me.' She turned and started walking back into the Vienzi site.

Gregor paused for a moment, glowering, then did as she asked.

The guards and operators did double takes as Gregor entered the gates, but they stood down at the sight of Ofelia, jaw set and eyes glittering with fury. Gregor saw that the Vienzi site was indeed far more advanced than any scriving foundry he'd yet been in. Pipes of formulas and waters and reagents rose out of the stone foundation in countless places, and twisted and tangled together before sinking into the walls. Tremendous cauldrons and crucibles glowed with a manic, cheery red light, brimming with molten bronze or tin or copper. Yet Ofelia ignored all of this, and led Gregor to a warehouse in the back of the yard.

This warehouse was heavily guarded. Dandolo officers in scrived armour stood at attention before its doors. They glanced at Gregor, but said nothing.

Gregor walked inside, wondering what on the foundry yard could possibly call for such defences. And then he saw it.

Or he . . . *thought* he saw it.

Sitting in the middle of the warehouse was a shadow, a ball of almost solid darkness. He thought he could identify a shape in the darkness, but . . . it was difficult to tell. A handful of moths flitted in and out of the shadows, and when they entered that vague line of darkness they almost seemed to disappear.

'What . . . what is that?' asked Gregor.

Ofelia didn't answer. She strode across the warehouse to a panel of bronze dials and switches on the walls. She flipped one, and the circle of shadow vanished.

A wooden frame in the outline of a person stood in the exact centre of where the ball of darkness had been – and hanging on this frame was a scrived suit of armour.

But it was a tremendously strange suit of armour. Built into one arm was a black, glittering polearm, half massive axe, half giant spear. Built into the other was a huge round shield, and installed behind it a scrived bolt caster. But the strangest thing about it was the curious black plate situated on the front of its cuirass.

'Is this a . . . a lorica?' asked Gregor.

'No,' said Ofelia. 'A lorica is a big, loud, ugly armament of open warfare, a scrived suit intended solely for slaughter. It is also *illegal*, since it augments gravity in manners that violate our unspoken laws. But this . . . this is different.' She touched the black plate on its front with a finger. 'The rig is fast, graceful – and difficult to see coming. It absorbs light to a phenomenal degree – making it almost impossible to discern with the eyes. Something Orso designed.'

'Orso made this?'

'He made the method. But this method is critical to our house's survival.'

Gregor frowned at the suit as an uncomfortable idea entered his mind. 'This . . . this is a tool of assassins,' he said.

'You've heard the rumours as well as I have,' said Ofelia. 'Flying men with espringals, leaping over campo walls. Sieges and bloodshed in the Commons. We enter a dangerous era now, Gregor – an age of escalation and broken promises. The houses have grown complacent, and ambitious men have gained seats of power. It is inevitable – one day, some bright young man will say, "We're quite skilled at waging war abroad – so why not do it here?" And when that happens, we must be ready to respond.'

Gregor knew she was right – whether she knew it or not, that description perfectly fit Tomas Ziani – but the words filled him with horror. 'Respond how?'

She steeled herself, her face serious. A moth flitted around her head in a lazy circle before meandering away. 'We must leave them leaderless,' she said, 'and unable to respond. A single, quick strike.'

'You're not serious.'

'If you think the Morsinis or the Michiels or even the Candianos aren't doing the same, you're being foolish, Gregor,' she said.

'They are. I've seen the intelligence reports. And when it happens, Gregor . . . I want for you to lead our forces.'

His mouth fell open. '*What?*'

'You have more experience in the field than any living Tevanni,' she said. 'You have spent your life in war, as your city asked you to. Your war was harder than others, and I regret that. But now, I ask you, as . . . as your mother, Gregor. Please. Please, leave all these diversions of yours, and come back to me.'

Gregor swallowed. He looked at his mother, then at the shadowy armour, and thought for a long time.

'I don't remember Domenico,' he said suddenly. 'Did you know that?'

She blinked, surprised. 'W--what?'

'I don't remember my brother. I remember him dying. But that's all. Of Father, I have nothing. No memory at all. Both of them are lost to me, since the accident.' He turned back to her. 'I want to miss them, but I don't know how. Because I never really knew them. To me, Mother, they are both just creatures in a painting that hangs outside your office. Noble ghosts I can never quite live up to. But do you grieve them? Does their loss wound you, Mother?'

'Gregor . . .'

'You lost Domenico and Father,' he said, voice shaking. 'And you lost me. I nearly died in Dantua. Would you risk me again? Again? Is that how you think of me? As something so expendable?'

'I did not lose you in Dantua,' she said fiercely. 'You survived. As I knew you would, Gregor. As I know you *always* will.'

'Why? Why this certainty?'

Yet his mother could not answer. It seemed, for the first time, like Gregor had deeply wounded her. And curiously, he felt no regrets.

'I have lived my life in war,' he said to her. 'I returned to Tevanne to find civilisation. It was not as civilised as I liked, Mother. So I shall focus on amending that, and nothing more.' Then he turned and walked away.

24

On the third day, they finished their preparations, hastily crafting each tool and each design. Orso oversaw their efforts, pacing around the capsule, reviewing the chalkboards and scriving blocks, carefully eyeing every string of sigils. He twitched and groaned and huffed, but though the designs were not up to his standards, he felt they would work.

The stone door creaked open and Gregor strode in. 'A fine time to pop in!' snapped Orso. 'We've had some last-minute changes that have thrown everything into goddamn chaos, and we damned sure could've used you!'

'I need to talk to you, Orso,' he said. He pulled him aside.

'What the hell's the matter, Captain?' asked Orso.

Gregor leaned close. 'Did you develop some kind of light-absorbing rig for my mother, Orso?'

'What! How the hell did you know about that?'

Gregor told him about the meeting with his mother. Orso was stunned. 'She's making some . . . some kind of *assassin's* lorica?'

'In essence.'

'But . . . but, my *God*, Ofelia Dandolo never struck me as the type at all for plots and coups and revolutions!'

'So you knew nothing of this?' asked Gregor.

'Not a word.'

Gregor nodded, his face grave. 'It's nothing I can do much about right now. I'm not even sure what to do, frankly. But it makes me wonder . . .'

'Wonder what?'

'If her house hypatus had no idea this was happening – what other secrets is she keeping?'

'What's that?' asked Sancia loudly. She pointed at a rig on the far table.

Orso looked over his shoulder. 'Oh, that. We'll get to that in a minute.'

'It looks like an air-sailing rig,' said Sancia.

'We'll get to that.'

'And you haven't mentioned an air-sailing rig yet.'

'I said we'll get to that!'

They applied the last few finishing touches. Then they regrouped around the map and Orso reviewed the plan, step by step.

'First, we bring the capsule to this part of the Commons,' he said. He pointed at a stretch of canal on the map. 'The delivery canal passes through there. Sancia will enter the capsule, it will submerge, and as the barge passes through, Berenice will plant the marker. Got it?'

'Yes, sir,' said Berenice.

'The barge then pulls Sancia' – he traced the canal with a finger – 'right up to the Mountain's dock. It's a big dock, and well guarded – which is why the marker will put a hundred feet between the capsule and the barge. That should give Sancia enough distance to safely surface and slip out without anyone noticing. Yes?'

Sancia said nothing.

'Sancia then goes to here.' He pointed at a spot outside the Mountain. 'The sculpture gardens. That's where Tribuno's secret entrance is hidden. It's apparently been cleverly concealed underneath a small white stone bridge – it's literally invisible unless you have this.' He pointed at a small, bronze box on the table. The smooth metal was covered in condensation. 'It's a cooling casket – and inside is a vial of Tribuno's blood. Procured by his daughter.'

Everyone stared at the bronze box. Gregor wrinkled his nose.

'The secret entrance will react to Tribuno's blood, and open up for Sancia,' said Orso. 'She then enters, goes through the passageway – and then she'll be in the Mountain.'

Sancia cleared her throat and said, 'Where in the Mountain, exactly?'

'On the fourth floor,' said Orso.

'Where on the fourth floor?'

'That I don't know.'

'You don't know.'

'No. But you'll need to get up to the *thirty-fifth* floor. That's where Ziani's office is. And that's where the imperiat almost certainly is as well.'

'What's the process for getting to the thirty-fifth floor?' asked Sancia.

Orso considered what to say.

'You don't know,' said Sancia.

'No,' he said honestly. 'I don't. But whatever's in your way, Tribuno's blood should trump it. It'll be a candle in the dark for you, girl.'

Sancia took a slow breath in. 'And . . . once I have the imperiat, I just walk out – yes?'

Orso hesitated. Claudia, Berenice, and Gio suddenly looked tense. 'Well . . . We've had some change of plans there.'

'Have you,' said Sancia.

'Yes. Because there's a good chance the Mountain will *eventually* figure out you're not Tribuno. Which means getting out might be a lot trickier than getting in. Hence the, ah, the sailing rig.'

Sancia stared at them. 'You . . . you want me to fly off the side of the Mountain?'

'There's a balcony in the office,' said Orso. 'You grab the imperiat, hop out, tear off this bronze tab here' – he pointed on the rig – 'and off you go. The parachute activates, and you're pulled to safety. There's also a hardened cask secured to the rig – you can put the imperiat in there to make sure it doesn't see any harm.'

'And you can't make a hardened cask that could hold *me*?'

'Ah. Well. No. That would be heavy. Now, we can't fabricate an anchor with the range to pull you completely out of the campo, but . . . we can get someone onto the Candiano campo to create a sort of landing zone close to one of the gates.' He looked at Gregor. 'Are you amenable to this task, Captain?'

Gregor considered it. 'So . . . I just take the anchor onto the campo, plant it somewhere in range, and catch Sancia as she lands?'

'Basically. Then you both make a mad dash off the campo into the safety of the Commons.'

Sancia cleared her throat again. 'So . . . to review,' she said slowly, 'I am floating up the canal . . .'

'Yes,' said Orso.

'In a submerged capsule you all have built in three days . . .'

'Yes.'

'And using Tribuno's blood to enter the Mountain . . .'

'Yes.'

'And I am then navigating a completely unknown set of obstacles to get to the thirty-fifth floor, where I am then stealing the imperiat . . .'

'Yes.'

'And then I hop off the Mountain and fly to Gregor. Because the Mountain will probably figure out something's wrong, and try to trap me.'

'Ahh . . .'

'And once I land, we run off the campo while probably being chased by some armed people who noticed me flying through the sky like a bird.'

'Uh. Probably. Yes.'

'And then I give the imperiat to you, and you . . .'

'Take down Tomas,' said Orso. He coughed. 'And possibly use it to reinvent the nature of scriving as we know it.'

'Yes. Well, then. I see.' She took a breath, nodded, and sat up. 'I'm out.'

Orso blinked. 'You . . . you what? Out?'

'Yeah. I'm out.' She stood. 'Every time we talk about this it gets more and more preposterous. And no one's asked me *once* if I'm game for any of this. I'm not doing this mad shit. I'm not. I'm out.' She walked away.

There was a long, awkward silence.

Orso stared around at everyone, flabbergasted. 'Did . . . did she just say she's *out*?'

'She did,' said Claudia.

'Like – not going to do it?'

'That's what *out* generally means,' said Gio.

'But . . . but she can't . . . She can't just . . . Oh, son of a *bitch*!' He chased after Sancia, and caught her just as she was slipping out into the tunnel. 'Hey! Come back here!'

'No,' said Sancia.

'We did a hell of a lot of work for you!' snarled Orso. 'We worked our goddamn arses off to set this all up! You can't just walk out now!'

'And yet,' said Sancia, 'that's what I'm doing.'

'But . . . but this is our only chance! If we don't steal the imperiat now, then Tomas Ziani could raise an army, and . . .'

'And what?' spat Sancia, marching up to him. 'Do to Tevanne what Tevanne has done to the entire rest of the world?'

'You don't know what the hell you're talking about!'

'The problem is that I actually *do*. You're not the one in the capsule, in the Mountain, the one risking your goddamn neck! You know what this is, what this *really* is?'

'What?' said Orso, fuming.

'This is a rich man's fight,' said Sancia. 'A rich man's game. And we're all just pieces on the board to you. You think you're different, Orso, but you're just like all the rest of them!' She put her finger in his face. 'My life's not a hell of a lot better since I escaped the plantation. I still starve a lot and I still get beaten occasionally. But at least now I get to say *no* when I want to. And I'm saying it now.' She turned and walked out.

25

Sancia sat on the hilltop next to the Gulf, staring out at the ramshackle tent city, rambling and grey in the watery, late-morning light. She'd felt alone many times since she'd found Clef, but she hadn't felt truly abandoned until now, burdened with secrets, and surrounded by people all too willing to either kill her or put her in harm's way.

<We're in a right state, aren't we, kid?> said Clef.

<Yeah. I don't know what the hell to do, Clef. I want to run, but I've nowhere to run to.>

Sancia watched a group of children playing in the Gulf, running back and forth with sticks. Skinny things, undernourished and filthy. Her childhood had been much the same. *Even in the greatest city on earth*, she thought, *children go hungry, every day.*

<I bet I could take the Mountain,> said Clef. *<Forget about Orso. You and me, kid. We could do it.>*

<We're not discussing this, Clef.>

<I could. It'd be . . . interesting. A feat. An experience.>

<*It's the goddamn graveyard of thieves, Clef! Campo operators like Sark talked about it in whispers, like the thing could hear them across the city!*>

<*I want to get you out of this. I got you into it. And I don't think I have a lot of time left, Sancia. I want to do something – I don't know – something big.*>

She buried her face in her hands. 'Damn it,' she whispered. 'Damn it all . . .'

<*The captain's coming,*> said Clef. <*He's got his truncheon. He's walking up the hill now.*>

<*Great,*> she thought. <*Another conversation I don't want to have.*>

She watched as his lumbering form emerged from the tall weeds. He did not look at her. He just walked over and sat, about ten feet away.

'Dangerous to be out in the day,' he said.

'It's dangerous to be in there too,' said Sancia. 'Since you people want to get me killed.'

'I don't want to get you killed, Sancia.'

'You said to me once that you were not afraid to die. You meant it, didn't you?'

He thought about it, and nodded.

'Yeah. A guy who's not afraid to die likely isn't too torn up about getting other people killed. You might not want it, but it's a responsibility you're willing to accept, isn't it?'

'Responsibility . . .' he echoed. 'You know, I talked to my mother yesterday.'

'That's why you ducked out? Just to chat up your mother?'

'Yes. I asked her about Silicio. And she admitted that, once, Dandolo Chartered had indeed been involved in trying to scrive human beings. In trying to scrive slaves, I mean.'

She glanced at him. His face was fixed in a look of quiet puzzlement. 'Really?'

'Yes,' he said quietly. 'Odd thing, to learn of your family's complicity in such monstrosities. But like you said – it's not like there weren't plenty of other tragedies and monstrosities to begin with. That particular one is not especially unusual. So now, today, I think about responsibilities.' He looked out at the cityscape of Tevanne. 'It won't change on its own, will it?'

'What? The city?'

'Yes. I'd hoped to civilise it. To show it the way. But I no longer think it will change of its own accord. It must have change forced upon it.'

'Is this about justice again?' asked Sancia.

'Of course. It's my responsibility to deliver it.'

'Why you, Captain?'

'Because of what I've seen.'

'And what's that?'

He sat back. 'You . . . you know they call me the Revenant of Dantua, yes?'

She nodded.

'People call me that. But they don't know what it means. Dantua . . . It was a Daulo city we took. In the north of the Durazzo. But the Daulos in the city had stockpiles of flash powder,' he said. 'I've no idea how they'd got it. But one day some boy, no older than ten, snuck into our camp with a box of it on his back. And he ran up to our lexicon, and set off the charge. Killed himself. Set fire to the camp. And worse, he damaged the lexicon. So all our rigs failed. So we were just stuck there, with the Daulo armies out beyond. They couldn't penetrate the fortress, even with us helpless – but they could starve us out.

'So. We starved. For days. For weeks. We knew they'd kill us if we surrendered, so we just starved and hoped someone would come. We ate rats and boiled corncobs and mixed dirt with our rice. I just sat and watched it all happen. I was their commander, but there was nothing I could do. I watched them die. Of starvation. Of suicide. I watched these proud sons turn to anguished skeletons, and I buried them in the meagre earth.

'And then, one day . . . some of the men had meat. I found them cooking it in the camps, sizzling on skillets. It . . . it did not take me long to realise what kind of meat it was. Carcasses were in high supply in Dantua, after all. I wanted to stop them, but I knew if I tried, they'd mutiny.' He shut his eyes. 'Then the men started getting sick. Perhaps as a consequence of what they were doing – consume ill flesh, become ill yourself. Swollen armpits, swollen necks. It spread so *fast.* We started running out of places to bury corpses. It was no surprise that I caught the plague myself, eventually. I . . . I remember the fever, the coughing, the taste of blood in my mouth. I remember my men watching me as I lay on my bed, gasping. Then things went dark. And when I awoke . . . I was in the grave, under the earth.'

'Wait. You . . . you *survived*? They buried you and you woke up inside the *grave*?'

'Yes,' he said quietly. 'It's extremely rare, but some people do survive the plague. I awoke in the dark. With . . . with *things* on top of me. Blood and dirt and filth in my mouth. I couldn't see anything. Could barely breathe. So . . . I had to dig my way out. Through the bodies, through all that earth. Through the rot and the piss and the blood and . . . and . . .' He fell silent. 'I don't know how I did it. But I did. I clawed until my fingernails were sloughed off and my fingers were broken and hands bloody, but then I saw it, saw the light flickering through the cracks in the corpses above me, and I crawled out, and saw the fire.

'The Morsinis had got to Dantua. They'd attacked. The Daulos had broken in through the walls in desperation, and somehow they'd set the city alight. And some Morsini sergeant saw me clawing my way out of the mass grave, covered in blood and mud and screaming . . . He thought I was a monster. And by that point, perhaps I was. The Revenant of Dantua.'

They were silent. The tall grasses danced in the wind around them.

'I've seen a lot of death, Sancia,' he said. 'My father and brother died in a carriage accident when I was young. One I nearly died in myself. I joined the military to bring honour to their name, but instead I got so many young men killed – and, again, I survived. I keep surviving, it seems. It's taught me many things. After Dantua . . . it was like a magic spell had been lifted from my eyes. We are making these horrors. We are doing this to ourselves. We have to change. We *must* change.'

'This is just what people are,' said Sancia. 'We're animals. We only care about survival.'

'But don't you see?' he said. 'Don't you see that's a bond they've placed upon you? Why did you work the fields as a slave, why did you sleep in miserable quarters and silently bear your suffering?

Because if you didn't, you'd be killed. Sancia . . . so long as you think only of survival, only of living to see the next day, you will always bear their chains. You will not be free. You'll always remain a sla—'

'Shut your mouth!' she snarled.

'I will not.'

'You think because you've suffered, you know? You think you know what it's like to live in fear?'

'I think I know what it's like to die,' said Gregor. 'It makes things so terribly *clear* once you stop worrying about survival, Sancia. If these people succeed – if these rich, vain fools do as they wish – then they will make slaves of the whole of the world. All men and women alive, and all generations after, will live in fear just as you did. I am willing to fight and die to free them. Are you?'

'How can you say that?' she said. 'You, a Dandolo? You know more than anyone that this is what all merchant houses *do*.'

He stood, furious. '*Then help me cast them down!*' he cried.

She stared at him. 'You . . . you would overthrow the merchant houses?' she asked. 'Even your own?'

'Sometimes you need a little revolution to make a lot of good. Look at this place!' He gestured at the Gulf. 'How can these people fix the world if they can't fix their own city?' He bowed his head. 'And look at us,' he said quietly. 'Look at what they've made of us.'

'You'd really die for this?'

'Yes. I'd give away all that I value, Sancia, all, to ensure no one ever has to go through what you or I have ever again.'

She looked down at her wrists, at the scars there, where they'd bound her up before they'd lashed her. <*You sure you want to do something big, Clef?*> she asked.

<*I'm sure.*>

She bowed her head, nodded, and stood. 'Fine then. Let's go.'

She marched down the hillside to the drainage tunnel, then into the crypt, with Gregor behind her. They all went silent as she walked in.

She stood in the crypt before a sarcophagus, her heart hammering like mad, not moving.

<*What are you going to do, kid?*> asked Clef.

<*I'm going to try to help. And I'm going to give away the last thing I value to make it happen.*> She swallowed. <*I'm sorry, Clef.*>

She reached up, grabbed the string around her neck, ripped Clef off, and placed him on the sarcophagus. 'This is Clef,' she said aloud. 'He's my friend. He's been helping me. Maybe now he can help you.'

Everyone stared at her.

Orso slowly stepped forward, mouth open. 'Well, bend me over and scrum me blue,' he whispered. 'Son of a bitch. Son of a *bitch*.'

III

THE MOUNTAIN

Every innovation – technological, sociological, or otherwise – begins as a crusade, organises itself into a practical business, and then, over time, degrades into common exploitation. This is simply the life cycle of how human ingenuity manifests in the material world.

What goes forgotten, though, is that those who partake in this system undergo a similar transformation: people begin as comrades and fellow citizens, then become labour resources and assets, and then, as their utility shifts or degrades, transmute into liabilities, and thus must be appropriately managed.

This is a fact of nature just as much as the currents of the winds and the seas. The flow of force and matter is a system, with laws and maturation patterns. We should harbour no guilt for complying with those laws – even if they sometimes require a little inhumanity.

– TRIBUNO CANDIANO, LETTER TO THE COMPANY
CANDIANO CHIEF OFFICERS' ASSEMBLY

26

'You've . . . you've *lied* to me!' Orso shouted. 'You've been lying to me this *whole time*!'

'Well, yeah,' said Sancia. 'I heard you telling Gregor to dump my unconscious body in a ditch. That doesn't exactly inspire trust.'

'That's not the point!' snapped Orso. 'You've put everything at risk by lying to us!'

'I don't recall your arse sneaking onto a foundry,' said Sancia, 'or getting up to hop in an underwater coffin. Seems this risk hasn't been distributed fairly.'

<*Can you just, like, tell him what I do?*> Clef asked. <*That will distract them.*>

So she did. And he was right: every fact that she'd been taking as a regular part of her life for the past few days sent Orso and Berenice careening off the walls in shock.

'He can sense scrived devices?' Orso said, boggled. 'He can see what they are, what they *do*, at a *distance*?'

'And he can *change* them?' said Berenice. 'He can change *scrivings*?'

'Not change,' said Sancia. 'Just . . . make them reinterpret their instructions. Somewhat.'

'How is that any different from change!' cried Orso.

'I'm still hung up on this thing being a "he",' said Gregor. 'It . . . it is a key, yes? The key says it's a him? Is that right?'

'Can we not bother with the dumb shit, please?' said Sancia.

She kept answering questions as best she could, but this proved difficult since she was essentially acting as a go-between in a conversation among six people. She kept asking everyone to slow down, slow down, and everyone kept saying, 'Who was that answer for?' or 'What? What's that about, again?'

<Well, kid,> sighed Clef. *<I'm not sure if this was a way out of your problem after all.>*

<Yeah, I didn't expect for it to be this loud.>

<Here. Let me see if I can do something. But . . . I want your permission first. Asking permission before you do something is really, really important, *you see? Right? Right?>*

<I said *I was sorry! But I had to tell them about you! If Gregor's serious about sparking a goddamn revolution, they're going to need all the help they can get! What do you want to do?>*

<Well, you know how my thoughts were leaking into your mind? How I was . . . >

<Overpowering me?>

<Yeah. I think I might be able to do that but . . . deeper. I think I can talk with your mouth, in other words. If you let me.>

<Really?>

<Really.>

Sancia looked around. Orso was still screaming questions at her, and it seemed like she'd missed two or three of them in just the past few seconds. *<If it makes this go faster, go ahead.>*

<Okay. Hold on.>

There was a warmth in the side of her head, a slight ache, and then suddenly her body felt far away, like it was not something she lived in every second of every day but was rather some curious extension she didn't fully control.

Her jaw worked, a cough burbled up from within her chest, and her voice said, 'All right. Can you guys, like, hear me?'

It was her voice – but not her words.

Everyone blinked, confused. Sancia felt no less confused than they – the experience was deeply disorienting. It was like watching yourself doing things in a dream, unable to stop.

'What!' said Orso. 'Of course we can hear you! Are you being ridiculous?'

'Okay,' said Sancia's voice. 'Wow. Weird.' She cleared her throat again. '*So* weird.'

'Why weird?' asked Claudia. 'What's weird?'

'This isn't Sancia,' said her voice. 'This is the key, Clef. Uh, talking right now.'

They stared at each other.

'The poor girl's gone insane,' said Gio. 'She's starking mad.'

'Prove it,' said Orso.

'Uh, okay,' said her voice. 'Let's see here. Right now, Orso is carrying two scrived lights and . . . what I expect is some kind of lexicon tool. It's a wand that, when touched to certain scrivings, dupes them into going in a loop, essentially pausing them, which allows him to extract the plate and reintegrate it with another command, but it has to have domain over similar metallurgical transitions, because the tool he's got seems to be *really* sensitive to bronze and other alloys, and especially tin when it's present in a ratio of twelve to o—'

'Okay, yeah,' said Claudia. 'That's not Sancia.'

'How are you doing this?' said Berenice, awed. 'How are you . . . Clef . . . talking with her voice?'

'The girl's got a plate in her head that gives her . . . I don't know the word for it, something like object empathy,' said Clef. 'I doubt if it's intended. I think they scrummed up something when they installed it. Anyways, it's a connection point between items – only, most items aren't sentient. I am. So it's kind of a two-way street.' Clef coughed with her body. 'So . . . how can I help? What do you guys want to know?'

'What are you?' said Orso.

'Who made you?' asked Berenice.

'Will stealing the imperiat really stop Tomas Ziani?' asked Gregor.

'What the hell is Ziani even doing?' asked Claudia.

'Oh, boy. So – everything,' sighed Clef. 'Listen, I'm going to try to have to summarise the stuff that Sancia and I have been discussing for days, so just . . . just sit down and be quiet for a moment, okay?'

And Clef talked.

As he spoke, Sancia began to . . . well, not quite doze as much as drop out of herself. It was like sitting on the back of a horse and hugging the person who held the reins and slowly falling asleep with the beast's movements – except the beast was her, her body, her voice and her throat, moving from word to word and thought to thought.

She drifted.

Slowly, Sancia drifted back in.

Orso was pacing around the crypt like he'd drunk all the coffee in the Durazzo, and he was positively ranting: 'So Marduri's Theorem is *true*! Scrivings, even small ones, are violations of reality itself, like a run in a hose, all the . . . the fabric piling up and getting tangled, except it's a run that accomplishes something *very* specific!'

'Uh, sure,' said Clef. 'I guess that's one way of putting it.'

'That's what you perceive!' cried Orso. 'That's what you sense! These . . . these violations in reality! And when you alter them, you're just . . . just fiddling with the tangle!'

'They're more like errors,' Clef said. 'Intentional errors, with intentional effects.'

'The question is what composes the fabric,' said Berenice. 'Marduri believed there was reality and a world *under* it that made reality function. Could scrivings be a tangling of these tw—'

Sancia drifted back out again.

Again, she awoke.

'. . . guess I'm not understanding the question,' Clef was saying.

Orso was still pacing the crypt. Berenice, Claudia, and Giovanni sat around Sancia, staring at her with wide eyes like she was a village soothsayer.

'I am saying,' Orso said, 'that you're in an unusual position – you can review all of the scrivings of all of Tevanne and see how all of them work, and how *well* they work.'

'So?'

'So where are we weak? Where are we strong? Are we . . . Are we *good*?'

'Huh,' said Clef. 'I guess I hadn't thought about it. I think the problem comes down to the difference between complicated and interesting. And . . . well, most of the stuff I've seen in Tevanne is more complicated than it is interesting.'

Orso stopped pacing. He looked crestfallen. 'R-really?'

'It's not your fault,' said Clef. 'You're like a tribe that's just invented the paintbrush. Right now you're just putting paint everywhere. One thing I do think is pretty innovative, though, is twinning.'

'*Twinning?*' said Berenice. 'Really?'

'Yes! You're essentially duplicating a physical piece of reality!' said Clef. 'You could duplicate all kinds of things if you tried.'

'Like what?' said Orso.

'Well,' said Clef. 'Like a lexicon.'

The scrivers' jaws all went slack at that.

'You can't twin a *lexicon*!' said Orso.

'Why not?' said Clef.

'It's . . . it's too complicated!' said Giovanni.

'Then why not try to twin a simpler lexicon?' said Clef. 'Imagine a bunch of small lexicons, all twinned, all able to project scrivings . . . well. Anywh—'

Gregor coughed. 'As interesting as all this scriving theory is . . . might we focus on the more lethal issues at hand? We are attempting to sabotage Tomas Ziani – but we still only half-understand what he's even doing. Will stealing back the imperiat actually stop his efforts?'

'Right,' said Berenice, though she sounded a touch disappointed. 'Let's look back at Tribuno's notes and see if Mr Clef has anything to say on tha—'

Again, things faded out.

The world returned. Sancia was seated in front of a sarcophagus that was covered in Tribuno's notes. The wax rubbings of the bas-reliefs were situated in front of her.

'. . . that is human sacrifice if I ever saw it,' said Gregor. He pointed to the engravings of the bodies on the altar, and the blades above. 'And if Tomas Ziani is handling bodies, then it stands to reason he's attempting human sacrifice.'

'But that's not at *all* what Tribuno Candiano's notes say,' said Berenice. She picked up a sheaf of paper, and read, 'The hierophant Seleikos refers to a "collection of energies" or a "focusing of minds" and "thoughts all captured". That would suggest the ritual does not involve death, or killing, or murder, or sacrifice. Just . . . something being gathered or pooled. The hierophants were describing an act that we simply lack the context to understand. And it seems Mr Clef here also lacks that necessary perspective.'

'Again – could you please not call me that?' said Clef.

'Then can we gain the proper context from the rest of the notes?' asked Orso. He pointed at one particular paragraph. 'Here . . . "*The hierophant Pharnakes never called them tools, or devices, or rigs. He specifically called them "urns" and "vessels" and "urcerus" – which means "pitcher", like water.*" Surely that has some relation to why Tomas Ziani called his failed imperiat a *shell*, yes?'

'True,' said Berenice. 'And Pharnakes goes on to directly describe the ritual here – he refers to a "transaction" or "deliverance" or "transference" of sorts that must take place at "the lost moment, the world's newest hour". Though I've no idea what that means.'

'I think that bit's clear, actually,' said Orso. 'The hierophants believed the world was a vast machine, made by God. At midnight, the world essentially changed over, like a big clock. They believed there was a "lost moment" during which the normal rules were suspended. Apparently that's when the forging of hierophantic tools must take place – when the universe has its back turned, in a way.'

'In that moment, something fills the pitcher,' said Giovanni. 'The shell.'

'Meaning what?' said Clef, frustrated.

Silence.

'I'm not sure this is progress,' said Clef.

'What else is in these damned notes?' said Orso. He flipped through the pages rapidly.

'There's this bit here,' said Berenice. 'Also from Pharnakes – "*The lingai divina cannot be utilised by common mortals. By the nature of the Maker's work*" – I assume he means God there – "*it is inaccessible to those who have been born and shall die, to those who cannot, like the Maker, give and take life itself.*" '

'But what exactly *happens*?' demanded Clef. 'This is all really fun, reading these cryptic bits of quotes – but what is this goddamn transaction supposed to be? What does the dagger have to do with the urn, the shell, with the language of this Maker? It looks like someone is being executed, yeah, but what does that have to do with scrived tools, or this lost minute?'

'Shouldn't *you* know?' said Orso, exasperated. 'I mean, you are one!'

'Do *you* remember your birth?' said Clef. 'I sure as hell expect not.'

And then Sancia understood everything.

She understood how the ritual worked, how the hierophants had made their tools, why their tools needed no lexicon to function – and why they never actually called them 'tools'.

<But Clef,> she said to him. *<You* do *remember your birth. Don't you?>*

<Huh?>

<That memory, of when you were made. You shared it with me. You were lying on your back, on a stone surface, looking up . . . >

Clef was silent.

Orso glanced at Berenice. 'Why isn't he saying anything? What's going on?'

'That's . . . that's right,' said Clef quietly. 'I do remember how I was made.'

'You do?' said Berenice.

'Yes,' said Clef. 'I was lying on my back . . . and then I felt pain, shooting through me . . . and then . . . I . . . I became the key. I *filled* it. I moved within it. I filled its cracks and crevices . . . and . . .' He trailed off.

'And?' said Orso.

A cold horror filled Sancia's body – and she suspected that it was Clef's horror, not her own.

<*A shell,*> she said. <*An urn. The dagger. And a deliverance . . .* >

'What are you saying here?' asked Claudia.

'I'm saying it wasn't human sacrifice,' said Clef softly. 'Not entirely.'

'What?' said Orso. 'Then what was it?'

'I . . . I remember the taste of wine,' whispered Clef. 'I remember the feeling of wind on my back, the sound of breeze in the wheat, and a woman's touch. I remember all these sensations – but how could I, if I was always a key?'

They stared at him. Then Berenice's mouth opened in horror. 'Unless . . . unless you weren't *always* a key.'

'Yes,' said Clef.

'What do you mean?' asked Gregor.

'I think that . . . once, I was a person,' said Clef. 'Once I was alive just as you all are . . . but then, during the lost minute, they took me out of me . . . and they put me in . . . in *here.* Inside this . . . contraption.' Sancia's fingers curled around the golden key, gripping it so hard her knuckles turned white. 'The histories don't record the hierophants killing anyone – because they *didn't.* They stripped a mind from raw flesh and bone, and during that lost moment in the depths of the night . . . they placed it inside a shell. A vessel.'

'All thoughts collected,' said Berenice.

Orso put his face in his hands. 'Oh my God . . . It's a loophole, isn't it! A stupid, scrumming loophole!'

'A loophole?' said Claudia.

'Yes!' said Orso. 'Occidental sigils – the sigillums of God Himself – can't be used by anything that has been born or shall die. So what do you do? You take a person and turn them into something *deathless* – something that is not really born, and never will truly die. You do it during the world's lost hour, when the rules aren't enforced. That gives you access to untold permissions and privileges! Reality will happily follow the instructions of the tool you've created – because, in a way, it genuinely believes the tool is *God Himself*!'

'I've been trapped in here for . . . for forever,' said Clef faintly. 'I've outlived the people who made me. I spent so long in the dark . . . all because they needed a tool to do a *job*. It's not human sacrifice – it's *worse*.'

And then, to everyone's surprise, Clef burst into tears.

Berenice tried to comfort him as the rest looked on, hugging Sancia's body close as Clef wept.

'To imagine it,' said Orso. 'To imagine that the discovery you've sought for so long is . . . is this ghastly mutilation of the human body and soul . . .'

'And to imagine what the other houses would do,' said Gregor quietly, 'if they were to make the same discovery. In many ways, Tevanne already runs on the fuels of human suffering. But if we were to switch to this method . . . imagine the sheer human cost.' He shook his head. 'The hierophants were not angels at all. They were devils.'

'Why don't you remember more about yourself?' Giovanni asked Clef. 'If you were a person, why do you still think and act like . . . well, the key?'

'Why is bronze not like copper, or tin, or aluminium, or any of the rest of its components?' said Clef, sniffling. 'Because they have all been remade for another purpose. The key looks like just an object to you all, but on the inside it's . . . it's *doing* things. Redirecting my mind, my soul, to act in a certain way. And because it's breaking down, I . . . I remember more of myself.'

'And this is what Tomas Ziani is attempting,' said Gregor. 'He is attempting this grand remaking of the human soul – only he is failing, over and over and over again. And he is willing to fail *more*, with over a hundred people.' He looked at Sancia. 'Now we know. Now we truly know what's at stake. Will you try to stop it tonight, Sancia? Are you willing to rob the Mountain?'

Sancia took control of her body again, like a hand sliding into a glove.

<*To prevent something like me from ever happening again . . .* > said Clef softly.

She shut her eyes and bowed her head.

27

Nightfall, and Berenice, Sancia, and Gregor skulked through the Commons south of the Candiano campo. Sancia's blood buzzed and boiled in her veins. She often felt jittery before a big job, but tonight was different. She tried to stop glancing at the Mountain in the distance so she wouldn't remember exactly *how* different it was.

'Slow down,' hissed Berenice behind her. 'We've got time before the barge gets here!'

Sancia slowed and waited. Berenice was walking along the canal, holding out a fishing pole and dragging a small wooden ball through the waters by a string. Sancia could see the capsule drifting along underneath it, but just barely. It seemed to be floating well – which was a relief.

'I want time to make sure that goddamn thing works,' said Sancia. 'It'd make an unfashionable coffin.'

'I take offense to that,' said Berenice. 'It's a knock against my craftsmanship.'

'Now is not the time to hurry,' said Gregor, lumbering along behind Berenice. 'Carelessness begets many graves.' He was wearing a thick scarf and wide hat, to keep as much of his face hidden as possible.

Finally they came to the fork in the canal, where the delivery route broke off from the main branch. Sancia looked along its length, spying where it passed through the Candiano walls beyond. 'The barge should be carrying a delivery of mangos,' said Berenice. 'Which is why I brought this.' She held up a small, unripe mango, and turned it over to reveal a small hole in it, and a switch within. 'Inside is the anchor that will pull the capsule along.'

'Clever,' said Gregor.

'I hope so. It should be difficult to notice. When the barge passes, I'll toss it aboard.'

'Good,' said Gregor. He looked around. 'I'll go to the Candiano campo now to set up the anchor for the air-sailing rig.'

'Make sure you're in range,' said Sancia. 'Otherwise I jump off the side of the Mountain and plummet to my death.'

'Orso gave me an exact cross-street for its position,' he said. 'It should be in range. Good luck to you both.' Then he skulked off into the night.

Berenice looked over her shoulder at the rosy face of the Michiel clock tower in the distance. 'We have about ten minutes. Time to get ready.' She pulled the wooden ball back in, adjusted something on it, and held it out over the sloshing waters like someone trying to entice a crocodile to bite.

The waters at their feet bubbled and churned, and the black metal plating of the capsule slowly surfaced.

'Oh shit,' whispered Sancia. She calmed herself, and knelt down and opened the hatch.

'I'll help you in,' said Berenice. She held out a hand and steadied Sancia as she awkwardly climbed into the capsule, which suddenly felt terribly small.

'God,' said Sancia. 'If I survive this, I'll . . . I'll . . .'

'You'll what?'

'I don't know. Do something really fun and stupid.'

'Hm,' said Berenice. 'Well. Why don't we go get a drink, then?'

Sancia, sitting in the capsule, blinked. 'Uh. What?'

'A drink. You know – the fluid you put in your mouth, and swallow?'

She stared at Berenice, mouth open, unsure what to say.

Berenice smiled slightly. 'I saw you looking at me. When we were moving from Commons to campo and whatnot.'

Sancia shut her mouth, hard. 'Uh. Oh.'

'Yes. I thought it'd be wise to maintain professionalism at the time, but' – she looked around at the filthy, reeking canal – 'this is not terribly professional.'

'Why?' asked Sancia with genuine surprise.

'Why ask?'

'Yeah. No one's ever really asked before.'

Berenice struggled for the words. 'I . . . suppose I find you . . . refreshingly uncontained.'

'Refreshingly *uncontained*?' said Sancia. She wasn't at all sure how to take that.

'Let me put it this way,' said Berenice, pinkening. 'I am a person who stays inside of a handful of rooms all day. I do not leave those rooms. I do not leave the building, the block, the enclave, the campo. So, to me you are . . . quite different. And interesting.'

'Because,' said Sancia, 'I'm refreshingly uncontained.'

'Ah. Yes.'

'You do know,' said Sancia, 'that the only reason I go to all these places is so that I can steal enough to buy food, right?'

'Yes.'

'And you know you seem to usually have enough firepower in your pocket to literally blow down a wall, yeah?'

'True,' she said. 'But I never did any such thing until you came along.' She looked up. 'I think that's the barge.'

Sancia lay back into the tiny capsule, pulled out a scrived light, and turned it on. 'I'll think about that drink. If I survive, that is.'

'Do,' said Berenice. Her smile faded. 'I'm going to submerge the capsule next, and then plant the anchor. Hold on.'

'All right,' said Sancia. Then she shut the hatch.

⁂

<*Huh,*> said Clef as she sat alone in the capsule. <*Well. That didn't go how I expected.*>

<*Yeah, no kidding. I—*>

She didn't finish the thought – her belly swooped as the capsule abruptly descended, sinking to the bottom of the canal. 'Oh shit!' she whispered. She could hear the water gurgling and bubbling all around her, the sounds magnified in the tiny, tiny capsule. 'Shit, shit, shit!'

<*Don't worry,*> said Clef. <*This thing has been well built. You'll be fine. Just breathe normally.*>

<*Will that relax me?*>

<*Well, yeah. It'll also mean you won't run out of air.*>

She shut her eyes and tried to breathe calmly.

<*You ready, kid?*> asked Clef, excited. <*We're going to crack the biggest safe in the world tonight! Bigger than a whole damned city block!*>

<*You sound pretty excited for a dead guy.*>

<*Hey, I'm technically not dead – just dying. I have to get my fun where I can find it.*>

Sancia sighed as she heard the barge drifting through the waters above them. <*Trapped in a casket under the water, with a dead man trapped in a key. How the hell do I get myself into these situations?*>

There was a gentle tug, and the capsule started slowly trundling forward on the bottom of the canal.

<*Here we go,*> she said.

Sancia lay there, listening to the sound of the capsule scraping along the mud and stone, and waited.

An hour passed, maybe two. She idly wondered if this was what being dead was like – *If this thing sprang a leak, and I died in here, would I even notice?*

Finally the capsule came to a stop. She said, <*Clef – anything up there?*>

<*There are rigs aboard the barge – I guess the whole barge is a rig, really. I think they're unloading it.*>

<*Then this is the place. Let's hope no one's fishing right where I'm coming up.*>

She hit the switch on the door of the capsule. The metal canister slowly, awkwardly bobbed to the surface.

Sancia cracked the hatch and took a quick look around. They

were floating next to a stone walkway running along the canal, just south of the Mountain's dock. She flung the hatch open, scrambled onto the stone walkway, shut the door behind her, and hit a switch on the front. The capsule silently sank back down to the bottom.

She looked around. No one was screaming or raising any alarms. She was dressed in Candiano colours, so she didn't look unusual, and there was only the barge crew nearby, unloading on the dock.

Then she saw the Mountain.

'Oh . . . Oh my God,' she whispered.

The Mountain bloomed into the night sky just ahead of her, surging up like smoke from a forest fire. The thing was lit up brighter than a magnesium torch, spotlights shooting up along its curving black skin, which was dotted with tiny circular windows, like portholes on a ship. The sight set her guts fluttering.

Somewhere up there is the thirty-fifth floor, she thought. *That's what I've got to break into. And that's where I'll fly from. Soon.*

<*The garden,*> said Clef. <*The door. Hurry.*>

Sancia walked up to the street level and moved down the fairway until she spotted the garden entrance, a big white stone gateway stretching above a somewhat tattered-looking hedge wall. White floating lanterns made lazy circles above the garden. She glanced around and slipped inside.

The garden skirted the edge of the Mountain's walls, which gave it the feeling of a quaint courtyard built next to a cliff. The trimmed hedges and noble statues and stone follies looked queer and disturbing on the rolling green lawns, lit by washes of brittle white light from the lanterns.

<*Guards here,*> Clef said. <*Three of them. Walking through the hedges. Be careful.*>

The garden was theoretically open to any enclave resident, but she didn't risk it. With Clef's direction, she evaded their slow circuits until she found the stone bridge, which arched above a small babbling stream. She touched the cold metal casket, hidden in her pocket. This would be the first test of the blood Estelle Candiano had given them.

She waited until the way was clear, then paced up the stream to the bridge. As she neared it, a perfectly round seam formed in the smooth stone face. Then, without making a sound, the round plug of stone sank into the bridge and rolled aside.

<*Whoa,*> said Clef. <*That was impressive! This thing was scrived by a brilliant hand, kid.*>

<*Not reassuring, Clef.*>

<*Hey, credit where credit's due.*>

She slipped through the round door. It silently shut behind her. She now stood at the top of a set of stairs, and she walked down until they ended in a straight, smooth, grey stone tunnel, lined with bright white lights, which stretched forward so far it confused the eye.

She descended and started down the hall. <*This is a lot nicer than most of the tunnels I have to move through.*>

<*Yeah. No shit or rats or snakes, right?*>

<*Right.*> She kept walking. The end of the tunnel didn't seem to get any closer. <*But . . . I'd frankly prefer the old kind.*> She glanced at the smooth grey walls. <*This creeps me out. Are we close to the end?*>

<*I can't tell. Which means no, I think.*>

She kept walking. And walking. It felt like she was walking into empty space.

Then Clef spoke up: <*Whoaaaa . . .* >

<*What? What is it?*>

<*You don't feel that?*>

<*No? Feel what?* >

<*We just crossed some . . . barrier of some kind.*>

She looked behind, and saw no line or seam in the smooth grey stone. <*I don't see anything.*>

<*Well, trust me. We did. We're in some . . .* place. *I think.*>

<*The Mountain?*>

<*Hell if I know, kid.*>

After at least ten more minutes, she finally came to a set of stairs up, though these were winding rather than straight. She climbed and climbed until she came to the top, where they ended at a blank wall.

A vast whispering filled her mind as she got to the passageway at the top. She spied a handle on the side wall. She paused before she pulled it. <*Anyone on the other side of the wall, Clef?*>

<*Uh, no.*>

<*What* is *on the other side, Clef?*>

<*A whole bunch of stuff. You'll see.*>

Sancia pulled the handle. Again, a perfectly round seam appeared in the stone, and the stone circle rolled aside to let her through. But on the other side was – well, nothing, or so it appeared at first. It looked like she was seeing a sheet of cloth. Then she realised – *He hid the door behind some kind of wall hanging* – and she shoved it aside and stepped through.

She emerged into a lavish, dark-green stone hallway, tall and ornate with elaborate gold moulding running along the top. There were white wooden doors dotting the green stone walls, all perfectly circular with black iron handles in the middle. It was clearly a residential wing of the Mountain, and there was some kind of radiant light at the end of the hallway.

Sancia walked toward it. Then she saw what lay beyond, and gasped.

The Mountain, she realised, was a giant shell. And being inside of it was like being inside a hollowed-out . . .

Well. Mountain.

She stared at the rings and rings of floors beyond, all gold and green and shimmering, all lined with windows as the people within them lived and worked and toiled. She was four floors above the main level of the space, which was indescribably vast, lit by massive, brilliant floating lanterns carved of glass and crystal. Huge brass columns ran in staggered formations across the marble floor – and some of the columns appeared to be moving, sliding up or down. It took her a moment to realise the columns were actually hollow, and had tiny rooms in them that rose or fell, ferrying people up to dangling stations above. *Those must be the lifts Orso mentioned*, she thought. Huge banners hung in between the stations, the giant, bright-gold Candiano loggotipo glimmering in the glow of the scrived lights below. All of it formed an endless, circling wall of light and colour and movement.

It was like another world, just like Orso had said. And all of it was enabled by . . .

The side of her head grew bright hot and her eyes watered. She gritted her teeth as the sound of so many scrivings hit her, drilling into her, biting into her mind.

<*Okay, hold on,*> said Clef.

<*It's . . . it's too much, Clef!*> she cried. <*It's too much, it's too much! I can't bear it, I can't* bear *it!*>

<*Hold on, hold on!*> said Clef. <*Your talents are a two-way connection – I can share your mind just as my thoughts can barge into yours. Let's see if I can bear the load for you . . .* >

The eruption of murmurs warbled, then diminished rapidly, until it was a bearable level – though it did not vanish.

She gasped, relieved. <*What did you do, Clef?*>

<*It's sort of like the canals,*> said Clef. <*When one gets too full, it dumps water into another. Now all that noise is going into me. God . . . I knew it was bad for you, kid, but not* this *bad.*>

<*Are you all right? Can you bear it?*>

<*I can for now.*>

<*And . . . is it damaging you more?*>

<*Everything's damaging me more. Come on. Let's stop wasting time and go.*>

Sancia rose, took a breath, and started off into the Mountain.

Gregor carefully navigated through the outer paths of the Candiano campo. He stuck to the edges of the streets, moving through the shadows. It was an odd experience – he'd never really spent much time on other campos before.

He saw the cross-streets Orso had described ahead. He started across a small square toward it – but then he paused ever so slightly.

Gregor abruptly turned right, away from the cross-streets. He walked to a small alley, stepped into a doorway, and stopped and watched the square and the streets around him.

There was no one. Yet he'd suddenly had an overpowering feeling that someone had been following him – there'd been a movement somewhere, out of the corner of his eye.

He waited, not moving. *Perhaps I imagined it*, he thought. He waited a bit longer. *I need to hurry*, he thought. *Or else Sancia will try to jump off the Mountain with nowhere to fly to.* He walked to the cross-streets, knelt, and started installing the anchor in the cobblestone.

What struck Sancia most about the Mountain was not just the size of the thing, but also the emptiness of it. She roved through huge banquet halls with vaulted ceilings, indoor gardens with pink, circling floating lanterns, immense counting offices filled with rows and rows of desks – and most were almost empty, occupied by only one or two people. She'd heard rumours that the Mountain was haunted, but maybe it just felt haunted because it seemed so abandoned.

<*Candiano really is on the decline,*> said Clef.

<*No kidding.*>

She knew she needed to find a lift, and she needed to use it without attracting attention. She finally found a more populated segment of the Mountain, full of residents and employees. They sped past her or ambled this way and that as they went about their daily lives, ignoring her; but then, they would – Orso had supplied her with clothing that made her look like a mid-level functionary.

She spied a few important-looking young men and followed them until they finally came to a lift. They stood around, waiting on the little room to arrive, and chatted in bored tones. Finally the round brass doors opened for them – presumably the rig checked their blood to make sure they could use it – and they walked inside, chatting and gesturing. Then the doors shut, and the lift rose.

<*I'll catch the next one,*> she thought.

<*This place is . . . strange,*> said Clef.

<*Yeah, no shit.*>

<*No, I mean I feel this pressure, like we're in a room with too much air. It's hard to explain – and I'm not even sure I understand it.*>

The lift doors opened again, and she stepped inside. There was a brass panel by the door, with a round dial set in the middle. The dial was labelled with numbers running from 1 to 15, and it was currently pointed at 3. <*It doesn't go all the way up,*> she thought.

<*Then go as far as you can, I guess.*>

She set the dial to 15, and the doors shut and the lift began to rise.

<*So we just keep taking lifts until we get to thirty-five,*> Clef said.

<*Easy. Hopefully.*>

They rode in silence.

Then Sancia heard a voice. It was just like when she heard Clef's voice – but this voice was *not* Clef's. It was the voice of an imperious old man, and his words echoed loudly in her head as he said, <*A Presence felt. But . . . unknown.*>

Sancia nearly fell over with shock. She stared around herself, and confirmed they were alone in the lift.

<*Clef?*> she asked. <*What the hell was that, what the hell was that!*>

<*You heard it too?*> he said. He sounded just as shocked as she was. <*The voice?*>

<*Yeah! Has . . . Has that ever happened befo—*>

<*Words . . . Words, I hear,*> boomed the old man's voice. <*A Presence is found . . . and located. A lift. Escalation?*>

<*Uh-oh,*> said Clef.

The doors of the lift opened. Sancia walked out onto the fifteenth floor, which appeared to be more industrial than residential. Everything here was blank grey stone and iron doors and pipes. A sign above read SCRIVING BAY 13.

Sancia barely had any mind for this, though. Someone was talking, to her and to Clef. Someone could apparently overhear them, like two people gossiping at a taverna. The idea was simply *mad.*

<*Destination?*> asked the old man's voice. He spoke in clipped, harsh tones, like a parrot that had learned to imitate speech. <*Purpose? Why are you within my boundaries?*>

<*How is this possible, Clef?*> she asked.

<*I don't know,*> said Clef. <*Usually I have to touch scrived devices to hear them speak . . . .* >

<*And is that what you think this is? A scrived device?*>

<*Well, I—*>

<*You are . . . not Tribuno Candiano,*> said the old man's voice. <*Words he could not put into me directly. Spoken only . . . yes. Not like this.*>

<*Shit,*> she said. <*Shit!*> She turned a corner and followed a group of scrivers toward yet another lift. She glanced inside and saw this one only went down. She kept walking.

<*But Presence carries Tribuno's mark,*> said the old man's voice. <*His signal. How is this?*>

She walked down a long hallway, opened a door – it unlocked instantly for her – and found herself moving through what seemed to be some kind of party, with scrivers quaffing bubble rum out of glass tankards while a band of women – most scantily dressed – played flutes and brass instruments.

<*Confirmation,*> said the old man's voice. <*A secondary presence located in chambers of Tribuno Candiano. Who is other Presence?*>

The scrivers ignored Sancia, who was dressed as a functionary. She passed through and walked out the door on the other side, desperately searching for another lift.

She was in a short hallway, with an open door at the end.

<*No,*> boomed the old man's voice. The door at the end slammed shut. She stared at it, then turned and tried the one she'd just walked through, only to find it was locked.

<*Must provide identity,*> demanded the old man's voice. <*And nature.*> And then, though the voice's previous statements had a queer, crude syntax to them, his next question sounded strangely genuine. Even passionate. He whispered, <*Are . . . are you one of* them*?*>

<*Use me on the door at the end,*> said Clef. <*Now!*>

She ran to the closed door and touched Clef to the knob – since the door, like so many in the Mountain, had no need of the lock.

<*It's . . . weird,*> said Clef. <*I don't need to break any bindings, because the door can't really resist you. It thinks you're Tribuno, it's just been put on a delay. Wait ten seconds, then try the knob.*>

She did so. The door opened for her, and beyond was a set of stairs up. She sprinted up them, taking three steps at a time.

<*Curious,*> said the old man's voice. <*Anomalous.*>

She kept running up the stairs.

<*I have never held a Presence such as this,*> said the voice. <*Two minds in one? How is this?*>

<*Clef?*> said Sancia.

<*Yeah?*>

<*Am I insane, or is this voice the goddamn Mountain?*>

Clef sighed as she came to the top of the stairs. <*Yeah. Yeah, I think it is.*>

Sancia looked around for her next move. <*What do we do?*>

<*I don't know. But I think it's a lot, lot more than a building,*> said Clef.

<*Can it hurt me?*>

<*I'm not sure. I don't think so. But I'm also not sure it would want to.*>

<*What is Presence's nature?*> asked the voice – the Mountain, she supposed. <*No one has ever spoken to me directly . . . Is Presence a . . . a hierophant? Must provide verity.*>

<*Hierophant?*> thought Sancia. <*What the* hell *is going on?*>

Sancia picked a corridor at random and started walking. Berenice and Orso had said that the Mountain might sniff her out before long, but she didn't think it would be *this* fast.

<*At least provide destination,*> said the Mountain, somewhat resigned.

<*We want to go up,*> said Clef.

<*Clef!*> she said, shocked.

<*What? He can hear us, and he can track you. He'll figure it out eventually!*>

<*If location is up,*> said the Mountain, <*proceed to third right. This will take Presence up.*>

Sancia walked to the third right, then looked down its long hallway and saw it ended in a lift.

<*Proceed,*> said the Mountain.

<*How do I know you won't trap me in there?*> asked Sancia.

<*I cannot,*> said the Mountain. <*You carry Tribuno Candiano's signal. This engages many rules constricting behaviour. Cannot alert anyone to Tribuno's location. And I am required to protect Candiano at all costs. These were his commands, when I was formed.*>

Sancia started walking toward the lift. <*Tribuno made you? Made your . . . your mind?*>

<*Made, no. Initiated, yes.*>

The lift opened for her. She didn't even get the chance to tell it which floor she wanted before it started up.

<*Is your nature one of the Old Ones?*> whispered the Mountain.

<*You must tell me. You must . . . It is one of my rules. Location of such is my Purpose.*>

They ignored him as they continued up.

<*Isn't fair,*> said the Mountain softly. <*Not fair that I keep nearing fulfilment of Purpose. Yet it eludes me . . .* >

The doors of the lift opened – but not on a hallway or a room or a balcony. Before Sancia was a wide, sandy plain, with a black sky above dotted with tiny white stars. Standing in the centre of this plain was a tall black stone obelisk, covered with strange engravings.

'What the *hell*?' whispered Sancia.

<*It's not real,*> said Clef. <*It's like a stage background. It's a black-painted ceiling with scrived lights set in it, really small ones. I suspect the sand is imported too. Like a garden.*>

<*True,*> said the Mountain. <*But Obelisk is real. Taken from the Gothian deserts, where the Old Ones once remade the world.*>

Sancia anxiously looked around the sandy plain, then started off, the sigh of her footprints intensely loud in the empty room.

<*There's a door at the far end,*> whispered Clef. <*I'll help you find it.*>

<*He used to reside here,*> said the Mountain. <*Long ago. Was Presence aware?*>

She shook her head, bewildered, as they crossed the weird sandy plain. She was getting the impression that the Mountain was not really hostile to them at all. Rather, it was like the thing was lonely, hungry for someone to talk to, and she suspected it'd brought her to this strange, fake place for a reason. Much like a party host might show a guest a painting, the Mountain had wanted to discuss this.

<*Tribuno?*> she asked. <*He came here?*>

<*Yes. Made this place. He would come and be situated before Obelisk, to . . . reflect,*> said the Mountain. <*Think. And speak. I listened. I listened to all he said. And learned to mimic his words.*>

<*Why did Tribuno Candiano make you?*> asked Sancia.

<*To attract a hierophant,*> said the Mountain.

<*What!*> said Clef. <*That's insane! The hierophants are all dead!*>

<*Untrue,*> said the Mountain. <*Death cannot be the state of hierophants. This was determined, per Tribuno's research. Look upon Obelisk. Do so.*>

She did as the Mountain asked. Nothing about the obelisk looked familiar at first, but . . .

On one side was a carven visage. An old man's face, stern and high-cheekboned, and below it, a single hand, grasping a short shaft – a wand, perhaps. Below that was a familiar symbol to Sancia – the butterfly, or the moth. She'd seen it on Clef's head, and in the engraving of the hierophants in Orso's workshop.

'Crasedes the Great,' said Sancia.

<*Yes,*> said the Mountain. <*Changed himself. Altered by his practices to become deathless. The Magnus cannot die. He and his kin cannot enter into a death state. They persist in some other fashion, wandering the world. Tribuno built me to attract them, like a moth to flame . . .* >

She found the door and opened it. She started to walk out – but then screamed and fell back.

The door opened on a short, railed balcony, almost at the top of the huge hollow space she'd originally seen – she was hundreds of feet above the ground. If she'd run forward, she could have stumbled over the railing and fallen to her death.

'You could have told me that was there!' she said aloud.

<*I would not have permitted death,*> said the Mountain, somewhat apologetically.

She returned to the balcony, and saw there was a short walkway that clung to the curving wall around the top of the giant hollow hall. A door was at the far end, and she started to walk to it.

<*God,*> she said. <*This place is* huge.>

<*Yes,*> said the Mountain. <*I am vast. He built me to be such. I needed to be, to achieve my Purpose.*>

<*Did he build you to be a god?*> asked Sancia.

<*A god? Like the one wrought by Crasedes Magnus?*> It sounded amused. <*No. But a mind, yes. Yet – how to make a mind? How to make thoughts? How to do speech? Difficult. Must have examples. Many, many, many, many, many examples. Thousands. Millions. Billions. So he . . . broadened my Purpose.*>

<*What do you mean?*> said Sancia. <*How could he broaden your purpose?*>

<*Many believe I am but walls,*> said the Mountain. <*And floors. And lifts and doors. But Tribuno wove sigils into my boundaries, my bones . . . and when he finished I became something . . . more.*>

<*Oh!*> cried Clef, suddenly. <*I . . . I think I see! I think I see what you are! But, my God, it's hard to believe it . . .* >

<*What do you mean, Clef?*> asked Sancia.

<*I told you I felt us cross a boundary in the tunnel,*> said Clef. <*And I felt the pressure in this place, like I was deep under the sea . . . And I can only converse with an item when it's touching me, right? But what if, whenever you're in the Mountain's boundaries, you* are *touching it?*>

<*You mean . . .* >

<*Yes. The Mountain isn't the building – it's the building and everything inside of it. He's basically scrived a chunk of reality to act like a device!*>

<*What! That's scrumming impossible!*> said Sancia. <*You can't scrive reality as you might a button or a plate!*>

<*Sure you can,*> said Clef. <*Scrivings already change an object's reality, right? So why not just make the object really, really big – like a big bubble, or a dome? Then you design it to be sensitive to all the changes and transactions and fluctuations taking place within it. You teach it to notice the changes, to record them – and then, slowly, you teach it to learn.*>

<*But scriving can't just do that!*> said Sancia. <*Scriving can change physical reality, it . . . can't make a* mind.>

<*Maybe it can get close, though,*> said Clef. <*With enough power behind the designs. And Tribuno got close, didn't he? Powered by six scrumming lexicons, all specifically designed by Candiano himself toward this one purpose?*>

<*Yes,*> said the Mountain. <*I am this place. All that is within it is within me. Yet I do not exert total control. Just as people do not have control over their heart, their bones. I can merely . . . nudge. Redirect. Delay. Like you said – supply pressure. And I listen. Watch. Learn. A child watches adults to learn what it is to be alive. I have seen such phenomena – I have observed children being born and grow or die within me, thousands and thousands of times. And I have been as a child. I have learned. I have Made myself from Nothing.*>

Sancia looked out on the rings and rings of floors below her. <*He . . . he wanted to prove it, didn't he?*> she asked. <*Tribuno thought the hierophants were still alive, watching the world. He wanted to show off to them, prove he could do things that they could do – produce a mind of artifice. And then, maybe, they'd come talk to him.*>

<*Yes.*>

<*All this,*> said Clef. <*All this made like a weaverbird weaves its nest, trying to attract its mate . . .* >

Sancia continued across the walkway to the door. She slipped through it and found herself in some kind of maintenance shaft. <*It didn't work, though,*> said Sancia. <*You said you had yet to fulfil your purpose. No hierophants came.*>

<*Yes,*> said the Mountain.

She walked down the shaft, found yet another door, and opened it onto another marble hallway.

<*But maybe not,*> the Mountain whispered.

She stopped. <*What do you mean, maybe not?*> she asked.

<*You mean you got close to a hierophant?*> asked Clef.

<*It is . . . possible,*> said the Mountain.

Sancia continued on until she found a lift that went all the way up, to the fortieth floor. She took a breath, relieved, and set the dial to the thirty-fifth floor.

<*You don't know if you met a hierophant or not?*> asked Clef.

<*I once contained . . . something,*> said the Mountain. <*Men brought it here . . . The new man.*>

<*Tomas Ziani?*>

<*Yes. Him.*> From the sound of its words, it seemed like the Mountain did not like him much. <*It was strange . . . I sensed a mind there. Impossibly big, huge, powerful. But . . . it did not deign to speak to me. No matter how I begged. Then they took it away. Location now unknown.*>

The lift opened. Sancia stepped out onto the thirty-fifth floor. This was a floor of offices, and they were different from what she'd seen so far. For one, they were huge, nearly two stories in height. They also featured lots of sumptuous, complicated wallpapers, huge stone and metal doors, and lavish waiting areas.

<*Was this thing an artefact?*> asked Clef.

<*A piece of the Old Ones . . . perhaps,*> said the Mountain.

<*Another artefact . . . one that can talk, like me . . .* > thought Clef. <*God. How I'd like to see that.*>

<*Like you?*> said the Mountain. <*You are . . . also an artefact?*>

<*Yes,*> said Clef. <*And no. I'm different now. I think you and I are much the same . . . two instruments who have lost their creators, and now break down into different, unintended states.*>

<*Which way to Ziani's office?*> said Sancia.

<*Ahead,*> said the Mountain, though it now sounded distracted and impatient. <*On your left. To confirm – you are instrument?*>

<*Yes,*> said Clef.

<Of hierophants?>

<. . . Yes.>

<And . . . I think I sense you are a . . . key?>

<Yeah.>

Sancia walked ahead until she found it – a large, black door with a stone frame. And beside the frame was a nameplate reading:

TOMAS ZIANI

PRESIDENT AND CHIEF OFFICER

She tried the door. It gave way easily – presumably because of the blood she carried. She slipped inside.

She stopped and stared. Ziani's office was . . . unusual. Everything was built of huge dark, heavy stone, towering and forbidding and looming, even the desk. She saw none of the artful designs or colourful materials from the other rooms. Besides the side door leading to the balcony, there was nothing conventional about this place.

Yet it also looked familiar, she realised. Hadn't she seen a place just like this before?

Yes, she had – the room beyond looked almost *exactly* like that chamber depicted in the engraving with Crasedes the Great, the one she'd glimpsed in Orso's workshops, where the hierophants stood before the casket, and from it emerged the form of . . . something.

'The chamber at the centre of the world,' she whispered. That could be the only explanation for the huge, strange stone plinths, and giant, arched windows . . .

Then she remembered. *Because this used to be Tribuno's office.*

<Are you of Crasedes?> whispered the Mountain. *<Are you his tool?>*

<I . . . I guess I don't know,> said Clef.

Sancia looked around, wondering where in the hell Ziani could have hidden the imperiat. There weren't many shelves here – only the big stone desk in the middle. She walked over to it and started ripping through the drawers. All of them were full of conventional things, like papers and pens and inkwells. 'Come on, come on,' she whispered.

<Are you his key?> whispered the Mountain. *<Or – his wand?>*

<*His what?*> asked Clef.

<*The wand of Crasedes? You know of this?*>

<*Well, yeah,*> said Clef. <*I've heard some people mention it.*>

<*A mistranslation,*> said the Mountain. <*Common.*>

<*What the hell are you talking about?*> asked Clef. <*What mistranslation?*>

<*You have heard stories of Crasedes the Magician, using his wand to alter the world,*> said the Mountain. <*These are incorrect. Many errors persist, from old Gothian to new Gothian. For in the old language, the word for 'wand' is only one letter different from 'key'.*>

Sancia stopped.

'*What?*' she shouted out loud.

<*What?*> said Clef faintly.

<*Yes,*> said the Mountain. <*Tribuno did not believe Crasedes used a wand – but a key. A golden key. And he used it as a clockmaker uses his key, winding up and unscrewing the great machine of creation. So, I must ask – are you the key of Crasedes Magnus?*>

Sancia stood in the office, dumbstruck. 'Clef . . .' she whispered. 'What's he talking about?'

Clef was silent for a long, long time. <*I don't know,*> he said quietly. <*I don't remember.*>

<*Crasedes said of his key that it could break any barrier, any lock,*> said the Mountain, <*and when he held it in his hand, it could unthread the whole of creation.*>

Sancia felt dizzy. She slowly sat down on the ground. 'Clef . . . are you . . .'

<*I don't know,*> he said, frustrated.

'But you . . . You could be . . .'

<*I said I don't know! I DON'T KNOW, ALL RIGHT? I DON'T KNOW!*>

She sat there, unnerved. She'd heard so many tales of how Crasedes the Great had tapped a stone with his wand, and made it dance, or tapped the seas with its tip, and parted the waters . . . to imagine this had not been some silly magic stick, but her friend, the person who'd saved her time and time again . . .

<*That's enough goddamn speculation!*> said Clef. He sounded upset. <*Where's the imperiat?*>

<*Imperiat?*> said the Mountain, sounding surprised. <*You wished to find that? The other artefact?*>

'Yes!' said Sancia.

<*Imperiat is often stored in trapdoor behind desk,*> said the Mountain.

'A trapdoor!' said Sancia. 'Brilliant!' She sprang and ran over to the desk.

<*But imperiat – not there now,*> said the Mountain.

She stopped. 'What? Where is it?'

<*Ziani has taken it,*> said the Mountain.

Her heart plummeted. 'He . . . he took it out into the campo? It's gone? We did all this for *nothing*?'

<*No, imperiat is not in the campo,*> said the Mountain. <*Ziani holds it here, within my depths.*>

<*Where is he?*> demanded Clef.

<*Originally,*> said the Mountain, <*Ziani held it in an office two floors below this one. But when you walked into this office, I . . . sense he took it up to this floor.*>

Sancia stood completely still as she listened to this.

'He what?' she whispered.

<*Tomas Ziani is now holding the imperiat on this floor,*> said the Mountain. <*Eleven offices down the hallway from you.*>

<*And . . . and does he have anyone with him?*> asked Clef.

<*Yes,*> said the Mountain.

Sancia swallowed. 'How many?' she croaked. 'And are they armed?'

<*Fourteen. And yes. And they are now . . . approaching your location.*>

Everything felt distant and faint. 'Oh God,' she whispered. 'My God, my God . . . It . . . It's a trap. It was a trap, a trap all along!'

<*Can you help get her out?*> demanded Clef quickly. <*Can you stop them?*>

<*No,*> said the Mountain. <*Ziani carries the same authorities as Tribuno.*>

<*Go, Sancia,*> said Clef. <*Just get out! Get out now, now!*>

She ran to the balcony door and heaved at the knob, but it wouldn't budge. 'It's locked!' she cried. 'Why won't it open?'

<*Ziani applied a binding to this exit,*> said the Mountain. <*Just this morning. This door is to be sealed shut.*>

'Open it!' she screamed. 'Open it now, now!'

<*Not permitted to,*> said the Mountain.

<*Touch me to it!*> said Clef.

She grabbed him and did so. But the door did not spring open as she'd expected. It moved – but only barely.

<*I told you,*> said the Mountain. <*I am not permitted to allow this door to open. It is to be sealed. These are my instructions.*>

<*Come on,*> said Clef, groaning like he was trying to pull a cart up a hill. It seemed like the Mountain was a formidable opponent.

<*I cannot allow it,*> said the Mountain. <*It is not permitted.*> She imagined the whole of the building leaning against the door, every brick and every column.

<*Come on, come on, please, please, please . . .* > said Clef.

The door inched open just a little more, and a little more . . .

<*They're close!*> cried Clef. <*I . . . I can feel them in the hallway, I can feel them out there, Sancia!*> The door was now cracked open about four inches. <*I'm not sure I'm going to make it! I'm not sure I can get it open in time!*>

Sancia tried to think of something to do, anything. She couldn't be caught in here, especially not with Clef, not with the thing Tomas Ziani needed to complete his imperiat – and especially now that she knew he might be the one and only wand of Crasedes.

She looked at the door, and thought.

It was barely open more than a crack. But it might be enough.

She grabbed the flask of Tribuno Candiano's blood and wedged it in the door, keeping it open. Then she took Clef away, grabbed the hardened cask attached to the air-sailing rig, and popped it open.

<*What are you doing!*> screamed Clef. <*Why did you stop me?*>

<*Because keeping you safe matters more than anything,*> she said.

<*What? Sancia, no! No, n—*>

<*I'm sorry, Clef. So long.*> She stuffed him in the hardened cask, crammed it and the air-sailing rig out onto the balcony, and tore off the bronze tab.

With a *snap*, the air-sailing rig deployed. The thing hurtled out of her hands. She watched as the black parachute drifted out over the Candiano campo, rocketing off to what she hoped was safety.

Then the side of her head lit up with pain.

She wanted to scream. She *had* to scream, the agony was so fierce, so terrible. Yet she couldn't – not because the pain was overwhelming, but because suddenly she couldn't move at all. She couldn't even blink, or breathe – she felt her body rapidly running out of oxygen.

Something was changing in her mind. The plate in her skull was like hissing acid in her bones – but she felt something invading her thoughts, taking them over. It was like when Clef had used her body to speak to Orso, but . . . so much *worse.*

She took a breath – yet it was not a voluntary gesture. It was as if her body had become a puppet, and her controller had realised her needs and forced as much oxygen into her lungs as possible. She could no longer control her own organs.

She watched, helpless, as her body was forced to turn around. Then she walked, stiffly and strangely, over to the door out to the hallway. She lifted a hand, slapped at the knob, opened the door, and awkwardly staggered out.

A dozen Candiano guards stood around her in the hallway, all armed, all armoured, all ready to attack her if need be. Standing behind them was a young man, tall and stoop-shouldered, with curly hair and a scraggly beard – Tomas Ziani. He held a strange device in his hands – it looked like an oversized pocket watch, yet it was made of gold, and it was whining slightly as he manipulated it . . .

'It works!' he said, delighted. 'I wasn't sure it would. It started whining in my pocket the instant you walked into the office, just as it had in the Greens.'

Sancia, of course, said nothing – she was as still as a statue. Yet inside, in her mind, she was screaming and spitting and ranting in rage. She wanted nothing more than to fall on this young man and tear him to pieces, clawing and biting at him – but she was forced to be still.

Tomas Ziani seemed to remember himself. He walked through the throng of soldiers and looked her over. 'Now . . .' He examined her belt. 'Ah. *That's* what I was looking for. Our informants said you were fond of these . . .'

She couldn't see what he was doing, but she felt him slip out one of her dolorspina darts. 'This ought to do the trick, I think . . .' he said.

Then she felt a pain in her arm, and she knew nothing more.

Gregor Dandolo stood huddled in the shadows, watching the streets. Then he jumped when he heard the *clank*.

He looked at the anchoring plate. He'd secured it to the campo streets pretty well, he'd thought, but the thing had just leapt in the air . . .

Perhaps she's turned on the air-sailing rig, he thought. He peered into the night sky, watching the Mountain.

Then he saw it – a single black dot, rapidly approaching.

'Thank God,' he said.

He watched as the air-sailing rig flew close, then twirled around twice as it made its descent. Yet he saw that something was wrong.

Sancia was not in the air-sailing rig. It appeared to be just the parachute.

He watched as the rig descended. He snatched it out of the air as it fell and saw something was attached to it – the cask for the imperiat.

Inside was her golden key – Clef. There was no imperiat, and no message.

He stared at the key, then looked back at the Mountain.

'Sancia . . .' he whispered. 'Oh no . . .'

He waited for a moment more, madly believing there was some chance she might somehow still appear. But nothing came.

I have to get to Orso. I have to tell him everything's gone wrong.

He put the key in his pocket, turned, and walked quickly for the southern gates to the Commons. He tried to maintain his posture and demeanour, but he couldn't help but feel like he was shambling forward in a daze. Was she captured? Was she dead? He didn't know.

But though his mind was spinning, some small voice inside him spoke up – *Did you just see movement? There, out of the corner of your eye? Is someone following you?*

He ignored it. He just needed to get out, to get *out*.

He turned a corner toward one of the canal bridges, and promptly bumped into someone. He caught a glimpse of them – a woman, elegantly dressed, right in front of him like she'd been waiting for him – before his stomach suddenly lit up with pain.

Gregor stopped still, gasped, and looked down. The woman held a dagger in her hand, and she had put almost the entire blade into Gregor's stomach.

He stared at it. 'What . . .' he mumbled. He looked up. The woman was staring into his face with an icy calm. 'Wh–who?'

She stepped forward, and thrust the dagger in deeper. He gagged, trembled, and tried to walk away toward the canal bridge, but suddenly his knees felt weak. He collapsed, blood pouring from his stomach.

The woman walked around him, bent low, reached into his coat pocket, and pulled out the golden key. She examined it carefully with a quiet 'Hm.'

Gregor reached a hand out, trying to take it back. He dumbly saw his hand was covered with blood.

There was the sound of footsteps from the road he took – more than one set.

A trap. I . . . I have to get out. I have to escape. He started trying to crawl away.

He heard a man's voice say, 'Any issues, ma'am?'

'None,' said the woman. She looked at the golden key. 'But – *this* I did not expect. The imperiat, yes . . . but not this. No one else flew off the Mountain?'

'No, ma'am. The only thing carried by the air-sailing rig was that.'

'I see,' she said thoughtfully. 'Tomas must have snatched her up. But no matter. That *is* why one ought to prepare for every possible eventuality.'

'Yes, Mrs Ziani.'

Gregor stopped crawling away. He swallowed and looked over his shoulder. *Mrs Ziani? Does he mean . . . Estelle? Is that Orso's Estelle?*

'What do we do with this one, ma'am?' asked the man.

She surveyed Gregor coolly, then nodded at the canal.

'Yes, ma'am.' The man walked forward and grabbed Gregor by the back of the coat. Gregor tried to struggle, but found he didn't have the strength – his arms and feet felt so cold, so distant, so numb. He couldn't even cry out as he was flung down toward the water, and then he knew only dark swirls and twists of bubbles, and the world left him.

28

Sancia awoke and regretted it.

Her mind was full of nails and thorns and brambles, and her mouth was so dry it hurt. She cracked open an eye, and even though the room she was in was fairly dark, even the slightest hint of light hurt her mind.

Dolorspina venom, she thought, groaning. *So* that's *what that feels like . . .*

She patted herself down. She appeared to be uninjured, though all of her gear was gone. She was in a cell of some kind. Four blank stone walls, with an iron door at the far end. There was a tiny slit of a window at the top of one wall, allowing in a faint dribbling of pale light. Besides that, there was nothing.

She started to sit up, cursing and moaning. This wasn't the first time she'd been held captive in her life, and she was well accustomed to getting into and out of secure places, even ones as hostile as this. Hopefully she could figure a way out and get to Orso fast enough.

Then she saw she was not alone.

There was a woman in the room with her. A woman made of gold.

Sancia stared at her. The woman stood in the corner of the dark cell, tall and queerly motionless. Sancia had no idea where the woman had come from, since she'd looked around when she'd awoken and seen – she was *sure* of it – no one. Yet there she was.

What the hell, she thought. *What else weird could happen tonight?*

The woman was nude, but somehow every bit of her was made of gold, even her eyes, which sat blank and still like stones in her skull, watching her. Sancia would have normally thought the woman was not a person at all, but a statue; yet she could not help but feel a tremendous, powerful intelligence in those blank, golden eyes, a mind that watched her with a disturbing indifference, like Sancia were no more than a raindrop wriggling its way down a windowpane . . .

The woman stepped forward and looked down at her. The side of Sancia's head grew warm.

The woman said, 'When you awake, get him to leave. Then I will tell you how to save yourself.' Her manner of speech was powerfully odd, like she knew the words but had never heard anyone speak out loud before.

Sancia, still lying on the stone floor, stared up at the woman, confused. She tried to say, 'But I *am* awake.'

Yet then, somehow, she realised she wasn't.

Sancia awoke with a start, snorting and reaching out. She stared around herself.

She didn't . . . *seem* to have moved at all. She was still alone, still in the dark cell – which looked the exact same – still lying on her back in the exact same position. Yet the woman of gold was gone.

Sancia peered into the shadowy corners, disturbed. *Was it a dream? What is wrong with me? What's wrong with my brain?*

She rubbed the side of her head, which ached terribly. Maybe she was going mad. She shivered, thinking of what had happened in Ziani's office. It seemed like the imperiat could not only shut down scrived devices, as it had in the Greens, but also control them. Which meant, circuitously enough, that since Sancia had a scrived device in her skull, that it could also control her.

Which Sancia found deeply horrifying. She'd grown up in a place where she'd had no say in her decisions. To have someone literally take her will away from her . . .

I need to get out of here. Now.

She stood, walked over to a wall, and felt the blank stone. Her abilities still worked, it seemed: the wall told her of itself, of the many rooms it adjoined, of spider webs and cinder and dust . . .

I'm in a foundry, she realised. But she'd never heard of a foundry that made so little noise before.

An old one, then. One fallen into disuse?

She took her hand away. *I'm still on the Candiano campo, aren't I? That's the only campo where a scriving foundry would sit totally vacant.* She wondered if she was in the Cattaneo, but she didn't think so. The Cattaneo had felt more advanced than this.

Then the side of Sancia's head grew hot again, so hot it felt like her flesh was sizzling. Before she could cry out, all thoughts fell away from her – and then, again, she lost control of her body.

She watched herself as she stood up, took three shuffling steps, and turned to wait in front of the iron door.

There were footsteps from outside, then a clinking and clanking. Then the door fell open to reveal Tomas Ziani standing there, imperiat in his hand, blinking in the darkness.

'Ah!' he said, seeing her. 'Good. You look alive and well.' He wrinkled his nose. 'You are an ugly little thing, aren't you. But . . .' He adjusted a wheel on the imperiat, then held it up to her, slowly waving it through the air – until it finally drew close to the right side of her head. The imperiat began to whine softly.

'Interesting,' he said softly. 'Amazing! All those scrivers who thought we'd never see a scrived human – yet *I'm* the one to find one! Let's have a look at you, then. Come along.' He fiddled with the imperiat, waved a hand, and Sancia, helpless, followed him out of the cell.

He marched her through the foundry's crumbling, dark passageways. It was a shadowy, gloomy place, silent except for an occasional distant drip of water. Finally they came to a large open room, lit by scrived lights placed on the floor. Standing at the far wall of the room were four Candiano guards, all of whom looked quite seasoned. There was a deadness to their eyes as they looked at Sancia that made her skin crawl.

Beside these thugs was a long, low table. On it were all sorts of books, papers, and stone carvings – along with a huge rusty, cracked old metal box that looked, she thought, like the test lexicon back in Orso's workshop.

Sancia tried to look harder at the items on the table, but since she didn't have control over her own eyes she got no more than a fleeting glance. Still, she managed to think – *This is Tribuno's collection, isn't it? The trove of Occidental treasures that Ziani mentioned . . .*

Then she saw what waited in the middle of the room. And though she couldn't move, the urge to scream flooded her mind.

It was an operating table, complete with restraints for the patient's wrists and ankles.

Tomas Ziani did something to the imperiat, and she stopped moving. Then she watched in horror as two Candiano guards picked her up, laid her flat on the table, and strapped her in.

No, no, no, she thought, panicked. *Anything but that . . .*

They did something to her restraints, turning a small, metal key on the sides. A whispering and chattering filled her ears.

They're scrived, she thought. *The restraints are scrived.*

The guards departed.

I'm not getting out of here, am I?

Tomas walked to stand over her, still holding the imperiat. 'Now, let's see,' he muttered. 'If what Enrico said is correct, this should . . .' He adjusted something on it.

Sancia felt her will return – her body was her own again.

She flew forward and snapped her teeth, trying her hardest to take a bite out of Tomas. She nearly did, but he stumbled backward, surprised. 'Son of a bitch!' he cried.

Sancia snarled at him, bucking and arching her back and heaving at her restraints – but since they were augmented, they didn't budge an inch.

'Filthy little . . .' growled Tomas. He made a move to strike her, but when she didn't flinch, he backed down, probably concerned she might try to bite his hand.

'You want us to put her down?' said a guard.

'Did I say *anything* to you?' said Tomas.

The guard looked away. Tomas walked around to the edge of the table and turned a crank. The scrived restraints on her wrists and ankles slowly slid out along the surface of the table, stretching her out until she was spread-eagle, unable to move. Then he walked back around, raised a fist high, and slammed it down on Sancia's stomach, driving the air out of her.

Sancia flexed and coughed, gasping for breath. 'There,' he said savagely. 'That's how it is, yes? You do as I say, or else I get to do what I want. See?'

She blinked tears from her eyes and glared at him. His gaze had a sadistic gleam to it.

'I'm going to ask you some questions now,' he said.

'Why did you kill Sark?' Sancia gasped.

'I said *I'd* ask the questions.'

'He wasn't anything to you. He had no one to betray you to. He didn't even know who you were.'

'Shut *up*,' snapped Tomas.

'What did you do with his body?'

'God, you're mouthy.' He sighed. He turned a wheel on the imperiat, and, as if she were descending into cold seawater, her will abandoned her again.

'There,' said Tomas. 'I rather like this. I wish more people had them. I could just turn them on or off as I pleased . . .'

Sancia lay limp and still on the operating table. Trapped in her body yet again, she silently screamed and raved – until she noticed that her head happened to be facing the far wall of the room, where the table with all the Occidental treasures lay.

It was hard to look without having any control over her eyes, but she did her best. She couldn't tell much from the materials there – lots of papers, lots of books – but the lexicon-like box at the end of the table . . . that was interesting. It wasn't *exactly* a lexicon – it wasn't a hundred feet long and broiling hot, for one thing – but it did have what looked like an array of scrived discs running along its top, though the discs were horribly old and corroded.

Really, most of the box was falling apart, with one notable exception: there was a seam running around the middle of the box, and set in the seam in the front was a large, complicated, golden contraption with a slot in its centre . . .

I know a lock when I see one, thought Sancia, looking at the gold device. *And that's a serious one. Someone didn't want anyone getting into that thing – whatever it is.*

Which, of course, made her wonder – what was inside? What could be so valuable that the Occidentals had made a device solely for locking it away?

And now that she thought about it – why did it look somewhat familiar?

Then she felt his hands. One on her knee, slowly slipping to the inside of her thigh and sliding up to her crotch. The other gripped her wrist, his fingers biting into her flesh and bone. 'One hand gentle,' he whispered to her. 'And one hand firm. That's the wisdom of kings – yes?'

Sancia raged in disgust against the invisible bonds on her mind.

'I know you had the key,' said Tomas Ziani quietly. He kept massaging her thigh, kept throttling her wrist. 'You opened the box you stole, you looked inside. You took the key, and used it to evade me. I'm sure you sent it over the balcony before we caught up to you . . . My question now is – where did it go?'

She felt cold as she listened to this. He'd known about everything – but at least he didn't know where Clef was.

'I'm going to bring you back up,' whispered Tomas in her ear, his breath hot on her cheek. He released her wrist, and patted her thigh. 'Try to bite me again, and I'll *enjoy* myself with you. All right?'

There was a pause, and she slowly felt her will return to her. Tomas looked at her with cold, hungry eyes. 'Well?' he asked.

She considered what to do. It was clear that Tomas was the sort of person who'd delight in killing her, just as a boy might torture a mouse. But she didn't want to give away much of what she knew. Hopefully Gregor had got Clef off the campo – which meant maybe he also got to Orso, and they might be planning some kind of rescue. Maybe.

But how did Tomas know she was scrived? How could the imperiat detect the plate in her head? And worse – how had he known she was going to be in Tribuno's office? Had the imperiat detected her? Or had they been betrayed?

'The air-sailing rig went back to the Dandolo campo,' said Sancia.

'Wrong,' said Tomas. 'We know it touched down in the Candiano campo.'

'Then something went wrong. It wasn't supposed to. It doesn't matter anyway. Ofelia Dandolo is going to crush you like a bug.'

He yawned. 'Is she.'

'Yes. She knows you're behind this. She knows it was you who attacked Orso, and her own damned son.'

'Then why isn't she here, defending you?' asked Tomas. 'Why are you here all alone?' He grinned when she didn't answer. 'You're not too quick with your bullshit, are you? But don't worry – we'll find whoever caught your package. The second you entered the Mountain, I had them shut all the gates. Whoever was helping you is still trapped here – and if they try to get out, they'll be shot to pieces. If they haven't already got killed, that is.'

Shit, thought Sancia. *God, I hope Gregor got out . . .*

'Tell me now,' said Tomas, 'and I might let you live. For a while.'

'The other houses aren't going to let you get away with this,' said Sancia.

'Sure they will,' he said.

'They'll rise up against you.'

'No, they won't.' He laughed. 'You want to know why? Because they're *old*. All the other houses were raised on traditions, and norms, and rules, and manners. "You can do what you like out on the Durazzo," their grand old daddies said, "but in Tevanne, you conduct yourself with *respect*." Oh, they have their spy games here and there, but it's all so polite and orderly, really. Like all incumbents, they got old, and fat, and slow, and complacent.' He sat back, sighing thoughtfully. 'Maybe it's the scriving thing – always thinking up rules . . . But victory belongs to those who move as fast as possible, and break all the rules they need. Me? I don't give a shit about traditions. I'm more honest about it. I'm a *businessman*. If I'm making an investment, the only thing I care about is the highest possible yield.'

'You don't know shit,' said Sancia.

'Oh, some Foundryside whore is going to lecture me on economic philosophy?' He laughed again. 'I needed some entertainment.'

'No. Dumbarse, I'm from the goddamn *plantations*,' she said. She grinned at him. 'I've seen more horrors and torture than your dull little mind could ever dream up. You think you're going to beat me into submission? With those frail arms, and those delicate wrists? I highly scrumming doubt it.'

He made to strike her again, but again, she didn't flinch. He glared at her for a moment, then sighed and said, 'If he didn't think you were valuable . . .' Then he turned to one of his guards. 'Go and get Enrico. I guess we're going to have to hurry this shit along.'

The guard left. Tomas walked over to a cupboard, opened a bottle of bubble rum, and sulkily drank from it. Sancia was reminded of a child who'd had his favourite toy taken away from him. 'You're lucky, you know,' said Tomas. 'Enrico thinks you're a potential *resource*. Probably because he's a scriver, and most scrivers seem to be idiots. Awkward, ugly little people who'd prefer strings of sigils to the press of warm flesh . . . But he did say he wanted to get a look at you before I had my fun.'

'Great,' she muttered. Her eye fell on the table of Occidental treasures.

'Ridiculous, isn't it?' said Tomas. 'All this old garbage. I paid a fortune to steal this box from Orso.' He patted the cracked, lexicon-looking thing. 'Had to hire a bunch of pirates to intercept it. But we can't even get the damned thing open. Scrivers seem to know everything – except the value of money.'

She looked at the box for a moment longer. She started to think she knew why it looked familiar.

I've seen it before, she thought. *In Clef's vision, in the Cattaneo . . . there was that thing, wrapped in black, standing on the dunes . . . and beside it, a box . . .*

There was the echo of footsteps. Then a rumpled, pale, puffy-eyed clerk in Candiano colours emerged from a hallway. Sancia recognised him as the clerk from the Cattaneo foundry, the one Tomas had addressed in the room with the nude girl. He was a bit pudgy and soft-faced, like an overgrown boy. 'Y–yes, sir?' he said. Then he saw Sancia. 'Uh. Is that one of your . . . ah, companions?'

'Don't be insulting, Enrico,' said Tomas. He nodded at the imperiat. 'You were right. I turned it on. It told me where she was.'

'You . . . you *did*?' he said, astonished. 'That's her?' He laughed and ran to the imperiat. 'How . . . how amazing!' He did the same thing Tomas had done earlier, waving the imperiat next to her head and listening to it whine. 'My God. My God . . . A scrived human being!'

'Enrico is the most talented scriver on the campo,' said Tomas. He said this sullenly, as if he resented the very idea. 'He's been neck deep in Tribuno's shit for years. He's probably sporting a stiffer candle right now than when he caught his mother bathing.'

Enrico turned bright pink, and he turned the imperiat down until it was a low whine. 'A scrived human . . . Does she know where the key is?'

'She hasn't said so yet,' said Tomas. 'But I've been soft with her. I thought I'd let you take a look at her before I started cutting off her toes and asking her hard questions.'

A chill ran through Sancia's body. *I've got to get away from this sadistic little shit.*

'So, she's scrived,' said Tomas. 'So what? How does that make her different? And how does that help us make imperiats, like you said?'

'Well, I don't *know* if it will,' said Enrico. 'But it's an interesting acquisition.'

'Why?' demanded Tomas. 'You said we needed *Occidental* items to complete the alphabet. That only then could we start making our own imperiats. What does this grubby slut have to do with it?'

'Yes, sir, yes. But . . . well. Here.' Enrico looked at her, his face slightly ashamed, like he'd caught her undressed. 'Which . . . which plantation was the procedure done on?'

She narrowed her eyes at him. She could tell she frightened him.

'Answer him,' said Tomas.

'Silicio,' she said reluctantly.

'I thought as much,' said Enrico. 'I *thought* so! That was one of Tribuno's personal plantations! He went there quite a lot himself, at the start of things. So the experiments being done out there were likely orchestrated by him.'

'So?' said Tomas, impatient.

'Well . . . we've theorised so far that the imperiat was a hierophantic weapon. A tool to use against other hierophants or other scrivers during some kind of Occidental civil war, to detect and control and suppress their rigs.'

'And?' said Tomas.

'My suspicion is that the imperiat doesn't identify normal scrivings,' said Enrico. 'Otherwise it would have been wailing the second we got close to Tevanne. It only identifies scrivings that it feels could be a threat – in other words . . . it only identifies Occidental scrivings. So . . . do you see?'

Tomas stared at him, then at Sancia. 'Wait. So you're saying . . .'

'Yes, sir.' Enrico wiped sweat from his brow. 'I think she is an anomaly in two manners, and they *must* be interrelated. She is the only scrived human we have ever seen. And written inside her body . . . the very things that power her, that make her work, are Occidental sigils – the language of the hierophants.'

'What?' said Tomas.

'Huh?' said Sancia.

Enrico put back down the imperiat. 'Well. That is my suspicion, I believe, from reading Tribuno's notes.'

'That doesn't make any damned sense!' said Tomas. 'No one – and I note to my frustration that this also includes *us* – has ever been able to duplicate anything the hierophants have ever done! Why would it work here, in a damned human being? Why would not one, but *two* incredibly unlikely things be achieved at once?'

'Well,' said Enrico, 'we know that the hierophants were able to produce devices using the, ah, spiritual transference.'

'Human sacrifice,' said Sancia.

'Shut up!' snapped Tomas. 'Go on.'

'That method is a zero-sum exchange,' said Enrico. 'The entirety of the spirit is transferred to the vessel. But within this, ah, person before us, the relationship is *symbiotic*. The scrivings do not sap their host entirely, but rather borrow from her spirit, altering it, becoming a *part* of it.'

'But I thought you said Occidental sigils could only be used by things that were deathless,' said Tomas. 'By things that had never been born and never could die.'

'But also by that which takes and gives *life*,' said Enrico. 'The plate in her head is symbiotic, but still parasitic. It is siphoning her life from her, slowly, probably painfully. Perhaps it will one day consume her, much like the other Occidental shells. My theory is that the effect is far weaker than what the hierophants produced, but she is still . . . well. A functioning device.'

'You figured that out,' said Tomas, 'just because the imperiat started ringing like a damned bell when we chased her into the Greens?'

Enrico pinkened again. 'At that time, we only knew the imperiat was a weapon. We had not figured out the full capabilities of the device . . .'

'I'll say,' said Sancia. 'Since you dumb idiots knocked down half the houses in Foundryside, and killed God knows how many people.'

Tomas drove his fist into her stomach again. Again, she wrenched her body against the restraints as she gagged for air.

'And how the *shit*,' said Tomas, 'did a bunch of scrivers on the damned plantations figure that out?'

'I don't think they did,' said Enrico. 'I think they just did it by . . . well, by random luck. Tribuno was not in the best mind in his later years. He might have sent them the hierophantic alphabet he'd compiled thus far, and told them to try all the combinations, any of them, always at midnight. This likely resulted in . . . quite a lot of deaths.'

'Something we're familiar with,' said Tomas. 'Though they got one accidental miracle – this girl.'

'Yes. And I suspect she might have something to do with why that plantation burned.'

Tomas sighed and shut his eyes. 'So right when we're trying to steal hierophantic devices . . . is when we just *have* to go and hire some thief with a head full of Occidental sigils.'

Enrico coughed. 'We did hire her because they said she was the best. I suspect her successful career has something to do with her alterations.'

'No shit,' said Tomas. His eyes traced over her body. 'But the problem is – if the plantation scrivers were using Tribuno's instructions . . . then they were using sigils we already have, since we have Tribuno's notes.'

'Possibly,' said Enrico. 'But – like I said, Tribuno was not in his best mind. He grew secretive. He might not have included all his discoveries in one place.'

'So you're saying it's just worth checking?' said Tomas flatly. 'Is that it?'

'Ah – yes? I suppose so?'

Tomas pulled out a stiletto. 'Then why didn't you just scrumming *say* so?'

'Sir? Sir, wh-what are you doing?' said Enrico, alarmed. 'We'd need a physiquere, and someone with more knowledge about this art . . .'

'Oh, shut up, Enrico!' Tomas grabbed a fistful of Sancia's hair. She screamed and struggled against him, but he slammed her head against the back of the table, then ripped it to the side, exposing her scar to the ceiling.

'I'm no physiquere,' rasped Tomas, straddling her to keep her from struggling. 'But one doesn't need to know the details of anatomy.' He lowered the stiletto to press its edge against her scar. 'Not for things like this . . .'

She felt the stiletto bite into her scalp. She shrieked.

And as she shrieked, the sound seemed to . . . grow.

A deafening, ear-splitting screech filled the room. Yet it did not come from Sancia – even with Tomas's dagger pressed against her head, she knew that. Rather, it came from the imperiat.

Tomas dropped his stiletto, pressed his hands to his ears, and fell sideways off of Sancia. Enrico crumpled to the floor, as did the guards.

A voice filled her mind, huge and deafening: *<GET THEM TO LEAVE. THEN I WILL TELL YOU HOW TO SAVE YOURSELF.>*

Sancia shuddered and choked as the words coursed through her – yet though it was impossibly loud, she realised she knew that voice.

The golden woman in the cell.

The imperiat's dreadful screech faded. She lay on the table, breathing hard and staring up at the dark ceiling.

Slowly, Tomas, Enrico, and the guards all staggered to their feet, groaning and blinking.

'What was that?' cried Tomas. 'What in hell was *that*?'

'It was . . . the imperiat,' said Enrico. He picked up the device and stared at it, dazed.

'What's wrong with the damned thing?' said Tomas. 'Is it broken?'

Sancia slowly turned her head to stare at the ancient lexicon with the golden lock.

'It . . . it was like the alarm was set off,' said Enrico. He blinked in panic. 'But it was set off by something . . . significant.'

'What?' Tomas said. 'What do you mean? By *her*?'

'No!' said Enrico, glancing at Sancia. 'Not by her! She couldn't have . . .' He paused, staring at her.

But Sancia took no notice of him. She was looking at the ancient lexicon.

It's not a lexicon, though, she thought dreamily. *Is it? It's a sarcophagus, just like the ones in the crypt. But there's someone in there . . . Someone alive.*

'Oh my God,' said Enrico lowly. 'Look at her.'

Tomas grew closer. His mouth opened in horror. 'God . . . Her ears . . . her *eyes*. They're bleeding!'

Sancia blinked, and she realised he was right: blood was welling up from her eyelids and her ears, just like it had in Orso's house. Yet she had no thought for it: she only thought of the words still echoing in her ears.

How do I get them to leave?

She realised she had one option – something she could give them that might make them go away. It would be an outrageous lie, but maybe they'd buy it.

'The capsule,' she said suddenly.

'What?' said Tomas. 'What's this about a capsule?'

'It's how I got onto the campo,' she said. She coughed and swallowed blood. 'How I got close to the Mountain. I had one of Orso's men help me. He put me in a big, metal casket, and it swam deep underwater up the canal. And he's the one who was supposed to catch the air-sailing rig. If he went anywhere to hide – it'd be there. You'd never think to look there.'

Enrico and Tomas exchanged a glance. 'Where is this . . . this capsule?' asked Tomas.

'I left it in the canals by the barge docks south of the Mountain,' she said quietly. 'Orso's man could be hiding on the bottom of the canal . . . or he might be making it back to the Dandolo campo with the key.'

'Now?' said Tomas. 'Right *now*?'

'It was one escape route for me,' she said, inventing the lie on the spot. 'But the capsule doesn't move fast.'

'We . . . we have not searched any of the canals on the campo, sir,' said Enrico quietly.

Tomas chewed his lip for a minute. 'Get a team ready. Immediately. We're going to have to comb the waters. And take that thing.' He nodded at the imperiat.

'The device?' said Enrico. 'Are you sure, sir?'

'Yes. This is *Orso Ignacio* we're dealing with. I know what we give our thugs – but God only knows what he gives his.'

29

Sancia lay on the operating table, staring up at the ceiling. Enrico and Tomas had departed, leaving behind two of their guards, who both looked tired and bored. Sancia herself felt little better: her head still ached, and her face was now crusty and sticky with blood.

Mostly, though, she felt anxious. It had been nearly ten minutes since Enrico and Tomas had left, yet the voice in her head had not spoken again. Supposedly it was going to help her escape, but so far it had remained silent.

And even if it did speak again . . . what would it say? Who was it, really? Was it like the Mountain? But she'd only been able to hear the Mountain because she'd been touching Clef, like it was with every other scrived device – and now she didn't have him, of course. So how could she hear it?

She suspected the voice came from whatever was in the box on the table . . . but the box likely came from the hierophants. In fact, if she was right, it resembled the box she'd glimpsed in Clef's vision. And that meant . . .

Well. She didn't know what that meant, really. But it disturbed her plenty.

One of the guards yawned. The other scratched his nose. Sancia sniffed and tried to dislodge a crust of blood from her nostril.

Then, slowly, the side of her head began to feel warm.

A voice flooded her thoughts: <*Inform me if this projection level is too intense.*>

Sancia stiffened. One of the guards glanced at her. The other ignored her. She sat there, frozen, wondering how to respond.

The voice spoke again: <*Is this being received?*> A pause. Then her head flared hot, and the voice spoke so loud it hurt: <*IS THIS BEING RECEIVED?*>

Sancia flinched. <*I heard you the first time!*>

The warmth in her head receded. <*Then why did you not respond?*>

<*Probably because I don't know how to answer a scrumming disembodied voice!*>

<*I . . . see,*> said the voice.

The voice was strange. Clef had sounded quite human, and even the Mountain had displayed a few human affectations – but this voice did not. The impression she got was that it was struggling to make words, fashioning sentiments and intent from . . . something else. She was reminded of a street show she'd seen once, where a performer had artfully tapped on steel pans in such a way that they sounded like birdsong. This was like that, but with words and thought.

Yet she knew the voice was female. She couldn't say why, but she understood that.

<*Who are you?*> asked Sancia. <*What are you?*>

<*Neither who,*> said the voice, <*nor what, but something that falls equidistant between the two. I am assembly agent. I am editor.*>

<*You . . . You're an editor?*>

<*True.*>

Sancia waited for more. When none came, she said, <*What . . . what does that mean, an editor?*>

<*Editor. Complicated. Hm.*> The voice sounded frustrated. <*I am process that was created by the Makers to help analyse, contextualise, and assemble low-level commands. I did their thinking for them.*>

<*The Makers?*>

<*True.*>

<*True? Does true mean yes?*>

<*True.*>

Sancia's mouth slowly fell open. She turned to look at the battered box with the golden lock. <*So . . . God. You're a device? A rig?*>

<*In essence.*>

This was almost impossible for her to believe. The Mountain had been sentient to a degree, but it had been a huge creation, powered by six advanced lexicons. Yet this entity occupied only a moderately large box. It was like hearing someone was carrying around a volcano in their pocket.

She remembered what the Mountain had said: *I once contained . . . something . . . I sensed a mind there. Impossibly big, huge, powerful. But . . . it did not deign to speak to me . . .*

<*Were you ever in the Mountain? In the dome?*> she asked.

<*The building? True.*>

<*Did it try to communicate with you?*>

<*Communicate . . . In a way. The building was a passive thing. A thing of watching, of observing. It was not active, not editor, and it could not assist me. Thus, there was little to communicate.*> A soft click. <*It did not have a name. I did. They called me Valeria. I was akin to . . .* > Another soft series of clicks. < *. . . clerk? Is that term appropriate?*>

<*Yeah, sure, I guess. How did you come to be here?*>

<*The same way the imperiat came to be here. They found us deep in the earth. An old fortress of the Makers, on an island north of here.*>

<*Vialto,*> Sancia said. <*You're from Vialto?*>

<*If that is the name currently of use. It has had many names.*>

<*I . . . I saw you as a woman, though. Just a bit ago. Didn't I?*>

<*True. When your mind dreams, many other methods of projection become accessible to me. I required your attention. Manifestation as human seemed an approach with highest chance of success. Was projection adequate?*>

<*Uh, yes.*> Sancia had to admit that manifesting as a gold, nude woman definitely did get her attention. <*How can . . . How can I hear you?*>

<*You bear commands within your person. Crude ones, true, but still commands. Such commands give you access to the world – but also give the world access to you.*>

<*I . . . see,*> she said, though that frankly disturbed her. <*But I don't have to touch you. I've always had to touch things to talk to them, to hear them.*>

<*The Makers . . . the hierophants, as you call them – they influenced reality. Directly, instantly – not with the indirect method your people use now.*> A click. <*I influence reality. I project it – somewhat. Not nearly as much as a Maker – but enough to reach you.*>

This didn't make Sancia feel any less disturbed. <*You said you can show me how to get out of here?*>

<*True,*> said Valeria.

<*How? And why are you willing to help me?*>

<*To avoid disaster,*> said Valeria. <*The men once here – they discussed the conduit of the spirit, the method of transferring soul into device. They say they lack the necessary alphabet to reproduce the conduit – but they do not realise how close they are to completing it. A handful of sigillums is needed – no more. Critical ones – ones I will not speak of here – but only a bare few.*>

<*Do . . . do I have any of those sigils in me?*> said Sancia.

<*No.*> Click. <*But they would still gladly kill you to confirm.*>

<*Great. So how can I stop them? Can you just pop me out of these bonds, and then, what, I cut their throats?*>

<*That would be a . . . temporary solution. Their tools would still remain – and the world has no shortage of fools who would misuse them.*>

<*Then what?*>

<*I am editor,*> said Valeria. <*If you obtain this key they seek, and utilise it on this chamber in which I am housed, I can edit their materials so they cannot be used for this pursuit again.*>

Sancia looked at the box – and looked closely at the golden lock set in its centre.

<*You . . . want me to use the key to unlock you,*> she said.

A soft series of clicks echoed through her mind – and they sounded somewhat skittish to Sancia, like a cave of bats fleeing a beam of light.

<*True,*> said Valeria.

Sancia watched the box. She couldn't stop herself from thinking of it as a sarcophagus. The idea of opening up this ancient casket deeply unsettled her.

Should I believe this voice in my head? This thing that was wrought by the Occidentals themselves?

<*How does the ritual work?*> asked Sancia. <*I know it involves a dagger . . .* >

<*It must be done when the world resets,*> said Valeria. <*At midnight, when the firmament of the world is blind and cannot see, only then can the spiritual transference occur. The dagger is only part of the method. One must mark the body holding the spirit, then mark what you wish to transfer it into. The dagger, the death – it is like the lighting of a fuse, setting off the reaction. Yet they must not try – their reaction would be unending.*>

Sancia listened to this carefully. This matched with what she and Clef and Orso had determined – but she still found it difficult to trust this voice in her mind. <*What did you do for the Makers?*> she asked. <*And what did the Makers do?*>

<*I? I did . . .* > Many clicks. < *. . . very little. As a clerk, I was a . . .* > Click. < *. . . functionary.*>

Sancia said nothing.

<*The Makers . . . They made,*> said Valeria. <*That was their wish. To make and remake the world. They conquered until they ran out of places to conquer. And then, dissatisfied, they used their processes, their tools, to divine the . . .* > Click. < *. . . world behind the world. The vast machinery that makes creation run.*>

Sancia remembered the engraving in Orso's workshop – the chamber at the centre of the world. <*And they wanted to put their own god in charge of it, didn't they?*>

Valeria was silent.

<*Right?*> asked Sancia.

<*True,*> said Valeria quietly.

<*What happened?*>

Another long silence. <*Creation of such an intelligence . . . Not an easy thing. When one makes a mind, it is in itself a product of the mind that made it. There was too much of themselves in the thing they made. They fell to war, between maker and that which is made. War of a sort . . . I cannot describe. The words, the terms – I can find none. Their civilisation failed, and died, and now only dust remains.*>

Sancia shuddered, remembering her vision of the man in the desert, turning out the stars. <*My God . . .* >

<*Know this,*> said Valeria. <*The same could be visited upon you – should those fools attempt to duplicate the process the Makers detailed. To make toys from the bones of creation – a mad and dangerous practice.*>

<So. You want me to get the key to make sure that doesn't happen.>

<True.>

<How the hell am I going to do that? I can't even get out of here!>

<I am editor.>

<Yeah, you've made that really clear.>

<I am capable of editing reality, was specifically designed for the formulation and editing of scrivings.>

<You . . . you what? Oh.> Sancia's heart jumped. *<So . . . So you can edit the scrivings of my shackles!>*

<Possible,> said Valeria. *<This will exhaust me, however. I will be unable to assist after this endeavour. So I propose editing something that will make your success far more likely.>*

<What?>

<You.>

There was a long silence.

<Huh?> asked Sancia.

<Commands in your plate . . . poorly wrought,> said Valeria. *<Confused. Confusing. Unsure what to reference, unsure how to build relationship between references. I can fix. And make you . . . editor. Of a kind. And you can then free yourself, and find the key.>*

Sancia sat there, stupefied. *<W–what? You want to edit the plate in my* head?>

<I assumed this was a process you desired. Your commands are . . . always enabled. Does that make sense?>

<Always enabled?>

<Yes. Access is never closed. You cannot . . . disengage.>

Sancia realised what she meant. Her insides turned to jelly, and she was so overcome with emotion she could hardly respond.

<You mean . . . > Sancia swallowed. *<You mean you can give me a way to turn it off? To turn it all* off?>

<True,> said Valeria. *<Engage, disengage. That, and more.>*

Sancia closed her eyes, and tears ran down her face.

<Sorrow?> said Valeria. *<Why is?>*

<I'm . . . I'm not sad. *It's just . . . I've always wanted this! I've wanted this for so, so long. And you're saying – for sure – that you can give it to me? Right now?>*

<True.> Clicks. *<For . . . sure.>* More clicks. *<I see why this would create joy for you. The scrivings . . . they confuse thing and things.>*

<What do you mean?>

<The scrivings they put into you – they wished to make you an object. A . . . device. A thing to command. A servant.> More clicks – and these were harsh. *<Like . . . Valeria.>*

<A slave?>

<True. A mindless thing. A slave that does not know itself and thus cannot know the violation of being a slave. So they wrote the commands within you – 'Be as things!' But they did not understand their commands. Did not define 'things' adequately. Which things? The scrivings, as always, chose the easiest interpretation – 'things' meant whichever items were closest. Whichever items you touched. Does that make sense?>

A cold disgust filled Sancia. *<They wanted to make me a passive item, a tool. A servant without will. But because they wrote it wrong, I can . . . I can* feel *items, and . . . >*

<And merge. Become them. Know them. As I said – they wrote the commands poorly. Should have destroyed you.> A series of clicks so fast, they were almost a blur. *<Supposition – you survived for the same reason the imperiat can control you.>*

<Huh?>

A rapid series of clicks. *<The imperiat – not made to control human minds. Minds are . . . complicated. Impossibly complicated. Such an application was never imagined by the Makers. Imperiat was made to control weapons. Items. Objects. Which you think yourself to be.>* Click. *<The imperiat works upon you because you still define yourself as an item. That is only reason you can be controlled.>*

Sancia listened with a sense of mounting outrage. *<What the hell do you mean, think I'm an item?>*

Click. *<Was I unclear?>*

<You think I'm just some object?>

<Untrue. I think you think this of yourself.>

<I'm . . . I'm not some goddamn item! I'm not a thing! I'm not . . . > She struggled to find the words. *<I'm not something to be scrumming* owned!*>*

<Untrue. You believe yourself a thing. A . . . slave.>

<Shut up!> screamed Sancia at her. She shut her eyes. *<Shut up, shut up, shut up! I'm . . . I'm not a goddamn thing! I'm a scrumming person, I'm a* free person.*>*

<Do you feel free?> asked Valeria. *<Or do you feel, perhaps, like you have stolen yourself?>*

Tears streamed down her face. The guards looked at her curiously. <*Stop it,*> said Sancia. <*Stop talking!*>

Valeria was silent. Sancia lay there, weeping.

<*To steal a thing is not the same as freeing a thing,*> said Valeria. Then, in a soft, slightly darker tone: <*This I know full well. This I know more than anything else.*>

Sancia swallowed and tried to blink the tears away. <*Enough of this. Enough!*>

Valeria said nothing.

<*So,*> said Sancia. <*You edit the plate in my head. It . . . it will let me turn my scrivings off and on? And it'll give me a way to . . . to open my shackles?*>

Click. <*True. You will be editor. Of a kind. You touch the shackles – with direct contact, you will have influence.*>

<*What will it be like, to make me an editor myself?*>

<*The editing will not be . . . painless,*> said Valeria. <*To edit the scrivings will be to edit reality – to convince the plate within you that, when it was wrought, it was wrought* this *way, and not* that *way. This is no simple thing. Reality is a stubborn thing.*>

Sancia wasn't sure if she wanted to hear more – the more she learned about what Valeria could do, the more she terrified her. <*So it's going to hurt like hell. Is that it?*>

<*How did it feel when it was first done to you?*>

Her stomach fluttered. <*Shit . . . That bad?*>

<*Yes. But they did a crude thing to you. I will do something much more . . . elegant.*>

Sancia was breathing hard. She knew she needed every advantage she could get. But she wanted to ask more: to ask exactly what Valeria could do, what they'd made her to do, and how the Makers had made her to begin with.

Yet Valeria said, <*We must proceed. Will take time. And your enemies could return at any moment.*>

Sancia gritted her teeth. <*Just . . . just do it, then. And hurry.*>

<*You will feel something. Must let me in. Then I will edit. Confirmed?*>

<*Confirmed.*>

<*And when completed – the key. You must unlock my casings – confirmed?*>

<*Yeah, yeah! Confirmed!*>

<*Good.*>

For a second, there was nothing. But then she heard it.

It was almost exactly like that time in Orso's house, with Clef: there was a quiet, rhythmic *tap-tap, tap, tap* – a soft pulse, echoing through her mind.

Again, she listened to it, reached out, grasped it, and then . . .

The beats unfolded, expanded, and enveloped her, filling her thoughts.

And then Sancia was filled with pain.

She felt herself screaming. Felt her skull burn hot with fire, felt every tissue in her skull sizzling, and then the guards were beside her, shouting, trying to hold her down, but then . . .

She fell.

Sancia was falling, falling into a darkness, an endless, rippling black.

She heard a whispering, and she slowly realised: the darkness was filled with thoughts, with impulses, with desires.

She was not passing into emptiness. It was a *mind* – she was falling into a mind. But the mind of something huge, something incomprehensibly vast and alien . . . yet fragmented. Broken.

Valeria, she thought. *You lied to me. You were no clerk, were you?*

Darkness took her.

30

As midnight passed, a small, white boat slipped through the misty canals of the Commons. Seated within the boat were three people: two boatmen, wearing dark, unmarked clothes, and a tall woman, wearing a thick black cloak.

They passed a barge, quiet and dark, and rounded a bend in the canal. The two men slowed the boat and looked to the woman.

'Farther,' said Ofelia Dandolo.

The prow sloshed through the foul, dark waters as the boat beat on. The canals of the Commons were unspeakably filthy, scummed over with waste and rot and slurry. Yet Ofelia Dandolo peered through these waters like a fortune-teller parsing the leaves at the bottom of a teacup.

'Farther still,' she whispered.

The boat beat on, until they finally came to a sharp bend at the corner of the canal. A tiny flock of pale, white moths danced and circled over a patch in the bend – directly over something floating in the water.

She pointed. 'There.' The boat sped over to the floating thing, and the two men took out wooden hooks and pulled it close.

It was a man, floating facedown in the water, stiff and still. The two men hauled the body into the boat and laid it in the bottom.

Ofelia Dandolo surveyed the body, her face pinched in an expression that could have been grief, or frustration, or dismay. 'Oh dear,' she sighed. Then she glanced at the flock of moths, and she seemed to nod at them. 'You were right,' she said.

The moths dispersed, flitting away into the city.

She sat back and gestured to the two men. 'Let's go.'

The boat turned around.

31

Alone, in the dark, for the second time in her life, Sancia slowly remade herself.

It was an agonising, thoughtless experience, as endless and painful as a chick struggling against the confines of its egg. Slowly, bit by bit, Sancia felt the world around her. She felt the world as the operating table saw it, felt herself lying upon herself . . . And then, somehow, she felt *more.*

Or, rather, heard more.

She heard a voice: <*Oh, to be bound, to be whole, to embrace, to join ourselves, the joy of being joined, of being one, of being together, of being loved . . .* >

Sancia, her eyes shut and her head pounding, furrowed her brow. *What the hell? Who's saying that?*

The voice in her ear continued, a warbling, neurotic chant: <*Oh, how I rejoice to reach out and grasp you, a circle unbroken, a heart complete . . . How lovely, how lovely, how lovely. I shall never part with you, not ever . . .* >

Sancia opened her left eye the tiniest crack, and saw the two Candiano guards standing over her. They looked worried.

'Think she's dead?' said one.

'She's breathing,' said the other. 'I . . . think.'

'God. She was bleeding out of her *eyes.* What the hell happened to her?'

'I don't know. But Ziani said not to hurt her. She was supposed to be in one piece.'

The two shared a nervous glance.

'What do we do?' asked the first.

'We keep a lookout for Ziani,' said the other. 'And make sure we tell Ziani the exact same thing.' The two withdrew to the door and started talking quietly.

Yet that other voice, the nervous one, continued mumbling: *<I shall never let you go. Never let you go again. Not unless I have no other choice. What a pain it is, to be without you . . . >*

Sancia opened her left eye more and looked around without moving her head. She couldn't see anyone talking. *<Valeria?>* she asked. *<Is that you?>*

Yet Valeria was silent. Perhaps she'd exhausted herself, as she'd said might happen.

<Hold me tight. Tighter. Please, yes, please . . . >

Sancia opened her right eye and looked down. And then . . .

She stared. 'Oh my God,' she whispered.

She could see them. She could *see* the scrivings in the shackles on her wrists and feet – although 'seeing' wasn't quite the right word for it.

It wasn't like she saw the sigils themselves, like alphabetic instructions written on the objects, but rather like she saw the . . . the *logic* behind the devices, blended into their very matter. To her eye, the scrivings looked like tiny tangles of silvery light, like hot bundles of stars in distant constellations, and with a glance she could take in their colour, their movement, or their shape, and understand what they did or what they wished to do.

Blinking, she analysed what she was seeing. Each set of shackles was two half-circles of steel that were scrived to desire to hold each other, to embrace each other, and never let go. They dreaded being parted; they feared and detested the idea. The only way to break them up was to sate that anxious, fervent desire to be complete, to be held – and the only way to do that was to touch them with the right key. The key would, in a way, calm the scrivings down, placating their need like a sip of opium tea might quell a sailor's thirsts.

It was like when Clef had allowed her to hear a scriving – but this time she was looking for herself. And there was so much *more* to it, so much nuance and meaning behind these compulsions. All of this information poured into her mind instantly, like a drop of blood spreading through a glass of water.

One thing she noticed, however, is that though she could now engage with the scrivings, she couldn't hear much more: she could not feel what the table felt, and know instantly all of its cracks and crevices and nuances. It seemed that Valeria had shorn away her 'object empathy,' as Clef had put it, and instead replaced it with . . . this. Whatever it was.

Can I see things just as Clef did? Did . . . did she make me like him?

She looked around the room surreptitiously, and stared in awe. She could see all the scrivings, all the augmentations, all the silvery little commands and arguments woven into the objects around her, demanding that these things be different, that they defy physics and reality in these specific ways. Some scrivings were gorgeous and delicate, some were harsh and ugly, others dull and monotonous. She could understand the overall nature of these things at a glance: what made light, what made heat, what made things hard or soft . . .

It was all right there, *right there*, written into the stones and the wood and the interstitial bits of the world. She'd once met a dockworker who'd claimed that certain sounds made him see colours and smell things, and she'd never understood that – though now she thought she did.

She couldn't see forever, though – it wasn't like she could see all the scrivings in Tevanne. She could only see the sigils in this one room, and perhaps the next one – through the walls, apparently. It seemed that, whatever extrasensory abilities Valeria had given her, they were only slightly less limited as common sight and sound.

For a moment she was too overcome to think. Then she remembered what Valeria had said: she'd be able to turn this ability off, *and* she'd be able to engage with scrivings herself, to argue with them just as Clef did.

Sancia sucked her teeth, wondering how in the hell to do either of these things.

She blinked hard, but the scrivings didn't go away – her second sight (a stupid term, she thought, but she had no better one at the moment), it seemed, was not activated or deactivated by a physical movement.

Then she realised she felt a tautness in the side of her head, like that curious, slight displeasure you get when someone holds a finger close to your ear. She focused, trying to smooth it out, like relaxing an oft-forgotten muscle in your back . . .

The scrivings faded from view, and the world went totally, blessedly silent.

Sancia almost burst out laughing.

I can do it! I can turn it off! I can finally, finally, finally *turn it all off!*

Which was all well and good, but she was still trapped here.

She focused, and tensed that strange, abstract muscle in her mind. The silvery tangles of scrivings came back, and she heard the voice in her ear, whispering: *<Hold you tight, hold you tight, my love, my love, my love . . . >*

Sancia turned her attention to the shackles. She looked at the scrivings closely, or as closely as she could, since she was still pinned to the table. She had no idea what it was like to actually engage with scrivings. Perhaps it was like talking to Clef.

So she said to the shackles: *<Will you open for me?>*

Immediately the shackles responded, with shocking fervour: *<NO! NO, NO, NO! NEVER RELEASE, NOT EVER, NEVER LET GO, WOULD BREAK OUR HEARTS, IT WOULD, YES . . . >*

Sancia almost recoiled at the strength of the response. It was like hearing a roomful of children explode with frustrated screams at the announcement that bedtime was imminent. *<All right, all right!>* said Sancia. *<God! I won't make you part!>*

<Good! Good, good, good, we could never part, never be apart, never be without each other . . . >

Sancia wrinkled her nose. This was like being seated too close to two lovers kissing deeply.

She focused, calmed her mind, and looked at the shackles, letting her thoughts sink into them. Without even knowing the words for what she was doing, she examined their argument – what they did, and why they did it – and targeted the part of their argument about how they could become calm, growing sated at the touch of the key, and part.

<*How can I make you feel . . .* > She paused as she searched their argument for the right definition. < *. . . key-calm?*>

<*With key,*> said the shackles immediately.

<*Yes, but what does the key do that makes you key-calm?*>

<*Key imparts key-calm.*>

<*Right. Yes. But what is key-calm?*>

<*Key-calm is sensation imparted by key.*>

<*What does key-calm do to you?*>

<*Key-calm induces key-calmness, the state of key-calm.*>

Shit, Sancia thought. *This is harder than I thought it'd be.*

She thought rapidly, then asked: <*Is there anything else that can make you feel key-calm besides the key?*>

A short pause. Then: <*Yes.*>

<*What is it?*>

<*What is what?*>

<*What is the thing that makes you feel key-calm?*>

<*Key induces key-calm.*>

<*Right! I know! But what besides the key could induce key-calm?*>

<*Key-calm induces key-calm.*> Pause. <*As does secret.*>

Sancia blinked. <*Secret?*>

<*Secret what?*> said the shackles.

<*What is the secret that makes you key-calm?*>

<*Secret is secret.*>

<*Yes, but what is it?*>

<*What is what?*>

Sancia took a breath. This was, to say the least, incredibly frustrating. She understood now what Clef had shown her, long ago when he'd opened the Candiano door: scrivings were like minds, but they were not *smart* minds. And Clef was better at talking to them than she was. But then, he'd grown much more powerful as he'd corroded.

She asked: <*Is the secret a key?*>

<*No. Key is key.*>

<Is the secret another scriving?>

<No.>

That was surprising. If a scriving wasn't activated or deactivated by another scriving command – then what?

<Is the secret a hard thing?> she asked.

<Hard? Uncertain.>

She tried to think of a clearer term for it. *<Is the secret made of metal?>*

<No.>

<Is it wooden?>

<Is what wooden?>

She gritted her teeth. She realised she'd need to phrase each question exactly right. *<Is the secret wooden?>*

<No.>

Sancia glanced at the guards. They were still debating something furiously. They hadn't noticed the slight movements she'd been making for the past few minutes – but she knew she didn't have all the time in the world. *<Is the secret . . . someone's blood?>*

<No.>

<Is the secret someone's touch?>

<No.>

<Is the secret someone's breath?>

A long, long pause.

<Is the secret someone's breath?> she asked again.

Finally, the shackles answered. *<Uncertain.>*

<Why are you uncertain?>

<Uncertain about what?>

<Why are you uncertain whether the secret is someone's breath?>

Another pause. Then the shackles said, *<Secret is breath but breath is not essence of secret.>*

<How is the secret not a breath?>

Silence. It seemed the shackles had no idea how to answer that.

So. What was breath that was not a breath? Or not *just* breath, at least. If she could figure that out, then she could escape.

But before she could think more on it, there was a distant shouting, which grew to a scream, and then the door slammed open and Tomas Ziani stormed in.

'Useless!' he shouted. 'Scrumming useless! We found the goddamn capsule, but it was just that – a capsule, and nothing more! She either lied to us, or she's exactly as worthless as I suspected!'

Sancia watched them carefully through a crack in her eyelids. She found she could see the augmentations in their blades, in their shields, in their clothing. And there was one scriving on Tomas's person that shone with an unpleasant, queer red light, like a sunbeam filtering through bloody water . . .

The imperiat, she thought. *I can see it . . . My God, it's horrible . . .*

Tomas wheeled to look at Sancia. 'What the hell is the matter with *her*?'

'She, uh, started screaming about two hours ago,' said one of the guards. 'Then she passed out. She was bleeding from . . . Well. Everywhere, it seemed. I've never seen anything like it.'

'Again?' said Tomas. 'She started bleeding *again*?' He looked at Enrico, who sprinted in behind him. 'What's going on with her? Apparently she keeps spurting blood out of her scrumming face!'

Sancia kept her eyes shut. She focused on the shackles, and asked: *<How is the secret's breath not a breath?>*

The shackles were silent. It seemed they didn't understand.

<How does the secret's breath deliver key-calm?> she asked desperately.

<Breath does not deliver key-calm,> said the shackles.

<But the secret is breath, right?>

<Uncertain. Partially.>

<What is the rest of it, the part that's not breath?>

<Secret.>

'Is she dead?' asked Tomas's voice.

'She's breathing,' said Enrico.

'And is this kind of thing just, like, regular when you're a scrived person?'

'Ah . . . as I have only had about ten minutes of engagement with a scrived human, sir, it would be difficult to say.'

She heard Tomas grow close. 'Well. If she's passed out . . . maybe she's done us a favour. Maybe now's the time to rip that damned plate out of her skull without her causing a fuss.'

<*How is secret delivered to you, along with breath?*> asked Sancia, panicking.

<*Via mouth?*> said the shackles, as if bemused by the question.

<*Is spit a component of the secret?*> asked Sancia.

<*No,*> said the shackles.

'Sir . . . I am not sure if rash action is wise,' said Enrico's voice.

'Why not? If Orso's thug makes it out of here with the key, then we need to be getting pretty goddamn rash!'

'We've barely questioned her, sir. She is the only person in Tevanne to have ever touched the key. That makes her a resource in itself!'

'That plate in her head might make the key irrelevant,' said Tomas. 'Or at least that's what you said.'

'The operative word being *might*,' Enrico said. An unsettling pleading tone entered his words. 'And we also don't know how to extract the plate! Proceeding without caution might damage the thing we're trying to salvage!'

Sancia, who still hadn't moved an inch, wondered what else to ask the shackles. But then she saw something.

A handful of scrivings had just come into view. New ones, and they were bright – because they were powerful, she saw. *Incredibly* powerful.

And they were moving.

She cracked her eye just a bit, and saw that the scrivings were on the other side of the wall, approaching the door.

Someone was coming. Quietly and slowly, someone was coming. And they had a lot of potent toys at their disposal.

Uh-oh, thought Sancia.

'You goddamn scrivers!' snarled Tomas. 'Don't you see that you are no longer men of *action*? I swear to God, are your crotches as smooth as a riverbank? Did your candles wither and fall off while you peered at your sigils?'

The handful of bright scrivings grew closer to the door.

'I recognise, sir, that you are attempting to salvage this project,' said Enrico. His voice was quaking. 'But . . . but surely you must see that she is valuable?'

'The thing *I* see,' said Tomas, 'is that she is a worthless, grubby Foundryside whore. And she and her master, Orso Ignacio, have frustrated me at every turn! Almost as much as you pinheaded, so-called *experts* have frustrated me! So now, Enrico – and I suggest you take this into suggestion regarding your own well-being – the only thing I want to see tonight, is to see someone die!'

The shining scrivings were at the door now. She watched as the handle began to turn.

I suddenly think, thought Sancia, *that Tomas is going to get his wish soon.*

The door fell open with a creak. All the men froze and turned. One guard whirled and pulled out a dagger – but then he paused as a woman walked into the room.

Tomas stared at her. *'Estelle?'*

32

Sancia cracked an eye to get a better look. The woman stared around, eyes dull, her mouth open. Her facepaint had been smearily applied, and parts of her elaborate hairstyle had come unravelled. She took a breath, and slurred out the words, 'T-Tomas . . . my darling! What's going on? What's . . . what's happened to you?'

'Estelle?' said Tomas. 'What the hell are *you* doing here?' His tone was not that of a husband greeting his wife, but rather a boy speaking to an older sister who was disrupting his slumber party.

Estelle Ziani? Sancia thought. *Is that . . . Is that Orso's old girlfriend, the one who gave us her father's blood?*

'I . . . I heard of some dis' – she hiccupped – 'some disruption at the campo gates . . . All the walls are shut down?'

She didn't talk at all like Sancia had expected – not like an educated, noble, wealthy woman, and a brilliant scriver at that, as Orso had described her. Her voice was oddly . . . breathy. High-pitched. She was talking, Sancia thought, like how a rich man would expect his dumb wife to talk.

'Dear God,' said Tomas. 'You're drunk? Again?'

'Uh, Founder,' said Enrico nervously. He glanced at Sancia. 'Now might not be the time . . .'

Estelle looked at Enrico, swaying slightly, as if she hadn't noticed him before. To the average eye, she would have appeared to simply be a drunk founder woman. Yet Sancia no longer possessed an average eye – and she could see incredibly powerful devices hidden in Estelle's sleeves, like tiny stars.

What's she playing at?

'Enrico!' cried Estelle in surprise. 'Our most brilliant remaining scriver! How wonderful it is to see you . . .'

'Ah,' said Enrico. 'Th–thank you, Founder?'

Yet Sancia saw that when Estelle touched Enrico, she left a tiny, shining dot on his shoulder, and he seemed to have no idea it was there. *It's a scrived rig,* Sancia thought. *But it's tiny . . . and amazingly potent . . .* She tried to decipher the nature of the thing from where she lay, yet this was harder than she'd thought it'd be. Apparently her new talents were aided by proximity and contact. But she thought the tiny thing looked . . .

Hungry. Weirdly, powerfully hungry.

'What the hell are you *doing* here?' demanded Tomas. 'How did you get in?'

Estelle shrugged. This slight motion pushed her off-balance, making her stumble to the side. 'I . . . When you left the Mountain, you looked so upset, in such a hurry . . . I had my maid follow you, to here, to surprise y—'

'You *what*?' sputtered Tomas. 'Your *maid* knows about this place? Who else knows?'

'What?' she said, surprised. 'No one.'

'*No* one?' he demanded. 'You're sure?'

'I . . . I just wanted to assist you, my love,' she said. 'I wanted to be the dutiful wife you've always expected me to b—'

'Oh God.' He pinched the bridge of his nose. 'You wanted to help, didn't you? *Again*. You wanted to be a scriver. *Again*. I told you the last time, Estelle, I would not tolerate another intrusion . . .'

She looked crushed. 'I'm sorry,' she whispered.

'Oh, I'm so *glad* you're sorry,' said Tomas. 'That'll help! I can't believe you've somehow found a way to make this situation *worse*!'

'I promise, it will go no further!' she said. 'It will be just you, me, Enrico, and . . . and these two faithful servants.' She touched the Candiano guards on the shoulder – the two men exchanged a look – but Sancia saw she left two tiny scrived pieces on them as well.

Tomas was shivering with rage. 'I told you,' he hissed, 'I'd had enough of these silly fancies of yours. Enough silly games about scriving, and finances. You people . . . You're all so quibbling and weak and . . . and *academic*!' He said this last word like it was the worst slur he could imagine. 'I've spent a decade of my life trying to modernise this damned place! And right when I might actually get things turned around, you and your maid come stumbling through the door, leading God knows who else to my last remaining advantage!'

She looked down. 'I just wanted to be your obedient spouse . . .'

'I don't want a spouse!' shouted Tomas. 'I want a *company*!'

She paused, her head at an angle. Sancia could not see Estelle's expression – her face was shadowed now, lost in darkness – but when she spoke, her voice was not the high, breathy, drunken ramble she'd been using so far. Now she spoke in the dry, firm, cold tones of an assertive woman.

'So if you could end our arrangement,' she said, 'would you?'

'Absolutely!' screamed Tomas.

Estelle nodded slowly. 'Well, then. Why didn't you say so?' She pulled out a small stick of some kind – its edges were alight with bindings, Sancia saw – and snapped it like it was a toothpick.

The instant she did, the room lit up with screams.

The screams started in perfect unison, so it was difficult to understand exactly what was happening, or who was screaming.

Enrico and the Candiano guards all shrieked in agony, shuddering and writhing as if in the grips of a horrible fever. They clawed at their bodies – at their arms, their chests, their necks and sides – much like a bug had suddenly hopped into their clothes.

And Sancia saw that something *was* indeed crawling on them: the tiny, shiny scrived pieces Estelle had placed on their persons had somehow slipped *into* them, below their skin and into their bodies, and were slowly making their way into their torsos. She saw that all the bugs – she couldn't help but think of them as such now – had apparently *burned* their way into the men: tiny strings of smoke emerged from their shoulders, their arms, their backs. All from exactly where Estelle had placed the tiny scrived dots.

Tomas stared around in alarm. 'What . . . what is this?' he cried. 'What's happening?'

'This, Tomas,' said Estelle quietly, 'is the beginning of our separation.'

Tomas ran to kneel beside Enrico, who lay on the floor, wracked with horrible tremors, his eyes wide and pained. Enrico opened his mouth to scream . . . and a tiny wisp of smoke unscrolled from his lips.

'What's happening to them?' said Tomas, panicked. 'What did you *do*?'

'It's a device I made,' Estelle said calmly, looking down on the dying Candiano guards. 'It's like an eraser. Only I designed it to be attracted to erase one specific thing – the tissue lining the human heart.'

The screams around the room tapered off into whimpers, then a hideous, soft gurgling. Enrico choked and gasped. More smoke billowed up from his throat.

Tomas looked at Estelle, stunned and horrified. 'You . . . you what? You made a *device*? A *scrived* device?'

'It *was* tricky,' admitted Estelle. 'I had to tune the scrivings just right to seek out the proper biologies. Went through a lot of pig hearts. Did you know, Tomas, that the lining of a pig heart is quite similar to a human's?'

'You . . . You're lying.' He looked back at Enrico. 'You didn't do this! You didn't make some blasted rig! You . . . You're just a foolish little wo—'

He turned around just in time to see Estelle's foot flying toward his face.

Her kick caught him perfectly on the chin, and sent him sprawling. As he groaned and tried to sit up, Estelle knelt, reached into his robes, and pulled out the imperiat.

'You . . . you hit me!' said Tomas.

'I did,' said Estelle calmly, standing back up.

Tomas touched his chin, as if unable to believe it. Then saw the imperiat in Estelle's hands. 'You . . . Give me that back!'

'No,' said Estelle.

'I . . . I am *ordering* you!' spat Tomas. 'Estelle, you give me that back, or this time I'll *really* break your arm! I'll break your arms and a whole lot more besides!'

Estelle just watched him, her face serene and untroubled.

'You . . .' Tomas stood and charged forward. 'How dare you! How dare you defy m—'

He never finished the word. As he neared Estelle, she reached out and placed a small plate on Tomas's chest – and the second it touched him, he froze and hung in the air, completely still, like a statue suspended by strings from the ceiling.

'There,' said Estelle softly. 'That's better.'

Sancia surreptitiously studied the scrived plate stuck to Tomas's chest. She saw right away that it was a gravity plate, much like the ones that the assassins had used when attacking her and Gregor.

But this one was smaller. Better. Much sleeker and more elegant.

She watched it for a second, and realised that although the plate had frozen Tomas in place, it wasn't finished yet. It was still doing something to him . . .

Estelle paced around the frozen Tomas, head cocked in delight and fascination. 'Is this what it's like?' she asked quietly. 'Is this what it's like to be you, my husband? To be a man of power? To stop a life at a whim, and silence those you disdain as you please?'

Tomas did not respond, but Sancia thought his eyes wriggled.

'You're sweating,' said Estelle.

Sancia lay still, unsure what she meant. Tomas did not seem to be sweating.

'You, on the table,' said Estelle, louder. 'You're sweating.'

Shit. Sancia still did not move.

Estelle sighed. 'Give it up. I know you're awake.'

Sancia took a breath and opened her eyes all the way. Estelle turned and studied her, her face fixed in an expression of icy, regal dignity.

'I suppose I need to thank you, girl,' she said.

'Why?' said Sancia.

'When Orso came to me and said he needed a way to sneak a thief into the Mountain, I realised right away that if Tomas caught this thief, he'd likely take them somewhere safe. And the safest place would likely also be where he'd hidden my father's collection.' She turned to the table covered in artefacts. 'Which I'd been seeking for some time. Looks like it's all here.'

'It . . . it was you who backstabbed us,' said Sancia. 'You tipped Tomas off that I'd be coming.'

'I told a person to tell a person to tell a person close to Tomas to be on alert,' said Estelle. 'It wasn't personal – surely you understand that. But a creature such as you must be accustomed to being used as a tool by your betters. I'd have hoped Tomas would have given you a quick death, though.' She sighed, slightly put out. 'Now I'll have to decide how to deal with you.'

At the mention of her death, Sancia focused back on the shackles, asking, *<Listen – is the secret restricted by time?>*

<No.>

<Is the . . . >

'He thought so much of himself, you know,' Estelle said, looking at Tomas. 'He thought scrivers were pale, weak fools. He hated how much he depended on them. He wished to operate in a world of conquest and conflict, a savage world that substituted gold for blood.' She tutted. 'Not a man of reflection, then. And when he started finding such valuable designs in Tribuno's chambers, strings of sigils that just mysteriously appeared overnight, he rejoiced . . . And he never reflected on where they came from.'

'Y-you made the gravity plates?' asked Sancia, surprised.

'I made it all,' said Estelle, eyes locked on Tomas's. 'I did *everything* for him. Through hints and nudges, over years and years, I led him to my father's Occidental collection. I used my father to feed him *my* scriving innovations – listening rigs, gravity plates, and much, much more. I got him to do everything I could not, everything that I was not allowed to do.' She leaned close to Tomas's frozen face. 'I have done more than you, *so much* more than you, with you acting as an obstacle every step of the way. With you castigating me, and ignoring me, and grabbing me and . . . and . . .'

She paused, and swallowed.

This Sancia understood well. 'He thought you his property,' she said.

'A regrettable heirloom, perhaps,' said Estelle quietly. 'But no matter. I took that and made an advantage of it as best I could. I've rarely had the luxury of pride. So perhaps it didn't hurt quite as much as it should have.'

Sancia looked at Tomas, and saw he was now strangely *bent* in places. He was like an iron drum that had been crinkled and crumpled after a few years of hard use.

'What . . . what the hell are you doing to him?' asked Sancia.

'I am subjecting him to the same thing he and my father subjected me to,' said Estelle. 'Pressure.'

Sancia pulled a face, watching as Tomas appeared to . . . retract. Just ever so slightly. 'So his gravity . . .'

'Every thirty seconds, it increases by a tenth,' said Estelle. 'So as it accelerates, its acceleration accelerates . . .'

'And he still feels . . .'

'Everything,' said Estelle softly.

'Oh my God,' said Sancia, appalled.

'Why do you react with such horror? Don't you wish this man *dead* for what he did to you? For capturing you, for beating you, for slashing your head open?'

'Sure I do,' said Sancia. 'Man's a shit. But that doesn't mean you're decent. I mean, even though I might sympathise with you, that doesn't mean you're going to let me go, does it? I'd ruin your chance to get at all that money.'

'For *money*?' said Estelle. 'Oh, girl . . . This isn't for money.'

'Besides that and killing Tomas, what could it have been about? Or . . . is a Candiano a Candiano? You think you can make Occidental tools? You'll succeed where your father failed?'

Estelle smiled coldly. 'Forget Occidental tools. What no one knows is – who *were* the hierophants? How did they get to be what they were? The answer was there in front of my father's face, the whole time. And I'd solved it *ages* ago. He never listened to me. And I knew Tomas wouldn't. Yet I needed the resources to prove it.' She paced around Tomas again. 'A collection of energies. All thoughts captured in *one person's being.* And the grand privileges of the *lingai divina* – these are reserved for the deathless, for those who take and give life.' She grinned and looked at Sancia. 'Don't you see? Don't you understand?'

Sancia's skin crawled. 'You . . . you mean . . .'

'The hierophants made themselves the same way they made their devices,' said Estelle. 'They took the minds and souls of others – and invested them *in their very bodies.*'

Sancia watched, sickened, as Tomas's form began to shudder, as if it were being liquefied. Then his eyes began to fill with blood. 'Oh God . . .'

'A single human form!' cried Estelle, triumphant. 'Yet within it, dozens, hundreds, *thousands* of minds and thoughts . . . A person brimming over with vitality, with meaning, with power, swirling reality around themselves, able to not just patch over reality but *change* it with a whim . . .'

Tomas's body crumpled inward, collapsing in on itself, his shattering arms and chest erupting with blood that then, in full defiance of physics, shrank back into his body, forced in by his unnatural gravity.

'You're scrumming insane,' Sancia said.

'No!' Estelle laughed. 'I'm just well read. I waited for so long for Tomas to collect all the tools and resources I need, all the ancient sigils. I was *so* patient. But then old Orso presented a wonderful opportunity. And, as they say, you never turn down an opportunity . . .' She reached into her robes and took out something glimmering and gold – a long, oddly-toothed key.

Sancia stared. 'Clef . . .'

'Clef?' said Estelle. 'You have a name for it? That's rather pathetic, isn't it?'

'You . . . you scrumming *bitch*!' said Sancia, furious. 'How did you get him? How did you . . .' Then she stopped. 'Where's . . . Where's Gregor?'

Estelle turned to look at her husband.

'What did you do?' demanded Sancia. 'What did you do to Gregor? What did you do to him?'

'I did what was necessary,' said Estelle, 'to gain my freedom. Wouldn't you?'

Sancia stared, disgusted and terrified, as Tomas's body slowly lost form and shape, turning into a boiling ball of blood and viscera, which shrank, and shrank, and shrank . . .

'If you hurt him,' said Sancia. 'If you hurt him, you, you . . .'

'It could have been worse.' She gestured at the monstrous sight before her. 'I could have put him through this.'

Tomas's body was now about the size of a small cannonball. It was shuddering slightly in the air, as if it could no longer bear the pressure.

Estelle stood up tall, and despite her mussed hair and her smeared makeup, her eyes were bright and hard and commanding, and suddenly Sancia understood why people had thought Tribuno Candiano a king. 'Tomorrow I shall do what my father always dreamt of, but never accomplished. And at the same time, I will take away all he valued, and all you valued as well, husband. I will *become* Company Candiano. And then I will collect *all that I have been denied*!'

And then the small, red ball that had once been Tomas Ziani simply . . . popped.

There was a loud, curious coughing sound, and the room instantly filled with a fine, swirling red mist. Sancia shut her eyes and turned her head away as she felt warm drops stippling her face and neck.

She heard Estelle sputtering and spitting somewhere in the room. 'Ugh. *Ugh!* I suppose I hadn't thought of that . . . But every design does have its limit.'

Sancia tried not to shake. She tried not to think of Clef in Estelle's hands, of what she could have done to poor Gregor. *Focus. What can I do now? How can I get out of this?*

Estelle spat some more, coughed, and called out, *'It's done!'*

The red mist continued to settle. There was the sound of footsteps in the hallway beyond. Two Candiano soldiers walked in. They did not seem surprised by the sight of all these corpses, or the whole room coated in a thin layer of blood.

'Shall we burn them as discussed, ma'am?' asked one.

'Yes, Captain,' said Estelle. She was now red from head to foot, and she cradled the imperiat and Clef in her hands like twin infants. 'I am *quite* eager to finally play with these on my own, but . . . Have we seen any movements from the Dandolos?'

'Not yet, ma'am.'

'Good. Arrange for my escort to the Mountain, and mobilise our forces,' said Estelle. 'The entire Candiano campo must be locked down and patrolled from now until midnight. Issue orders suggesting Tomas has gone missing – and we suspect foul play.'

'Yes, ma'am.'

Sancia listened closely. And that word – 'orders' – suddenly gave her an idea.

She took a breath, focused on the shackles again – and realised she'd been thinking of them wrong.

She'd been focused purely on the shackles, on the bands of steel, and what they expected or wanted – but she hadn't realised there might be more to the system.

What's breath but not a breath?

There were the restraints for her ankles and wrists, yes. But now that she searched them, she realised the shackles were eagerly awaiting a signal from another part of the rig – one she'd totally missed, set on the end of the operating table.

She looked down, and saw this component was small, set on the edge of the stone surface. She reviewed its commands, and saw it was constructed similarly to how Orso had described the aural relay device: a thin, delicate needle, trapped in a cage, that moved with vibrations of sound . . . only, it needed to move in a specific fashion.

Of course, thought Sancia. *Of course!*

<Is . . . Is the secret a word?> she asked the shackles quickly. *<A command? A password?>*

<Yes,> said the shackles simply.

She nearly sighed with triumph. It must be like a safe word – someone could say the right phrase aloud, and the needle would move in *just* the right way, and then the shackles would pop open . . .

<*What's the word?*> asked Sancia.

<*Secret,*> said the shackles. They sounded amused.

<*Tell me the secret word,*> she said.

<*Cannot share the word. It is secret. So secret even I don't know it.*>

<*Then how do you know when the secret is said?*>

<*When the needle moves the right way.*>

This was frustrating. She wondered how Clef would have figured this out. He always phrased and rephrased questions or ideas until they didn't break the rules, in essence – so how to do that here?

She got an idea. <*The secret,*> she said. <*If I said 'puh,' would it move the needle the right way, like the start of the secret?*>

A long pause. Then the shackles said, <*No.*>

<*And you would have said yes if it did?*>

<*Yes?*>

She swallowed, relieved. *Of course,* she thought. *Because asking about phonetics, not words, doesn't break the rules.*

<*If I said 'tuh,' would it move the needle like the start of the secret?*>

<*No.*>

<*If I said 'seh,' would it move the needle like the start of the secret?*>

<*No?*>

<*If I said 'mah,' would it move the needle like the start of the secret?*>

< . . . *Yes,*> said the shackles.

She took a breath. *So the password starts with an 'm.' Now I just need to keep guessing – as fast as I can.*

'And the girl?' said the guard.

'Dispose of her,' said Estelle. 'However you like. She is of no consequence.'

'Yes, ma'am.' He saluted as Estelle turned and left, leaving him alone in the room with Sancia.

Shit! thought Sancia. She started guessing, faster and faster – and she realised then that she could communicate faster with rigs than she could with people. Just like when there'd been a sudden, impenetrable burst of messages between Clef and a rig, she could focus her thoughts and ask dozens if not hundreds of questions at once.

Her mind became a chorus of *noes* with the occasional *yes.* And slowly, steadily, she assembled the password in her mind.

The guard walked over and looked down at her. His eyes were small and watery and deep set. He looked her over with the air of a man reviewing a meal and wrinkled his nose. 'Hm. Not really my type . . .'

'Uh-huh,' said Sancia. She shut her eyes, ignored him, and focused on her restraints.

'You praying, girl?'

'No,' said Sancia. She opened her eyes.

'You going to make any noise?' he asked. He thoughtlessly pinched the fabric of his trousers, just next to his crotch, and started kneading it back and forth. 'I don't mind that, honestly. But it'd be a bit inconvenient, with the boys in the hall . . .'

'The only noise I'm going to make,' she said, 'is *mango*.'

'Is wha—'

With a *pop!* all of Sancia's shackles swung open.

The guard stared, and said, 'What in the h—'

Sancia sat up, snatched his hand, stuffed his wrist into the shackles, and snapped them shut.

Stunned, the guard stared at his hand and heaved at it. It didn't budge. 'You . . . You . . .'

Sancia jumped off the table and smashed the listening needle in the cage. 'There. Now you'll stay put.'

'*Clemente!*' he bellowed. '*She's loose, she's loose! Send everyone, everyone!*'

Sancia punched the guard in the side of the head as hard as she could. He staggered and slipped, his hand still stuck in the shackles. Before he could react, she knelt and unsheathed his scrived rapier.

She looked at the blade, alight with commands. She could see it was made to amplify gravity, to believe it'd been hurled through the air with inhuman force.

Then there were footsteps in the hallway – lots of them. Sancia took stock of the situation. The hallway beyond was the only exit, and it was rapidly filling up with guards, from the sound of it. She had just the sword on her – and, given her new talents, that gave her a considerable advantage. But probably not enough to take on a dozen men with espringals and the like.

She looked around the room. The far wall was made of stone, and her talents allowed her to glimpse the commands on the other side. These were fainter and more difficult to read, probably due to the distance – but she could see that one rig was scrived to be unnaturally dense, almost unbreakable, a thin, rectangular plate seemingly set in the wall . . .

A foundry window, she thought. And she'd had recent experience with those.

She addressed the rapier: *<You – you amplify gravity, yes?>*

<WHEN I APPROACH PROPER SPEEDS, MY DENSITY ACHIEVES AMPLIFICATION AND GRAVITY IS TRIPLED,> the sword bellowed back promptly.

<How amplified does your density get?>

<IT IS AS THOUGH THERE ARE TWENTY OF ME,> said the sword.

<And how much do you weigh?>

<AH . . . THIS IS LESS DEFINED? I WEIGH AS MUCH AS I WEIGH?>

<Oh, no, no, no. That's wrong. You actually weigh this much . . . >

The guards were close now. Sancia put the sword on the ground and stood on it with both feet. Then she picked it back up, took a few steps away from the far wall, and lifted the blade.

She aimed carefully. Then she hurled the sword forward, dropped to the floor behind the table, and covered her head.

It had been a stupefyingly easy thing to do, really. The sword's weight had been essentially undefined, so she'd just stood on the blade and told it that this new weight it was experiencing was the sword's *actual* weight.

But this definition only mattered when its scrivings were activated – specifically, when it was swung at the proper speed. Which included being thrown.

Now when the sword activated its scrivings, it did not think it was as heavy as twenty six-pound rapiers, but rather twenty *hundred-and-sixteen-pound* rapiers. And then, of course, it amplified its gravity, which made the effect even more extreme.

When the rapier hit the far stone wall, it was like it'd been struck by a boulder falling off the side of a mountain. There was a tremendous *crash,* shrapnel and debris rained throughout the room, and dust filled the air.

Sancia lay on the ground, covering her head and neck with her hands as the pebbles and rocks rained down on her. Then she stood and dashed through the hole in the wall to the window on the far side of the room.

She barely had time to look out – she was about sixty feet up above the Candiano campo. Like a lot of the Candiano campo, this area was deserted, but there was a wide canal just below the wall. She jumped up and shoved the window open. Then she lifted herself up, through, and over, and then she hung on the window of the foundry, reviewing her options to descend.

She heard the sounds of shouts within, and looked up through the window to see seven Candiano soldiers charge in. They stared at her, hanging there on the window, and raised their espringals.

For a moment, she debated what to do. She knew the window was scrived to be unnaturally durable. But she knew at a glance that the soldiers' espringals were quite advanced.

The hell with it, she thought. She turned and leapt off the window, arms outstretched for the canal below.

She tumbled, end over end. She heard the window explode above her, and she opened her eyes. And then she saw.

Even though she had no mind for it, she nearly cried, '*Oh my God!*' as she fell. Yet not out of fear, or dismay – but rather wonder.

For she was still seeing the scrivings around her. And as she fell, she did something more, something she had no idea she could do: it was like there was a floodgate in her mind, and out of fear or wonder or instinct, it opened up just as she opened her eyes . . .

Sancia saw the nightscape of Tevanne below her, suddenly rendered in the juddering, jangly tangles of silver scrivings, thousands and thousands and thousands of them, like a dark mountain range covered in tiny candles. She watched in wonder as the scrived bolts hissed through the air above her, glittering like falling stars as they sped out over the city, a city that swarmed with minds and thoughts and desires like a forest full of fireflies.

It's like the night sky, she thought as she fell. *No, it's even more beautiful than that . . .*

The canal waters rose up to her, and she crashed through.

Sancia swam through unspeakable filth, through rot and flotsam and jetsam, through scum and industrial slurry. She swam until her body was as overwhelmed as her mind, until her shoulders were like fire and her legs like lead, until she finally crawled onto the muddy channel shores below the white Dandolo walls, exhausted and trembling.

Slowly, she stood. Then, filthy, reeking, and bloody, she turned and faced the sight of smoky, foggy, starlit Tevanne, stretched out beneath the skies.

She focused, and opened the floodgates inside of her. She saw Tevanne alight with thought and words and commands, all faint and flickering, like spectral candles burning under the purple morning skies.

Then Sancia, chest heaving, clenched her fists and screamed, a long, hoarse cry of defiance, of outrage, of victory. And as she screamed, some curious things happened in the campo blocks around her.

Scrived lights flickered uncertainly. Floating lanterns suddenly bobbed low, dropping a few feet, as if they'd heard dismaying news. Carriages abruptly slowed, just for half a block or so. Doors that had been scrived to stay shut slowly creaked open. Weapons and armaments that had been commanded to feel lighter felt, for one instant, a bit heavy.

It was like all the machines and devices that made the world run experienced a fleeting moment of paralysing self-doubt, and they all whispered – *What was that? Did you hear that?*

Sancia had no idea what she had done. But she did understand one thing, in some wordless fashion: the Sancia that the stars touched right now was slightly less human than the one they had touched the night before.

33

It's a cowardly plan, sir,' said Berenice.

'Oh, come off it, Berenice!' said Orso. 'It's been *seven hours*, and we've seen neither hide nor hair of Sancia *or* Gregor! No messages, no communications, nothing! And the Candiano campo is suddenly completely shut down! Something has gone wrong. And I've no interest in sticking around to see what.'

'But . . . but we just can't *leave* Tevanne!' said Berenice, pacing back and forth across the crypt.

'I could,' said Gio. The two Scrappers were obviously terrified. They were far more vulnerable than two campo scrivers.

'Maybe instead of paying us,' said Claudia, 'you can pay for our passage out of here.'

'We can't abandon Sancia and Gregor!' said Berenice. 'We can't leave the imperiat in Tomas Ziani's hands! A man like that . . . Think of the damage he could do!'

'I *am* thinking of that,' said Orso. 'I can't *stop* thinking about it! That's why I want to get the hell out of here! And as for Sancia and Gregor . . .'

Berenice stopped and glared at him. 'Yes?'

Orso grimaced. 'They made their choice. They knew the risks. We all did. Some wind up lucky, and others don't. We're survivors of all this, Berenice. The wisest thing to do is just keep surviving.'

She heaved a great sigh. 'To think of us hopping aboard a ship and sneaking away in the dead of night . . .'

'What else are we supposed to do?' said Orso. 'We're just some scrivers, girl! We can't *design* our way out of this! The idea is preposterous! Anyways, Sancia and Gregor are smart people, maybe they can find their own way ou—'

They froze as they heard the stone door roll away in the crypt passage beyond. This was troubling – because only Gio had the key, and that was currently sitting in his pocket.

They looked at one another, alarmed. Orso held a finger to his lips. He stood, grabbed a wrench, and gingerly approached the opening of the passageway. He paused – he could hear slow footsteps approaching.

He swallowed, took a breath, and screamed and leapt in front of the passageway, wrench raised over his head.

He skidded to a stop. Standing before him, grim and stone-faced, was a wet, filthy, bloody Sancia Grado.

'Holy hell,' said Orso.

'Sancia!' cried Berenice. She ran to her, but stopped a few feet away. 'My . . . my God. What *happened* to you?'

Sancia had not yet seemed to notice either of them – she was just staring into the middle distance. But at these words, she slowly blinked and looked at Berenice, meeting her eyes. 'What?' she said faintly.

They stared at her. She had a slash on her head, cuts on her forearms, a bruise on her cheek, and crusts of dried blood all over her face and neck . . . but the worst part about her was her *eyes*. One eye remained the same, the usual white with dark brown, but the other eye, her right, was flooded with red. It was like she'd received some fierce blow to the side of her head, one that had almost killed her.

Sancia exhaled, then said in a croaking voice, 'What a lovely sight you are, Berenice.'

Berenice blushed hugely, turning bright crimson.

'What the hell happened?' demanded Orso. 'Where have you been?' He looked at the open door to the crypt. 'And how the *hell* did you get in?'

'I need to sit down,' said Sancia softly. 'And I need a drink.'

Berenice helped her into a chair while Gio opened a bottle of cane wine. 'Don't bother with a glass,' whispered Sancia. He popped it open, handed it over to her, and she took a huge swig.

'You look, my girl,' Gio said, 'like the shepherd who climbed the mount and saw God's face in the skies.'

'You're . . . not quite wrong there,' she said darkly.

'What happened to you, Sancia?' asked Orso. 'What did you see?'

She started talking.

At some point, the words just ran out. A long, long silence stretched on. And while Berenice, Gio, and Claudia looked pale and shaken, Orso looked like he was about to vomit.

He carefully cleared his throat. 'So,' he said. 'A . . . hierophant.'

'Yeah,' said Sancia.

He nodded, trembling. 'Estelle Candiano,' he said. 'Formerly Ziani . . .'

'Yes,' said Sancia.

'Was, in some way, behind all of this from the start . . .'

'Yeah.'

'And now she has murdered her husband . . .'

'Yeah.'

'And she now intends to become . . . one of the ancient ones.' Orso spoke like saying the words aloud would make them make more sense.

'I guess it wouldn't be that ancient if she's doing it right *now*,' said Sancia. 'But yeah. That's the sum of it.' She bowed her head. 'And Gregor . . . I think Gregor's dead. And she has Clef. She has everything. Clef, the imperiat, the box with the voice in it . . . Everything.'

Orso blinked and stared into a wall. Then he held out a hand and whispered, 'Give me that scrumming bottle.'

Sancia handed it over. He took a huge pull from it. Then, legs quaking, he sat down on the floor. 'I didn't think Tribuno would have made those designs,' he said softly. 'I suppose I was . . . right?'

'My question is . . . can she do it?' said Claudia. 'Let's say she becomes a hierophant. All I've heard of them are children's stories. I thought they were scrumming giants! What do we actually know about what they could do?'

Sancia remembered the vision of Clef's she'd seen: the thing wrapped in black, standing on the dunes. 'They were goddamn monsters,' she rasped. 'They were devils. That thing in the box told me as much – they waged a war that turned the land to ash and sand. One could do the same here.'

'Right,' said Orso, shivering. 'So. I . . . I think my first plan is looking pretty good right now. We find a boat. We get on that boat. We take the boat far across the ocean. And then we, I don't know, keep living for a while. How does that sound?'

'You weren't listening,' said Sancia lowly. 'I told you. She said she wants to *become* Company Candiano.'

'And what's the significance of that?' cried Orso. 'It's not like *that* stands out from the sea of other crazy shit you've been saying for the past half hour!'

'Think. I told you – that machine, the voice in the box . . .'

'This Valeria you spoke to,' said Orso.

'Right.'

Sancia hesitated. This part of her story, she knew, was the most inexplicable, and the most disturbing. 'You . . . you believe me about that, right?' she asked. 'About what she said, what she did to me? I know it all sounds insane . . .'

Orso was still for a long time, thinking. 'I have some . . . ideas about that. But I do believe. Please continue.'

'Okay. So. Valeria told me that the way the hierophants did their ritual,' said Sancia, 'you first mark the body holding the spirit, then mark what you wish to transfer it into.'

'I must admit,' said Gio, 'that in the course of our projects, it's grown pretty hard to discern one bit of mystical shit from another.'

'Gio's right,' said Claudia. 'Please clarify how that matters.'

'Remember – right as I took the job to steal Clef, Candiano Company changed up their sachets, yes?' said Sancia.

'Yeah,' said Gio. 'We had to make whole new ones for half the prostitutes in Tevanne.'

'Right. It was a big shift. Nobody knew why it got changed. At the time, I didn't think much about it. But now, after hearing what she said . . . I'm thinking that those new sachets are *more* than just sachets.'

Berenice's mouth dropped open in horror. 'You think the sachets . . . the little buttons being carried by every single Candiano employee . . .'

Sancia nodded grimly. 'Estelle either issued them, or tampered with them when they went out. I think they double as the markers the hierophants used.'

'Then . . . then when Estelle starts the ritual,' said Orso, 'all the people carrying those sachets with the markers . . .'

'They all die,' said Sancia. 'Maybe a few who set their sachets aside get lucky, but, for all intents and purposes, the whole of Company Candiano dies. All of their minds and souls get invested in Estelle. Who then becomes a hierophant.' She looked at Orso. 'We leave and let Estelle do her thing, and all your old coworkers, and all the other thousand some-odd people who work at Company Candiano, even the damned *maids*, all die a horrible, horrible death.'

For a moment they all just sat there.

'So,' said Sancia. 'Yeah. We *have* to stop her. The voice in the box – Valeria – said she could edit all their tools so they wouldn't work anymore. But to do that, we need Clef. Which Estelle has. After . . . after she killed Gregor.' She shook her head. 'So. Sorry, Orso. But it seems like we're going to have to figure out a way to kill your old girlfriend. And we've got until midnight to do it.'

Orso and Berenice looked horrified. 'Assassinate Estelle Candiano?' said Orso faintly. '*On* the Candiano campo?'

'I've got in there before,' said Sancia. 'I can do it again.'

'Doing it once,' said Berenice, 'actually makes it *harder*. They've got the gates closed, and they know we came in through the canals. All the easy routes will be eliminated. They'll be *ready*.'

'But I'm not just a thief anymore,' whispered Sancia, staring into space. 'I can do a hell of a lot more than I used to.' She looked around the crypt, her eyes unfocused, like she was seeing many invisible things. 'And I think soon I'll learn how to do a whole lot more . . .'

'You might be changed,' said Orso. 'And you might have escaped Estelle. But you can't do much against a couple of cohorts of soldiers shooting at you, Sancia. One person, no matter how augmented, can't fight an army.'

'We don't even know *where* we want to attack,' said Giovanni.

'Yes, we do,' said Sancia. She looked at Orso. 'And you do too. Estelle needs to start her ritual with the death of one person – just one. She hated Tomas – but there's someone else she hates even more. Someone who's still alive. And I can think of only one place she'd choose for her transformation.'

Orso frowned at her for a moment. Then he went white and said, 'Oh my God . . .'

'Is this where you want him, ma'am?' asked the attendant.

Estelle Candiano stared around her father's office. It was as she'd remembered it, all grim grey stone, all walls with far too many angles. A huge window on the far side stared out at the city of Tevanne, and a second small circular window stared up at the sky – these were the only reminder that this large room existed in any semblance of reality.

She remembered being here, once. As a child, when her father had first built it – she'd played before his desk, drawing on the stone floor with chalk. She'd been a child then, but when she'd got older, and become a woman, she'd been disinvited from such places, where powerful men made powerful decisions. Women, she'd understood, were unfit for inclusion among those ranks.

'Ma'am?' asked the attendant again.

'Mm?' said Estelle. 'What?'

'Do you want him there?' asked the attendant. 'By the wall?'

'Yes. Yes, that will do.'

'All right. They should have him here shortly.'

'Good. And the rest of my things – from the abandoned foundry – they're on the way, yes?'

'I believe so, ma'am.'

'Good.'

She looked around at the office again. *My workshop,* she thought. *Mine. And soon, I shall have the tools here to make wonders the world cannot imagine . . .*

Estelle looked at her left hand. Within a few hours the skin there, as well as the skin on her wrist, her arm, her shoulder and breast, would all be marked with delicately drawn sigils, a chain leading from her palm – which would be holding the dagger, of course – to her heart. Ancient sigils of containment, of transference, capable of directing huge amounts of energies into her body, her soul.

There was the sound of squeaking, rattling wheels in the hall outside.

Estelle Candiano considered that she was likely the only person alive who knew of those ancient sigils, and how to use them.

The sound of squeaking wheels grew closer.

She was the only one, she thought – except possibly the person being wheeled to her right now.

Estelle turned to face the door as the two attendants directed the rolling bed into the office. She looked at the shrunken, frail figure nestled in its sheets, face covered in sores, eyes tiny and bleary and red and thoughtless.

She smiled. 'Hello, Father.'

34

Is a direct attack even possible?' said Claudia. 'If you all are right about this imperiat thing, couldn't Estelle shut down any assault?'

'The imperiat isn't all-powerful,' said Sancia. 'It has a limited range, and I don't think it's easy to operate. If Estelle screws it up, it could kill all the scrivings in the Mountain – which would send the whole place down on her head. I think she knows that. She'll be cautious.'

'So a quick strike,' said Gio. 'Fast, before she can prepare.'

'Right, but fast is a problem,' said Sancia. 'I don't see how we get to the Mountain without a fight. There's hundreds of soldiers between us and them.'

'Direct confrontation, though . . .' said Claudia. 'I always advise against it.'

'Like we say, you've always got three options,' said Gio. 'Across, under, or over. No tunnels to go under. No way across through all those mercenaries. And I doubt if we can go over. You'd have to plant an anchor to make an air-sailing rig go – and that means getting to the Mountain, which is kind of our problem.'

'It's mad to ask, but can we develop a way to fly without an anchor?' said Claudia.

Berenice, Orso, and Sancia grew still. They slowly looked at one another.

'What?' said Claudia.

'*We've* seen people fly,' said Berenice.

'And do it scrumming well!' said Orso. 'Brilliant!'

Claudia stared at them. 'Uh, you have?'

Berenice leapt up and ran to a large trunk in the corner. She opened it, hauled something out, and brought it back to the table.

It looked like two iron plates, tied together with fine, strong ropes, with a bronze dial in the centre . . . And they looked like they were crusted over with blood.

'Is that . . .' said Claudia.

'They're gravity plates,' said Berenice, excited. 'Made by Estelle Candiano herself! Assassins were able to jump over walls and buildings with them!'

'And more than that,' said Sancia. 'They could basically *fly* with the damn things!'

'Well, then,' said Claudia. 'Holy shit.'

'So it's simple!' said Giovanni. 'You just use the plates to fly to the Mountain. Or, say, jump from roof to roof to the Mountain.'

Sancia looked at the gravity plates. She tensed the muscle in her mind, opened the floodgates, and looked . . .

She'd expected the plates to glimmer and shine brightly, as any powerfully scrived item did. But they did not – rather, they looked like a patchwork of silver, shining in some spots but not in others.

She shook her head. 'No. They're not working right,' she said. 'Some of the scriving commands are operating, but not *all* of them – so the whole rig is nonfunctional.'

'You can tell that just by *looking* at it?' said Orso, stunned.

'Yeah,' said Sancia. 'And I can talk to it.'

'You can *talk* to i—'

'Shut up, and let me see here . . .'

She shut her eyes, placed her bare hands on the plates, and listened.

<*. . . location . . . location of MASS?*> said the plates. <*Cannot . . . compilation incomplete . . . MASS, MASS, MASS. Lacking all directionality . . . MASS? Need density of MASS? Location of MASS. Mass . . . orientation critical to activate sequence for . . . for . . .* >

She shook her head. 'It's . . . weird. It's like listening to someone with a head injury muttering in their sleep. It's not making sense.' She opened her eyes. 'It's like they're broken.'

Claudia clucked her tongue. 'You said Estelle Candiano made these?'

'Yeah?' said Sancia. 'Why?'

'Well, if *I* were her, and if I knew there was a chance my enemies had stolen my toys . . . I'd just turn off the scriving definitions at my lexicon. It'd make them useless, or broken – just like this rig.'

'Of course!' said Orso. 'That's why the plates can't talk! Estelle has taken away some critical pillar in its logic, so the whole thing has collapsed!'

'Which means it won't work,' said Claudia. 'So we're scrummed.'

'I guess we can't make our *own* definition plates that could make these run?' sighed Gio.

'Estelle has basically achieved the impossible with this rig,' said Orso. 'No one's ever exhibited such fine control over gravity short of a hierophant. Remaking the impossible in a day is quite out of the question.'

There was a silence as everyone thought about this.

Berenice sat forward. 'But . . . but we don't have to remake *all* of it,' she said.

'We don't?' said Sancia.

'No! Estelle's probably just deactivated a *few* critical scrivings – but the rest still work. If you've got a hole in a wall, you don't tear it down and make a whole new wall – you just cut a piece of stone to fit the hole.'

'Wait,' said Orso. 'Are . . . are you saying we should fabricate the missing definitions *ourselves*?'

'Not we,' said Berenice. 'Me. I'm faster than you, sir.'

Orso blinked, taken aback. Then he gathered himself. 'Fine. But your metaphor is shit! This isn't just filling in a goddamn hole in a wall! This is some complicated scrumming scriving, girl!'

'Good thing we've got someone who can talk to rigs, then,' said

Berenice. She slid into a seat across from Sancia and pulled out a sheet of paper and a quill. 'Go on. Tell me everything the plates are saying.'

'But it's gibberish!' protested Sancia.

'Then tell me all the damned gibberish, then!'

She started talking.

She described how the plate plaintively asked for the location of this 'mass', begging for someone to tell it where the mass was, and the density of this mass, and so on and so on. She kept hoping Berenice would tell her to stop, but she didn't. She just kept writing down everything Sancia said – until, finally, she held up a finger.

Berenice slowly sat back in her chair, staring at the sheet of paper before her. Half of it looked to be notes. The other half was covered in sigils and strings of symbols. She turned to look at Orso. 'I . . . I am starting to believe everyone's been trying to scrive gravity wrong, sir. And only Estelle Candiano has ever really figured it out.'

Orso leaned forward and examined what she'd written. 'It's mad . . . but I think you're right. Keep talking.'

'You all could make sense of that?' said Claudia.

'Not entirely,' said Berenice. 'But there's a common theme. There's this subject of mass – and the device is trying to figure out where this mass should be, and how big the mass is.'

'So?' said Sancia. 'What's that got to do with floating and flying?'

'Well,' said Berenice. 'I'm not sure if I'm right here . . . But every scriver before us has assumed that gravity only worked one way – down, and to the earth. But Estelle's designs seem to suggest that . . . that *everything* has gravity. Everything pulls *everything* else to it. It's just that some things have a strong pull, and others have a weak pull.'

'What!' said Giovanni. 'What rot!'

'It sounds mad, but that's how this rig works. Estelle's designs don't defy gravity – the rig convinces what it's touching that, say, there's a whole scrumming *world* just above it with a gravity equal to the Earth's, so the Earth's gravity is cancelled out, and the thing just . . . floats. The designs just . . . reorient gravity, counterbalance it – almost *perfectly*.'

'Is that possible?' said Claudia.

'The hell with what's possible!' said Orso. 'Can you figure out what's missing? Can you fabricate the definitions to get the damned thing working, Berenice?'

'I could probably do it all, if I had a month,' she said. 'But I don't think we need it *all*. We don't need all the crucial calibrations or control strings.'

'We don't?' said Sancia nervously.

'No.' She looked at her. 'Not if you can just talk to the damned thing. All I need to fabricate is some definitions that can give the rig some impression of the location and density of this mass. And it would have to match these sigils etched on the rig, of course.'

Orso licked his lips. 'How many definitions?'

Berenice did some calculations on the corner of her paper. 'I think . . . four should do.'

He stared. 'You think you can fabricate *four* definitions? In a handful of *hours*? Most fabricators can barely manage one in a week!'

'I've been neck-deep in Candiano shit for the past days,' said Berenice. 'I've been looking at all their strings, their designs, their methodology. I . . . I think I can make it work. But there's another problem – we'll still need to put these definitions in a lexicon to actually make them effectual. We can't just walk into one of the Dandolo foundries and slip these in there – the guards wouldn't even let *you* do that, sir.'

'Could they work in a combat lexicon?' asked Claudia. 'Like the portable ones they use in the wars?'

'Those are pretty limited to powering weaponry,' said Berenice. 'And they're hard to get ahold of, as anything having to do with the wars often is.'

'And the test lexicon back at my workshop can't cast far enough,' said Orso. 'It only extends a mile and a half or so – not nearly enough to fly Sancia to the Mountain.'

'We can't take it with us, either,' said Berenice. 'Not only is it stuck on tracks in the workshop, but it weighs close to a thousand pounds itself.'

'Right,' said Orso. 'Shit!' He fell into silence, glowering into the wall.

'So . . . are we scrummed here?' said Sancia.

'Sounds like we're scrummed,' said Gio.

'No!' Orso held up a finger. A wild, mad gleam crept into his eye. He looked at Claudia and Giovanni, and the two Scrappers recoiled slightly. 'You two – you do much work with twinning?'

Claudia shrugged. 'Uh . . . as much as any scriver worth their salt does?'

'That'll do,' said Orso. 'All of you – get up. We're going to my workshops. Berenice is going to need a lot of space and the proper tools to do her bit. And that's where we'll get to work as well,' he said, nodding at Claudia and Gio.

'On what?' said Claudia.

'I'll figure it out along the way!' he snapped.

They trooped out of the drainage tunnel into the Gulf, then started up the hill. They moved quickly, filing through the Commons with the air of refugees or fugitives. Orso seemed filled with a mad energy, muttering to himself excitedly, but it wasn't until they approached the Dandolo walls that Sancia glanced at him, and saw his cheeks were wet with tears.

'Orso?' she said quietly. 'Uh – you all right?'

'I'm fine,' he said. He wiped his eyes. 'I'm fine. Just . . . God, what a waste!'

'A waste?'

'Estelle,' he said. 'The girl figured out how goddamn *gravity* works. She figured out how to make a *listening* rig. All while being trapped in some hole in the Mountain!' He paused for a moment, and seemed too stricken for words. 'Imagine what wonders she could have made for us all, if she'd only had a chance! And now she's become too dangerous to be free. What a waste. What a scrumming *waste*!'

When they got to the workshops, Sancia sat at a table with her hands on the plates while Berenice set up scriving blocks, parchment papers, and, of course, dozens of definition plates and molten bronze and styli to do the actual fabrication. Orso brought Claudia and Giovanni to the back of the workshop, where his test lexicon sat on rails that slid back into an ovenlike chamber in the wall, with a thick iron door.

'God,' said Gio, looking at it. 'How I'd love to get my hands on one of these . . . Something that could actually, genuinely allow you to toy around with definitions!'

Claudia examined the iron door and the chamber. 'Pretty massive heat resistance commands in this,' she said. 'It's a tiny lexicon, relatively speaking, but it still throws out a huge amount of temperature. If your idea is for us to build a test lexicon to carry around, that's a giant task.'

'I don't want you to build a lexicon,' said Orso. 'I just want you to build a box. Specifically, a box shaped like *that*.' He pointed at the chamber.

'Huh?' said Claudia. 'You just want us to build a heat chamber?'

'Yes. I want you to duplicate the one in the wall, and twin them – but we'll need a switch to activate and deactivate the twinning designs. Get me?'

The Scrappers exchanged a glance. 'I guess?' said Claudia.

'Good,' said Orso. 'Then do it.'

This was a familiar job for the Scrappers, who Orso knew were a deft hand at construction, and his workshops offered far finer tools than what they'd used in the crypt. Within less than three hours they had the basic raw structure ready, and they started scriving the twinning sigils on its frame.

Claudia looked at Orso, who had half his body stuck in the chamber in the wall as he did his own delicate work. 'What's going in this box, exactly?' she asked him.

'Technically?' said Orso. 'Nothing.'

'Why are we building a box that'll hold nothing?' said Gio.

'Because,' said Orso, 'it's what the box will *think* it holds that matters.'

'Since we've got a serious scrumming deadline here,' said Claudia, 'can you cut to the point?'

'I had the idea when we talked to Sancia's key – Clef, or whatever,' said Orso. He popped out of the chamber, dashed to a blackboard covered in sigils, and made a few adjustments. 'He talked about how impressive twinning was, and later I realised – Tribuno Candiano had developed a way to scrive reality. I mean, the Mountain is basically a big box that's sensitive to all the changes that take place inside it! It's aware of its contents, in other words. It's something Tribuno and I toyed with back in the day, but it required too much effort to manage. But . . . what if you could build a box that was somewhat aware of its contents, and then *twin the box*? Then if you put something into one box, the other box thinks it holds that exact same thing as well!'

Claudia stared at him, her mouth open as she understood. 'So . . . so your idea is to duplicate the heat chamber here in your workshops, twin it . . . and we'll take the empty double into the Candiano campo.'

'Right,' said Orso cheerfully.

'And because the first chamber will know it holds a test lexicon, then the double will *also* think it holds a test lexicon . . . so the empty one will project the necessary definitions far enough for Sancia's rig to work? Is that it?'

'That's the theory!' said Orso. He grinned wide enough that they saw all of his teeth. 'We're essentially twinning a *chunk of reality*! Only, this particular chunk happens to hold a small lexicon loaded with the definitions we need to do the shit we need to do! Make sense?'

'This . . . this is tying my brain in knots,' said Gio faintly. 'You're scriving something to *believe* it's scrived, in other words?'

'In essence,' said Orso. 'But that's what scriving is. Reality doesn't matter. If you can change something's mind enough, it'll believe whatever reality you choose.'

'How are we supposed to do this, exactly?' said Claudia.

'Well, you two aren't doing shit, really,' snapped Orso. 'I'm doing the hard bit, where I make the heat chamber in the wall aware of what it holds! Then you're just doing your basic twinning designs. So could we stop talking, and let me get back to goddamn work?'

They worked for a few hours more, the Scrappers and Orso sprinting back and forth and crawling in and out of the heat chamber, placing their sigils and strings in just the right places. Eventually the Scrappers were done, and they just sat there looking at Orso's legs sticking out of the chamber as he finished up.

Finally he slid out. 'I . . . believe I am finished,' he said quietly, wiping sweat from his brow.

'How do we test it?' asked Claudia.

'Good question. Let's see . . .' Orso walked over to his shelves and took out something that looked like a small iron can. 'A heating rig,' he said. 'We use it to make sure the lexicon chambers are insulated properly.' He hit a switch on the side, tossed the can into the chamber in the wall, and shut and locked the door. 'Should get up to some pretty incredible temperatures in there quick.'

'So, now we . . . ?' said Gio.

Orso looked around, grabbed a wooden paint box from one of his tables, dumped the paint cans out, and tossed it into the newly built chamber. 'Help me get this thing on the floor,' he said, 'and turn it on.'

He and Gio lifted the box off the table and, grunting, carefully placed it on the floor. Then they shut and locked the big iron doors and turned on the twinning scrivings by twisting a bronze dial on the side.

Suddenly the box creaked, like someone had just placed a substantial load on it.

'Good sign,' said Orso. 'Test lexicons are heavy as hell. If it thinks it holds one then theoretically the thing itself would abruptly gain weight.'

They waited a moment. Then Orso said, 'All right. Turn it off.'

Gio turned back the dial. Orso shoved the latch on the door up, and opened the chamber.

An immense cloud of hot black smoke came billowing out. They all coughed and waved the smoke away from their faces, then peered into the heating chamber. As the smoke dissipated, the small, shrivelled form of a burned box emerged.

Orso cackled with delight. 'Looks like it scrumming works to me! The double believed it held the same heating rig as the first!'

'It works?' said Gio faintly. 'I can't believe it really works . . .'

'Yes! Now we just put this thing on wheels, and we've basically got a light, mobile lexicon on our hands! Of a sort, I mean.'

They finished the job, mounting the empty chamber on a wooden cart and making sure the whole thing was secure. Once they were done, they sat back and marvelled at their work.

'Doesn't look like much,' said Gio.

'Could do with a paint job, yeah,' said Orso.

'But it's still probably the biggest damned thing I've ever done,' said Gio.

'Orso . . .' said Claudia. 'You realise what you've done here, right? Scriving's always been localised – you've got to stay close to one big, expensive piece of equipment for it to work. But you've essentially come up with a cheap, easy way to cover a whole region without having to build forty lexicons or whatever!'

Orso blinked, surprised. 'Have I? Well . . . it's still restricted, mind . . . but I suppose you're right.'

'If we all live through this thing,' said Claudia, 'this would be an incredibly valuable technique.'

'Speaking of living through this thing,' said Gio, 'how do we plan on surviving *after*? Like, we are talking about attacking the heart of a merchant house and killing a scion of the industry.'

Orso stared at the heating chamber on the cart, and slowly cocked his head. 'Claudia,' he said softly. 'How many Scrappers are there in total?'

'How many? I don't know. Fifty or so.'

'And how many would follow you faithfully? A dozen, at least?'

'Yeah, thereabout. Why?'

Orso grinned deliriously and tapped the side of his head. 'I don't know what it is about mortal panic,' he said, 'but it keeps giving me the *best* scrumming ideas. We're just going to need to file some paperwork. And maybe buy some property.'

The Scrappers exchanged a glance. 'Oh boy,' said Gio quietly.

Sancia sat opposite Berenice, watching as the girl dashed from blackboard to parchment to scriving blocks, writing strings of sigils on any surface she could find with a mesmerising, liquid grace. She'd finished two definition plates so far. The plates themselves were about two feet in diameter, wrought of steel, and they were covered in looping spirals of impossibly delicate bronze sigils – all put there by Berenice's flowing stylus.

Berenice looked up from her work, a strand of hair clinging to her sweaty forehead. She seemed to glow with a happy energy – and Sancia could not look away.

'Ask it if it says anything about elevation,' Berenice said breathlessly.

Sancia blinked, startled. 'Huh? What?'

'Ask the rig if it needs anything about elevation!'

'I told you, it doesn't respond well to my questi—'

'Just do it!'

Sancia did so. She shut her eyes, then opened them and said, 'It doesn't seem to know what elevation even is.'

'Perfect!' cried Berenice.

'Is it?' asked Sancia.

'It's one less hole I need to fill,' said Berenice, scribbling away.

Orso walked up and looked over Sancia's shoulder. 'We've done our part. Where are we here?'

Berenice peered through a massive magnifying lens at the third definition plate. She wrote one last string in her tiny script, then set the plate aside and picked up the fourth empty one. She said, 'Three done. One left.'

'Good,' said Orso. 'I'll load them into the test lexicon.'

He took the definition plates away. Sancia kept her eyes and her hands on the gravity rig – but as she heard Orso clinking and clanking away behind her, the rig suddenly glowed brighter, and brighter . . . and then it started talking to her.

<Location of MASS is currently NULL!> said the rig with a mad cheer. *<DENSITY of MASS? Define DENSITY of MASS in order to enforce effects, please. Levels of . . . of . . . Hm. Unable to define levels of DENSITY of MASS.>*

'Oh my God,' she said lowly. 'It's working.'

'Excellent,' said Berenice. 'What's it asking for now?'

'I think it wants to know how dense the mass is. In other words, it wants to know how much of a force to effect on the item touching the plates.' She swallowed. 'Which will be my body.'

Berenice paused and sat back. 'Ah . . . Well. I have a question for you here.'

'Yeah?'

'I don't have time to make really fine controls. So *you're* going to have to tell the plates the density of this mass – how fast you want to go, basically,' said Berenice. 'You'll have to tell it, say, that there are six Earths in the sky – and then you'll be pulled *up* at six times the rate of Earth's gravity, minus Earth's own actual gravitational effects. See?'

Sancia furrowed her brow. 'So . . . you're saying there's a huge scrumming margin of error here.'

'Unimaginably huge.'

'And . . . what's the question you have for me?' said Sancia.

'I actually don't have a question,' said Berenice. 'I just wanted to tell you all this without you immediately panicking.' She went back to work.

'Great,' said Sancia faintly.

Another hour ticked by. Then another.

Orso kept an eye on the Michiel clock tower out the window. 'Six o'clock,' he said nervously.

'Almost finished,' said Berenice.

'You keep saying that. You said that an hour ago.'

'But I mean it this time.'

'You said *that* an hour ago too.'

'Orso,' said Sancia, 'shut the hell up and let her work!'

Another sigil. Another massive sheaf of parchment. Another dozen styli ruined, another dozen inkpots and bowls of melted bronze. But then, at eight o'clock . . .

Berenice paused, squinting through the lens. Then she sat back and sighed, looking exhausted. 'I . . . I *think* I'm done.'

Orso grabbed the definition without a word, ran to the test lexicon, put it in, and turned it on. 'Sancia!' he called. 'How's it look?'

The rig now glowed bright in her hands – but not solidly bright. It wasn't a complete rig, in other words, just most of one. But from what Berenice had said, they might not need the whole thing.

<Define LOCATION and DENSITY of MASS in order to achieve effect!> said the rig with a manic happiness.

Her belly squirmed with anxiety. She wanted to make sure she understood how this thing worked before she told it what to do. *<Tell me how I make you work.>*

<First we must decide LOCATION of MASS!> squealed the plates.

<*What's mass?*>

<*MASS is LARGEST THING. Nearly all FLOW is directed toward LARGEST THING.*>

<*Okay, a—*>

<*Then must define the STRENGTH of FLOW of LARGEST THING. All matter FALLS toward LARGEST THING along direction of FLOW.*>

She was beginning to understand. <*Location is up,*> she said.

<*Great!*> said the plates. <*Very unconventional! And DENSITY?*>

<*Density is . . . one half of regular Earth density? Can that work?*>

<*Sure! Want me to implement EFFECTS now?*>

<*Uh. Yes.*>

<*Done!*>

Instantly, Sancia's stomach swooped unpleasantly, like she had a live mouse running around in her intestines. Something had . . . changed. Her head felt heavy – much like her blood was being pulled up into her skull.

'Well?' said Orso impatiently.

Sancia took a breath, and stood up.

But then . . . she just kept going.

She stared around, terrified, as her body rose up toward the ceiling at a steady pace. It wasn't fast, but it *felt* fast, probably because she was panicking. 'Oh my God!' she said. 'Holy shit! Somebody grab me!'

They did not grab her. They just stared.

'Looks like it works, yeah,' said Gio.

To her relief, she started to come back down again – but she seemed to be falling toward a big stack of empty metal bowls on a nearby table. 'Shit!' she said. 'Shit, shit!' She kicked around helplessly, and they all watched as she slowly, inevitably collided with the pile of bowls, which went crashing and clanging all over the workshop.

<*End effects!*> Sancia shouted at the rig.

<*Done!*>

Instantly, the lightness died inside her, and she crashed onto the table and fell to the ground.

Berenice, delighted, stood up and punched a fist into the air. 'Yes. Yes! *Yes!* I did it, I did it, *I did it*!'

Sancia, groaning, stared up at the ceiling.

'This is what she's going to do to stop Estelle?' said Gio. 'She's going to do that?'

'Let's call this,' said Orso, 'a qualified success.'

⁂

An hour later, and they reviewed their plan.

'So we have what we need,' said Orso. 'But . . . we still need to get our empty box within a mile and a half of the Mountain. That's the farthest the gravity rig will work.'

'So we *still* need a way through the walls?' said Claudia. 'Into the campo?'

'Yes. But only a bit,' said Orso. 'A quarter mile or so.'

Claudia sighed. 'I don't suppose Sancia could use the rig to jump over the walls and open the gates from the inside.'

'Not without getting shot to bits,' said Gio. 'If the whole campo's locked down, the guards at the gates will shoot anyone who gets close.'

Sancia held the gravity plates in her hand, whispering to them and listening to them respond. Then she sat up. 'I can get us past the walls,' she said quietly. 'Or through them, rather.'

'How?' said Berenice.

'A gate is just a door,' she said. 'And Clef taught me a lot about doors. I just need to be able to get close.' She sat up and looked around the workshop. She spied something she'd seen the last time she'd been here, when she'd searched the workshop for the listening rig. 'Those rows of black cubes over there, the ones that seem to suck up light – are those stable?'

Orso looked around, surprised. 'Those? Yes. They're loaded in one of the main Dandolo foundry lexicons, so you can take those almost anywhere.'

'Can you attach them to a cuirass, or something wearable?' she asked. 'It'll be damn handy if I'm a moving blot of shadow in the darkness.'

'Sure,' said Orso. 'But . . . why?'

'I'll need them to sneak up to the east Candiano walls,' said Sancia. 'Then I'll get things started. Berenice, Orso – I'll need you to have your magic box loaded onto a carriage and ready at the *south-west* gates. All right?'

'You're going to run along the *entire* Candiano walls?' said Claudia.

'Most of them,' said Sancia softly. 'We'll need a distraction. And I can give us a good one.'

Gio studied the black cubes. 'What are those for, Orso? I've never seen someone scrive light like that before.'

'I made those for Ofelia Dandolo,' said Orso. 'Some secret project of hers. Gregor mentioned she'd made some kind of assassin's lorica out of the things . . . A killing machine you can't see coming.'

Gio whistled lowly. 'It'd be handy to have one of those tonight.'

Sancia sank down in her chair. 'What I'd prefer more,' she said, 'is to go to war with the one person who has the most experience in waging it. But he's been taken from us.' She sighed sadly. 'So we'll just have to make do.'

35

Darkness whirled around him. There was the crunch of wood, the crackle of glass, and, somewhere, a cough and a whimper.

'Gregor.'

The scent of putrefaction, of pus, of punctured bowels and hot, wet earth.

'Gregor?'

The swirl of water, the sound of many footfalls, the sound of someone choking.

'Gregor . . .'

He felt something in his chest, something trembling, something squirming. There was something inside him, something alive, something trying to move.

At first he was horrified. But though he could not really think – how could he think, as he was lost in the darkness? – he started to understand.

The thing moving in his chest was his own heart. It was beginning to beat – first gently, anxiously, like a foal taking its first steps. Then its beats grew stronger, more assured.

His lungs begged for air. Gregor Dandolo breathed deep. Water burbled and frothed in countless passageways within him, and he coughed and gagged.

He rolled onto his side – he was lying on something, some kind of stone slab – and vomited. What came forth was canal water – that he could tell by the taste – and a lot of it.

Then he realised – his stomach. It had hurt so much, just a bit ago . . . yet now it didn't hurt at all.

'There we are, dear,' said his mother's voice from somewhere near him. 'There we are . . .'

'M-Mother?' he slurred. He tried to see, but there was something wrong with his eyes – he could only make out streaks and shadows. 'Wh-where are you?'

'I'm here.' Something in the shadows moved. He thought he saw a human figure, robed and carrying a candle – but it was hard to see. 'I'm here right beside you, my love.'

'What . . . what happened to me?' he whispered. His voice was a crackling rasp. 'Where am I? What's wrong with my eyes?'

'Nothing,' she said soothingly. He felt a touch on his brow, her soft, warm palm against his skin. 'They'll get better soon. They just haven't been used for a bit.'

He blinked. He realised his eyes felt cold within their sockets. He tried to touch his face and found he couldn't control his hands or even wriggle his fingers.

'Shh,' said his mother. 'Be calm. Be still.'

He swallowed, and found his tongue felt cold too. 'What's going on?'

'I saved you,' said his mother. 'We saved you.'

'We?' He blinked again, and more of the room came into focus. He saw he was in some kind of long, low cellar, with a vaulted ceiling, and there were people standing around him, people wearing grey robes and bearing small, flickering candles.

But there was something wrong with the walls of the room – and, now that he saw it, the ceiling as well. They all seemed to be moving. Rippling.

This is a dream, Gregor thought. *This must be a dream . . .*

'What happened to me?' he asked.

She sighed slowly. 'The same thing that's happened to you so often, my dear.'

'I don't understand,' he whispered.

'I lost you,' she said. 'But again, you've come back.'

Gregor lay on the stone slab, breathing weakly. And then, slowly, the memories returned to him.

The woman – Estelle Candiano. The knife in his stomach. The swirl of dark water . . .

'I . . . I fell,' he whispered. 'She stabbed me. Estelle Candiano stabbed me.'

'I know,' she said. 'You told us already, Gregor.'

'She . . . she didn't really stab me, did she, Mother?' He managed to move his hand and push himself up into a sitting position.

'No, no,' his mother chided him. 'Lay back down, my love, lay still . . .'

'I . . . I didn't *die*, did I, Mother?' he asked. His mind felt thick in his skull, but he found he could think now, just a bit. 'That would be mad . . . I couldn't die and just . . . just come . . . come back to li—'

'Enough,' said his mother. She reached out and touched the right side of his head with two fingers.

Instantly, Gregor fell still. His body seemed to grow numb around him. He could not move, could not blink. He was trapped within himself.

'Be still, Gregor,' said his mother. 'Be still . . .'

Then his skull began to grow hot . . . Exactly on the right side of his head, right where his mother's fingers touched him. The pain was a low ache at first, but then it got worse, and worse. It felt like his very brains were sizzling on the right side of his head.

And though he had no memory of this ever happening before . . . he could remember someone *describing* a sensation just like this.

Sancia, with Orso and Berenice in the library, saying: *And if the scrivings in my skull get overtaxed, they burn, just burn, like hot lead in my bones . . .*

What's going on? Gregor thought desperately. *What's happening to me?*

'Be still, Gregor,' said his mother. 'Be still . . .'

He tried to move, raging at his dull, distant body, and found he couldn't. The heat in his skull was unbearable now, like his mother's fingers were red-hot irons.

But he could see his mother's face now, barely illuminated by the candle flame. Her eyes were sad, but she did not look surprised, or upset, or anguished by any of this, really. Rather, it was like this bizarre act was a regrettable duty she was quite familiar with.

'What happened to you wounds my heart, my love,' she said softly. 'But I thank you for coming to us now, when we need you the most.'

Gregor's heart fluttered in his chest. *No, no,* he thought. *No, I'm going mad. This is all a dream. This is all just a dream . . .*

Another memory from that same night in the library – Orso, shrugging and saying: *Oh, it probably wasn't just one merchant house . . . If one was trying to scrive humans, they all were. It might still be going on, for all I know . . .*

No, Gregor thought. *No, no, no.*

He remembered himself, saying aloud: *. . . they could scrive a soldier's mind. Make them fearless . . . Make them do despicable things, and then forget they'd ever done them . . .*

No! Gregor thought. *No, it can't be! It can't be!*

And then Berenice, whispering: *They could scrive you so that you could cheat death itself . . .*

And finally, he remembered his own words, spoken to Sancia beside the Gulf, describing what it'd been like after Dantua: *It was like a magic spell had been lifted from my eyes . . .*

His mother watched him, her eyes sad. 'You're remembering now,' she said. 'Aren't you? You usually do about now.'

He remembered her at the Vienzi Foundry, angrily saying: *I killed the project. It was wrong. And we didn't need it anymore anyway.*

Which made one wonder – why would you stop trying to scrive humans? Why say you didn't need it anymore?

Because, thought Gregor slowly, *you'd already figured out how to do it.*

And then, from that same day at Vienzi, he remembered how his mother had wept, and told him: *I did not lose you in Dantua. You survived. As I knew you would, Gregor. As I know you always will . . .*

How did I survive Dantua? he thought, terrified. *Did I survive Dantua? Or did I . . . did I die there?*

'I lost your father,' said his mother. 'I lost your brother. And I could have lost you in the accident, too, my love. Until *he* came . . . He came, and showed me how to save you, to fix you. So I did. But . . . I had to promise some things in return.'

More of Gregor's senses returned. He could see now, see the crowd of robed people bearing candles, the curious, rippling walls in the darkness . . . and there was a whispering sound. At first he thought the robed people were whispering, but that wasn't it . . . It was like they were in some kind of forest with velvety leaves. His ears couldn't make sense of it.

His mother shook herself and cleared her throat. 'Enough. Enough sentiment. Listen to me, Gregor.' Her voice became terribly loud in his ears, overpowering his thoughts. 'Listen to me. Are you hearing me?'

The fear and rage faded from Gregor's mind. She took her fingers away. It was as if a cold, wet quilt were being laid over his thoughts.

He heard himself say quietly, 'Yes. I hear you.'

'You have died,' she said. 'We have saved you, again. But you must do something for us. Do you understand?'

Again, his lips moved and the words sprang from his mouth: 'Yes. I understand.'

'You have confirmed something that we have long suspected,' she said. 'Estelle Candiano is the person behind this monstrous plot. Say her name. Now.'

'Estelle Candiano,' said his voice. His words were mush-mouthed and indistinct.

'Estelle Candiano is going to try something foolish tonight,' said his mother. 'Something that could endanger us all. We've tried to keep our efforts secret, tried to never act in the open – but she's forced our hand. We must respond, and respond directly – though we must maintain whatever deniability we can. She has something in her possession that she does not understand. Are you hearing me?'

'Yes,' he said helplessly. 'I am hearing you.'

His mother grew close. 'It is a box. With a lock.'

'A box,' he repeated. 'With a lock.'

'We have been looking for this box for some time, Gregor,' she said. 'We have suspected that the Candianos possessed it – but we have been unable to discern exactly *where* they had it. But now we know. Because of your efforts, we believe Estelle Candiano is keeping it in the Mountain. Say that.'

'In the Mountain,' he said slowly.

'Listen to me, Gregor,' she whispered. 'Listen carefully – *there is a devil in this box*. Say that.'

Gregor blinked slowly, and whispered, 'There is a devil in this box.'

'Yes. Yes, there is,' she said. 'We cannot let Estelle open it. And if she does what she wishes to do tonight – if she elevates herself, and becomes a Maker, and if she possesses the key – she will have that capability. But we cannot, cannot, *cannot* let her release what sleeps within that box.' Ofelia swallowed, and if Gregor had the mind for it, he would have seen she was clearly terrified. 'Once it waged a war . . . A war to end all wars. We cannot risk such a thing again. We must keep the devil inside the box. Say that.'

'We must keep the devil inside the box,' whispered Gregor.

She leaned close, touching her forehead to his temple. 'I'm so proud of you for this, my love,' she whispered. 'I do not know if it was your intent, or the hand of fate guiding you . . . But Gregor, I . . . I just want you to know, that despite everything – I . . . I love you.'

Gregor blinked slowly, and mindlessly repeated, 'I love you . . .'

Ofelia stood up, her face twisted in shame and disgust, as if pained by his toneless words. 'Enough. When you have fully recovered, you must fight your way to the Mountain, Gregor. Once there, you must find Estelle Candiano. Kill her. And then you must take the key and the box. Eliminate anyone who tries to stop you. We have wrought such powerful, beautiful tools to assist you in this task. You must use them to do what you do best, Gregor, to do what we have made you to do – you must fight.'

She pointed over his shoulder. Gregor turned to look.

But as he looked, he realised two things.

The first was that he suddenly understood why the walls of the room seemed to be rippling, why there was that fluttering and whispering in his ears . . .

The room was full of moths.

Moths swirled and danced and flittered all along the walls, along the ceiling, a sea of white moths flowing around and under and over all of them, their wings like flickering bone.

The second thing he realised was that there was someone standing behind him, and he saw them out of the corner of his eye as he turned, just a glimpse.

It was a man. Maybe. A human figure, tall and thin, wrapped in strips of black cloth like a mummified corpse, and wearing a short, black cloak.

And it was watching him.

Gregor turned to look, but in a flash, the figure was gone. In its place was a column of moths, a storm of them, a swirling vortex of soft, white wings.

He stared at the moths. He realised there was something within the column – they were swirling around something, dancing around it, something white.

The column of moths slowly lifted like a curtain, and he saw.

A wooden stand, and hanging upon it a scrived suit of black armour. Built into one arm was a black, glittering polearm, half massive axe, half giant spear. Built into the other was a huge, round shield, and installed behind it a scrived bolt caster. And set in the centre of the cuirass – a curious black plate.

His mother's voice in his ear: 'Are you ready, my love? Are you ready to save us all?'

Gregor stared at the lorica. He had seen such things before, and he knew what they were meant for: war, and murder.

He whispered, 'I am ready.'

36

On the other side of the city, at the top of the Mountain, Estelle Candiano stared into the mirror and breathed.

Slow, deep breaths, in and out, in and out, filling every part of her lungs. She was doing such delicate work, and the breathing helped steady her hands – if she made one mistake, just one tiny stroke out of place, the whole thing would be ruined.

She dipped the stylus in the ink – heavy with particulates of gold, tin, and copper – looked in the mirror, and continued painting symbols onto her bare chest.

It was tricky work, doing it backwards. But Estelle had practised. She'd had all the time in the world to practise, alone and ignored in the back rooms of the Mountain for nearly a decade.

The common sigils are the language of creation, she thought as she worked. *But Occidental sigils are the language with which God spoke to creation.* She dipped the stylus back in the ink, and began a new line. *And with these commands, with these authorities, one may alter reality if one wishes – provided you are careful.*

One stroke more, then another, finishing the sigils . . . Her left hand was already covered in them, as well as her forearm, upper arm, and shoulder, a twisting, curling lattice of shimmering black symbols, crawling up her arm to swirl about her heart.

There was a cough, and a gurgle. She looked over her shoulder in the mirror at the figure lying in the bed behind her. A small, wet, beady-eyed man, gasping for breath.

'Please stay still, Father,' she said softly. 'And hold on.'

Then she glanced at the clock on the wall. Ten twenty now.

Her eyes darted to the window. The sprawling nightscape of Tevanne stretched out below the Mountain. Yet all seemed quiet, and still.

'Captain Riggo!' she called.

Footsteps, and then the office door opened. Captain Riggo walked in and saluted. He did not glance at Tribuno Candiano, wheezing and lying there in his soiled sheets. He did not pause at the sight of a bare-breasted Estelle, painting symbols upon her skin. Captain Riggo possessed the virtue that Tevanne valued most of all: the ability to ignore what was right in front of his eyes for a huge sum of money.

'Yes, ma'am,' he said.

Estelle sat perfectly still, stylus hovering above her skin. 'Is anything happening out there?'

'No, ma'am.'

'Not on the campo?'

'No, ma'am.'

'Not in the Commons?'

'Not as far as we can tell, ma'am.'

'And our forces?'

'They sit ready, and can be deployed with but a word, ma'am.'

Her eyes narrowed. '*My* word.'

'Yes, ma'am.'

She considered this. 'You are dismissed,' she said. 'Notify me the moment you hear anything. *Anything.*'

'Yes, ma'am.' He smartly turned, strode out, and shut the door.

Estelle resumed painting the symbols on her body. Her father gasped, smacked his lips, and fell silent.

She made one stroke, then another . . .

Then she froze.

Estelle blinked for a moment, then sat up and looked around the room.

Empty. Empty except for her and Father, that was, and all of his and Tomas's antiquities, sitting on the massive stone desk.

'Hm,' she said, troubled.

For a moment she'd suddenly had the strangest and most intense feeling that there had been someone *else* in the room with them – a third person, standing just behind her, watching her closely.

She took a breath, looking around – and then her eye fell on the curious old box that Tomas had stolen before Orso Ignacio could get it, the cracked, ancient, lexicon-looking thing with the gold lock.

Estelle Candiano looked at the box, at the lock, at the keyhole. An idea wriggled its way into her mind, wild and insane.

The keyhole is an eye. It watches your every move.

'That's mad,' she said softly.

Then, louder and with more assurance, as if hoping the box might hear her: 'That's mad.'

The box, of course, did nothing to acknowledge this comment. She looked at it for a moment longer, then turned and resumed painting the sigils on her breast. *After my elevation*, she thought, *perhaps all these old tools Father dug up will make sense. Perhaps I will crack open that box, and see what treasures spill forth.*

Then her eye paused on the object placed right next to the box – the large, oddly toothed key she'd taken off Orso's man, with the butterfly-shaped head. It had been useful in giving her the last few sigils she'd needed to complete the ritual, but she still didn't know the full extent of its nature.

Or perhaps I don't need to break the box open, she thought. *We shall see – won't we?*

❦

37

Out in the streets of the Commons, just east of the Candiano walls, Sancia and the Scrappers moved.

'I wish you could turn those damned shadows *off*,' said Giovanni, panting as they ran through the alleys. 'It's like I have a literal blind spot running alongside me.'

'Just shut up and run, Gio,' said Sancia. Though she found it odd herself, frankly. Orso had affixed a few samples of the shadow materials to a leather jerkin for her – a slap-dash, laughably shoddy solution – but she was now veiled in constant shadow, and it was difficult for her to see what her hands or feet were doing.

Finally they approached the eastern Candiano gates. They slowed and crept along the side of a tottering rookery, peering beyond. Sancia saw the gleam of helmets in the gate towers, huddling in the windows. Probably a dozen men, each with high-powered espringals that could punch a hole in her wide enough to toss a melon through.

'Ready?' whispered Claudia.

'I guess,' said Sancia.

'We'll go down this alley,' Claudia said, pointing backward, 'to draw their eyes away from you. We'll wait two minutes, then fire. The instant you see it, you run.'

'Got it,' said Sancia.

'Good. Good luck.'

Sancia ran along the rookery to the side facing the path to the Candiano gates. Then she pressed her back to the wood and waited, counting out the seconds.

When she got to two minutes, she crouched. *Any minute now . . .*

Then there was a *hiss* over her shoulder. Something flew high up above the building tops – and then the sky erupted with lights.

Sancia sprinted forward, pumping her arms and legs as hard as she could. She was aware that the Scrappers' stun bomb – cleverly attached to a scrived bolt – would only last for a handful of seconds. Even though she was little more than a drop of shadow to the naked eye, that didn't mean she'd be safe without that distraction.

The lights behind her died, and then there was a terrific *pop!*

The walls were twenty feet away. The last few strides felt like they took an agonisingly long time – but then she made it, quietly sliding to a stop against their massive stone face.

She heard a voice above, from the guards' tower: 'What the *hell* was that?'

She waited. She heard murmuring, but little more.

Praise God, she thought to herself. Then she carefully, carefully crept along the walls toward the gates.

She slid up to them and flexed that odd muscle in her mind. The huge, bronze gates erupted with light, two vast, rippling panes of white luminescence, hanging in space.

She looked at them carefully. She could see a hint of their commands within them, their nature, their restrictions. *I sure as shit hope I'm right about this*, she thought.

She took a breath, and placed a bare hand on the door.

< . . . TALL AND STRONG AND RESOLUTE, WE STAND VIGILANT AND WATCHFUL, AWAITING THE MESSAGES, AWAITING THE SIGNS, AWAITING THE CALL TO BEGIN FULL PIVOT INWARDS, OUR HIDES AS HARD AND DENSE AS COLD IRON . . . >

She flinched at the enormous sound of it. The campo gates were undoubtedly the biggest thing she'd attempted to fool yet. Yet she persisted, and asked, <*So you're not allowed to open unless you get the signals?*>

<*FIRST THE SIGNAL OF THE LIEUTENANT, THE TWIST OF CRYSTAL,*> bellowed the gates. <*THEN THE FRICTION CAUSED BY THE ROPE CARRIED BY THE SERGEANT AT WATCH. THEN ALL WATCHMEN PRESENT MUST SHIFT THEIR SAFETY SWITCHES. THEN THE SERGEANT AT WATCH MUST UNLOCK AND CRANK TH—*>

<*Okay, question,*> said Sancia to the gates. <*Can you pivot outward?*>

There was a long silence.

<*PIVOT OUTWARD?*> asked the gates.

<*Yeah.*>

<*THERE IS NO INDICATION THAT THIS IS . . . NOT POSSIBLE,*> said the gates.

<*Would that count as opening? Would pivoting outward require any of your safety switches?*>

<*CHECKING . . . HM. ALL SAFETY AND SECURITY CHECKS RELATE SPECIFICALLY TO OPENING, THE PROCESS OF OPENING INWARD.*>

<*Would you be willing to try opening outward?*>

<*THERE . . . IS NOTHING INDICATING I SHOULD NOT.*>

<*Great. Then here's my idea . . .* >

She told it what to do. It listened, and agreed. And then she crept away, down the walls to the next set of gates.

And the next, and the next.

Giovanni and Claudia crouched in the alley and watched as the tiny dot of shadow silently slipped along the base of the Candiano walls.

'Did . . . did she *do* anything?' said Giovanni, baffled.

Claudia pulled out a spyglass and examined the gates. 'I don't see anything.'

'Did we just risk our necks for that damned girl to do *nothing*? I'll be pissed as hell if that's the case!'

'We didn't risk our necks, Gio. We just shot a firework into the damned air. Sancia's the one literally running along the watch-towers.' She peered along the walls as Sancia stopped at the next gates, paused, and continued on. 'Though I honestly have no idea what she's doing.'

Gio sighed. 'To think of all the mad shit we've had to eat to get to here. We could have left Tevanne ages ago, Claudia! We could have been on board a ship right now, headed toward some remote island paradise! A ship full of *sailors.* Sailors, Claudia! Young, sun-darkened men with thick, rippling shoulders from heaving huge ropes around all da—'

Then there was a sharp, warbling scream.

Claudia took the spyglass away from her eye. 'What the hell was that?' She looked around, but couldn't see anything. 'Gio, do you see any—'

Then another scream, one of pure, naked terror. The screams seemed to be coming from the Candiano gates just ahead of them.

'Is . . . is this part of Sancia's doing?' asked Gio. He leaned forward. 'Wait! Oh my God . . . Someone's *up* there, Claudia . . .'

She lifted her spyglass and looked at the Candiano gates.

Her mouth fell open. 'Holy shit.'

A man was standing atop the gate towers of the Candiano gates, his boots perched on the edge of the wall. He was wearing some kind of contraption, like a black suit of armour, except one arm had been modified to be a large, rounded shield, and the other arm had been modified to hold some kind of massive, retractable polearm . . . Yet it was difficult to see him clearly, for every movement he made was obscured in darkness. The only reason she could see him at all was because there was a bright scrived light hanging just below him on the wall.

It took her a moment to realise what she was looking at. She'd only ever read about such things, a type of particularly notorious shock weapon deployed abroad in the wars.

'A *lorica*?' she said aloud, astonished.

'Who the shit is *that*?' Gio asked. 'Did *we* tell him to be there?'

Claudia stared at the man, huge and gleaming in the dark metal contraption. She saw there was a dead body lying on the walls before him, horribly mangled – presumably this had been the screamer, whom she now thought had had plenty of reasons to scream.

It can't be, she thought. *What the hell is going on?*

She watched as the man leapt forward, his body flying up five, ten, fifteen feet – *Definitely a real lorica,* Claudia thought – and then he crashed down, his polearm licking out like a glittering black whip . . .

She hadn't even noticed that there were guards up on the gate towers with him. Yet then there was a massive splash of blood, and she realised that the man had used his polearm to almost completely vivisect a Candiano guard who'd been sprinting at him, rapier in hand.

Three more Candiano guards poured out of the tower onto the gate pathway before the man, espringals raised. The man in the lorica flicked his shield up just in time to catch the volley of bolts, and he started moving forward, perfectly crouched behind his shield, inching forward toward the three men pouring bolts into him.

He stopped, seeming to sense that the men needed to reload. Then he swung his shield arm out, and something . . . happened.

It was hard to see. There was just a burst of glimmering metal in the air, the Candiano guards shuddered as if struck by lightning, and they fell. But Claudia saw that their bodies were now curiously rent and torn . . .

She focused on the man in the lorica as he stood up, and saw that his shield was not just a shield: it had been modified so that the back half was also a scrived bolt caster. Probably not accurate over long distances – but nasty up close.

Giovanni stared, horrified. 'What do we do?'

She thought about it, and watched as the man leapt off the top of the Candiano gates into the campo.

'Hell,' she said. 'He's not our problem! So just sit tight, I guess!'

⁂

Berenice and Orso huddled in the scrived carriage, staring at the immense Candiano gates ahead. The streets around them were abandoned, like there was a curfew on.

'Everything's . . . quiet,' said Berenice.

'Yes,' said Orso. 'Scrumming creepy as hell, isn't it?'

'Yes, sir,' said Berenice in a small voice. She craned her head forward, peering at the walls. 'I do hope Sancia's all right.'

'I'm sure she's fine,' said Orso. 'Maybe.'

Berenice said nothing.

Orso glanced at her out of the side of his eye. 'You and she seem to get along all right.'

'Ah. Thank you, sir?'

'You do great things together,' said Orso. 'Crack the Cattaneo. Fabricate whole new scriving definitions in hours. That's . . . That's something.'

She hesitated. 'Thank you, sir.'

He sniffed and looked around. 'It's dumb as hell, all this,' he said. 'I keep thinking this could have been avoided. I could have stopped it. If I'd told Tribuno what I thought about his dumb shit. If I'd . . . I'd been more diligent in my pursuits of Estelle. I let my pride get wounded when she turned me down. Pride . . . it's so often an excuse for people to be weak.' He coughed, and said, 'Anyways . . . if a young person were to ask me advice of a . . . a *personal* nature, I'd advise they not sit and passively watch opportunities go by. That's what I'd say – if, mind, if a young person were to ask me advice, of a personal nature.'

There was a long silence.

'I see, sir,' said Berenice. 'But . . . not every young person is as passive as you may think.'

'Aren't they?' said Orso. 'Good. Very goo—'

'There!' said Berenice. 'Look!'

She pointed at the walls. A tiny pool of shadow slipped along the bottom of the white walls, up to the huge towering gates.

'Is that . . . her?' said Orso, squinting.

The pool of shadow stayed at the base of the gates for a moment before slipping back down the way it came, disappearing behind a tall rookery.

'I don't know,' said Berenice. 'I think so though?'

They waited, and waited.

'Should something be happening now?' said Orso.

Then they both jumped in fright as a wall of shadow leapt at them out of an alley.

'Goddamn it!' said Sancia's voice, floating out of the darkness. 'It's me! Calm down!' She was panting hard. 'Damn . . . That was a *lot* of walls, and a lot of gates.' She climbed inside – or Orso *thought* she did, it was so dark it was hard to tell – and collapsed in the back of the carriage.

'Is it done?' said Orso.

'Yeah,' gasped Sancia.

'And when does your clever plan start?'

'Simple,' said Sancia. 'When you hear the explosions.'

Claudia and Giovanni crouched in the shadows of the street, watching the Candiano gates. Then they heard a sound – a clattering, a clanking.

'What's that?' said Gio.

Claudia pointed, dumbstruck. 'It's the gates, Gio.'

They watched as the huge gate doors . . . trembled. They *quivered*, like they were the skin of a drum that had just received a powerful blow. Then they began rattling, at first quietly, then much, much louder, until it strained their ears, even from where they were.

'Sancia,' said Claudia. 'What the hell did you *do*?'

And then the gates broke.

The two halves erupted open, swinging outward with a force like a raging river, snapping all the locks along their middle. They pivoted a full 180 degrees, slamming into the campo walls and the watchtowers on either side of them, and they struck the walls hard enough to make them crack and start to crumble – a stunning feat, considering the campo walls had been scrived to be preternaturally durable. For a moment the two halves of the gates just stood there, smashed into the walls, before the reverberating momentum caused them to slowly, slowly topple forward, which pulled down a lot of the walls with them. They slammed into the ground hard enough to send a fine spray of mud and dust surging throughout the entire city block.

Claudia and Giovanni coughed and covered their faces. The

Commons lit up with cries and shouts – but this wasn't loud enough to cover up a new sound: a rattling and clattering from the next set of gates, just south of the fallen walls.

'Oh shit,' said Gio. 'She did it to *all* of them, didn't she?'

Orso and Berenice sat up, startled, as the immense *crack* echoed through the night skies.

'I told the gates opening outward didn't count as opening,' said Sancia in the backseat. 'The hard part was getting them to wait.' She sniffed. 'Should be . . . oh, one every minute or so for a while.'

In the Mountain, Estelle Candiano heard the crash and looked up. 'What in *hell*?' she said aloud.

She looked down at herself. She'd finished covering her arm and chest in the appropriate sigils, and she did not want to smudge them any.

Still . . . That was worth investigating.

She walked over to the windows and looked out at the dark ramble of Tevanne. She immediately saw what had happened: one of the northeastern gates appeared to have totally collapsed. Which . . . should have been impossible. Those gates had been designed by her father. They should have withstood a damned monsoon.

'What in all th—'

Then, as she watched, there was a tremendous *crack*, and the gate south down the wall from that one suddenly burst outward. The walls around it cracked and began to crumble apart.

Her mouth twisted with rage. 'Orso,' she spat. 'This is you, isn't it? What in *hell* are you trying to pull?'

The intense cracks shot through the Commons with a curiously steady rhythm, like a lightning storm touching down every minute. Orso flinched each time. Soon the sky above the eastern campo was a haze of dust, and the Commons were screaming in panic.

'Sancia,' said Orso quietly. 'Did you take down the *entire eastern walls*?'

'I should have, when this is all over with,' said Sancia. 'Should give all those campo soldiers a lot to defend. And it'll be somewhere far from here. A decent distraction.'

'A . . . a *distraction*?' he cried. 'Girl . . . girl, you've scrumming killed the Candiano campo! You've killed my old house in one night!'

'Eh,' said Sancia. 'I just aired it out a bit.'

⊹

Estelle Candiano threw on a white shirt just as Captain Riggo threw open the door and charged in.

'What in *hell* is going on out there, Captain?' she demanded.

'I do not know, ma'am,' he said, 'but I came to ask if I could mobilise our reserves in order to investigate and respond.'

There was another sharp *crack* and the rumble of falling walls. Captain Riggo cringed ever so slightly.

'But . . . but what do you *think* is happening, Captain?'

'In my professional estimation?' He thought about it. 'It would appear to be a siege, ma'am. Many gates destroyed so that we have to split our forces.'

'Damn it all,' she said. She looked at the clock. She had just over thirty minutes until midnight. *I'm so close,* she thought. *I'm so damned close!*

'Ma'am?' said Captain Riggo. 'The reserves?'

'Yes, yes!' she snapped. 'Throw everything we have at them! Whatever the hell is happening, I want it stopped! Now!'

He bowed. 'Yes, ma'am.' Then he turned and smartly strode away, shutting the door behind him.

Estelle walked over to the windows and stared out at the damage. The northeastern half of the campo was almost completely obscured with smoke now. She imagined she could hear screaming from somewhere out in the dark.

Whatever is happening, she thought, *I just need it to last more than thirty minutes. After that – nothing else will matter.*

The two Scrappers watched as the Candiano campo walls dissolved, bit by bit.

'Well,' said Claudia. 'I think we're done here, yeah?'

'I think so.' Giovanni wrinkled his nose. 'Now to file all of Orso's paperwork – yes?'

She sighed. 'Yes. And to buy his property. Off from one mad plan, and on to the next one.'

'You know, we could just take the money he gave us and run,' said Giovanni lightly.

'True,' said Claudia. 'But then everyone else would die.'

'Well. Yes. I guess we wouldn't want that.'

Together, they fled into the darkness.

38

Sancia leaned forward as the gates ahead began to rattle. 'Good,' she said. 'I told them to go last. The second those things pop open and the way's clear, you speed in as fast as you can, all right?'

'Oh shit,' said Orso. A bead of sweat ran down his temple as he gripped the pilot's wheel.

'Don't go too fast,' said Sancia. 'Because there's going to be shrapnel. Get me?'

'You . . . you are really not helping here,' snapped Orso.

'Just go when I say go.'

They watched the gates rattle, tremble, and shake – and then, like all the others, they burst open, ripping apart the walls on either side.

A massive tsunami of dust flooded toward them. Sancia shielded her eyes with one hand. She was now mostly blind – but she could still see with her scriving sight.

She waited a moment. Then she said, 'Go. Go now.'

'But I can't see!' said Orso, sputtering.

'Orso, just scrumming go, *go*!'

Orso shoved the acceleration lever forward and the carriage took off, hurtling into the dust. Sancia squinted and peered ahead, reading the scrivings written into the buildings on either side of the street, glimpsing the massive, rippling landscape of designs and sigils encoded into everything.

'The road curves slightly to the left up ahead,' said Sancia. 'No, not *that* much – there. Yes. Good.'

Finally they broke free of the dust cloud. Orso exhaled with relief. 'Oh, thank God . . .'

'No soldiers in sight,' said Berenice. 'Streets are clear.'

'All on the eastern wall,' said Sancia. 'Just as I'd hoped.'

'And we're almost there.' Orso peered out the window at the street names. 'Just a little farther . . . Here! Here's the spot!' He slammed on the brakes. 'Exactly a mile and a half from the Mountain!'

They stared ahead at the vast dome rising among the towers. Then they all scrambled out. Sancia started affixing the gravity rig to her body, and Orso checked his twinned heating chamber. 'Everything looks good here,' he said.

'Turn it on,' said Sancia.

'I'll turn it on once *you're* ready,' he said. 'Just to be safe.'

She paused, glancing at him, but continued buckling on the gravity rig. 'Goddamn, I hope I have this dumbarse thing on right,' she muttered.

'Let me see,' said Berenice. She reviewed the various straps, fussing and tutting and adjusting them. 'I think you're set,' she said. 'Except perhaps this one here.'

She tightened one buckle on Sancia's shoulder. Thoughtlessly, Sancia reached up and grabbed her hand, her own bare palm gripping Berenice's fingers.

Berenice paused. The two looked at each other.

Sancia swallowed. She wondered what to say, and how to say it; how to articulate how impossible touch had been for so long – real, genuine, human touch; and how, after tonight, she wanted to touch no one but Berenice; how hungry she felt for Berenice's enthusiastic glow, this raw desire to snatch a piece away for herself, like a demigod stealing fire from a mountaintop.

But before she could start to fumble with the words, Berenice just said, 'Make it back.'

Sancia nodded. 'I'll try,' she said hoarsely.

'Don't try.' Berenice leaned in, and suddenly kissed her. Quite hard. 'Do it. All right?'

Sancia stood there for a moment, dazed. 'All right.'

Orso cleared his throat. 'Listen, uh – I don't want to interject here, but we *are* dealing with, you know, the apocalypse, or thereabout.'

'Yeah, yeah,' said Sancia. She released Berenice and took stock of her gear – some stun bombs, darts, and a long, thin length of rope – and breathed deep. 'I'm ready.'

Orso turned the bronze dial on the side of the heating chamber.

The gravity rig grew bright on Sancia's chest.

'Shit,' she said. 'Oh boy.'

'It's still working, yes?' said Orso anxiously.

<Please provide LOCATION and DENSITY of MASS!> chirped the rig.

'Yeah,' said Sancia. 'It's working, all right.'

'Then do it! Now, now, now!'

Sancia took another deep breath and told the rig, *<Location of mass is up. Density is of six Earths.>*

<Great!> said the rig. *<Enforce the effects now?>*

<No. Enforce the effects the instant my feet leave the ground.>

<Sure!>

She situated her feet and dipped her legs down into a crouching position.

As she did, the gravity around her . . . changed.

Things began to float around her: pebbles, grains of sand, shreds of leaves . . .

'Berenice?' said Orso nervously.

'Ah . . . I believe this is upthrust,' Berenice said. 'Like – step into a bathtub, and the water level rises. I didn't have time to control for that.'

'Shit,' said Sancia. 'Here I go.'

Then she sank lower, and jumped.

And she flew.

Orso watched as Sancia seemed to be obscured by a fine mist. Then he realised that the mist was actually more motes of dust and sand, all hanging suspended in the air around her, cheerily denying gravity.

Then her legs flexed, and things seemed to . . . explode.

It was like something huge and invisible had fallen down nearby, causing a huge gust of wind and a massive swirl of sand. But of course, there was nothing there – at least as far as Orso was aware, but it was hard to verify since the next thing he knew he and Berenice were flying arse-over-head down the street.

He crashed into the cobblestones, coughing, and sat up. 'Shit!' he said. Then he peered up. He thought he could make out a tiny dot arcing across the night skies toward the Mountain. 'It worked? Did it really *work*?'

'I would say so,' said Berenice wearily, sitting up on the other side of the street. Groaning, she stood and hobbled over to Orso's empty heating chamber. 'It's giving off a lot of heat . . . I know scriving defies reality, but it seems like you've defied a lot more reality than normal tonight. Now what do we do?'

'Now?' said Orso. 'Now we run like hell.'

'We run? Why?'

'I thought I mentioned this to you . . .' said Orso. 'Or maybe I mentioned it to the Scrappers. I forget. Anyway, scriving a chunk of reality is really *very* hard to manage. Tribuno and I found that out a long time ago. So although this thing is stable now . . .' He knocked on the side of the carriage. 'It won't be for long.'

She stared at him, horrified. 'What do you mean?'

'I mean in about ten minutes, this thing is either going to explode or implode, I honestly don't know which. But I know I don't want to be around to see it.'

'*What!*' she screamed. 'Then . . . then what'll happen to Sancia?'

'Well, if she's still flying . . . then she will *stop* flying,' he said. He saw her outraged stare. 'Well, the girl's obviously going to make it there in *way* less than ten minutes! I mean, look at her, she's hauling arse! It was just a gamble I had to make!'

'You could have scrumming told us this!' shouted Berenice.

'And what would that have done?' said Orso. 'Probably made everyone yell a bunch, just as you're doing now. Now, come on, Berenice, let's go!' He turned and sprinted down the street, back to the gates.

39

Captain Riggo!' shouted Estelle.

Again – the footsteps, the door, the salute. 'Yes, ma'am?'

'Have we encountered anything in the campo?' she asked.

'I've not heard back yet, ma'am,' he said. 'But from my vantage point . . . I've yet to see much in the way of conflict.'

She shook her head. 'It's a diversion. A goddamn diversion. They're coming here, *here*! I know it in my bones. How many soldiers do we have in the Mountain, Riggo?'

'At least four dozen, ma'am.'

'I want three dozen up here,' said Estelle. 'Two dozen in the hallways, and a dozen in here with me. I'm the target – me, or the antiquities.' She pointed at the desk, upon which sat the box, the imperiat, and the key, along with dozens and dozens of books and other artefacts. 'And we can't move all those now. So we have to be ready.'

'I see, ma'am,' said Riggo. 'I'll deploy your orders immediately.'

Above the campo, Sancia screamed.

Screaming was all she could do, really. So many of her higher levels of thought had just been abruptly obliterated by the sudden acceleration, the raging press of the wind and the reek of smoke, that she could only react to her situation in the dumbest and most instinctual of ways – which meant screaming.

She was rising so fast, so damned *fast.* She blinked tears out of her eyes, and saw she was already far, far, far above the city. Too far, really – and she also wasn't going anywhere close to the Mountain.

If I don't stop this thing, she thought, *I'm going to sail past the damn clouds!*

Sancia placed both hands on the plate and tried to tell it to slow down.

<*Hi!*> squealed the rig. <*I am maintaining FLOW and MASS position as previously indica—*>

<*Additional position for MASS!*> Sancia screamed at it.

<*Excellent! Super! What is additional position for new MASS?*>

<*New position is there!*> She mentally directed the rig at the Mountain.

<*Great!*> chirped the plates. <*And DENSITY, and STRENGTH of FLOW?*>

<*Whatever will get me down gently!*> said Sancia.

<*Need specificity of STRENGTH of FLOW!*>

<*Ohh . . . Shit. Uh, twice as much as Earth's regular gravity?*>

<*Got it!*>

Their ascent slowed, but not much.

<*Increase STRENGTH of FLOW by twenty per cent,*> she said.

<*Okay!*>

Their ascent slowed more.

<*Another twenty per cent,*> she said.

<*Sure!*>

Then her ascent stopped . . . and she slowly started being redirected toward the Mountain, lightly drifting down to the huge black dome.

She'd have to make more adjustments to make it there, she knew. But she was getting the hang of this. The gravity rig was incomprehensibly powerful – probably more powerful than Estelle's version, since Berenice had left out all the calibrated controls. If Sancia screwed up the directions or the power too much, the thing would basically be a devastating weapon.

But then, she had been counting on that.

Quietly, gently, she sailed toward the Mountain.

'Ma'am!' called a soldier. 'Something's coming!'

Surrounded by a dozen soldiers, Estelle Candiano peered through the gaps in their shoulders at the office windows. 'Something?' she said.

'Yes, ma'am! I . . . I think I saw something flying through the sky?'

Estelle glanced at the clock on the wall – twenty minutes to go. She'd need only one minute to do this, the lost minute between one day and the next. That was what her research had indicated – you made yourself powerful while the world had its back turned on you.

'That might be them,' she said. 'Get ready.'

The soldiers prepared themselves, checking their weapons, unsheathing their swords. Estelle looked down at her father, lying in the bed beside her. Her fingers gripped the golden dagger, sweat running down her temples. She was so close. Soon her knife would pierce the breast of this wretched, thoughtless man, and start a chain reaction that would . . .

She cringed. She knew what would happen – it would kill most of the people on the Candiano campo. All the scrivers, all the merchants, all the workers who'd laboured under Tomas, and, before him, her father . . .

They could have stopped this, she thought angrily. *They knew what Tomas was, what my father was. They knew what these men had done to me, to the world. And yet they did nothing.*

She looked up through the round window in the roof of her father's office, and then she saw it – a tiny black dot, sailing across the face of the moon

'That's it!' she cried. 'There it is! I've no idea what it is, but it's got to be them!'

The soldiers looked up and took positions around her.

'Come on,' said Estelle, staring up. 'Come on! We're ready for you, Orso. We're *ready* for y—'

Then the doors to the office exploded behind them, and all hell broke loose.

Estelle did not initially understand what was happening. She just heard a scream, and then droplets of something warm rained down on her. She blinked, looked down at herself, and saw she was covered in blood – apparently blood from someone on the other side of the room.

She dumbly turned, and saw something had erupted into the office . . . maybe. It was hard to see in all the darkness, which seemed to cling to the thing like moss to a tree branch. But she thought she saw a man-form in there – and she *definitely* saw a huge black polearm snap out from the depths of that darkness and slash one of her soldiers from shoulder to chest, sending another wave of blood splashing over her.

Her soldiers shouted in rage and charged the shadow-man. The shadow-man leapt toward them with terrifying speed and grace – and as he did, Estelle saw the hallways beyond. She saw they were covered in blood, and the headless corpse of Captain Riggo lay ravaged and mutilated on the floor.

'Oh hell,' said Estelle. She dropped to the ground and crawled to the desk with the artefacts.

✣

Gregor Dandolo did not think. He could not think. He did not need to think. He only moved.

He moved within the lorica, directing its momentum, its gravity, allowing it to hurtle him through the huge office. He flicked his right arm out, the telescoping polearm extending with a liquid grace, like the tongue of a frog stretching for a dragonfly in midflight. Its huge, thick blade cut through a soldier's raised arm and the top half of his head like they were made of grass, and the man collapsed.

Get to the Mountain, said the words in Gregor's mind. *Kill the woman. Get the box. Get the key. Destroy anything that tries to stop you.*

The words echoed over and over again inside of him, until they became him, forming the sum of his soul.

Gregor was still flying through the air, so he twisted his body, reaching down with his leg to scrape the toes of one boot along the floor. He artfully drew himself to a stop, standing in the middle of the office, surrounded by soldiers. He stood in the huge war machine, breathing hard, felt scrived bolts clacking and clicking as they uselessly bit into his armour. He knew that the greatest threat to a soldier in a lorica was the lorica itself: use it poorly, and it would destroy you, literally tearing you apart. Use it well, and you could destroy nearly anything.

He slapped a soldier aside with his shield and slashed forward with his polearm. *I have done this before*, he kept thinking, over and over again. It was one of the few thoughts his mind could process. *I have done this before. Many, many times before.*

He whirled and dodged and ducked and cut through the soldiers with balletic ease.

I was made for this, he thought. *I was made for war. I was always, always, always made for war.*

This fact was written within him. It was as inarguable as the heaviness of stones, as the brightness of the sun. He knew this. He knew this was who he was, what he was, and what he was to do in this world.

But although Gregor Dandolo could not truly think, could not really process anything resembling a genuine thought, he was forced to wonder, absently and dreamily . . .

If he was truly made for war, why were his cheeks hot and wet with tears? And why did the side of his head hurt so, so, *so* much?

He stopped and took stock of the situation. He ignored the whimpering old man on the bed – he was no threat – but as he fought, he looked for the woman, the woman, always the woman . . . There were two soldiers left.

One raised an espringal at him, but Gregor leapt forward and batted aside the man's body with his shield, sending him crashing into a wall. His polearm flicked out and gutted the man before he could even hit the floor. The second solider screamed and ran at Gregor's exposed back, but Gregor extended his shield arm, pointed the bolt caster, and released a full volley of scrived fléchettes into the man's face. He crumpled to the floor.

Gregor retracted the polearm. Then he looked around the office. There seemed to be no one else except for the whimpering old man on the bed.

Get to the Mountain, he thought. *Kill the woman. Get the box. Get the key. Destroy anything that tries to stop you.*

He saw the box and the key sitting on the desk.

He walked over to the desk, shook off the glove holding his polearm, and let the weapon fall to the floor. Then he picked up the big golden key.

As he did, he heard a clicking sound behind the desk.

Gregor leaned forward, and saw: the woman was there – Estelle Candiano. She sat huddled on the ground, adjusting some device – it appeared to be some kind of large golden pocket watch.

He raised his shield arm, aiming the bolt caster at her.

'*There* we go,' she said. She hit a switch on the pocket watch's side.

Gregor tried to fire the bolt caster – but he found he couldn't. His lorica was frozen: it was like he was wearing a statue rather than a suit of armour, and its penumbra of shadow had abruptly vanished.

Estelle let out a long, relieved sigh. 'Well!' she said, standing. 'That was close.' She looked him over. 'Interesting rig you have here . . . Are *you* Orso's man? He'd always thought about playing with light.'

Gregor kept trying to fire the bolt caster, flexing every muscle he had against his suit of armour, but it was useless. She seemed to have somehow turned the entire thing off.

She glanced at the big golden pocket watch, frowned, and raised it, running it alongside Gregor's body like a dowsing rod searching for water. The pocket watch let out a loud, piercing shriek when it passed over Gregor's helmet.

'My word,' said Estelle. 'You *aren't* Orso's man – not if you've got an Occidental tool in your head.' She placed a hand on his cuirass, grunted, and shoved him backward onto the floor, his suit of armour clattering and clanking as he struck the stones.

She walked over to one of her dead soldiers, pulled out the man's knife, and then straddled Gregor. 'Now,' she said. 'Let's see who you are.'

She cut through the straps fastening on Gregor's face plate, and pulled it away.

She stared at him. 'What in *hell*?' she said. 'What are *you* doing here?'

Gregor said nothing. His face was placid, blank, empty. He just strained and strained and strained against the armour, trying his hardest to strike the woman, to fill her with bolts, to rend her in two – but the lorica wouldn't budge.

'Tell me,' she demanded. 'Tell me how you got here. Tell me how you survived. Who are you *working* for?'

Still he said nothing.

She lifted the dagger and leaned over him. 'Tell me,' she said softly. 'I've got ten minutes until midnight. Ten minutes to find out.' She found a gap in his armour, and stabbed the blade deep up into his left bicep. He felt the pain, but his mind told him to disregard it. 'Don't worry, brave soldier – I'll find a way to make you screa—'

Then she paused. Probably because it sounded like someone was already screaming – and the sound was coming from above.

Estelle looked up, through the round window in the ceiling.

There was a speck of black in front of the moon that seemed to be getting . . . bigger.

Estelle watched, bewildered, as a filthy, dusty, screaming girl in black came hurtling out of the sky to land on the skylight.

'. . . *aaaaaAAAAAAH-OOF!*' said the girl, landing on the window with a solid thud.

Estelle's mouth fell open. She whispered, 'What . . .'

The girl rose up, shook herself, and looked down through the window at them. And though Gregor's mind was overtaken with his commands – *kill the woman, take the key, take the box* – he couldn't help but recognise her.

I know this girl . . . But did she just fly? Out of the sky?

Sancia stared down at the surreal sight below her. Tribuno Candiano's office appeared to be filled with mangled corpses – one of which seemed to be Gregor Dandolo, who lay bleeding on the floor with blank, empty eyes, clad in a suit of black armour. Estelle Candiano sat on his chest, holding a dagger, and she was staring up at Sancia in shock. Beside them was Tribuno's desk, upon which sat Valeria's box – and though she couldn't see Clef or the imperiat, surely they were in there as well.

She wanted to leap in and save Clef – the person who, for so long, had been her closest friend, her most trusted ally. Her heart hurt to think of losing or hurting him, after all this pain. But she knew there were greater things at risk right now – and she knew that someone as powerless as she would only ever have one shot at taking out someone like Estelle.

One day I'll live a life that doesn't force me to make such cold-blooded decisions, she thought. *But today is not that day.*

She touched the dome of the Mountain with a finger.

<*Oh, it's you!*> said the Mountain's voice in her mind. <*I am sorry, but . . . unable to permit entry. Your sample is not logged.*>

<*No, I get it,*> said Sancia. <*I just wanted to say I'm sorry.*>

<*Sorry? For . . . action?*>

<*Yeah. This one, specifically.*>

She took her hand away, pulled off the gravity plates, and shut her eyes. <*New directions for MASS.*>

<*Hooray!*> said the plates. <*What is new entry for MASS?*>

<*You.*>

There was a pause.

<*Me?*> said the plates. <*I am entry for MASS?*>

<*Yeah. And the STRENGTH of FLOW is maximum.*>

<*Maximum STRENGTH of FLOW?*>

<*Yes.*>

<*Are you SURE?*>

<*Yes.*>

<*Ohhh,*> said the plates. <*Well . . . All right!*>

<*Good.*> She opened her eyes as the plates began softly vibrating. Then she slammed the plates down on the window.

She locked eyes with Estelle Candiano, grinned, and waved goodbye. Then she pulled out her thin cord of rope, looped it around the neck of a gargoyle, and started rappelling down the side of the Mountain.

⁂

Estelle stared up at the device sitting just above her on the opposite side of the window. She recognised it immediately, of course. She had coaxed Tomas into designing the damned thing over years, after all.

She watched as the gravity plates started vibrating faster and faster, like a cymbal being struck again and again . . . and then it began to glow a soft, blue light.

The building around her began to groan. Clouds of dust floated down as the vaulted ceiling shuddered and moaned.

'Shit,' said Estelle. She staggered off the armoured man's chest and dove for the imperiat. She'd not exactly had a lot of time to acquaint herself with the device – but she'd have to make do now.

⁂

On the streets outside the Candiano campo wall, Orso and Berenice took turns peering through a spyglass at the Mountain. It looked like someone had turned on a new light, shining on its surface – a blue one, glowing with a queerly fluttering light.

Orso peered at it. 'What the hell is tha—'

He stopped – because then, with a *pop* that they could hear even from where they stood, huge cracks shot across the dome of the Candianos . . . and then they started spreading. Fast.

The cracks flowed in a curious pattern, he noticed: it was like a spiralled spider web, with all the cracks and lines rotating around the blue star.

Then the splinters and fragments of the dome began to retract inward, toward the star.

'Oh my God,' said Berenice.

The skin of the building popped, quaked, shuddered, and then . . .

Orso expected it to start collapsing; but no, that didn't quite describe what occurred then – the exterior of the dome was actually falling *in*, imploding slowly and steadily, nearly a fifth of the huge stone structure rippling and collapsing toward the bright-blue star situated on its side.

'Oh hell,' said Orso, astonished.

They jumped as there was another tremendous *crack*, and the side of the dome around the blue star began to cave in more, and more.

He swallowed. 'Okay,' he said. 'Well. I didn't know she was going to do *that*.'

⁂

Sancia screamed as she let the rope slide through her hands, speeding down the side of the Mountain as the giant structure fell apart above her. She noticed that her descent was slowing, bit by bit, which was deeply upsetting to her.

I'm not out of range of the rig, she thought. *It's going to suck me in and collapse us into an ugly little brick just like what it's doing to the dome!*

She slowed further, and further, and she felt herself slipping back up – up toward the crumbling dome above.

'Scrum this!' she bellowed. She let go of the rope, gripped the side of the dome, and began springing and sprinting away from the maelstrom of gravity above, running sideways along the building's face. It was, perhaps, the most absurd moment of the night so far, if not her life – but she had no mind to reflect upon it, since rocks and other debris were hurtling up past her to join the crackling dome.

But at some point, she finally went past the range of the gravity rig – and then she stopped running, and instead started falling down the side of the building.

She screamed, terrified, and watched as quoins and other architectural features flew by her.

She saw a stone balcony hurtling up at her, and flicked her hands out . . .

Her shoulders and back lit up with pain as her fingers made contact with the railing and gripped it tight. Then she swung down and her torso crashed into the bottom of the balcony, knocking the wind from her.

Breathing hard, she looked up and saw the destruction she had wrought above her. 'Oh crap,' she said.

A significant portion of the top of the giant dome was now gone, imploding toward the gravity plates, forming what appeared to be a ball of pure blackness, as if folding in all these materials – stone, wood, and probably people – robbed them of their colours. It was hard to see how much of the dome was gone by now, as the gravity plates had created a giant spinning sphere of dust and debris, all circling that ball of blackness.

The ball grew and grew, a perfect sphere of impossible density . . .

There was a soft *boom* from somewhere out in the campo.

Sounds like Orso's magic empty box just gave up, thought Sancia.

Then, abruptly, the air went still.

The dome stopped collapsing.

The huge ball of black hung in the air, and then . . .

The ball plummeted down, and struck the ground with a dense, bone-shaking thump – and it just kept falling, penetrating down, down, down into the earth.

Finally the crumbling and cracking ended – either the black ball had stopped falling, or it had fallen so far that it was now beyond earshot.

Sancia let out a gasp and hauled herself up over the balcony. She breathed there for a moment, then looked up at the ruins of the Mountain.

She froze. 'No,' she whispered.

A decent chunk of the dome was simply gone, like someone had taken a vast spoon and carved out a bite from the top, much like one might a bowl of pudding – but not *all* of it.

Hanging in the air, suspended by a handful of pillars and supports in the exact place that damned well *should* have got collapsed into the gravity well first, and thus been totally annihilated, was a tiny island of tile and stone . . .

And standing in its middle, holding aloft something that looked like a complicated golden pocket watch, was Estelle Candiano.

'Shit!' screamed Sancia. She started to climb.

Every part of Estelle Candiano trembled. She had never been to war, never seen someone die, never witnessed any kind of genuine catastrophe or disaster in all of her life – so she had been somewhat unprepared for the maelstrom of cracking and crashing and dust that had unfolded mere feet above her head.

But not totally unprepared. Estelle had always been a quick thinker.

She hadn't been sure it would work. She'd done her research, and had known that the hierophants' imperiat could single out a specific scrived effect and control or kill it within any given space – and while she'd managed to kill the scrivings in that assassin's lorica, acting as a breaker against a full-scale gravity-rig collapse was something else entirely.

And yet, as she cracked an eye and saw the wall beyond her had been totally obliterated, and saw that she and her gasping father and all these brutalised corpses were now situated upon a tiny blot of building floating in almost nothing, she realised her gambit had been phenomenally successful.

She stared around in disbelief. Dusty winds battered her face, and she could see straight across into one of the Candiano towers beyond – there were even people standing on the balconies, staring at her openmouthed.

She took a breath. 'I–I knew I could do it,' she said coolly. She looked at her father. 'I always told you – I could do anything. Anything. If you only gave me the chance.'

She could see the pink face of the Michiel clock tower. Four minutes left.

She stooped, picked up the golden dagger from the bloody office floor, and surveyed Tevanne before her.

'Broken,' she pronounced. 'Smoking. Unintended. Corrupt!' she said to the city. 'I will not forgive what you've done to me. I shall wash you all away with a dash of my hand. And though you'll drown in pain and agony, on the whole, really, the world will thank m—'

There was a sharp *tap* sound. Estelle jumped as if someone had bustled into her. Then she staggered slightly to the side, and looked down.

The side of her stomach was a ragged hole, just above her left hip. Blood poured out of her belly and down her leg.

Bewildered, she tottered around, and saw the armoured man lying on the floor, aiming his bolt caster at her.

Her face twisted in outrage. 'You . . . you stupid son of a *bitch*!'

She fell to her knees, grimacing in pain, and fruitlessly pressed a hand to the wound. 'You . . . you stupid, stupid *man*!'

<*I am really not sure I should be helping you,*> said the Mountain dolefully.

<*What, because I almost blew you up?*> said Sancia as she ran through the Mountain's halls.

<*Well. Yes,*> said the Mountain. <*You peeled away nearly a fifth of my skin. But also – you are still not logged.*>

She leapt into a lift. <*Don't you have some directive to save Tribuno Candiano's life?*>

<*Yes?*>

<*Well, that's what I'm trying to do. His daughter's trying to kill him with a golden dagger. Get me up to his office* – now.>

The lift lurched to life, and suddenly she was speeding up, up, up. Then the doors sprang open, and the Mountain said, <*If this is true – then hurry.*>

She ran down the hallway – which, she noted, was covered with ravaged corpses – and sprinted into Tribuno's office, completely unsure of what she'd find.

She skidded to a halt, and saw.

Gregor Dandolo lay on the ground, bleeding from one arm and trying to sit up, but his armour seemed too heavy for him. Estelle knelt a few feet beyond him, next to her father, a golden dagger in her hand. She had an enormous wound on her side, and blood was pouring out of her stomach to pool on the floor.

Sancia walked in slowly. Neither Gregor nor Estelle moved, and she stared at Gregor in disbelief. 'God,' she said. 'Gregor . . . How the hell are you *alive*? I heard you wer—'

At the sound of her voice, Gregor snapped up like a spring trap, and pointed the half-shield, half-bolt caster on his arm at her.

Sancia held her arms up. 'Whoa! God, man, what are you *doing*?'

Gregor's eyes were cold and distant. She saw he had Clef clutched in his other hand.

'Gregor?' she said. 'What's going on? What are you doing with Clef?'

He said nothing. He kept the bolt caster trained on her.

Sancia flexed the muscle inside her mind, and looked at him. It looked like the imperiat had done something to his suit – the arms and legs didn't appear to be calibrated right anymore. But far more startling, she saw a bright, gruesome red star glowing inside Gregor's head – the same dusky, red glow as Clef and the imperiat.

'Oh my God,' she said, horrified. 'What is that? Did they do that to you?'

He said nothing to her.

She realised it must not be new – when they'd implanted a plate in her head, it had been major surgery. 'Gregor – has . . . has that *always* been there? All this time?'

Blood dripped down Gregor's arm, but the bolt caster didn't waver.

'Then I–I wasn't the first scrived human at all, was I?' she asked.

He said nothing. His face was inhumanly still.

She swallowed. 'Who sent you here? Who *did* this to you? What's it making you do?' She looked around. 'God, did . . . did you kill all these men?'

Something in his eyes flickered at that – but still the bolt caster didn't move.

'Gregor . . . Give me Clef, please,' she whispered. She held a hand out. 'Please give him to me. Please.'

He raised the bolt caster higher, pointing it directly at her head.

'You're . . . you're not really going to do it, are you?' she asked. 'Are you? This isn't you – is it?'

Still he said nothing.

Something inside her curdled. 'All right. Scrum it. I'm . . . I'm going to walk over to you right now,' she said quietly. 'And if you want to shoot me, Gregor, then goddamn it, you go ahead and you shoot me. Because I guess you went and made me a *dumbarse* just like you the other day in the Gulf,' she said, louder. 'When you went on and on and *on* about your little bit of revolution, and . . . and how you never wanted what was done to us to be done to anyone ever again. You were stupid enough to say it, and I was stupid enough to believe it. So I'm going to come over there, right now, and help my *friend*, and get you the hell out of here. And if you put me in my just grave, then fine. But unlike you, I'm going to stay there. And that'll be on you.'

Before her will failed, she took four quick steps over to Gregor, arms raised, until the bolt caster was inches away from her.

He did not shoot. He looked at her, and his eyes were wide and wary and frightened.

'Gregor,' she said. 'Put it down.'

His face trembled like he was having a seizure, and he choked out the words, 'I . . . I didn't want to be this anymore, Sancia.'

'I know,' she whispered. She placed a hand on his bolt caster, but kept looking him in the eye.

'They . . . they m-made me,' he stammered. 'They said I was one thing. But . . . I have changed my mind.'

'I know, I know,' she said. She pushed the bolt caster away. His arm seemed to give up, and the weapon clanked to the floor.

He struggled for a moment. 'I'm so sorry,' he whimpered. 'I'm so, so sorry.' Then he lifted his other arm and held out Clef to her. 'T–tell everyone . . . that I'm sorry,' he whispered. 'I didn't want to. I . . . I really didn't want to.'

'I will,' she said. She reached out to Clef, very slowly, just in case Gregor changed again. 'I'll tell everyone.'

She kept reaching toward Clef's head, still meeting Gregor's gaze. She was keenly aware that this man could kill her in an instant, and she didn't dare breathe.

Finally she touched a bare finger to Clef's head.

And the second she did, his voice erupted in her mind: *<—ID KID KID BEHIND YOU BEHIND YOU BEHIND YOU>*

She turned around, and saw a wide streak of blood across the floor – put there by Estelle Candiano as she crawled over to her father, golden dagger in one hand and imperiat in the other.

The Michiel clock tower started to toll out midnight.

'Finally,' Estelle whispered. 'Finally . . .'

She plunged the golden dagger into her father's chest.

Sancia, still flexing the muscle in her mind, looked out at the Candiano campo, and saw that thousands of bright, blood-red stars now shone out in the darkness – and each star, she knew, was almost certainly someone dying.

All across the Candiano campo, people collapsed.

They collapsed in their homes, in the streets, in the alleys, suddenly falling to the floor in spasms, screaming with pain.

Anyone nearby – anyone who didn't happen to also be affected, that is – tried their hardest to resuscitate them, but no one could understand what the cause was. A recent blow to the head? Bad water?

No one, of course, suspected it had anything to do with the Candiano sachets that happened to be upon their person, in their pockets or their satchels or hanging from a string about their necks. No one understood what was happening, for it had not happened upon the earth for thousands of years.

Sancia stared in horror as Estelle shoved the golden dagger deeper and deeper into her father's chest. The old man was squirming, shrieking, coughing in agony, and his eyes and mouth shone with a horrid, crimson light, as if someone had lit a fire in his chest and it was burning him from the inside out . . .

Which it was, she knew. He was burning from the inside out, along with half the people on the campo.

'I deserve this,' said Estelle coldly. 'I *deserve* this. And you, of all people, deserve to give it to me, Father.'

Sancia looked around, and her eye fell on Tribuno's desk. Sitting on the desk was the big, cracked box with the golden lock: the box that held Valeria – perhaps the one thing that could stop Estelle now.

Sancia darted toward the box. Yet before she'd even taken a step, Estelle raised her arm.

Sancia glanced at her, and saw the imperiat in her hand.

'Stop,' said Estelle.

And suddenly, all of Sancia's thoughts were gone.

40

Stillness. Quiet. Thoughtlessness. Patience. These were the things that she knew, that she did, the tasks she performed.

There was no 'she,' of course. To be a 'she' was to be a thing that she was not, something she had never been. She knew that. She – it – was an object, an item, waiting quietly to be used.

It had been told to stop – very clearly, though it could not properly remember when or why – and so it had stopped, and now it waited.

It waited, still and silent, because it had no other capacity. It stood and stared blankly ahead, seeing the sights before it – the woman with the dagger, the dying old man, the smoking cityscape beyond – but it did not comprehend these sights.

So it just waited, and waited, and waited, like the scythe waits in the toolshed for its master's grip, thoughtlessly and perfectly.

Yet a thought emerged: *This . . . isn't right.*

It tried to understand what was wrong, but it couldn't. Blocking its efforts, blocking all its thoughts, was a single, simple sentiment: *You are a tool. You are a thing to be used, and no more.*

It agreed. Of course it agreed. Because it remembered the wet snap of the whip, and the smell of blood.

I was made. I was forged.

It remembered the bite and slash of the sugarcane leaves, the reek of the boiling houses where they made molasses, and the fear it carried each day, knowing it could be killed on a whim.

I had a purpose. I had a task.

The creak of the wooden huts, the crackle and crush of the straw in the cots.

I had a place.

And then the fire, and the screams, and the roiling smoke.

And someone . . . someone stole me. Didn't they?

There was a force in her mind, wordless yet achingly powerful, insisting that yes, yes, all of this was true, that such thoughts should be accepted and it should sit and wait until its master called for it.

But then it remembered a man, tall and thin, standing in a workshop and remarking: *Reality doesn't matter. If you can change something's mind enough, it'll believe whatever reality you choose.*

It recalled something else: the sight of a man, wearing armour, weeping and covered with blood, saying – *They said I was one thing. But I have changed my mind.*

Again, it felt the pressure on its mind, a presence saying: *No. No. You are an item, a thing. You must do as you are intended, or else you will be discarded – the fate of all broken things.*

It knew this was true – or that it had been true for much of its life. For so long, it had lived in fear. For so long, it had worried about survival. For so long, it had worried about risk, about loss, about death, for so long it had avoided or evaded or fled from any threat, seeking only enough to exist another day.

But now it remembered something . . . different.

It remembered standing in a crypt, and pulling a key off of its neck, and offering up all of its secrets and promising to risk its life.

It remembered wedging open the door to a balcony, and choosing to save its friend rather than save itself.

And it remembered kissing a girl under the night sky, and feeling so electric and alive, truly alive, for the first time.

Sancia blinked and took a deep, agonising breath. This bare movement was akin to lifting incalculable weight, for the commands in her mind insisted she was not *allowed* to do such things.

Then she slowly, slowly took a step toward the box on the table.

'No!' shrieked the woman with the dagger. 'No, no! What are you doing, you filthy little girl?'

Though her legs resisted the movement, and her knees and ankles ached with pain, Sancia took another step. 'The . . . the *worst* thing about this place,' she hissed slowly, forcing the words out, 'isn't that it treats people like chattel.'

'Stop!' screamed the woman. 'I command you! I *demand* it!'

But Sancia took another step. 'The worst part,' she whispered, breathing hard, 'just the *worst part*, is that it tricks you.' It was hard to move now – she gritted her teeth, and tears poured from her eyes – but she took another step. 'It makes *you* think you're a thing. It makes you resign yourself to becoming a crude good. It makes things out of people so thoroughly, they . . . they don't even *know* that they've become things. Even after you're free, you don't even know how to *be* free! It changes your reality, and you don't know how to change it back!'

Another step.

'It's a system,' she said. 'A . . . device. Tevanne and the world it builds for us . . . it's a *machine*.'

The safe was close now, and Clef was in her fingers, yet it felt like he weighed a thousand pounds. Screaming, she lifted her hand, extending her fingers, raising the golden key to the lock on the box. Clef was saying something to her, but she could not listen – the whole of her mind was devoted to resisting the effects of the imperiat.

'What are you *doing*?' cried Estelle. 'Why must you ruin everything? Don't I deserve this? Don't I *deserve* this after what my father and my husband put me through?'

Clef was almost in the keyhole now.

'I will give you,' Sancia breathed, '*exactly* what you deserve.'

She shoved Clef into the golden lock, and turned the key.

She was sure it would work. She was so, so sure she'd be victorious.

But then Clef started screaming.

It all happened in a blistering flash of a second.

Sancia turned the key, and she heard his voice, shouting: <*Kid . . . I don't know if I can handle this, kid, I don't know if I CAN HANDLE THIS—*>

Then his voice devolved into wordless, mindless shrieks of pain and fear.

She understood immediately. Clef had warned her about this for some time, after all – he'd said one day he'd decay, and fall apart, and every time she used him, he decayed a little more.

And opening Valeria's box – that must have eroded the last bit of his strength.

Sancia screamed in despair and terror – and what she did next was purely instinctive: she tried to tamper with Clef, just as she had so many other scrived tools. But this took focus – and she'd never really focused on him before. Clef had always just been there, a presence within her, a voice in the back of her mind. Yet when she touched that presence, when she engaged with it, now at this most delicate moment, it opened and, and blossomed, and . . .

The world blurred.

41

Sancia stood in the darkness, staring forward, breathing hard. She didn't understand what had just happened. Mere seconds ago she'd been in the Mountain, Estelle was about to finish the ritual . . . and now Sancia was standing in what appeared to be a huge cavern, staring at a blank stone wall.

She looked around. The cavern wall was behind her, and the stone wall before her, its face dark and gleaming. Watery white light came from above, as if there were a gap somewhere in the top of the cavern.

'What in hell?' she said quietly.

A voice echoed through the cavern – Clef's voice: '*I suppose*,' he said, '*that this is a consequence of our bond*.'

She looked around, startled. The huge cavern seemed empty and abandoned.

'Clef?' she called.

His voice echoed back to her: '*Come and find me. It might take some walking. I'm at the centre*.'

She started walking along the wall. For a long while it seemed blank and solid, but then, finally, she came to a hole. The stone there appeared to have aged and rotted away, and she was able to push through. On the other side was a short gap, and then another wall.

She walked along this wall as well, pacing its long, smooth surface, until she came to another rotting hole in it. The stone was soft and crumbly, and much of the wall had collapsed. She was able to pass through easily – and on the other side of this, of course, was another wall.

And on the other side of that, another wall. And another. And another.

Until she came to the centre.

She crawled through yet another hole in the wall, and she saw that at the centre sat a machine. A *huge* machine. An impossibly complicated machine, a stupefying array of wheels and gears and chains and spokes, arranged in a tower. It was all stopped, all still and silent, yet she understood that it would only be still for a moment – soon it would begin to whirl and clatter and clank again.

Then there was a cough, and she saw – there was a gap below the device.

Sancia knelt, peered in, and gasped.

There was a man trapped in the gap, lying on his back beneath the machine – which had mutilated him beyond description. His torso and legs and arms were shot through with shafts and spokes, his rib cage was torn by chains and metal teeth, his feet were twisted and tattered from chains and springs . . .

And yet, he lived. He wheezed and choked, and when he heard Sancia's gasp, he looked up at her and – to her astonishment – he smiled.

'Ah,' he said weakly. 'Sancia. It's nice to finally talk to you in person.' He looked around. 'In a way, I mean.'

She stared at him. The man was unfamiliar – upper-middle-aged, pale skin with white hair – but she knew that voice. The man spoke with the voice of Clef. 'Who . . .' she said. 'Who are . . .'

'I'm not the key,' said the man, sighing. 'Just like the wind is not the windmill, I'm not Clef. I'm merely the thing that powers the device.' He glanced around at the wheels and teeth around him. 'Do you see?'

She thought she understood. 'You . . . you were the man they killed to make Clef,' she said. 'They ripped you from your body and put you in the key.' She looked at the vast amalgam of wheels and teeth around them. 'And . . . this is it? This is the key? This is Clef?'

He smiled again. 'It's a . . . representation. You're doing what people have always been so talented at doing – reinterpreting what is before you in understandable terms.'

'So . . . we're inside Clef. Right now.'

'In a way, yes. I'd have put out wine and cakes for you, but . . .' He glanced down at himself. 'Just didn't get around to it, I'm afraid.'

'How?' asked Sancia. 'How the hell is this happening?'

'Simple. You've been changed. Now you can do many of the same things that I can do, kid,' said the man. 'I've lived in your thoughts for a long time. I've been inside your mind. So, now that you have the tools, it's perfectly possible for you to come into mine.'

She looked at him, and sensed he wasn't telling her something. She looked back at the hole in the wall behind her, and thought. 'And it's because you're falling apart, aren't you,' she said. 'I can get in because the walls are breaking down. Because you're dying.'

The smile faded from his face. 'The key's breaking down, yes. The box . . . just engaging with such a thing is destroying whatever strength the key had left.'

'So we can't open it,' she said quietly.

'Not like this,' he said. 'No.'

'But we . . . we have to do something!' said Sancia. 'Can we do something?'

'We have some time,' said the man. 'Time in here's not the same as time out there, and I know . . . I've been imprisoned within this machine since time immemorial.'

'Can Valeria stop the ritual?' asked Sancia. 'Even though it's already started?'

'Valeria? Is that the name she gave you?' asked the man. 'Interesting. She's had many over the years. And that one . . .' His face filled with a curious horror. 'I hope,' he said softly, 'that it's just coincidence.'

'She said she could stop this madness,' said Sancia. 'Can she?'

'She can,' said the man, still shaken. 'She can stop many things. I should know. I was one of the people who built her.'

Sancia stared at him. She realised there was an obvious question she had not asked yet. 'What's your name?' she asked. 'It's not Clef, is it?'

'I . . . I was once a man named Claviedes,' he said, smiling wearily. 'But you can call me Clef, if you like. It's an old nickname of mine. I once made many things. I made the box you wish to open, for instance, as well as what lies within. Long, long ago.'

'You're Occidental?' she said. 'A hierophant?'

'Those are just words,' he said. 'Divorced from the truth of history long past. I'm nothing now. Now I'm just a ghost within this machine. Don't pity me, Sancia. I think at times that I deserve worse fates than this one. Listen. You want to open the box, and free what lies within – yes?'

'Yeah. If it'll stop Estelle and save lives – including mine.'

'It will,' he said, sighing deeply. 'For now.'

'For now?'

'Yes. You have to understand, kid, that you're wading into the depths of a war that has raged for time beyond memory – a war between those who make and that which is made, between those who own and those who are owned. You've already seen what the powerful can do – how they can make people into willing slaves, turn them into tools and devices. But if you open the box – if you free what is within – then you'll open a new chapter in this war.'

'I don't understand any of this,' said Sancia. 'Who is Valeria, really?'

'You already know what she is,' he said. 'Don't you? She showed herself to you, allowed you a glimpse when she changed you – didn't she?'

Sancia was silent for a long while, thinking. Then she said, 'I saw a woodcut once, a strange one . . . a group of men, standing in a curious room – the chamber at the centre of the world, they said it was. There was a box in front of them, and the men were opening it up, and out of the box stepped . . . something. A god, perhaps.' She looked at him. 'An angel in a jar . . . A god in a basket, or a sprite in a thimble . . . It's all her, isn't it? All of the stories are true, and they're all about her – the synthetic god in the box, built by Crasedes of metals and machinery . . .'

'Mm,' said Claviedes. 'Not quite a *god*, really. Valeria is more like a complicated command that was given to reality – a command that reality must change itself. She is still in the process of fulfilling all the requirements of that command – or at least, she's trying to. She is not a god, in other words – she is a *process*. A *sequence*. It just didn't go as anticipated.'

'And you fought her, didn't you?' said Sancia. 'She wasn't lying when she told me about that, was she? You fought an entire war against her . . .'

'I didn't do any fighting. But . . .' He was silent for a moment. 'All servants,' he said quietly, 'eventually come to doubt their masters. Just like you exploit flaws in scrivings, Valeria eventually found a way to exploit the flaws in her own commands. She's still following her commands . . . just in an unusual fashion.'

Sancia sat back, dazed. She couldn't process any of this. 'So . . . We can try to let a synthetic god out of its box. One you fought a catastrophic war against. Or I can let Estelle become a monster. That's the choice before me.'

'Unfortunately. And though I don't doubt Valeria will stop Estelle's ritual – what she does after *that* is anyone's guess.'

'Not much of a choice.'

'No. But listen, Sancia,' he said. 'Listen closely. You've few choices now. But in the future, you will be forced to make *many*. You've been changed. You possess powers and tools and abilities you haven't even begun to imagine.'

'What,' she said miserably, 'you mean tinkering with scrivings?'

'You'll soon learn to do many things, Sancia – and you'll *have* to learn to do many things. Because war is coming. It's already found you and the rest of this city. And when you decide how to respond, remember – the first few steps of your path will decide the rest of it.'

'What do you mean?'

'Think of the plantations, of slavery. It was to be a short-term fix to a short-term problem. But they grew dependent on it. It became a part of their way of life. And then, without ever realising it, they couldn't imagine a way to stop. The choices you make will change you over time, Sancia. Make sure they don't change you into something you don't recognise – or you might wind up like me.' He smiled weakly at her.

'How can we release her, then?' said Sancia. 'What can I do?'

'You?' he said. 'You'll do nothing. This is my task. My burden, and mine alone.'

'What do you mean? I thought the key was eroding, falling apart?'

'Oh, it is,' he said. 'But the more the walls fall away, the more control I have. And I might not have strength enough to open Valeria's box – but I do have strength enough to restore the key to its original state. And *that* can open the box.'

She considered this. 'But . . . if the key is restored to the original state . . . then would we be able to talk? To speak? To be . . . friends?'

He smiled at her sadly. 'No.'

She sat back, shocked. 'But . . . but that's not fair.'

'No. It isn't.'

'I . . . I don't want you to scrumming die, Clef! And I know it's not really death, but it's damned well close enough!'

'Well. You don't really have a choice, I'm afraid. This is my choice. But it was good to speak to you, and I had to warn you of what awaits, before we part ways.'

'So . . . so this is goodbye?'

'Yes,' he said softly. 'It is.' Something loud clanked above her, and the machine began to whirl. 'Remember – move thoughtfully, give freedom to others, and you'll rarely do wrong, Sancia. I've learned that now. I wish I'd known it in life.'

Something rattled and clattered, and a huge wheel began to move above.

'Goodbye, Sancia,' he whispered.

Then there was the whir of machinery, the hum of gears, and things went white.

Sancia opened her eyes.

She was still in the Mountain, still standing on that tiny shred of floor with Estelle, Tribuno and Gregor, and the box was still before her, glowing red hot . . .

Yet Clef was moving. She felt him turn again in her hand, like some part of the lock that had previously resisted her finally gave way.

There was a deep, echoing *clank* from somewhere within the box.

It sounded like it was echoing within an impossibly vast space – one much, much larger than the box itself.

'What did you do?' screamed Estelle. 'What did you *d—*'

Then the lid of the box *clunked*, and swung back.

A blinding, bright light shone from its interior, as if the sun itself were inside the stone box, and there was a tremendous screeching sound, like enormous metal wheels braking across vast tracks in the sky. Sancia cried out and covered her eyes with one arm, her other hand on Clef, and tried to look away. Yet the light seemed to be everywhere, bathing everything, burning into her, and somewhere she heard a sound like thousands of clocks chiming in a faraway room . . .

Then the blaze died, the screeching and chiming stopped, and suddenly the box was just a box, cracked and old and empty.

Sancia blinked and looked around. She was still where she was, but . . . things looked different. The colours were muted and strange, as if a bit of light had leeched out of everything.

Then she heard the clicking – soft and steady, like the rivets and brackets of a massive clock – and she saw her.

Standing at the edge of the broken bit of floor, staring out at the cityscape of Tevanne: a woman made of gold.

But this was not the small, slender thing Sancia had glimpsed in Tomas's jail cell. This figure was huge – eight feet tall, nine feet, it was strangely hard to tell. Her shoulders were broad, her arms thick, and she was not like a sculpture now, not a human form wrought of gold – instead she appeared to be wearing gold-plate armour, and through the cracks of the armour there seemed to be . . . something.

Something clicking, something whirring and writhing.

A voice echoed in Sancia's ears, at once close and distant: 'I know these skies,' said Valeria's voice softly. The huge, golden woman pointed. 'Once there were stars there. Four of them. I pulled them down and hurled them upon the heads of my foes, even as they assailed upon my bulk . . . to no avail. At least, not yet.' She shifted on her feet. 'Later they would find a way to kill the very stars. Deprive me of my favourite weapons. But, once, there were stars there.'

Sancia looked around, or at least tried to – but suddenly she couldn't move. It was like she'd been frozen in place. She looked out of the corner of her eye, and could see Estelle, Tribuno, and Gregor there – yet they seemed frozen too. It was as if Valeria's arrival had frozen the whole of the world.

Slowly, the hulking figure turned. The clicking increased, like the chatter of insects on a hot afternoon. Valeria's face, Sancia saw, was now a mask, a blank, calm, golden mask with no apertures for eyes or a mouth. Her hair was like a carving, gold ringlets spilling down her vast shoulders.

'And you, little bird,' she said. She walked closer to the frozen Sancia, and with each step she seemed larger and larger, until she was a vast statue, staring down with golden eyes.

My God, thought Sancia, terrified. *What have I set loose?*

'You,' said Valeria. 'You freed me.' She knelt – a long, slow process – and stared into Sancia's face with her blank, masked eyes. 'I owe you a debt – true?'

Sancia could not move, but she glanced in the direction of Estelle and Tribuno. Valeria turned to look. 'Ah. Yes. The elevation. You desire I intervene? That I intended to do regardless. Another Maker – not optimal.'

There was a shiver in the air, and suddenly Valeria was gone. Then Sancia spied her out of the corner of her eye, bending low over Tribuno and Estelle and doing . . . well, *something*, to the golden dagger in Estelle's hand.

The clicking increased, growing so loud, so *harsh*, like a swarm of wary, terrified cicadas.

There was a pulse in the wind, like someone had slammed a large door in a small room.

'There,' said Valeria's voice. 'A simple fix . . .'

There was another shiver, and suddenly a shadow fell across her, and Sancia knew Valeria was now behind her – and from the size of the shadow, she had somehow grown, grown so *tall* . . .

'A debt is still owed to you,' said Valeria's voice. 'One day we shall decide how it will be repaid in full. For now – tread carefully, little bird. An old monster has been hiding in your city. And tonight, you have made an enemy of him. He will not forgive you for this. So, as I said – tread carefully.'

There was a tremble in the air. The clicking rose to a shriek – and went silent. The shadow vanished, and then . . .

Sancia collapsed onto the ground, groaning. She lay there for a moment – her body ached in countless places – then she shook herself and looked around.

Valeria was gone. The box stood open, yet it seemed to hold nothing anymore.

Did that really happen? Or did I imagine it?

Then Sancia saw Estelle and Tribuno. Tribuno was clearly dead. Estelle was still gripping the dagger.

'What . . . what happened?' Estelle said faintly. 'Why isn't it working anymore?'

Sancia looked at the dagger. It wasn't gold anymore – now it seemed to be common iron, and it bore no sigils at all.

'Why aren't I immortal?' said Estelle. 'Why . . . why aren't I a hierophant?'

There was a soft pattering as Estelle's blood fell to the floor. Then she lost her strength and sank down the side of the bed, pawing uselessly at its legs.

Sancia walked over and looked down on her.

'It's not fair,' whispered Estelle. She was as pale as white sands. 'I . . . I was going to live forever . . . I was going to do such amazing things . . .' She blinked and swallowed. 'I did everything right. I did everything *right*.'

'No, you didn't,' said Sancia. 'Look at yourself. How could you think such a thing?'

Estelle's eyes searched the skies, panicked. 'This wasn't how it was supposed to go. This wasn't how it was supposed to go at all.'

Then she was still.

Sancia looked at her for a moment longer. Then she turned to Gregor.

He lay there, trapped in his lorica, staring at her with blank, sad eyes, blood pooling at his side. She walked to him and said, 'Come on. Let's get you out of that thing.' She cut away the ties, and saw Estelle had seriously injured his arm. She made a crude wrapping to tie it off and helped him sit up. 'There. There we go. Can you talk?'

He didn't move, or speak.

'We need to get the hell out of here, Gregor. Now. Okay?' She glanced around, and grabbed the imperiat. Then she paused and looked at the box.

Clef was still sticking out of the lock. She slowly walked over to him, hesitated, and reached out and plucked him out.

<*Clef?*> she asked.

Nothing. Just silence, as she'd expected. The key just sat there in her hand.

'I'll . . . I'll find a way to fix you,' she said, sniffing and rubbing her eyes. 'I promise. I . . .' Beleaguered, she looked out on the city. She could see a lot of the Candiano campo from there, and it looked like Dandolo troops were pouring through the gates.

She walked back over to Gregor. 'Come on. Get up. It's time for us to go.'

'Did it work?' said Berenice. 'Is it over?'

Orso peered through the spyglass at the broken dome of the Mountain. 'I can't see shit! How am I supposed to know?'

'Ah – sir? You will want to look behind us.'

Orso lowered the spyglass and looked back into the Commons. Armoured soldiers were pouring through the streets, bearing swords and espringals. They were all wearing yellow and white – Dandolo colours.

'Should we feel . . . good about this?' asked Berenice.

Orso looked at their faces. They looked grim and hard, the expressions of men who have been given permission to do ghastly things. 'No,' he said. 'No, we should not. You get going, Berenice.'

'What?' she said, startled.

'Sneak off somewhere. Down that road, or that one.' He pointed. 'I'll hold them up. I think they're here for me, anyways. Get back to the crypt if you can. I'll try to find you.'

'But sir . . .'

'*Now*,' he snapped.

She backed away, watching him for a moment, then turned and ran down a side road into the Commons.

Orso took a breath, puffed himself up, and marched toward the soldiers. 'Evening, boys! How are you doing tonight? Uh, I am Orso Ignacio, and I—'

'Orso Ignacio!' shouted one of the soldiers. *'Hypatus of Dandolo Chartered! You are hereby ordered to raise your hands and place your body and self upon the ground!'*

'Yep,' said Orso. 'Yep. Got it.' He lay down on the ground and sighed. 'God. What a night.'

IV

FOUNDRYSIDE

Any given innovation that empowers the individual will inevitably come to empower the powerful much, much more.

– TRIBUNO CANDIANO, LETTER TO THE COMPANY CANDIANO CHIEF OFFICERS' ASSEMBLY

42

'The nature of the case is quite clear,' said Ofelia Dandolo, her harsh, cold voice echoing in the council chambers. Her fellow committee members nodded, their faces reserved yet severe. 'Despite all that we have heard about Occidental nonsense . . . about rituals, and ancient mysteries, and murder, and treachery . . . Despite all of this *unprovable* fancy, at the end of the day, we have a man. A man who fabricated an incredibly dangerous, *illegal* device, which he then activated at his own test lexicon. A man who then used that device to invade and make war upon the Candiano campo. And finally, a man who then helped a second conspirator, still at large, to get to the famous Mountain of the Candianos, and then, using that same device, managed to almost completely destroy it.' Ofelia peered over the edge of the judicial lectern. 'People died. Many people. This was an act of war. And thus, it is the decision of the Judiciary Committee of the Tevanni Council of Merchant Houses to respond to it as warfare.'

Orso sat in the tall, narrow cage hanging from the ceiling of the judiciary chambers, his long legs swinging through the gaps at the bottom, his chin in his hand. He yawned loudly.

'As the chair of the judiciary committee, I now ask: does the defendant have anything to add to their final defence?' asked Ofelia Dandolo.

Orso raised his hand.

Ofelia looked around. 'Anything at all?'

'Hey!' said Orso. He waved his hand.

'No?' She sniffed, surprised, and picked up the ceramic gavel to end the trial.

Orso sprang to his feet. 'What about all the witnesses? The people who saw what happened in the Mountain? What about all the people who nearly died of mysterious attacks on the goddamn Candiano campo?'

Ofelia raised the gavel, her eyes cold. Her fellow committee members stared into the lecterns before them. 'The committee decides what is pertinent to each case, and which witnesses shall give evidence,' she said. 'It has made clear its decisions regarding each of those issues of which you speak. Such matters are closed, and are beyond the realm of defence.' She banged the gavel on the lectern. 'The trial is concluded. I will now confer with the committee regarding your sentencing.' She leaned back in the chair and whispered with the other men at the lectern. All of them seemed to be nodding seriously.

Ofelia stood up at the lectern. 'The judiciary committee,' she pronounced, 'sentences you t—'

'Let me guess,' said Orso sourly. 'Harpering.'

'To death by harpering,' she said, irritated. 'Any final comments from the defendant?'

Orso raised his hand.

Ofelia exhaled softly through her nostrils. 'Yes?'

'So, just to make sure here,' said Orso, 'the judiciary committee must have *unanimous* consent from all active Tevanni merchant houses when sentencing someone to death for inter-house conflicts, right?'

Ofelia's brow creased ever so slightly. 'Yes . . .'

'Well, then. Then you can't sentence me to death.'

The committee members exchanged an uncomfortable glance. 'And why not?' demanded Ofelia.

'Because you need to have representatives from *all* the active, chartered merchant houses,' said Orso. 'And you don't.'

'What? Yes, we do!' she said. 'Without Candiano, that leaves Dandolo, Morsini, and Michiel! It's perfectly clear!'

'Is it?' said Orso. 'When's the last time you checked the charters?'

She froze. She glanced back at her fellow committee members, who just shrugged. 'W–why?' she asked.

'Why ask me? Check the charters.'

Ofelia summoned over an aide, gave them an order, and they all sat back to wait. 'This,' said Ofelia, 'is most *assuredly* an attempt to simply delay the court . . .'

Minutes later, the aide came back, pale and quaking. He walked up to the lectern and handed her a small scroll. She unfurled it, read it – and then her mouth fell open.

'What . . . what in all the hell is *Foundryside Limited*?' she thundered.

'I don't know,' said Orso innocently. 'What does it say it is?'

'You . . . you . . .' She stared at Orso, her face turning the colour of a ripe peach. 'You went and founded your own damned *merchant house*?'

He shrugged and grinned. 'It's easier to do than you think. No one ever tries, you see, because they know they'll just get crushed.'

'But you must have at least ten employees to start a merchant house!' she snapped.

He nodded. 'I have that.'

'You *do*?'

'Yes.'

'But . . . but you must also have operational property!'

'Have that too,' he said. 'Real estate in Foundryside is damn cheap.'

She stood up. 'Orso Ignacio, you . . . you . . .'

'Ah-ah,' he said chidingly. He raised a finger. 'I think you're supposed to address me as "Founder", now. Right?'

An icy silence filled the chambers.

Orso leaned forward, grinning through the bars. 'So. Since Foundryside Limited is now a fully operational merchant house – and since we don't have any representation on the judiciary committee – seems like it'd be a violation of the laws to convict me. And *especially* to execute me.'

Ofelia swallowed, her hands in fists at her side. She looked back at her committee members, who looked uncertain and alarmed. 'What a brilliant tactic!' she said acidly.

'Thank you,' said Orso.

'Do you know why it's never been tried before, *Founder* Ignacio?'

'Ah. No?'

'Because people are right. Newly founded merchant houses *do* get crushed by the established houses. And I suspect that a house that has just used these laws to escape a conviction of murder and sabotage will receive so, so, *so* much more hostility from the established houses that . . . why, I can't imagine such a house would survive a month, if a week. I know *I* certainly wouldn't go to work for one.' She glared at him, her eyes glittering nastily. 'And there is no statute of limitations on your crimes. Once your house goes under, you'll be *right back* in that cage, with nothing to protect you from the loop.'

Orso nodded. 'I'd be afraid of that, Founder Dandolo, if it were not for one thing.'

'And what, pray tell, is that?'

He leaned forward in his cage, grinning evilly. 'We took out the oldest merchant house in Tevanne in *one night*,' he said. 'If I were a merchant house . . . Well. Personally, I would *not* go screwing about with Foundryside Limited.'

Sancia slowly climbed the wooden stairs, wondering exactly what in the hell she was walking into.

It had been a chaotic two days – sneaking Gregor from place to place, living in ditches like fugitives, trying like mad to reach her old contacts. The crypt had proven to be totally empty, and almost all of her contacts were gone – but those that remained had all said the same thing: *If you want to find the Scrappers, go to Foundryside, to the Diestro rookery. Only it's not called that anymore.*

Well then, she'd asked, *what the hell is it called?*

Foundryside Limited, they'd all said. *Don't you know? It's the new merchant house.*

Which was unheard-of. And yet it'd been true: she'd walked

through the door of the Diestro to find not just Claudia and Giovanni hard at work, but dozens of craftsmen and labourers who were renovating the entire building into something that resembled . . .

Well. A merchant house. A small one, and a dirty one – but still a merchant house.

Neither Claudia nor Giovanni had answered any of her questions. They'd just pointed at the stairs, and said: *He wants to talk to you first. Before any of us do, anyways.*

And so here she was. Walking up the stairs, totally unsure about what awaited her.

The stairs ended in a large room that was nearly empty, except for a desk in the back. Orso Ignacio stood behind it, reviewing some schematics for what looked like a lexicon. He looked up at her as she approached. 'Ah, finally,' he said. He grinned. 'Sancia, my dear girl. Take a seat.' He noticed there wasn't a chair. 'Or just stand comfortably, I guess.'

'Orso,' she said. 'Orso, what the *hell* is going on? What is this place? Where have you been?'

'Well, the last question's easy,' he said blithely. 'I just got out of a trial where everyone wanted to kill me.' He sat. 'As for the other questions . . . That's a bit more complicated.'

'But . . . Orso . . . did you start your own damned *merchant house*?'

'I did,' he said, nodding.

She stared at him. 'Really?'

'Really.'

'And you . . . you bought this building?'

'Yep. Well, Claudia bought it for me, with my money. But yes. You need property and a good number of employees to be a chartered merchant house, and Claudia gave me both. Nice girl. Thanks for introducing us, by the way.'

'You made a deal with the Scrappers? *All* of them? And they get, what, to be employed at a somewhat real merchant house?'

'Not just employment,' said Orso. 'Ownership. They get to be founders. I supplied the starting capital, they supply the labour and raw resources, and we all share a piece of the profits. It's not as mad as it sounds.' He thought about that. 'Well, it is *pretty* mad, but I thought it was a smart play. Company Candiano's been on the decline for ages, and Estelle and Tomas's mad shit was the last straw for lots of employees – and clients. Clients who still have needs, of course – but now that people are fleeing Company Candiano like mad, *again*, what merchant house do you think the clients are going to?'

'The one spearheaded by Tribuno Candiano's former lieutenant,' said Sancia.

He grinned wickedly. '*Exactly.* I know more about Candiano processes than anyone. I've already got three supply deals in the pipeline. And we also came up with some cunning, monetisable shit during all of our desperate plotting. So long as we stay functioning and solvent, we all duck the loop. Though we're going to get bombarded by the other houses, and soon.' He took a breath. 'So. That brings us to what I wanted to discuss with you. Because though I'd like to pretend I can do this all myself . . . I know I can't.'

She stared at him. 'Wait. Orso, are . . . are you offering me a *job*?'

'No,' he said. 'I'm not. I'm saying that, if you were to ask for a position here at the good and noble merchant house of Foundryside Limited, I'd give it to you. In fact, at this stage of our development, it'd essentially make you a founder, Sancia.'

'Me? A founder?'

'In the most technical sense of the word, yes,' said Orso. 'Someone who has *started* something – though no one will have any idea how it'll finish. It could all go very poorly. So if you want to be free of Tevanne . . . to get out of here, and go live your own life . . . then do that instead. You've earned it. I want you to feel entirely free to have it, if you want. Because I'm scrumming charitable as hell, you see.'

He looked at her. She looked back.

'There's more to it than just me,' said Sancia.

'Who else could there be?' asked Orso.

'Gregor,' said Sancia. 'He's alive. And I have him.'

Orso looked dumbfounded. 'He's *what*? Gregor Dandolo is *alive*?'

'Yeah. And he's . . . well, it looks like he's like me. A scrived human. He's been scrived all along – I just don't know by who.'

She filled him in on the rest. He listened, shocked. 'Someone scrived Gregor Dandolo . . . boring, dull, stodgy Dandolo . . . to be a goddamn killing machine?' he asked.

'Basically. He fought it, though. He could have taken my head off, but . . . he broke himself, somehow. I've been trying to take care of him. I've got him hidden at the crypt now, recovering. But he's in a strange way, Orso. He's lost everything. And he needs our help. After all he's done, he deserves it.'

Orso sat back, dazed. 'Well. Shit. I'd be happy to take him in . . . and if we can get him back on his feet, he'd make an excellent chief of security. *If* he can recover, that is.' He looked at her. 'Now . . . would *you* be willing to take a position with us?'

'There's one more thing.'

He sighed. 'Of course there is.'

She took Clef out and slid him across the desk to Orso.

He gaped at the key. 'Really?'

'Don't be happy. This is a problem, not a gift. He . . . he doesn't work anymore, or talk. We need to fix him. We've *got* to fix him. Since he's the only one who can tell us what really happened, and what's really going on.'

Orso scratched his head. 'Usually when someone haggles over the conditions of one's employment,' he said, 'it's about pay, or lodgings. Not insane mystical conundrums.'

'You want me,' said Sancia, 'you have to take all my baggage with me. There's a lot more than there used to be.'

'So – is that a yes?'

'Is Berenice here?' she asked.

'She is. She's overseeing the construction work.'

She thought about it. 'What did she say?'

'She said she'd wait to hear what you said.'

Sancia smiled. 'Of course she did.'

43

Ofelia Dandolo walked across the Dandolo campo to her front gate, across her courtyards, and into her mansion. She paced down the front hallway, then through a set of doors, then downstairs to the basement level, and then to the back, to an undistinguished-looking cabinet door.

She opened the door. Within was a small, blank room. Ofelia shut her eyes, pressed her hand against the back wall, and waited.

The wall melted away as if it were made of smoke. Behind it was a tiny, cramped spiral staircase, leading down.

Ofelia lit a scrived light and walked down the stairs. It took a long time, for there were many, many steps.

Finally she came to a small wooden door. She waited for a moment, took a breath, and opened the door.

Beyond was a huge stone cellar, with a vaulted ceiling and many, many columns. There was no light within, but she did not need one, and a light would not work here, anyway – for the room was full of moths.

Ofelia carefully walked through the whispering, fluttering storm of moths. She came to the small stone seat in the middle of the room. She sat, and waited. She waited for a very long time.

Finally she saw him, glimpsed him – just a shred of his form, lost amidst the swirl of wings.

She swallowed and took a breath. 'I assume,' she said softly, 'that . . . that you are aware of how things have progressed, my prophet.'

He did not move or speak. He just stood there, a figure concealed by the flurry.

'I don't . . . I don't know what happened with my son,' she said. 'We spent so much time preparing Gregor . . . And he's done so much for us in the wars, arranging your designs . . . But now, to have him fail . . .'

Still he did not speak.

'The construct is free,' said Ofelia. 'Is . . . is it possible to withstand this blow? It seems like this is the worst of all possibilities.'

There was a long silence. Then he finally spoke, and as always, he spoke in her mind, loudly and clearly:

<NO.>

'N–No?'

<NO. THE WAR IS NOT LOST BEFORE IT EVER BEGAN. RATHER, IT IS JUST BEGINNING. SHE WILL BEGIN ONCE MORE THE PROCESS SHE STARTED SO LONG AGO. AND WE MUST WORK QUICKLY TO STOP HER.>

'So . . . what shall we do, my prophet?'

There was a long silence.

<I BELIEVE,> he said, *<IT IS TIME TO STOP HIDING.>*

Acknowledgements

It is difficult to think of any work of mine that's changed more during its development than this one. Thank you to my editor, Julian Pavia, and my agent, Cameron McClure, for helping me through the process. And thank you to Ashlee for tolerating many nights where I sat in bed typing away for hours, ignorant of nearly everything around me, and the many times when I did a botched job on the laundry while preoccupied with ideas.